00013536

FLORA SEGUNDA

OF CRACKPOT HALL

ABOUT THE AUTHOR

YSABEAU WILCE was born in the City of Califa at the age of one. While her parents were on a diplomatic mission to the Huitzil Empire, she was cared for by an uncle what brought her up by hand. She attended Sanctuary School as a scholarship girl and then spent three years at the University of Califa where she took a double degree in Apotropaic Philosophy and Confabulation.

She then became laundress to Company C, Enthusiastic Regiment of the Army of Califa, and accompanied her unit to Fort Gehenna, where she was bitten by a wer-flamingo. Only the timely intervention of the local curandero saved her from an awful skin-shifting pink fate.

After returning to Califa, Ysabeau was employed by the Califa Society for Historiography and Graphic Maps as an archivist. It was then she first developed an interest in the history of the Republic and began researching the City's past.

In her spare time, Ysabeau enjoys chewing, sleeping, gossiping, and folding paper-towels into napkins. She currently resides in the City of Porkopolis with her husband, a cheese-swilling financier, and a dog that is not red. She does not have a butler.

FLORA SEGUNDA

OF CRACKPOT HALL

Being the Magickal Mishaps of a Girl of Spirit,
Her Glass-Gazing Sidekick,
Two Ominous Butlers (One Blue), a House
with Eleven Thousand Rooms, and a Red Dog

Ysabeau Wilce

MARION LLOYD BOOKS

FOR TWO FURIES, OOO & MY

www.crackpothall.com

First published in the UK in 2007 by
Marion Lloyd Books,
An imprint of Scholastic Ltd
Euston House, 24 Eversholt Street
London, NW1 1DB, UK
Registered office: Westfield Road, Southam, Warwickshire, CV47 0RA
SCHOLASTIC and associated logos are trademarks and or registered
trademarks of Scholastic Inc.

Text copyright © Ysabeau S. Wilce, 2007
First published in the US by Harcourt, Inc., 2007
The right of Ysabeau Wilce to be identified as the author of this work has
been asserted by her.

10 digit ISBN 1 407 10237 0
13 digit ISBN 978 140710237 5

A CIP catalogue record for this book is available from the British Library

Typeset by M Rules
Printed by Bookmarque Ltd, Croydon, Surrey

Papers used by Scholastic Children's Books are made from wood grown
in sustainable forests.

1 3 5 7 9 10 8 6 4 2

www.scholastic.co.uk/zone

CONTENTS

THE DRAMATIC PERSONS

AT CRACKPOT HALL

Flora Fyrdraaca, called Flora Segunda *A girl of spirit*
General Juliet Buchanan Fyrdraaca, called Buck *Her mother*
Major Reverdy Anacreon Fyrdraaca, called Hotspur *Her father*
Idden Buchanan Fyrdraaca *Her older sister*
Flynn *Her red dog*
Bonzo *Her horse*
Udo Lanðaton *Her glass-gazing sidekick and best friend*
Mouse *Udo's horse*
Valefor *Butler of Crackpot Hall*

IN THE ARMY OF CALIFA

Nyana Keegan, called Nini Mo, the Coyote Queen
A famous Ranger
Boy Hansgen *Her sidekick*
Lieutenant Aglis Sabre *General Fyrdraaca's aide-de-camp*
Sergeant Carheña *A clerk in General Fyrdraaca's office*
Captain Honeychurch *Commanding Officer of Zoo Battery*
Lieutenant Samson *Adjutant at Zoo Battery*
Jam & Hendricks *Privates at Zoo Battery*

AT SAETA HOUSE

Florian Abenfarax de la Carcaza *Warlord of the
Republic of Califa*
Conde Rezaca *The Warlord's Chief of Staff*

AT CASA MARIPOSA

Lord Axacaya *The spiritual head of the City*
Axila Aguila *Chief of his quetzal guard*
Sitri *Servitor of Casa Mariposa*

APPEARING IN THIS NARRATIVE

AT BILSKINIR HOUSE
Paimon *Butler of Bilskinir House*
Alfonzo Guadaquevilla Perilla y Requesta *A malicious servitor*
General Banastre Haðraaða, called Hardhands *A corpse*
Parzival *A dog*

AT SANCTUARY SCHOOL
Madama *The Headmistress*
Archangel Bob *Her factotum*
Archangel Naberius *Arch-Librarian*

MISCELLANEOUS PERSONS OF INTEREST
Firemonkey *A Radical Chaoist revolutionary*
The Dainty Pirate *Scourge of the Pacifica*
The Horses of Instruction *A rowdy band*
The Viriena of Huitzil *The Republic of Califa's Overlord*

HISTORICAL PERSONAGES & ENTITIES MENTIONED
Butcher Brakespeare *Former Commanding General of the Army of Califa, now dead*
Califa *The Goddess after whom the City is named*
The Pontifexa of Califa *Last Haðraaða ruler of the City, deposed by the Warlord*
Barbizon *A Fyrdraaca war-horse*
Moxley Sorrel ov Lanðaton *Udo's birth-father*
Azucar Fyrdraaca *Founder of the Fyrdraaca Family*
Relais Evengardia *A famous actor*

> The Maiden caught me in the Wild
> Where I was dancing merrily;
> She put me into her Cabinet,
> And Lock'd me up with a golden Key.

WILLIAM BLAKE

Crackpot Hall:
The Fyrdraaca Family at Home

A Speech by Flora Nemain Fyrdraaca
ov Fyrdraaca on the Occasion of her
Fourteenth Birthday

~~Crackpot Hall has eleven thousand rooms, but only one potty.~~

~~The Warlord freed all the slaves, but he forgot to free me.~~

~~Like Crackpot Hall, the Fyrdraaca family used to be glorious, but has now fallen on hard times.~~

Blasted heck, I'm supposed to be writing my Catorcena speech, where I am supposed to be celebrating the fabulousness of my House, the glory of my family, the fantasticness of my future. But I can't think of what to write because Crackpot Hall isn't fabulous, and the Fyrdraaca family is not much glorious any more, and my future is hardly going to be fantastic. In my speech, I'm supposed to write the truth.

1

Well, here's some truth.

Let's start with the fabulousness of my House. So there are four great Houses in the City of Califa, and every one of them but Crackpot Hall has a magickal Butler. At Saeta House, your hat is taken by Furfur's floaty hands. At Sanctuary School, Archangel Bob wafts through the hallways, his red wings fluttering blanket-like behind him, and not one mote of dust or one smudge of dirt escapes his eye. Bilskinir House is closed now, since the Haðraaða family died out years ago, but they say Paimon is there still, waiting for a family that will never come home again.

And then there is our House, Crackpot Hall.

At Crackpot Hall I take your hat, and I try (mostly unsuccessfully) to watch out for dust motes, and I make sure the lamps are lit at night. No Butler, just me, Flora Nemain Fyrdraaca ov Fyrdraaca, last on the Fyrdraaca family list, slaving away at endless chores that should be done by our Butler. But thanks to Mamma, we don't have a Butler any more.

They don't call my mamma the Rock of Califa for nothing. Mamma doesn't like swirling décor and shifty rooms any more than she likes swirling clothes and shifty people. Mamma prefers things that do not change, and a House with a mind of its own often does just that. Also Mamma hates magick; it's a trick, she says, a cheat, an easy way to do hard things. Mamma is *all about* the hard things. So she banished our Butler, and now Crackpot Hall is quiet and still.

Quiet and still and falling apart.

Ayah so, this quietness is good for Mamma's peace of mind, but it's awful for the rest of us. When it rains, water leaks through the windows and puddles on the floor. Crackpot's fancy front gates are too heavy to open, so we have to use the delivery gate, like servants, and our garden is an overgrown jungle. Most of the House we can't even get to – doors do not open, stairs stop on the first step, hallways end in darkness. Crackpot Hall has eleven thousand rooms, and my family lives like squatters in just a few of them. The toilet in the one potty we *can* get to is always overflowing, and when it does, we have to go outside to the bog, where it is dark and cold, and the wooden seat is splintery.

The Butler was banished before I was born, so I don't remember Crackpot Hall's glory, but my sister Idden does. According to Idden, before, when you entered a room, the lights flickered on and the fire rose up to greet you. Before, when you reached for a towel, it was clean and fluffy and smelled of lemony sunshine. Before, delicious dinners appeared on command and dirty dishes disappeared. Before, rooms shifted with your desire, so it was only ever a short step away to the potty, and you had *dozens* of potties to choose from. Now, all gone. That's the truth about Crackpot Hall.

The truth about the glory of my family. From the outside, I guess the Fyrdraacas look pretty glorious

3

still – some of the Fyrdraacas, anyway. There used to be many more Fyrdraacas, but like the House itself, we've dwindled. Now we are just four.

Mamma is Juliet Buchanan Fyrdraaca ov Fyrdraaca, the Warlord's Commanding General. She helped broker the peace with the il Empire, thus saving the Republic from certain defeat and ruin. That was almost fourteen years ago, just after I was born, but crowds still cheer Mamma in the street, and she hasn't paid for a drink since. The Warlord is really old now and has only one leg, so he relies on Mamma for everything.

Idden graduated with honours from Benica Barracks, joined the Enthusiastics, the most prestigious regiment in the Army of Califa, and has already been promoted to captain. She has perfectly straight teeth, can rhyme sonnets on the fly, and will probably make colonel before she's thirty.

Of our five gazehounds, two (Flashingly Fine and Dashingly Handsome) have won the Warlord's Cup at the Saeta Kennel Club Dog Show. Two others (Lashings in Wine and Crash Worship) are champion hunters and once brought down a bear.

And then there is Flynn.

Flynn is the youngest gazehound pup. He is as burnished red as his siblings and has the same caramel-coloured eyes. But as the runt, he did not come out right. He's prone to overheating and falling over, piddling when he gets excited, and yapping like a little poodle.

And then there is Poppy.

Poppy is Reverdy Anacreon Fyrdraaca ov Fyrdraaca, and he used to be the glory of the Fyrdraaca family. He was a champion shot and a champion steeplechase rider. No man in the Republic could fight harder, shoot straighter, dance longer, or bust heads harder than my father. He was renowned for spirit and devilry, a real Hotspur, and so he was dubbed by the press, and so everyone calls him. But during the Huitzil War, he got captured, and the Virreina of Huitzil convicted him of war crimes. He spent three years in a Huitzil prison, and when Mamma finally ransomed him, he was broken.

Once my family had another Flora Fyrdraaca, and by all accounts she was fabulous. This was before I was born, so I never knew her. When she was lost, Mamma destroyed everything in the House she had ever touched; now no trace of her remains at Crackpot. But Idden managed to hide one of Flora's images from Mamma's purge, and in this portrait, Flora has golden curls and pink rosebud lips, the spitting image of Mamma. Even Idden, who can be pretty sour, allows that the First Flora was supercute, a real doll, sunshiny and happy all the day long. Adorable.

But the First Flora is gone now, lost in the War, and I'm hardly a replacement. I'm only the Second Flora.

Flora Segunda. I don't have golden curls or rosebud lips, nor do I look the slightest bit like Mamma. I'm not adorable, and I'm certainly not sunshiny, and I don't see

5

there is much in life to be happy about. Particularly not now. That's the truth about the glory of the Fyrdraaca family.

And that brings me to the truth about the fantastic-ness of my future. *Fyrdraacas are soldiers*, Mamma says. We are born to the gun. So when Fyrdraacas turn fourteen and celebrate their Catorcena, and are then adults in the eyes of the Warlord, off we go to Benica Barracks to learn to march, to learn to ride, to learn to shoot, to learn to die.

But I do not want to go to the Barracks and learn to be a killer, a servant, a slave. To learn to follow orders, like Idden, and to learn to kill, like Poppy, and to learn to give everything for my country, like Mamma. Not me!

I want to be a ranger, a scout, a spy. Rangers don't follow orders; they slide around the rules, scoot around the edges of the law. They hide and they listen and they uncover things that are concealed. They discover the truth though it be surrounded by a bodyguard of lies.

Rangers act with cunning and with clarity of Will, and absolute focus – and magick. Nyana Keegan, the greatest ranger who ever lived, could turn her thoughts outside in, and when she turned her thoughts inside out again, she was someone else entirely. Nini Mo, as everyone called her, could read signs on the air, smell someone's thoughts, and twist broken glass into fire. She was a great adept who turned the Current to her Will and used magick to further her aims.

When the War started, Nini Mo organized the Ranger Corps to act as the eyes and ears of the Army, to go where no soldier could go, and to use cunning and cleverness – and magick – to win the kinds of battles that are not fought with guns and swords. No one but Nini knew who the rangers were, and this secrecy made them deadly. But as part of the peace accord with the Huitzil Empire, the Ranger Corps was disbanded, its rangers dispersed, some arrested, some killed. They say there are no rangers any more, although I don't believe that. Rangers are sly and hard to catch, like coyotes, and I am sure that some of them got away.

So I can't join the Ranger Corps on my own, but I could be a ranger alone, as rangers really prefer to be. Then, why not satisfy Mamma, satisfy family tradition, and go to Benica Barracks, anyway? Be a soldier publicly and a ranger in private?

Because soldiers cannot practise magick, of course. Adepts have one foot in the Waking World and one foot Elsewhere, and that's hardly conducive to military discipline. Adepts are loyal to their Art first, the Warlord second – if at all. There's no honour in magick, and a soldier, says Mamma, is nothing without honour. A soldier caught meddling in the Current would be shot.

I can't be a soldier and a ranger, too. But I don't dare tell Mamma that I will not go to the Barracks. Mamma never raises her voice or threatens, but her disapproval *hurts*, and she expects so much to be obeyed that everyone obeys her. Every Fyrdraaca for generations has gone to the Barracks, even the dogs. For my whole life, Mamma has spoken of duty and how important it is to be true to your family honour and to your country.

Even if this means being untrue to yourself.

I

Mamma. Sleeping Late.
An Overdue Library Book.
The Elevator.

As Commanding General of the Army of Califa, Mamma is in charge of just about everything, so she is not much home – she's always off on an inspection, or manoeuvres, or at a grand council somewhere, or just working late. Thus, Crackpot's crumbling is no particular bother to her. Idden, too, is nicely out of it, even if her current post, Fort Jones, is the back end of Nowhere. At least she can count on having someone else do her laundry and cook her supper.

Mostly just Poppy and I are stuck home alone, which really works out to just me alone, because Poppy only comes out of his Eyrie when the booze and cigarillos run out. Then he's just a thin shadow in a worn cadet shawl and bloodstained frock coat creeping out the back door, off to buy more booze, so he hardly counts at all. Thus, it is me who reaps all the inconvenience.

When Mamma *is* home, she gets up at oh-dark-thirty and makes me get up with her, so that we can have family time at breakfast. This, of course, is not really family time, since Poppy isn't there, and Idden isn't there, and the First Flora isn't there. On these occasions, it's just Mamma and me, half a family, having half-a-family time. And since that's all we are ever going to have, that's what we have to learn to like.

It makes Mamma happy to pretend we are a happy family, so I sit and suffer through warmed-over take-away and café au lait, and she asks me about school, and I ask her about work, and this morning time makes up for the fact that she stays at the War Department every night until ten and I usually eat supper alone.

But when Mamma is off on one of her trips, I sleep until the very last minute and rush off to Sanctuary School without my breakfast, but with an extra half hour of snore.

Now, the Butler may be banished, but that doesn't mean that the House is entirely dead. Occasionally it groans and thrashes a bit, like a sleeping person whose body moves though her mind drifts far away. But it never moves like you would want it to, like before, when the potty would be next to your bedroom in the middle of the night, but tucked Elsewhere otherwise. Sometimes the long way is the short way and the short way is the long way, and occasionally there is no way at all.

This does not happen too often, because Mamma is

strict that it should not. Before, the Butler kept Crackpot in order, but now it's Mamma's Will alone that keeps the House in line. She likes to be in control of things and usually is. But when Mamma is gone, her grip slips a bit, and then so does the way downstairs, or to the back door, or maybe even to the potty. The House moves not in a good and useful way, but in a horribly inconveniently annoying way. Sometimes you have to be careful.

Like the Elevator. Our rooms are spread along three floors, and it's a bit of a hike to get from the kitchen in the basement up to my second-floor bedroom. The Elevator would be much quicker, but we aren't supposed to use it without Mamma. Once, when I was just a tot, Poppy tried to take the Elevator back to his Eyrie. Mamma warned him not to, but he was drunk, and he roared that he would see her in hell before he'd take another order from her, General Fyrdraaca, *sir*! When he staggered on to the Elevator, the iron grille slammed just like an eyelid snapping shut in fear, with Poppy still cursing blue as the cage moved upward.

The Elevator came back empty a few minutes later, and for a full week, we could hear distant howling and shouting drifting around us, but always out of our reach. Poppy finally staggered out of the Door of Delectable Desires, dishevelled and pale, and, without a word, started the long climb up the Stairs of Exuberance to his Eyrie, from which he did not stir for the next six months.

11

After that, Mamma made Idden and me swear not to use the Elevator without her. With her, the Elevator goes where it should: it wouldn't dare do anything else. But she doesn't trust it with the rest of us, and so I have to climb up and down a zillion stairs, which is a chore, particularly when you are loaded down with laundry.

And that's where everything started – with the Elevator.

Mamma was gone on an inspection of Angeles Barracks, and I woke up on the sharp edge of running extremely late. I had been up until nearly three trying to write my stupid Catorcena speech – a total waste of time, for the speech is supposed to celebrate your family and future, and what about my family and future is there to celebrate? But I had stayed up half the night trying, and here was the result: I had overslept.

Tardiness is not encouraged at Sanctuary School. Most of the kids sleep there, and that I do not is a benefit Mamma arranged due to the need for someone to keep an eye on Poppy during her frequent absences. Of course, I'd rather sleep at Sanctuary, for Poppy is not someone you want to get stuck keeping an eye on. When he is good, there's nothing to see, for he keeps to the Eyrie and is silent. When he is bad, he screams like a banshee and crashes furniture. But there are the dogs to consider, as well. If Poppy were left alone to feed them, they'd starve.

But anyway, I still have to be at Sanctuary on time, so

12

I was in a tearing hurry. I'd already been late three times in the past month, which had got me only detention. But a fourth strike meant more than just detention. First, it meant a trip to the Holy Head-mistress's office, where Madama would sit me down and look at me sorrowfully, and tell me I must be mindful of my time because I was all that my mamma had left now that Idden had gone, and she *relied* on me. That would make me feel guilty, and I hate feeling guilty.

But even worse, then Madama would write Mamma a letter. And Mamma would come home and get that letter, and she would be superannoyed. Mamma super-annoyed is fearsome. She doesn't scream or whack, but she would give me the Look that has reduced colonels to tears, and then she would remind me about duty, honour, and responsibility. I would feel worse than guilty – I would feel ashamed. Having Mamma give you the Look is about the worst thing in the world. It means you've failed her. And she was sure to mention, too, how sad it was that I had failed her so close to my Catorcena.

My Catorcena was only a week off. It's a big deal, turning fourteen, age of majority, legally an adult, wah-wah, suitable now to be received by the Warlord, wah-wah, and so it's celebrated in big-deal style. There's an assembly where you have to make a public speech about your family's history and obligations and the responsibility of adulthood. There's a reception where the Warlord greets you by name, thus acknowledging you as his loyal subject. It's all very tedious, over-wrought and complicated – a big whoop-de-do.

For some kids, this is the highlight of their lives, maybe the only time they get to see the Warlord in his courtly glory (you can see the Warlord propping up a bar South of the Slot any old time you care to look), the only time they have a fancy party at which no one looks anywhere but at them, the only time they get huge gifties. But I don't care about the Warlord in his courtly or noncourtly glory, and I don't care about huge gifties, and I don't care about fancy parties. And I certainly don't care about making a stupid speech about the history of my horrible, sad, decaying family.

Most kids want to be adults; then they are in charge of themselves. But not Fyrdraacas. Mamma is always in charge of Fyrdraacas, no matter how old they are, and for me, being an adult means only that I will be old enough to go to the Barracks next semester, whether I want to or not. And I certainly do not, although I have not yet got up the nerve to tell Mamma so.

So, I dreaded my birthday, and because of dreading was avoiding, and because of avoiding was nowhere near ready. My dress was still in pieces, my speech was still idle scribbles, and my invitations were still mostly uninvited. Instead of getting ready, I'd been avoiding, but now I was going to have to get cracking. Mamma was coming back in two days and if I wasn't ready, and there was a sorrowful letter from Madama tattling my tardiness, I would be in what Nini Mo, the Coyote Queen, called A World of Hurt.

So, when I opened my eyes and realized the sun on the wall was the wrong angle to be *early*, I flew out of bed, flew through the bathroom, squeezed into my stays, threw on my kilt and pinafore, flew to the kitchen, and chucked the sleepy dogs out into the garden. I paused at the foot of the Stairs of Exuberance, but all was quiet in the Eyrie above. Perhaps Poppy was actually sleeping for once.

I grabbed a stale bun for breakfast, yanked my boots and redingote on, snatched up the dispatch case I use for a book bag, gave the dogs their biscuits, herded them into the mudroom, then flew to the stables. (Guess who mucks those out?) I fed Bonzo and Mouse and was about to pound towards the back gate when I remembered I had forgotten the overdue library book that I had sworn to Arch-Librarian Naberius I would return that very day. Not just any old library book, either, but a very rare copy of Nini Mo's autobiography from Sanctuary's special collections. If I didn't get it back, he wasn't going to let me borrow volume 2, and I'd never find out how she escaped from the Flayed Riders of Huitzil. The book still lay on the settee in my bedroom, where I'd been reading it after I gave up on the stupid speech.

So I turned and flew back to the House. And in my hurry, I decided that rather than go the long way back through the mudroom, into the Below Kitchen, up the

Below Stairs, down the Upper Hall, up the Second Stairs, down the Hallway of Laborious Desire, by Mamma's bedroom, by the potty, and finally to my room, I would take the Elevator. The long way is more certain, but it's not called the long way because it is short.

If Idden had kept her promise to not use the Elevator, I don't know, though she has always been a good one for doing what she is supposed to. But I don't believe in following orders. If Idden hadn't followed orders, she wouldn't be rotting away in the back end of Nowhere, getting shot at by people hiding behind bushes. If Poppy hadn't followed orders, he wouldn't today be locked in his Eyrie, drunk as a hatter and twice as mad.

There's a whole series of illustrated yellowback novels about Nini Mo called Nini Mo, Coyote Queen, and I've read every one more than once. The novels are a bit trashy and, of course, probably exaggerated for some effect, but not entirely untrue, for Nini Mo did have an exciting life. She was always having adventures and excitement and narrow escapes. I wouldn't mind having adventures and excitement and narrow escapes, and you certainly don't have those by following orders. Nini Mo didn't follow orders.

So I don't, either. When Mamma is not around, I use the Elevator all the time, and never have I had the tiniest lick of trouble. In fact, I wouldn't mind if the Elevator showed me something new, but annoyingly it only ever goes two floors up. Poppy had been gone for a week – where did he go? How did he get back? What did he see? The part of Crackpot I can reach is small, but I know the House is much bigger, because from the stable roof, you see a wide spread of gables and buttresses, which I have never been able to reach.

What Mamma doesn't know can't hurt me, I thought. I was going to be late, but I didn't dare go without that book, because Naberius is death to those who don't bring his books back on time. I rushed back into the House, through the Below Kitchen, and up the Below Stairs.

I had forgotten the First Rule of Rangering: *never let down your guard.*

2

LOST. MANY EMPTY ROOMS.
VERY DUSTY TOWELS.

If the Elevator had let me off where it was supposed to, at the Hallway of Laborious Desire, I would have been able to nip right into my bedroom, grab the book, and still make the 7.45 horsecar, and, hopefully, Archangel Bob wouldn't even notice me creeping into morning assembly late. I am very good at creeping, although it's quite a challenge to sneak by an eternally vigilant denizen.

But the stupid Elevator did not let me off at the Hallway of Laborious Desire. No, the stupid Elevator had slowly and silently borne me upward, gently floating as on a summer swell, and though I banged and shouted, the Elevator did not slow or stop. Past the second floor it went, past a third floor – we'd never had a third floor before – upward and upward it went, smooth and steady, until, with a grinding whine, it

18

stopped. The golden outer doors opened to a thick darkness.

I had matches in my dispatch bag (among other useful things). *Be prepared*, says Nini Mo, but why use a trigger when there are other, more clever methods of gaining light?

"⟨sigil⟩," I said. The Ignite Sigil was the only Gramatica Invocation I had mastered, but I had mastered it well, and now a spurt of magickal coldfire flowered in the darkness like a sparkler and illuminated the blackness beyond the closed grille of the Elevator. The wan light showed the hollow shadows of bulky furniture, abandoned and forlorn.

"This is not the Hallway of Laborious Desire," I said crossly.

The Elevator did not answer.

Act as though you mean it, and you will, Nini Mo says. I said firmly, "I want to go to the Hallway of Laborious Desire. And I am in a hurry, so let's be snappy."

No response.

"I'm going to tell Mamma."

Idle words, really, because it would be my hide tacked up on the wall of Mamma's study if she found out that I had disobeyed her. But bluff is always worth a try. The threat made no impact upon the Elevator's smug silence.

"Well, if you are going to leave me here, at least give me more light." *Sweetness is its own sticky trap*, says

19

Nini Mo, so I added sweetly, "Please. Very pretty please, beautiful Elevator."

Nada. So much for good manners. I gave the golden grille a good kick, then pulled it open, stepping out on to the creaky wooden floors into a cloying darkness smelling of dust, decay and the distant sea. The pouty Elevator snapped its grille shut behind me. I turned and grabbed, but it yanked out of my grip and vanished into the murk. Now I was stuck.

I held my hand underneath the coldfire spark and focused all my Will upon its hazy gelid glow. A tiny pinpoint of pain tingled above my right eye, but the light winked and brightened. Now I could see hulking furniture draped in tattered dust covers, floating whitely in the darkness like ancient ignored ghosts.

There's no way out but through, Nini Mo said when she was lost in the Maze of Woefulness and Gloom in the yellowback novel *Nini Mo vs. the Flesh-Eating Fir Trees*.

I cautiously stepped forward. Somewhere there had to be stairs down and out – I just had to find them. My feet stirred up a haze of mould and frothy dirt, which glittered in the coldfire light that I now carried before me, floating above my open palm.

And I thought *our* rooms were a mess! Mamma is too busy or too gone to pay much attention to house-keeping, and though I usually manage to keep the actual filth at bay, it's hard to keep after the dust and spiders and all those dogs. Between laundry, cooking, cleaning and homework, I can only do so much, and so our rooms are always dreadfully untidy. Judging just by our rooms, you might think Crackpot was only lazy.

But here it was obvious that the House was worse than lazy. Here, there were cracks in the walls, and the floor beneath my feet felt dangerously creaky, as though it might splinter and give way, plunging me down, down – to where? I wandered in the darkness, through room after room, and saw nothing but decay and dirt. Piled furniture and cobwebby chandeliers. Wallpaper peeling off in long curling strips. Parquet floors so dirty that the dust was as thick as a rug.

Sometimes there was evidence of earlier grandeur: an orangery, though the stunted orange trees were all spindly and grey, their fruit withered to dry husks that crunched under my feet. The glass ceiling above was black with dirt and let no daylight in, for want of which, I guess, the poor trees had slowly died. A long echoing room, its ceiling held aloft by tall tree-shaped pillars, most of its floor space taken up by an enormous swimming pool. The shallow end of the pool was empty, its green and blue mosaic glinting sadly in my coldfire light. There was still a bit of water in the deep end, sludgy black water smelling of yuck.

But despite the occasional glimpses of grandeur, there was mostly just mess.

Mess, and no stairs, no way out. Rangers never get lost. They always know where they have been, where they are going, and all the bits in between. Nini Mo navigated her way from Puento to Angeles, with both hands tied behind her back and a sack over her head, by sense of smell alone – that's fifteen hundred miles of burning desert! It was stupid, then, that I couldn't even find a doorway out or a staircase down. I knew Crackpot was big, but I'd never imagined it could be *this* big.

A tiny idea was forming in my brain that maybe Mamma had been right about the Elevator. I remembered Poppy and his shouting and the pinched look on Mamma's face as she waited for him to return. Only now did it occur to me that she had not gone looking for him herself—

Wah! A ranger would never think such things. A ranger must look with utmost logic at where she is and what she is doing, not succumb to dire fantasy. Nini Mo had not panicked when the Up-Drawn Bandana Society tied her to a log and threw her into the Dellenbaugh Gorge in *Nini Mo vs. the Cattle Coolers*. She had coolly sawed through the ropes with a spur and used her kilt as a parachute, then climbed back up the ravine and garroted every last ruffian. She had survived because she had been cool-headed and considering. I would be so, too, if only I could get my hand to stop quivering. The coldfire light was getting dimmer, and this time my Gramatica Invocation had no strengthening effect. I remembered that First Rule of Rangering, *never let down your guard*, only too well now – now that it was too late.

The Second Rule of Rangering: *take your bearings*. I had walked into a narrow closet, its walls tiered with drawers that went up over my head. I pulled one open, and a burst of dusty lavender boiled upward. Inside lay the legendary towels. Idden is pretty fastidious, and in her stories of Crackpot's glory, she always dwelled on those wonderfully fluffy towels. Now they didn't look so fresh and clean.

I went to the window and rubbed away the grime with my free hand. All I could see was my smudgy reflection. How could it be dark outside? Had I been lost so long that the day had gone by and night fallen, and now I wasn't only late for school, I had missed it entirely? I had to get out of here, and fast.

The Third Rule of Rangering: *consider your options*. I did not want to climb out of the window into darkness. Goddess knew what hungry uglies were lurking down there, just waiting for a tasty little snack to plummet into their gaping maws. I had no option but to continue on. The dribble of panic I had been trying to swallow was turning into a torrent, and the coldfire light was almost gone. Though I tried to rekindle the Invocation, it would not spark again. A lone match would not be much aid against such very *dark* darkness.

So on I continued, down a short staircase, covered with well-torn carpet, and through a narrow corridor lined with empty chairs whose leather seats had rotted away. Then ahead – a thin slant of light.

I hastened towards it, passing through a room whose

emptiness was indicated by the hollow echo of my footsteps. As I got closer, I could see that the light slanted from a slightly opened door.

But not just a normal door, normal-sized and everyday ordinary. This door was one of a pair, and these two doors were enormous, each as wide as a coach and twice as tall. They were smoothly silver, with no decoration of any kind, not even doorknobs or lock plates. The flat metal reflected the tiny spark of my coldfire light, getting dimmer by the second, and my own unflattering reflection, squat and wavery.

It was lucky for me that that door was slightly ajar; never would I have had the strength to push that mammoth weight open. My coldfire light winked out, but the brilliant summery shimmer coming through the crack kept the darkness at bay.

"There's no way out but through," I said, my voice thin and whispery. I had to suck my tum in and hold my breath, but I could just squeeze through.

3

SURPRISE. DENIZENS & BUTLERS. MANY, MANY BOOKS.

After so long in darkness, the bright light was blinding. For a second I saw nothing, then blurring grey spots swam across my eyes. After a few seconds the spots faded, and I found myself in a library.

And what a library! I had thought the Library Rotunda at Sanctuary was huge, but it was a tiny broom cupboard compared to this room, whose length seemed to go on for ever, disappearing into a distant sunny haze. The width of the room was not so distantly long, but it was still plenty wide.

Like the doors I had squeezed through, all the surfaces of the room were sleek and silvery, the floor like polished steel, the bookcases angular and slick. To my left, the wall was one long sheet of glass, through which the hot sun spilled, making the dazzle that had so blinded me at first. The opposite wall was nothing but bookshelves, marching into the haze, climbing upward until they reached the round arch of a cloudy dragon-entwined ceiling far above.

But the books! Never had I seen so many books. Hundreds of sizes, colours and shapes filled the bookshelves, and their brilliant bindings were the only contrast to the glittering silver monotone. More slick cases – these fronted with glass – stood freely about the room, and these contained more books, and there were still more piled on the floor in haphazard stacks. More books than I could read in a lifetime, even if I sat down in one of the stiff metal chairs that stood at intervals along the enormous windows and started reading right that very second.

I went over to the table that marched the length of the room. It was larger even than the Grand Council Table at the War Department – which means it was *big* – and it was covered in scattered papers, stacks of books, inky-pen wipers. Chewed pens lay haphazardly, as though they had been tossed down in disgust, and there was a lovely big glass inkwell shaped like a turtle, half empty.

The papers were covered with thick black writing in the style called Splendiferous. It's an old script, and very flourishing, with many long sweepy bits both above and below. Back in the day, it had been the official hand for writing official documents such as laws and proclamations. Now it's just old-fashioned and rarely used. It's an extremely hard script to read, and I couldn't make out any of the writing.

"Hey, don't touch that," a voice hissed in my ear.

My heart nigh to jerking right out of my chest, I snatched my hand back from the book I had been about to pick up, then turned around.

A boy stood behind me, glaring, his arms crossed. He was tall, his gangliness wrapped in a tattered black gown with trailing torn sleeves. Greyish hair straggled around a narrow, starving face; colourless eyes peered over a pointy snuffling nose.

"That book is older than this City and even more fragile," he said, "so keep your dirty paw to yourself." The boy shivered and huddled deeper into a thick black woolly shawl, which was liberally dusted with shreds of torn paper.

"Says who?" I demanded. "Who the heck are you? And what are you doing here?"

"This is *my* library," the boy said menacingly. He widened his flat white eyes and scowled. "I should ask what *you* are doing here!"

"Nayah," I answered. "This is *my* House, or rather my mamma's House, and therefore this library is hers. And so is the book."

The boy's scowl turned into a snarl. "Your mamma lives in this House by my leave."

"Ayah? Says who?"

The boy puffed up like an adder and bellowed, "I say so – I, Valefor, the Denizen of House Fyrdraaca – I say so and so it is!"

At least, I think he tried to bellow. Really he just

kind of hooted in a loud reedy voice and ruined the effect by sputtering into a cough at the end. The windmill arms and the scraggly hair did not help his bombast, either.

Although I am ashamed to admit it, I laughed. He had tried to look so important and had only succeeded in looking silly. He coughed and coughed. I tried to swallow my laughter; he raised his head and gave me a look to cut glass.

"You are mean, Flora Fyrdraaca." The boy wheezed again, a terrible sound that made my own throat hurt in sympathy.

"And you are not our Butler," I said. "Mamma banished our Butler."

The boy stuck his pointy chin in the air. "Ha! I am an egregore of the fifth order – I can hardly be banished! Though Buck did try to get rid of me, this is as far as I can go, here to the Bibliotheca Mayor. If she banished me completely, the House would fall right down."

Could this actually be Valefor, our Butler? My excitement was tempered by scepticism. Praterhuman entities such as denizens, at least in my experience, tend towards the fantastic. At Sanctuary, Archangel Bob stands seven feet tall, and his crimson wings flutter behind him like two giant flags. Poor Furfur, at Saeta, even though he is run ragged by the hordes of lobbyists and sycophants always hanging around the Warlord, has a noble hound-dog head and is always perfectly dressed. Bilskinir House has been shut for years, but legend has it that the notorious Paimon is hugely and fabulously phosphorescent, and always hungry. This boy did not look fantastic at all, only scraggly. If he was our Butler, I guess he had fallen on hard times, like the rest of us at Crackpot Hall. But could it really be him?

"I know who you are, Flora Nemain Fyrdraaca ov Fyrdraaca the *Second*. Why do you not know me?" the boy said, scowling.

"Because I've never seen you before, and you sure don't look like a Butler."

He deflated a bit and wrung his bony hands melodramatically. "I know, I know. I'm really not in good shape. You should have seen me in my early days, before your dear mamma sucked me dry and cast me aside. Under Azucar Fyrdraaca, I had the mane of a lion and fingernails of gold. When Anacreon Fyrdraaca was Head of the House, I had six of the most perfect arms, and I was fifteen feet tall—"

"You must have banged your head a lot on the doorways then."

He stuck his lip out at me. "My hallways were taller then, too. You are a snippy one, Flora. I'm surprised at you, and disappointed, too. Surely you are the shortest Fyrdraaca that I can recall, and my memory is pretty good. And those little blue eyes – don't squint like that. It only makes you look mean. That hair – do you ever comb it? And that coat you are wearing! What a mess, those wide lapels and awful—"

Now I was not excited at all, just stung. It is true that I'm not pretty; my hair is rusty red and curly, with a tendency to frizz, and I am rather plump. But rangers don't want to be beautiful; they want to be anonymous. Nini Mo wasn't beautiful; she was strong and fast and clever, and those qualities are more important than looks. But it's irksome to have a complete stranger comment so personally on personal things.

"There is nothing wrong with my redingote," I said. "It's the latest style in coats."

"A slave to fashion, too! Fyrdraacas set the fashion; they don't follow it—"

"Well, you don't look so great yourself," I interrupted, to sting back.

"You should have seen me before. Then, I was the best House in the City – the brightest and most awesome. You could see my gleaming silver roofs all the way from the Alameda Hills, and at night, the glow of my lamps was visible even through the thickest fog. I was terrific. Until your mamma became Head of the House and cast me out of my rightful place, and struck me to this sorry state. Now look at me, this starveling, this! I am the House—"

"Prove it."

He stopped mid-speech. "Prove it?"

"Ayah so. Prove you are our Butler. You say you are, but saying means nothing. You could be anyone."

"But I am Valefor Fyrdraaca!" he protested.

"So you say. Do something Butlery."

"But I can't. I am proscribed!"

"That's convenient," I said maliciously, as payback for his snarky comments regarding my clothes and cuteness. Of course he had to be Valefor – who else could he be?

He wrung his hands and said, agonized, "I *am* Valefor. How would I know you otherwise? My Will is Fyrdraaca Will—"

"Butlers have no Wills of their own. They are just servitors to their Houses."

He puffed. "Some servitors never gain power, and remain trapped for ever within the Wills of those who made them, always stuck within their duty. But I, Valefor, have evolved so that I can act within my own Will, as it serves the good of the House."

"But if you have your own Will, how could you be banished?"

Another puff, almost a huff. "I am an egregore of the *fifth* order. I'm good, but I'm not perfect. I exist to serve the Head of the Fyrdraaca House, your dear lady mother, whose stubbornness knows no bounds. She banished me to this prison, but she did not dare abrogate me completely. I was not created to care for Fyrdraaca House – I *am* Fyrdraaca House, the very bricks, the marble, the mortar, the tile, the shingle, the nails, the crossbeams, the gold paint; to destroy me is to destroy your family—"

I should have been superexcited to have made such

a fantastic discovery: our Butler, hidden away in our House. And at first, I was. But now that excitement was fading. Our Butler was not glorious and fantastic – he was weak and paltry and a whiner to boot. The disappointment was acute. It's like when Idden had such a crush on Relais Evengardia, the matinee idol, and spent hours mooning about the Cow Palace stage door, hoping for his autograph. But when she finally got to meet him, he was a complete and utter git, and her romantic love for him (and the stage) was squashed for ever.

And with this surge of acute disappointment, I suddenly remembered that I was late-late-late, and now getting later.

I interrupted, "I am sorry, Valefor. Normally I would love to stay and chat, but I am very late, and I'm going to be in B-I-G trouble when I finally get to Sanctuary, because I don't have my library book, and this isn't helping any."

"Overdue library book, eh? And Naberius is a fiend on library books, too. I'd be surprised if he doesn't eat you."

"I will be surprised, too. So if you don't mind, I gotta get my book and get to school. I'm sorry I can't stay longer."

"What book?"

"*High Jinks in Low Places: The Autobiography of Nini Mo, Coyote Queen*, volume 1."

Valefor sniffed. "That's awful tripe, you know. You

should read something more educational. I have a lovely book on eschatological extensions and their role in immanentizing the—"

Ignoring Valefor's ramblings, I looked around the room, hoping for a way out other than the way I had come in, and there, set deeply within one of the massive bookcases, was a small silver doorway. It swung open at my touch, revealing a rickety flight of wooden stairs.

"You can't get down that way," Valefor said. "Those stairs lead to the Cellars of Excruciations. At least, I think they do. Thanks to your dear lady mamma, I don't know anything for sure any more. But anyway, I wouldn't go down there unless I were feeling lucky. Are you feeling lucky, Flora Segunda?"

After my earlier encounter with the Elevator, I was definitely not feeling lucky. I stared into the dank tunnel leading downward and decided to try the windows instead. I am an extremely good climber.

The windows overlooked a sunlit yard, thick with snarled rosebushes and dusty green hedges. From the length of the Elevator ride, I would have thought we were at least five or six storeys up, but it didn't look that far to the ground. Beyond, I could see the crenulated edge of another roof just beyond a cluster of eucalyptus trees. Judging from the angle of the sun, I was on the west side of the house, and that roof was probably the stables. When I took out my compass to check my guess, the needle spun like a broken top.

"It won't work here," Valefor said, breathing over my shoulder. "I am the lodestar of the House, and the needle will always point to me."

"It's spinning like a wheel."

"Well, then it's broken."

Huh, I thought. The compass was an award for Best Rope Climber at last year's Gymkhana Exhibition, and it was not broken. Anyway, I was pretty sure I recognized the stables, and outside was outside. I'd rather wander through the daylit garden than go back into the musty darkness. I climbed on to the broad expanse of the window seat and fumbled with the catch.

"What are you doing?" Valefor demanded.

"Getting ready to climb down that ivy vine," I said. "The one that is about to tear most of this wall away."

"Well, it's not my fault. Blame your dear mamma. If she let me do my job, then I would have this wall fixed, and all the other walls, too. And you wouldn't have to muck out the stables any more."

"How do you know I muck out the stables?" I asked.

"Your boots have horse hoo all over them. Anyway, why are you leaving so soon? Didn't you just get here? Come and sit with me for a while and let's have a nice chat," Valefor said, suddenly all nicey-nice and beguiling.

"I have to go. I am late for school. I'm sorry, Valefor."

"When you take the dæmon on board, you must row him ashore." Valefor grabbed my sleeve with a hand

that had about as much substance as a piece of paper. His flesh – if that is what it was – was faintly translucent, so I could see the wavering shade of my purple redingote through his thin fingers. I yanked but his grip was strong.

I was caught.

4

VAL'S STRONG GRIP. EXPLANATIONS. A KISS.

Valefor looked like a high wind could blow him away, but if a high wind came along, it would take me, too, because although I pulled hard, he would not let go. It was like being pinned by a shadow. I should have been able to just pull free of his diaphanous hand, and yet I could not.

"Let me go, Valefor—"

"I am so very, very hungry, Flora Segunda," he whined. "Can't you feed me?"

With my free hand, I fumbled in my dispatch case. You never know when you suddenly might feel a wee bit faint, so I make it a practice to keep a few little snackie things about me at all times. "Here, I have a chocolate bar. It's kinda squished, but you can have it. Take it and let me go." I pulled, but his grip did not slacken.

"Yuck – it's not nasty chewy food I want." The sunlight gleamed off Valefor's eyes and made them look as opaque as milk. I had never before wondered what Butlers ate, but suddenly the wonder was foremost in my mind – and not in a good way, either.

"If you hurt me, I will really tell Mamma," I said, more stoutly than I felt. I didn't like the way he was licking his lips.

"And then we'll both be in trouble, but whose trouble will hurt the most?"

Good point. *If force doesn't get you free*, said Nini Mo, *then fall back on surprise.*

"⚡⊗♯♭ ⊶⟷ '⟁⟍!" I shouted. The Invocation filled my mouth with a sour taste. And instead of sparking a small coldfire light, which I had hoped would startle Valefor enough to let loose his grip, a huge fuzzy ball of brilliant green coldfire flared, then dwindled into a tiny little green dot that vanished into itself with a brain-rattling, percussive *POP*.

My ears rang, my eyesight went black, and the world went fuzzy. When the blackness cleared and my sight came back into focus, I saw that Valefor had collapsed on the floor in a heap of dusty rags. I didn't feel so good myself; there was a heavy metallic taste in the back of my throat, like iron filings, and my teeth were buzzing.

"Where did you learn such an awful Word, Flora Segunda?" Valefor said, coughing out a huge cloud of dust. Now he looked even worse than before, as though he'd been left out in the rain and all his colours had run into a giant blur.

I clenched my teeth in an effort to get them to stop jittering around in my mouth. "It was supposed to just spark a little light."

"You shouldn't light a match in a powder magazine, Flora Segunda, then be surprised if the gunpowder explodes. Your Gramatica pronunciation is terrible. If you meant to Exhort an Ignition you should have used the Nominative case, not the Vocative. The Nominative lights, the Vocative implodes."

"It worked before just fine," I sputtered.

"You were lucky! Look what you have done to me – I was hardly here already, and now, thanks to your atrocious accent, I am almost gone! I haven't even the energy to rise!"

A tiny bad feeling was growing in me. Poor Valefor, trapped all alone in the library, and when he finally gets a visitor, she is mean to him and almost turns him into soup.

"What do you want me to do, Valefor?" I asked, relenting.

He perked up. "Just a wee little thing."

"What wee thing?"

"A tiny teeny thing that will be so small you won't even notice it."

"Such as?"

"Tiny teeny—"

"Plainly, Valefor, or I'm out of here!"

"Your Anima. If you gave me just a tiny teeny bit, it would go so far, and I would feel so much better, and you would be so nice."

"My Anima?"

"Ayah, your Anima – you know, your magickal essence, inside you, your spiritual energy—"

"I know what Anima is, Valefor, but how can I give you some?"

He sighed. "You have so little control over yourself, Flora Segunda, that every time you breathe out, you let a bit of your Anima blow away. Why waste it when you could give it to me? Please, I'll be your best friend, and it would taste so good."

Compassion is the vice of queens, Mamma always says, and she thinks I should toughen up. She says that I let the dogs take advantage of me and hog the bed, when they should sleep on the floor, and that I give too much of my pocket money to beggars, and that if I am to get along in this world, I need to harden my heart.

Well, I don't want my heart to be hard, and even if I end up like Poppy, trying to drink my heart to death, or like Mamma, trying to work my heart to death, at least I will know that I have a heart and I used it honestly. And maybe I owed Valefor something for making him worse. I couldn't really resist the poor Butler sitting there so forlorn and famished, too weak even to get up out of the heap that I had blown him into.

He said eagerly, "It's very easy – see, all you have to

do is breathe out and I shall breathe in, thus I shall be fed. Easy as pie."

"All right." I knelt down beside him, and he reached for me with thin shivery hands. We bent our heads together. I closed my eyes, took a deep breath, and felt the featherweight touch of his lips against mine. Slowly I breathed out, then felt his shoulders shake under my hands.

"Ah, that is so happy," Valefor whispered. "One more time?"

I drew in another breath, and again exhaled. His lips grew warmer, and now I was shivering – not with cold, but with a skittery feeling deep inside, not entirely unpleasant. I opened my eyes. His pupils had dilated to enormous purple circles, bright as coldfire. Glittering. A faint tinge of colour was creeping across his face.

"Just once more. The last, I promise."

I sucked a deep breath into my lungs, which suddenly felt deflated and small. Valefor's grip was much stronger this time. As I breathed out, a great darkness opened up before me, swirling with streaks of colour. The skittery feeling inside turned warm, then hot, and suddenly I couldn't breathe at all. I yanked back, gasping.

Val said, distantly, "Thank you. You don't know how much better I feel."

I leaned against the window seat, sputtering. The room spun about me in fragments of light and colour. I closed my eyes again, and the spinning slowed. I felt as though something had punched me in the gut. Something delicious.

"What a drama queen you are, Flora," Valefor said. "I didn't take that much."

I opened my eyes. The fragments slid back together with a click, and there was Valefor, looking an awful lot better. His face had rounded out, and his eyes were now iridescently purple. He shook out his gown and twirled it around. The fabric, now black and satiny, flared around his knees. "Isn't it nice?" he said.

It *was* rather nice, but I didn't want to admit it. The tight feeling of anxiety and gloom that I usually carry around in the pit of my stomach seemed less tight, less gloomy.

Still twirling, Val was giving off little sparks. He stopped suddenly, and his glittery eyes crinkled as he frowned. "You taste different, though. There's some unfamiliar spark about you. What can it be?"

"I don't know and I can't wait for you to figure it out," I said, standing up. A whirl of dizziness made me almost slide back down.

"Rebellion! That's it, Flora Segunda. You are full of irresponsible thoughts. So you want to be a ranger, join the Ranger Corps?"

"There is no more Ranger Corps. They were disbanded at the end of the War."

"Oh, that silly war, ayah, I remember. A ranger! Secret and sly, the rangers are. Other than Nini Mo, who knows a ranger? Who can tell where a ranger will be,

41

who a ranger will be? I'm surprised at you, Flora, for harbouring such deviant thoughts. Fyrdraacas go to the Barracks, you know."

I did not want to be reminded of this, particularly by a denizen who was making that remark with a superior little grin. "I gotta go. Ave, Valefor."

"Will you come back, Flora Segunda?" he asked anxiously.

"I don't know if I will be able to find you again."

"I'll mark the way," he promised. "And now that I feel better, I will make sure you land in exactly the right place!"

"I will try." I pushed the window open, swung down the uneven stone wall, lost my grip on the ivy, and fell, with a great puff of dust, into a pile of leaves.

Something thumped next to my head. When I got my wind back, I dug through the crackling leaves until I felt the spine of my overdue library book, which I had left on the settee in my bedroom. Just like Idden had said, Valefor and his magicking were helpful! Rolling to my feet, I looked up. The window was now closed, but I thought I could see a faint pale hand, waving at me frantically. I waved back and ran to catch the horsecar, feeling almost cheerful.

POPPY THROWS A CAKE.
BARKING DOGS. BROKEN GLASS.
TEMPER TANTRUM.

That evening, I sat in the Below Kitchen, having a late dessert and thinking. Somehow, I had been lost for less time than I had thought. By running as fast as my short legs could carry me, I had made the 7.45 horsecar in time, and slid into the Round Rotunda just as the first bell was ringing. By the time the second bell tolled, I was safely in line, ready for Morning Assembly. At lunch, Librarian Naberius accepted my fifty-one-glory fine with a fishy grin, and handed over volume 2 of Nini Mo's autobiography.

No visit to Madama, no letter to Mamma. A narrow squeak, but a squeak all the same.

The rest of the day had been productive. In Dressmaking, I got the bodice of my Catorcena dress cut out. In Scriptive, I finished almost all the invitations, and in Literature, I got 100 per cent on the pop vocab test. And all the while, my mind had spun around on the topic of Valefor, and it was spinning now still.

Poor Valefor, all alone and forlorn. I know a little something about feeling all alone and forlorn. Ayah so, he was pompous, that's true, but he was our Butler, and a part of our family. He was a magickal entity and must therefore know a lot about the Current, and therefore could probably be mighty helpful to me in my rangery aspirations. I wished that Udo, my best friend, were available to discuss, but – so annoying – he'd been under house arrest for two weeks and thus incommunicado for anything non-school-related. I wondered if the Elevator really would take me directly back to the Bibliotheca. I wouldn't mind talking to Valefor some more, but I didn't relish being lost again.

My thoughtful chewing was interrupted by thundering from above. When the dogs started to howl out a welcome, all the joy went right out of my chocolate hazelnut cake. Suddenly the luscious cake felt as heavy as a pair of shoes in my stomach. The dogs bolted out of the kitchen and up the Below Stairs, yelping joyously.

Once in a red moon, Poppy staggers down the Stairs of Exuberance and causes a lot of commotion. I always hope that he will save his acting out for when Mamma is home, because she puts up with nothing. The first sign of trouble from him and out comes her pearl-handled revolver and whack goes the barrel on the side of his head. Then she carries him back to the Eyrie, and we don't hear much from Poppy for a while.

I have a harder time handling him, because I don't believe in whacking people to make them behave, even though I admit that it seems to work for Mamma. She is a soldier and soldiers are prone to whacking, so it's understandable that she would feel comfortable with it. I have found that cajoling people and making nice is as effective as whacking, but it's hard to cajole someone who is drunk and half mad.

"Where's Buck?" Poppy demanded, materializing in the doorway like a dæmon from the Abyss. He pushed a dog down off his chest and nudged another one out of his way with a grimy bare foot.

"Mamma's on inspection," I said warily, from behind my fork. Like I said, I don't believe in whacking, but I was glad that I was closer to the knife board than he was. "Are you hungry, Poppy?"

Poppy doesn't eat much – crackers and cookies mostly, which I leave at the bottom of the Stairs of Exuberance or Mamma takes up to him. But sometimes he comes looking for something more substantial, and maybe that was all he wanted tonight.

"Where's Idden?" He sat down in the chair opposite me. His hands were steady and his eyes, sunken deep in the black stripe of the mourning band painted across his face, did not seem as bleary as usual. I had the sudden bubbling hope that he might be sober.

"She's gone back to Fort Jones," I said. "Her leave was over."

"Lucky her. You can taste the sky at Fort Jones," he said, reaching for my cake plate. "Get the hell down, Flynnie; you know that dogs can't have chocolate. It will kill you for sure." He paused the plate in mid-air and looked down at Flynn's begging face, considering.

"Here, Flynnie, here, pup," I said hastily, dangling a cinnamon cookie. You never can guess what Poppy will do next, and among all the dogs, Flynn is my favourite. Sometimes he sprays, and always he quivers, but he is my darling boy.

After Flynnie snatched the cookie, I tossed cookies to the other dogs, herded them all into the mudroom, locked the door, then put the key in my pocket. I wouldn't have minded sitting in the mudroom with them, myself, but it probably wasn't a good idea to leave Poppy alone.

"Where's Flora?" Poppy asked, shovelling the cake in. The last time he had come down from the Eyrie, I hadn't been home, so I hadn't seen him for about two weeks. He looked the same, though: like hell. His face was sharp as a blade, and his clothes were filthy.

"I'm right here, Poppy," I said, hoping he meant me, but pretty sure he did not.

"Not you. Flora. Where is she?"

He wasn't sober. My heart sighed, and I tried to distract him. "When was the last time you changed your clothes, Poppy?"

He paused mid shovel. "What's wrong with my clothes?"

"Well, they are awfully grungy, Poppy. Wouldn't you feel better if you had some clean clothes? I'll get you some if you want."

"Where's Flora?" he demanded again.

"Do you want ice cream with your cake, Poppy?" I asked. "I got three kinds: chocolate, peach—"

"Where is Flora?" His voice was getting louder.

"She went with Mamma on inspection," I lied. I went to the icebox for the peach ice cream. He took the carton from me but, a moment later, abandoned the ice cream and sat silently, shoulders slumped, staring.

"What's wrong, Poppy?"

"I lost her, Flora," he said sadly. At least he recognized me again. "The Birdies took her from me."

"I know, Poppy, but it wasn't your fault." By Birdies I knew he meant the Huitzils. Huitzil means hummingbird and Birdie is the not-so-nice Califa nickname for our overlords.

"Your mother will never forgive me."

"She will, Poppy, but you must forgive yourself." Sometimes it is better to lie. Mamma never would forgive Poppy for losing the First Flora, but I privately felt that she deserved some of the blame herself. War is no place for a kid, yet Mamma had sent Flora to Poppy, and when he was captured, so was she. They were both taken to Anahautl City as prisoners. But although Poppy was ransomed, the First Flora was never seen again.

47

"Why didn't your mother leave me there? I deserved the darkness. I broke faith, Flora, I broke my word. I swore I'd never leave her and I did. I left her behind."

I didn't know what to say. I swallowed hard, blinking. The chocolate torte had become a huge wad in the back of my throat.

"Do you want some more ice cream, Poppy?" I asked lamely. Mamma would have known what to say, but Mamma wasn't there. At least, I thought dolefully, he wasn't throwing things. I kept an eye on the door, anyway. A good ranger knows how to make a swift exit.

He put his elbows on the table, and the sleeves of his tattered cardigan fell away, showing livid knife stripes along his inner arms, one so fresh it still oozed. "Do you think she will ever forget what I did?"

I wasn't sure which "she" he was referring to, but I said, "I am sure that she would understand."

"How can she understand in the dark? I never saw her after that, they kept us apart, but I could hear the screaming, maybe that was me, it was so far off that I couldn't quite make out the words, they gave me Moxley's heart on a soup plate, with barley broth and carrots, and I have always hated cooked carrots. They make me *sick*!"

He flung the plate against the wall, and the cake exploded into chocolate and hazelnut shrapnel. After that, he screamed and yelled and got the dogs all into a huge barking uproar, and then escaped the kitchen.

Although I couldn't cajole him back up the Stairs of Exuberance to his Eyrie, I finally corralled him upstairs, in the Garterobe of Resolution, our only working potty, then locked the door.

I brushed back my messy hair and plopped down on the hall settle to catch my breath. In the dust-up, I had knocked my elbow against a case full of ancient family artifacts, and now the bone throbbed in time to my newly pulsing headache. For a moment I thought I might throw up. Rangers do not cry, but my nose was running in a most unprofessional way.

"I had a ghost who was that noisy once, but you can bet that I got rid of him quickly." It was Valefor.

"I thought you couldn't leave the Bibliotheca." Despite the bad timing, I was a little pleased to see him. He was company, after all. I wiped my nose on the edge of my kilt. "Are you still banished?"

He smirked. "Ayah so, but I'm feeling a bit better. Not completely myself, but stronger."

Although his voice sounded less scratchy, the rest of him bordered on the transparent. I could see the wall behind him, through him. But the coldfire violet eyes still glittered.

"I can see through you," I said.

"Yes. I may be feeling better, but it's still a lot of effort for me to get out. I could use another sip." He looked at me hopefully.

"*Flora!*" Poppy roared from the potty. "*Unlock this door right now!*"

"He needs a good thumping," Valefor said. "That would shut him up."

"I don't believe in thumping people," I answered. "And besides, it's not Poppy's fault that he is this way. So thumping him would hardly make him better. He's sick."

"Hotspur's drunk," Val said. "It's the curse of the Fyrdraacas. You'll probably go that way one day yourself."

I said hotly, "I don't drink."

"Not drunkenness, pinhead. I mean the madness. It's been bred in the bone; you are all high-strung, like good hunting dogs. The Fyrdraacas make magnificent soldiers and fantastic lawyers, but it's the madness in them that makes them great."

"Mamma's not mad!"

"There is more than one way of being crazy, Flora," Valefor said. "Some people are crazy for glory, some crazy for drink, some crazy for duty. You'll see."

I doubted it. I had no intention of becoming a drinker like Poppy, or a workaholic like Mamma, or a self-righteous git like Idden. Being a great ranger requires many qualities, but madness and drunkenness aren't among them.

Valefor continued, "Ah, poor Hotspur. He was so glorious once. The best of all the Fyrdraacas and the most beautiful, too. Who would have thought this day would come? I remember, when he was just a tot—"

"Flora, damn you, let me out!"

That crashing sound was probably Poppy throwing a chair against the door. Mamma was going to be very angry if she came home to find the Garterobe of Resolution trashed. We only have access to one indoor loo, and I hate going outside to the bog.

"You could threaten his life with a railway share," Valefor offered. "I have a huge collection of them in the Bibliotheca Mayor, and some of them are sharp as razors. Oh no, I forgot, you are a *pacifist*. I would suggest charming him with smiles and soap, then. That would be a good non-violent approach. Honestly, I can't see how you can be a Fyrdraaca and be a pacifist, too. It's an absolute contradiction in terms."

I was not happy to see Val any more. He was a snippy snapperhead and he was not helping at all. I ignored his happy pontificating and went back to the potty door. Poppy's fits usually do blow over quickly. He screams and shouts for a while, and then he is done until the next time.

"Poppy?"

The hurtling noises abruptly stopped.

"Flora, please let me out." His voice sounded weak and far away.

"Are you done screaming and shouting?"

"Yes, Flora," he said meekly.

"Promise?"

"*Flora*—"

"Poppy, I have the key and I am not going to let you out until you promise to be good."

51

He turned threatening. "I'm going to tell your mother."

"Tell her what? That I locked you in the Garterobe of Resolution because you were screaming and shouting and that you threw my cake against the kitchen wall?"

There was a brief pause, and then his voice, less muffled, drifted through the keyhole. "I promise, Flora. Just please let me out. I need to get back to the Eyrie. I am feeling rather sick."

"I wouldn't," said Valefor, breathing down my neck. "Let him stew for a while."

"Get off." I pushed him away, my hand shredding through his arm like a knife through smoke. I gingerly opened the door and Poppy wobbled out. He sat patiently on the settle while I bandaged up the cuts on his hands. He had smashed the mirrors with his bare fists.

"My eyes are too green. I can't stand the way they stare in my face," Poppy said, as though that was an explanation.

"I shouldn't wonder," Valefor muttered. "*Look on my face, I have become death, murderer of calm.*"

Poppy turned his head sharply, noticing Valefor for the first time. "What the hell are you doing down here?"

Val shrank behind me, wavering.

"If Buck catches you out, she'll cut you up and use you for a raincoat," Poppy warned.

"Hold still, Poppy," I ordered. He was shaking so

52

hard that I kept smearing the Madama Twanky's Cut-Eze on his shirt instead of his arm.

"Ouch, careful with that stuff, it burns."

"Good on it," I said. "Serves you right. Who's going to clean up all that mess now, Poppy?"

"Make your little friend do it. After all, it is *his* House," Poppy said sarcastically.

Valefor snorted. "Hardly any more. Your darling lady wife locked me up in the Bibliotheca Mayor, and this is the first time I've been out in I don't know how long."

"How *did* you get out?" Poppy asked.

"Poppy," I said, before Val could get me in trouble, "you should go back to your Eyrie and lie down for a while. I'm sure you'll feel better, then—"

"Watch him, Flora," Poppy interrupted. "He is bound to spit and that's going to burn. I warn you."

Whatever *that* meant. "Ayah so, Poppy, don't worry. I'll take care of everything."

Poppy shambled to his feet. "You'd better get back to the Bibliotheca before Buck gets back, Valefor."

Val sniffed. "I am not afraid of Buck."

Poppy looked at him sombrely. "You are the only one. And you are a fool."

6

CLEANING UP. VAL MAKES AN OFFER. WIGGLING FINGERS. ANOTHER KISS.

"I could help you clean up," Val said, trailing behind me as I went downstairs to the kitchen to fetch a broom and let the dogs out.

The dogs slunk out of the mudroom dejectedly, then slunk off into the garden. Flynnie pressed up against my legs sadly and pushed his head into my hand to be petted. I hugged his solid meaty bulk, and he licked my face before squirming free to follow his sibs into the darkness.

"How can you do that? I thought you were diminished and without any ability." I got the broom and a garbage sack out of the mudroom, and Val followed me back up the Below Stairs.

"I am still weak, it's true, but you have lent me enough to allow me some freedom. So now we are friends and I stick by my friends."

The Garterobe of Resolution was a wreck. Shards of glass winked like fallen stars on the floor and in the bathtub. The sink was full of tooth powder and bath salts, and the walls and ceiling were stuck with soggy toilet paper. FOR THIS WE ARE SOLDIERS was scrawled in red lip rouge across one of the walls. Even if I got the mess cleaned up, I could not replace the mirrors before Mamma returned. Both Poppy and I were going to be in big trouble.

"My beautiful loo," Val moaned, peering over my shoulder. "My beautiful loo. Do you have any idea how long it took me to make those mirrors? Weeks of utter concentration and focused desire. And the tiles – oh, the energy to make them the most perfect shade of bleachy blue, after which I was almost invisible with exhaustion – now all cracked, and filthy, too. Hotspur made a mess, but he didn't have far to go. Don't you ever wash the bathroom floor, Flora Segunda?"

"Well, can you do something about the mess?" I demanded, ignoring his crack. Valefor might not be afraid of Mamma, but I was. I did not want her to see this mess and say that I had not watched Poppy closely enough.

"Well, if I were to have more Anima—"

"How much?"

He grinned at me hopefully. "Not a lot, just more. What did you have for dinner tonight?"

"General Chow's tofu."

He wrinkled his long nose. "I'm not that fond of

such spicy food myself, but all right. It's better than nothing."

"But be careful," I said. "You almost made me pass out last time."

"I'll be sweet as pie," he promised. His lips brushed mine and then parted to take my breath. A slow tingle started in my toes and wiggled its way upward, as though my blood had turned fizzy.

"That's enough," I said, breaking away. "You are making me dizzy."

Val grinned. "Ah, I feel so much better, you cannot believe it!"

His hair, I realized, was not black. It was dark purple-blue, the colour of a damson plum, and little threads of silver sparked in the thick curls now springing around his shoulders.

"Just clean this place up, Valefor. It's late and I have to go to bed. Tomorrow's a school day."

"You are a busy one, aren't you?" Valefor said. "Always rushing from here to there and there to here. You ought to just slow down and enjoy life. It's short enough as it is without you hurrying."

Ha! As though there was anything about life to enjoy. "Clean it up. Now!"

Valefor flourished a long finger. " ᘓᐧᗁᑊᗕ!"

When the sparkly purple Invocation faded, not only was the Garterobe of Resolution tidied up, but it was actually clean. The silver taps gleamed and the porcelain sparkled. The broken loo chain had been

56

replaced, Mamma's cut-glass bottles were lined up neatly above the bath, and the towels were soft and fluffy. The mirror showed my astonished face and Valefor's smug smile.

"See how helpful I can be?" Valefor said happily. "The mirror is not exactly the same, of course. I don't have enough for that, but I don't think Buck's subtlety will extend to noticing the difference."

Valefor *was* helpful. While I let the dogs in, he whisked about the Below Kitchen, humming Gramatica under his breath and wiggling his fingers. When he was done, the kitchen was so clean that it almost sparkled. The copper pans hanging from the ceiling shone like stars, the stove glowed like a polished black pearl, and the floor looked clean enough to eat off.

"There we are! Let's have popcorn!" Valefor said when he was done.

"I thought you didn't eat food."

"Well, I don't eat to live, but sometimes it is fun to live to eat. Come on, Flora, tra-la-let's have a party! Oh please, let's!"

"I have to go to bed."

"Pah! Bed! There's time enough to sleep when you are dead, Flora."

"I am tired." Dealing with Poppy is exhausting and sick-at-heart-making, and now I wanted nothing more than to crawl into bed and stay there a week. It was a relief to have the mess cleaned up, and popcorn was tempting, but I still wanted my bed.

"You are a stick, Flora, that's what you are, an absolute stick," Valefor said.

I did not give in, but Valefor would not give up. Still begging, he followed me as I turned down the lights, banked the stove, and went upstairs. He leaned over me as I stopped by the Stairs of Exuberance, to listen for noise coming from Poppy's Eyrie. (Dead silence.)

"You are *bugging* me!" I shouted, after I had shut my bedroom door in his face and he had floated right through, anyway.

He looked hurt. "But I thought you liked me."

I threw my boots into the wardrobe and pulled my nightgown out from under my pillow. "I just need to go to bed and get some sleep. And I can't do that if you are following me everywhere. Can't you leave me alone?"

"I told you, Flora, we are connected now, and I can go where you go, at least around the House. I will be very quiet," he said, sitting down on the settee. But of course he wasn't. He chattered on about this and that, and that and this. Having someone around to clean things up was nice, but I could see now that it had its cost. *The meal's not free if you still have to leave a tip*, Nini Mo said.

". . . and a shame that a Fyrdraaca should be sleeping in a broom closet—"

"This was a broom closet?" I interrupted. My room is not fancy, but it's not tiny, either. It has a fireplace surmounted by a mantel carved with cunning little

58

monkeys, two big windows that overlook the kitchen garden, a cushy settee, and a banged-up wardrobe big enough to play house in. Sure, it is messy, but that was nothing against the room, only against my interest in keeping it tidy.

"Well, not this room. This room was, I think, where I stored extra toilet brushes or something; I don't remember. Anyway, I mean there—" Valefor pointed to my bed. "That closet!"

At first glance around my room, you wouldn't see my bed at all, and you'd think maybe I slept on the settee. But then you would notice a set of doors on one wall, and when the doors slid open, there was my bed, tucked inside a little alcove, all snuggly and secret. I love my bed; when the doors are closed and you are pillowed down into your comforters with a dog at your feet, you are hidden and no one can get you. Had my bed been a broom closet?

"See how it is that the Fyrdraacas are constrained," Valefor said. "I am as wide as the sky when it comes to space, and here the Fyrdraacas are, crouching in utility rooms. Even your kitchen is just an extra kitchen I made in case some guest brought his own cook, and these rooms, all of them, spare servants' quarters for spare servants, and here you are living as servants in them. Or in your case, a slave, Flora Segunda."

Valefor was right. Why were we living in servants' rooms, like servants? Because we couldn't get to the rest of the House without the Butler. Whom Mamma had banished. Another thing to hold against her, I supposed. But not tonight. "I really have to go to bed, Valefor," I said. "Are you going to shut up or shall I kick you?"

"All right, all right!" He settled down on the settee and began to read one of my Nini Mo yellowback novels. I climbed into bed, pulled the door mostly closed, and put my nightgown on. The dogs had already settled in, and they shifted around to make room for me.

"Must you throw your clothes on the floor?" Valefor asked without looking up from his reading. He waved one hand and my stays and chemise drifted upward, then floated over to the wardrobe, tucking themselves inside. My kilt and pinafore wafted into the dirty-clothes bin, and my pullover flitted over to Valefor, who put down the yellowback to receive it.

"There's a giant hole in the elbow!" he said, accusingly. I'm terrible at darning. I can sew fine, but somehow when it comes to knitting, my stitches get muddled. Valefor smoothed the sweater between his palms, and when he held it up, smugly, the hole was gone. "You are welcome!"

"Thank you, Valefor."

"You *are* welcome."

"Well, then, if you are going to stay, at least turn the lights down."

The lights dimmed accordingly, and I slid the bed door shut and snuggled into the nest of dogs. Flynn squirmed his boniness between my feet, and Flash and

Dash curled together against the wall. The sheets were doggy warm, but they could have smelled fresher.

I lay there and let the darkness overwhelm me. Sometimes it is very hard not to sink. Udo calls this feeling the little black ghost in my head, and while sometimes its wheedling is muted, I can never quite completely pull free of its influence. Sometimes it seems as though there will never be an end. Poppy will continue to be drunken, Mamma will continue to be gone, and I will march off to the Barracks and fulfil the Fyrdraaca family destiny, which is nothing but ruin and sorrow.

"Why are you crying?"

My heart jerked, and I lifted my head. The dogs hadn't moved, but Valefor's eyes, faint coldfire sparks, glimmered next to me.

"Pigface Psychopomp! I think I just lost ten years off my life."

"Fyrdraacas die young, anyway," Val said. "Where's your nightcap?"

I wiped my eyes on the pillowcase. "Go away and let me go to sleep."

"But you weren't sleeping," he pointed out. "You can't sleep and cry at the same time. And if you cry yourself to sleep, you'll only wake up with a headache tomorrow morning."

"I wish you would mind your own business."

"This *is* my business. I mean, I'm the House Fyrdraaca and you are a Fyrdraaca, so that makes it my business. Besides, you are getting my sheets wet. If anyone should be crying, it's me, over the decline of our family. Once so numerous and distinguished, oh, we had generals and lawyers, artists and statesmen, we were the beauty of the world, and now down to four Fyrdraacas, and none of you particularly distinguished compared to the Fyrdraacas of old."

He was a snapperhead, and for a savage sudden minute, I wished he'd stayed in his library and rotted. Cold feet squirmed against my ankles and I yanked away. Flynn growled and crawled to the other edge of the bed.

"Aw, finally, toasty. I get so very cold," Valefor said. "I remember when your great-great-great-grandmother Idden Fyrdraaca made this comforter. She cut up captured battle flags to make the quilt pieces, and when it was finished, she stuffed it with the hair of her enemies. Took her four years to get enough to fill the quilt. That's why it is so nice and warm."

Ugh! I had come across the quilt, brilliantly coloured and crazily sewn together with bright swatches of silk, in one of the huge clothespresses in the laundry room. It had been on my bed ever since, and it was very warm, but I resolved now to burn it in the morning.

"Don't you have to get back to the Bibliotheca?" I asked hopefully.

"Oh no." Valefor laughed. "I feel so much better right now, I just can't believe it. Isn't this fun? It's just like one of those slumber parties I have read about. The girls lie in the dark and tell sad stories of the deaths of kings, and eat popcorn, and then they give each other green facials."

"You are not a girl."

"Oh. Well, yes, I suppose you are right, but now that I feel better, I could be a girl, if you wanted me to be—"

"No," I said hastily. He was confusing enough as he was. "Just stay the way that you are."

"Don't you want any popcorn?" the whiny dark asked.

I sat up, disrupting dogs and kicking aside cold feet. "Look, I am trying to go to sleep. I have had a long day and I have to get up early in the morning. All right? For Pigface Psychopomp's sake, can't you shut up?"

"Well, fine," said the darkness, snippily.

I flopped down, turned my back to the sulky silence, and pulled the covers over my ears. At least I didn't feel like crying any more.

7

SICKNESS. MED-I-CINE.
WAFFLES. VAL PROPOSES.

Valefor was gone when I awoke, and I did not feel so well. My head ached, my bones ached, and generally I felt punk. Rangers suck up pain and sickness; they don't let a little thing like weakness of the body get in the way of their obligations, so I dragged myself out of bed, did my morning chores, and got to Sanctuary just in time for first bell.

But the day was such a horrible loss; I should have stayed at home. In my furry brain-haze, I left my Lit vocab list at home, so I got a zed on the hand-in, which meant that even though I got a plus-ten on the pop quiz, there went a fourth of my grade. In Scriptive, I knocked over the ink bottle and flooded out an entire stack of Catorcena invitations – twenty-five to do over. And after much finger-pricking, thread-snapping, and swearing in Dressmaking, I discovered that I had put the left sleeve of my Catorcena dress in upside down.

Every time I passed Archangel Bob in the hall, he would give me the eye, as though he had noticed I was not up to snuff and was wondering if he should send me to the Infirmary. With Mamma due home on Monday, I had too much to do to go to the Infirmary, and anyway, that was not where I wanted to spend my weekend, swallowing nasty medicine and eating nothing but oatmeal mush with spelt flakes. If you have to die in bed, it's better that that bed be your own. Nini Mo didn't say that, but I'll bet she would have agreed. Of course, she didn't die in bed, but it's the principle.

It seemed like the day would never be over, but finally it was, and before Archangel Bob could make up his mind and grab me, I schlepped home. I kicked the dogs into the garden, hung the laundry out, and mucked the horses. The dogs came back in, and I shut them in the parlour, leaving the terrace door open so they could let themselves out. I blearily climbed the zillion stairs up to my bedroom, where I flopped on to the settee and fell into a snuffling sleep.

Time became a sickly blur of waking, stumbling to the potty, stumbling back to the settee, and sleep. Waking, stumbling down to feed the dogs, back to the settee, and sleep. Sometimes it was daylight when I woke, sometimes it was night. Always I was shivery cold, shaky and miserable.

Finally, I woke up feeling a little better, not nearly as shivery, but still terribly cold. And hungry, too. I didn't have the energy to get up, light a lamp, check on the dogs, find some chow. I didn't have the energy to do anything at all. I lay on the settee, staring miserably up into the darkness.

Then I remembered Valefor.

"Valefor," I croaked.

A thin wavery cloud coalesced at the end of the settee. I could barely make out Val's narrow face. The cloud crept down over me, and I shivered at the coolness. I put my palms up and he put misty hands against mine, and he immediately brightened into a more solid shape. He bent over and I breathed a deep breath into him, feeling him grow concrete, sucking the ache from me. For a few seconds, my insides felt airy, as though my skin were filled with nothing but a tingling purple light.

When Valefor stood upright, he looked the best yet, not at all a starveling. In fact, if it weren't for the purple eyes and his purple hair, he could have been a normal boy. He wasn't exactly pretty, but he sparkled.

Valefor grinned at me and waved his arms about. "Thank you, Flora Segunda. I feel much better. You don't taste so good right now, but still, it's enough."

I flopped back on the pillows, feeling like I had inhaled little sparks of fire. I suddenly felt a lot more perky, albeit a tad breathless. "You are welcome."

With a gentle hiss, the radiators came on, even

though I hadn't shovelled any coal in over a week. In the fireplace, the fire flared up, bright and friendly.

"This is much, much better," Val beamed, balancing on the settee arm. "Why didn't you call me earlier? You shouldn't be lying around like this, Flora. It's bad for your mental state. Once you lie down, you might not get up again for ages. Great-uncle Gussie once spent four years lying on the sofa in the Drawing Room of Depredations. You don't know how hard it was to dust around him."

"I've been ill."

"Ah . . ." Val fished around in his long hanging sleeves, then came up with a small green bottle. "I have just the trick."

"What is it?"

He proffered a spoonful of pinkish liquid. "Open up. It will make you all better."

I recoiled. I knew from experience that liquids that promise to make you all better usually make you wish you could die. "What does it taste – oof."

Valefor had shoved in the spoon. I started to choke and then the lovely buttery syrup flowed down my throat and seemed to settle into a warm fuzzy haze in my wheezing chest. Now I was really feeling pretty good.

"What was that?"

"Madama Twanky's Sel-Ray Psalt Med-I-Cine," Valefor replied. He'd replaced both bottle and spoon inside his flowing sleeve.

"It tasted like maple syrup." The Madama Twanky's Sel-Ray Psalt that Mamma forces me to take when I'm ill tastes like lamp oil.

"Well, I did improve a bit on the original, but it will fix what ails you."

"When is it?" I asked, pushing myself back up on the pillows. Ah, the lovely warmth puffing from the radiator. Ah, the lovely warmth in my bones.

"All times are alike to me, so monotonous and boring, but –" Valefor considered. "I think it's Sunday for you."

"Sunday!" Panic gurgled in my throat, in my voice. Sunday! The entire weekend gone. My dress, my invitations, my speech, the fifty tamales I had to make and distribute to the poor! Everything I was going to get done this weekend, just in the nick of Mamma coming home. And now she would be home tomorrow and I had done nothing. Even if I started immediately, I wouldn't have time to get it all done. "I've wasted the whole weekend. I'll never get all my chores done!" I slumped back down into gloom and felt babyish tears prickle at my eyes.

"Never you worry," said Valefor soothingly. "Valefor is here and he specializes in getting things done. But first, teatime!"

Out of Nowhere, Val produced a plate of waffles and a giant pot of orange tiger tea. While I gobbled the first solid food I'd had in for ever, he started tidying. He twinkled his fingertips and suddenly my bedsheets were clean and the bed was made. (Pigface, I'd forgotten to get rid of that horrible comforter!) He waved a hand and my scattered Nini Mo yellowbacks hopped into a neat stack, and the painting of Mamma and Idden hanging over the fireplace straightened. He flapped my socks and they were hole-free. He fixed the upside-down sleeve of my Catorcena dress with a flip of one finger, and hemmed it with a wave of another. He tapped pen to paper and soon enough had a full stack of invitations completed, without a smudge or an ink blot. It was so wonderful to lie there, warm and full, and watch someone else do all the work. In just a few short minutes, my bedroom was cleaner than it had been in years and my Catorcena chores were nearly done. *Mamma, why are you so darn stubborn?*

"Well," Val said, finally, after I had drunk the last drop of tea and he had eaten the last waffle. He tossed the tea tray up in the air, and before I could shout, it was gone. "I have been thinking."

I yawned again. Between the medicine and all those waffles I was feeling awfully sleepy, but in a yummy tired way. "About what?"

He leaned over the back of the settee and grinned ingratiatingly at me. "I don't think the Elevator was being obdurate when it brought us together, Flora. That Elevator, that part of me, that is, knew what it was doing, even if you and I were slow to pick up on it."

"Hmm..." My eyelids weighed fifty pounds, and they kept dropping closed.

"Are you listening to me?" Val's breath smelled like nutmeg. I opened my eyes. His face was so close to mine that I could see the faint shimmer of golden freckles on his skin, which was as smooth as rubber.

"Do you have bones?" I murmured.

He said snippily, "Of course I have bones. Every stone in this house is part of my—"

"No, I mean, inside your skin, do you have bones? Do you have a liver?"

"What would I need a liver for – disgusting organ – of course not! But as I was saying. I could help you further, if you help me further, Flora."

"Ayah so?" I yawned again.

He continued, "You just don't know how boring and lonely it is to be so diminished, me who once had the world begging for favours. And it's not right, either, to close up such a House and let it moulder away just because you are afraid—"

This woke me up some, indignantly. "Mamma is not afraid of anything." In her youth, my mamma killed a jaguar with a shovel. She's won the Warlord's Hammer twice. She's fought three duels, one bare-knuckled, and won them all. And, of course, she's been married to Poppy for twenty-eight years, which alone takes an awful lot of sand.

"Pah. You can be as brave as a lion on the outside,

70

Flora Segunda," Val answered, "and fight bears with your fingernails and stare down monsters until they melt into little puddles of goo at your feet and still be a coward inside, in your heart, where it counts."

I rolled over and turned my back to Val. He was lucky I didn't believe in violence; otherwise, I would have punched his lights out for maligning Mamma so. The comfy feeling of chores done was receding into the more familiar feeling of gloom. Why did Valefor have to remind me of all this when I had been feeling so nice?

Val's nutmeg breath tickled my ear. "Don't sulk, Flora Segunda. It is not becoming to your lineage. I mean no disrespect to your dear lady mamma, but you have to face facts – this is not the way things should be."

"That's not my mamma's fault," I said into the cushion. "She does the best she can." *Which isn't good enough*, my brain whispered.

"No doubt she does, but that's not helping me, and it's not helping you, either. If we got together, we could help each other, and help your dear mamma, and even help darling Hotspur, too."

I rolled back over and stared up at Val's looming head. The coldfire burned purple in his eyes, like sparks of light deep in a black well. His lips were a faint shade of lavender, like very pale blueberries. He cocked his head and grinned at me, very sweet.

"What do you mean, help Mamma and Poppy?" I asked.

"You know," he said, "I remember the night the First Flora was born. It was strange weather. First came huge rain, then loud thunder, then an earthquake. An omen, don't you think? The First Flora was a stubborn little thing, and she was not going to come out. Such screaming and shouting and rushing to and fro, and, ah, the blood – I was never so strong, I think, as I was that night. Your mamma almost died. And you know why she didn't?"

I shook my head. Mamma never speaks of the First Flora.

Val looked smug. "Your father wasn't there, or I suppose he would have tried to help her, being a great one with the knife, Hotspur, always hoping to find something or someone to carve up. Your mamma was spewing blood and her eyes were growing dark. A doctor could not have helped her. But for me, for Valefor, what is a truculent baby and a dying mother? I just reached right in with one slender hand and I took a hold of that bad little girl's feet and she popped like a cork out of a bottle. Flora knew she'd met her match in me and there was no more insolence from her, I tell you."

"You are so full of hoo," I said. "Anyway, so what?"

"You ask your dear lady mamma," Val said, wounded. "And she will tell you I am saying nothing but the truth. I am the power of this House, Flora. The point is you all *need* me."

"Mamma is the power of this House. You are just the Butler."

"You decline without me. You dwindle. I told Buck, two wasn't enough, but did she listen to me? Of course not. See – she's already had to replace one!"

There were fewer Fyrdraacas in Califa than there had once been, but that didn't mean that we were in decline, did it? Fyrdraacas tend to die young, in all sorts of glamorous ways. It's not so good for the bloodline if people keep getting killed in duels (Great-aunt Arabelle), breaking their necks in cross-country horse races (Great-uncle Anacreon), drowned trying to swim across the Bay's Gate (Great-aunt Anacreona), or bit by a rattlesnake during a bar bet (Cousin Hippolyte), and not leaving any heirs behind. Pretty soon the family tree is pretty thin.

I answered, "Says you! There's still me and Idden. We aren't chopped mackerel."

"You are thin-blooded and miserable, that's what you are."

"We aren't." But my protest was half hearted. I *was* a replacement, wasn't I?

"Suit yourself, then," he said, shrugging. "Whether you believe it or not does not affect whether it is the truth. It's not fair. I am oppressed, and nothing more than a slave to Buck's Will."

"You are just the Butler, a denizen – you *should* be subject to Mamma's Will. It was what you were made for, to serve her, as the Head of the Fyrdraaca family," I said meanly, for he had completely spoiled my happy mood.

Valefor glared at me. "Fyrdraacas come and go, but I alone of this House stand for ever. Buck should understand that and treat me with the respect that I deserve. And anyway, it's not just me – we are *all* slaves to Buck's Will. Hotspur, Idden, you—"

"I have my own Will," I protested.

"Then why are you studying for the Benica Barracks entry exam?" Val asked slyly.

"I'm not." I wasn't, but I was supposed to be. I half hoped that if I failed the exam I wouldn't get in, although I'm sure that I would get in no matter if I passed or not. The Fyrdraaca estate may be worthless, but the Fyrdraaca name still has value.

"Why are you acting a slavey in your own home? Why do you have to get stuck dealing with Hotspur? Stuck with all the chores – the housework, the horses, the laundry?"

Each of Valefor's questions burned, for they were questions I had asked myself so many times but had never dared voice aloud. Underneath my gloom, there was the pinprick of anger. Why did Mamma have to be so unfair? Why couldn't she think of the rest of us for once?

He continued, "While I – whose Will it is to do those tasks – am locked away like a criminal."

"Anyway, we are both stuck, Valefor," I said, pulling the blanket up to my chin. "There's nothing we can do."

"Isn't there?" Val asked. He had perched on the settee

arm, above my feet, and now he leaned forward, eyes gleaming.

"What do you mean?"

Valefor grinned at me hopefully. "I could be restored."

8

DISCUSSION.
THE ESCHATANOMICON.

Suddenly a tiny lick of excitement was kindling against my gloominess. Could Valefor be restored? What if every day were like today, with working radiators and clean sheets? With delicious waffles and hole-free socks? The Elevator would always work, and there would be not a single dog hair anywhere. Could Valefor manage Poppy? I could live at Sanctuary and my nights would be blissfully scream-free. We would have our House back, in all its glory, and we'd be a normal family again, just like everyone else.

Then I remembered. "Mamma would never allow it."

"Why would Mamma have to know? I'd be very silent, just a little secret between you and me. I'd help you out, and Mamma would think you so clever, and no one but us would need to know." Val leaned in again, and again I saw the stars in his eyes. "Just think.

Warm sheets, fresh waffles, no more stable duty, clean towels, you wouldn't have to clean the bathroom any more, which I know you hate. No more dirty dishes or ancient leftover takeaway. Wouldn't that be heavenly?" The runnels of silver in Valefor's dark curls glittered. He wiggled a long finger enticingly at me. "And I can handle young Hotspur. I know where he lives. He'd be no trouble at all to me."

I closed my eyes to Val's enticements, which were mighty enticing. Clean rooms and no chores. Fluffy towels and yummy snacks. And Poppy, handled.

Val's voice purred in my ear, deliciously. "In a little wink, I could have all those tamales made and your dress done. Your invitations sent and your speech written. Everything would be ready, and with no trouble to you. Everything in perfect order."

It *was* a delicious thought, and the more I thought about it, the more delicious it became. Oh, how blissful it would be to have order in the House and things working as they should. Valefor could do all the work, and I could get all the credit, and Mamma would never be the wiser. Maybe Val *was* the power of our family; after all, didn't everything start falling apart right when he was banished?

"But could you be restored, Valefor?"

"Of course. I am here, but weakened. Of course I could be made strong again."

"What would it take?"

"Ayah so? It would be easy, Flora, I know it would,"

Valefor said eagerly. "I mean, you want to be a ranger, right? I can taste it on your Anima. It's your heart's desire, your True Will, so what a place to start! Even Nini Mo would not have dared to jump in so quickly, but I know you can do it."

"I'm not an adept, though. Surely I would have to be."

"Well, Buck's not an adept and she was able to banish me," Valefor said. "Ayah, there's skill, it's true, but also the right Working."

"I don't know a Working that strong."

"Not yet, that is. See, Flora, I am so kind and generous. I have a giftie for you, and one I think you will like real well. Look here –"

He reached up and plucked Something from Nothing, then offered that Something to me: a red book, small as a deck of cards, with a glittery soft cover trimmed in golden emboss and studded with small pearls. A gilt hasp kept the book closed, but the hasp opened easily when I tugged on it. I flipped to the title page.

The Eschatanomicon,
OR,
Rangering for Everybody!

An Invaluable Collection of Eight Hundred
Practical Receipts, Sigils and Instructs

FOR

Rangers, Adepts, Sorcerers, Mages, Bibliomantics,
Scouts, Hierophants, Gnostics, Chaoists, Priestesses, Sibyls,
Sages, Archons, Anthropagists, Avatars, Trackers,
and People Generally,
Containing a Rational Guide to
Evocation, Invocation, Augoeides, Smithing, Epiclesis,
Camping, Divination, Equipage, Retroactive Enchantment,
Mule Packing, Geas, Adoration, Cutting for Sign,
Bibliomancy, Transubstantiation, Hitches, Vortices,
Prophecy, Libel & Dreams, etc.

by

NYANA KEEGAN OV ADMOISH

"Free the oppressed!"

Valefor said, "It's a first edition. The later versions were expurgated, of course, which took all the fun out of them. But this one is intact, complete, and it's terribly rare. It's worth more than half the City, Flora. Don't read it in the bath. And look – it's signed."

The frontispiece showed a sketch of Nini Mo in a coyote-skin cape, rifle in one hand, pen in the other, and there on the flyleaf was a thick black scrawl. Her calligraphy was very hard to read; each letter looked like a spiky thistle, and some had very long tails, but her signature was unmistakable.

Nyana Macslyn Keegan or Admosh

"What does the inscription say?" I asked.

Val squinted, then read: "'To Little Tiny Doom and Fig. Dare, Win, or Disappear!'"

"Who is that? Little Tiny Doom? And Fig?"

"I have no idea; I don't remember exactly where I got the book. But see, Flora – _The Eschatanomicon_ contains everything you need to know about rangering, or magick, or both, and I'm sure it has the perfect Working to fix me fine as I ever was before."

I stared at the book in my hand, stared at the thick slant of Nini Mo's handwriting. This book she had held in _her_ hand; that black lettering had come from her pen. My head knew that Nini Mo – Nyana Keegan – was a real person, that she had once lived and breathed and died, as I lived and breathed and would one day die. I knew people who had known her, seen her, and talked to her. But yet, in my heart she was as fantastic as the stories that were told about her, and thus she seemed completely unreal.

But she had held this book in her hands, as I held it now. This selfsame book. Her flesh-and-blood hands. A small blot of ink followed her signature where her pen had slipped, as mine so often does. She had touched this book before, as I touched it now. These thoughts made my heart feel fluttery.

I flipped through _The Eschatanomicon_'s pages,

which were as thin as lettuce leaves. The first few chapters were very rangery, indeed. "How to Make a Fire with Rocks." "Fording a River with a Rope." "Making a Mule Mind." "The Charm of Charm." "Sleeping in a Heavy Rain." "Tracking Backwards." There were illustrations, too: tiny line-drawings of rangers fording rivers on rafts, rangers riding bucking horses, rangers hypnotizing rattlesnakes, rangers dancing the gavotte and doing other rangery things.

But then, after chapter 11, the headings changed. "Retroactive Enchantments." "Sigils to Bind." "Sigils to Break." "The A–Z of Banishing." "Interior Evocations." "Exhalative Invocations." "Fun with Charms." The illustrations changed, too; now they showed rangers making Invoking Gestures, rangers wrestling with dæmons, rangers tossing lightning bolts, rangers turning into coyotes.

I flipped to the index, and there found what I was looking for:

"Restoration Sigils."

9

WAITING. UDO'S HAT.
THE ELEVATOR AGAIN.

I sat on the edge of the Immaculata Piazza, leaning against one of the immense pillars that held up the main dome of Sanctuary, throwing scraps of bread to the doves. The Immaculata Piazza is protected from sun by the looming dome above, and sheltered from wind by large support pillars. It's a pleasant place to sit and wait for someone, which was good for me, because I had been waiting over half an hour for Udo, who was massively late.

Udo was finally out of the lockdown he'd earned by punching his horrible sister Gunn-Britt in the nose in a fight over the last tortilla. That sounds pretty bad, but Gunn-Britt is a pincher, and I had no doubt she gave as good as she got. There are seven kids in the Landaðon family, and they fight over everything. Seven kids, one mother, and three fathers. It's a terribly famous love story in Califa, and there was even a play written about it: how Udo's mamma was wooed by identical triplets and, having no way to decide among them, married all three. Udo's birth-father was in prison in Anahuatl City with Poppy and died there, but Udo still has two fathers left.

I've known Udo since we were tots. When I was too large to be easily portable on Mamma's trips but not large enough to stay home alone with Poppy, I would stay at Case Tigger (the Landaðon family home), which was fun and friendly, even with all those kids. Case Tigger is not a Great House, and it has no Butler, but it's homey and clean, and I love it there. But now that I have to Poppy-sit, Udo stays with me to keep me company. He would have done so this time, too, if he hadn't gotten popped for punching Gunn-Britt.

Although Udo is not destined for the Barracks like me, his parents are just as strong-willed about his future fate as Mamma is about mine, and he's just as annoyed at their planning as I am about Mamma's. The Landaðons are all lawyers; Madama Landaðon is on the Warlord's Bench, and Major Landaðon and Captain Landaðon are in the Judge Advocate General's office. As eldest, Udo should carry on the family tradition, but he'd rather go back to the original family profession: piracy.

His grandmother Gunn-Britt Landaðon had sailed with the Warlord, back in the days when the Warlord himself was a pirate and he hadn't yet scored his biggest prize: Califa. Now the Warlord is a warlord, not a pirate, and the Landaðons are lawyers, not pirates, and piracy in general is frowned upon, but that hasn't stopped Udo in his ambition.

If Nini Mo is my lodestar, then Udo's is the Dainty Pirate, whose exploits in the waters up and down the Califa coastline are notorious. The Dainty Pirate flouts the Warlord's Authority and refuses to sail with a Letter of Marque, which means if he ever gets caught, he'll be hanged. They call him the Dainty Pirate because his manners are exquisite, and so, too, his wardrobe. Udo thinks he's fabulous.

I had briefed Udo on Valefor during lunch, and he had demanded to see Val for himself, so we had agreed to meet after school and go back to Crackpot together. Which would have been fine, if he'd been on time, but Udo has a problem with punctuality that many detentions have not straightened out.

While I waited, I thought about *The Eschatanomicon*. I had stayed up most of the night reading it front to back. It really is a terrific book, full of all sorts of useful information and written in a friendly style, as though Nini Mo were sitting down next to you, talking to you as an equal. Magick books, in my experience, tend to be arcane and complicated, full of tortuous explanations and run-on sentences, and most adepts are superfond of superbig words. But Nini Mo eschewed the fancy words and spoke plainly. I didn't understand why the book was so rare, or why I'd never heard of it before. It was the best book on magick I'd ever read.

And after reading it, I was sure that I could restore Valefor, although a few details needed to be ironed out first, if only Udo would hurry up and arrive so we could go back to Crackpot and start ironing.

I was just about to give up and go to the Tuckshop for a mocha, and then let Udo arrive and wait for *me,* when at last there was a hollering *yahoo,* and here he came, resplendent in a black-and-white-striped frock coat over an emerald green kilt. Perched on his head was an emerald green hat the size of a wheel of cheese, well festooned with black and white ribbons and cruelly surmounted by an iridescent green-and-gold bird wing. Udo is the most conscientious dresser I know; half the time you need to put your sunshades on just to look at him. He is what the *Califa Police Gazette* would call a glass-gazing font of frivolity. If he weren't so disgustingly handsome, he'd look ridiculous. Instead, he looked glorious.

"Nice hat, Udo," I said. "I feel sorry for the bird that had to die so you could be stylish."

"Well, ave to you, too, Flora," he answered, reaching up as though to make sure the hat was still on his head, which it was, thanks to a hatpin longer than my arm. "I dug the bird out of Granny's old clothes-closet. It's been dead longer than we've been alive, and don't you think it's nice to make sure it didn't die in vain?"

"What took you so long?"

"Sorry. I got caught up in Arts Logic. Here, I brought you a mocha."

I took the cup he offered. Just what I needed, so lovely warm and chocolatey. "How much do I owe you?"

"Nayah, it's on me," he answered, airily.

I was shocked. Udo is notoriously cheap. Other than the money he spends on his clothes, most of which he buys second-hand or makes himself, every glory he gets goes straight into his Letter of Marque fund. (Udo has no intention of paying for his piracy with his neck.)

"To what do I owe this honour?"

"Well, I missed you, Flora."

I had missed him, too, but I hate soppiness, so I said, all business-brisk: "So you should have."

Udo rolled his eyes and sat down on the bench next to me. "I can't stay out late tonight. Mam and the Daddies are going to the opera, and somehow I got stuck with squirt-wrangling. And I got six pages of cyclotomy to do for turn-in tomorrow. You'll be so lucky when you have Valefor doing your homework, Flora. Gunn-Britt was doing all my maths, but she just raised her prices out of spite over the nose thing, and now I can't afford her. Do you think Valefor would do my homework, too? I guess you could just order him to—"

"I don't have a lot of time, either. I have to meet Mamma at the Presidio for dinner. She's finally back from Angeles."

"You are so lucky, Flora, that Buck is gone all the time. I wish *los padres* would go and take all those nasty kiddies with them. How bliss it would be to have no one to look after but blissful me."

"And Poppy, and the horses, and the dogs, and the chores—"

"The Warlord freed all the slaves but you, Flora."

"Don't I know it. Come on. We're burning daylight."

Crackpot was as I had left it some hours earlier, with no sign of either Poppy or Valefor. A few stray smashing sounds drifted down from the Eyrie, but we pretended not to notice. Let Mamma deal with Poppy when she got home later; let him be *her* job, not mine. Or better yet, let him be Valefor's job.

The Elevator was waiting, grille ajar. I jumped in so quickly that it rocked back and forth slightly, squeaking at my weight. Udo followed and pulled the grille shut behind him.

"Take us to the Bibliotheca," I demanded, but the Elevator did not move. "Come on, chop-chop. Take me to Valefor in the Bibliotheca."

The Elevator remained stubbornly stationary, even when I stamped my foot.

"Maybe you should press a button?" Udo suggested.

"I never did before, but maybe so."

Together we peered at the buttons, which were less than helpful, listing:

"This House is bigger than I thought," Udo said, and before I could stop him, he reached out and punched the LIBROS button.

The Elevator jolted a bit, dropping a few inches. I grabbed at Udo, and Udo grabbed at me, and we both fell against the wall.

"Udo! Who knows where we'll end up now!" I found my footing and stood up.

"It said *books* and a library has books, don't it?"

The Elevator recovered and began to slide downwards.

"I thought you said the Bibliotheca was up," Udo said.

"It was, blast it all." I pushed all the buttons, some of them twice, but the Elevator just kept dropping, slowly picking up speed as it went. "But maybe this book place is entirely different."

"Hit the STOP button," Udo said helpfully.

"There is no stop button." I pressed all the other buttons again, and then, for good measure, thumped on the panel.

"That red one –" Udo leaned in front of me. "There –"

"That doesn't say anything about stopping – don't – Udo –"

He pressed the button. The Elevator stopped abruptly, sending Udo careening into me and down to the floor, where his elbow crushed my liver painfully.

"Get off me –" I pushed him off and stood up, holding my hand against my side.

"See – I told you!" Udo looked pleased with himself.

"Ayah so, but now we are stuck between floors."

With a horrible groan that set my teeth to grinding, the Elevator bounced once, upwards. Udo staggered against me again, almost pushing me off balance. The light went out. The Elevator shrieked like a baby.

And then it dropped like a stone.

Downwards we plummeted, in pitch darkness. The roar of rushing air filled my ears to near bursting, or maybe that was just the pressure of our fall. Dimly, behind the rush, I could hear howling – maybe it was Udo, or maybe it was me. It was so dark that I couldn't tell if my mouth was open or not. I was pressed into the floor, feeling the Elevator shudder and leap beneath my hands and knees, my head swimming with nausea. I closed my eyes tightly against the darkness, and so dark was it that even the sparks of light you normally see when you squinch your eyes up were extinguished.

After a while, maybe it was for ever even, it seemed like we were not moving at all, that we were suspended in a black void, and it was the Void itself that was moving, rushing by us in a howl. Perhaps this is what the Abyss is like, I thought, the impenetrable blackness, the scream of air; perhaps it was not the air screaming, but—

The Elevator hit hard and bounced upwards, and so did I, catching my tongue painfully between my teeth. Something knobbed into my side, bright and hard. I jerked away and whacked my noggin into a stony object, which complained, "Owwww, that was my chin."

I opened my eyes. Grey light hazed in through the Elevator's open door. Udo sat on his heels, rubbing his chin with one hand and patting his hat with the other. The foot-long hatpin had kept it on his head, but now it was quite cockeyed. My head felt as though a hundred million goldfish were flapping their fins inside my skull. I tried to stand, but my knees wobbled me back down again. The grille stood open, so I did the easy thing and crawled out of the Elevator, into the huge expanse of the Bibliotheca.

10

NAUSEA. DISCUSSION.
TEA. SIGILS.

The floor bobbed and jumped with imaginary motion, and the mocha in my tum was threatening to abandon ship. Every time I raised my head, the Bibliotheca swirled into a blur of steel grey, and closing my eyes was worse: then the darkness itself whirled and lurched. If I stared directly at one fixed point, my head started to slow down, but the second I moved my eyes, everything began to spin again.

Udo moaned, "Are you OK, Flora?"

I tried to look back to the Elevator without actually turning my head to look back at the Elevator, and I realized that Udo had crawled up next to me. I risked a glance and saw that his face was almost as green as his hat.

"I'm going to urp," Udo complained.

"Don't do it on me—"

"Floooooooooooora!"

"Valefor?" I risked another turn of the head and saw that the Bibliotheca was shrouded in gloom. Today the light filtering through the windows was weak and grey, and rain skimmed the outside of the glass. It hadn't been raining earlier.

"Floooooooooooora!"

"Valefor – where are you?"

This time the only response was a wracking cough. I pushed up off the floor and stood, staggering over to the nearest table, to grab for balance. The floor tipped up and then down again, and for a moment my mocha was poised to spew. But then I got enough balance back to stand straighter and to see Valefor wavering, as thin and pale grey as newsprint. He looked terrible, much worse even than when I had first seen him. His hair stuck out like thistledown and his eyes gleamed wetly white.

"I am receding again, Flora," he moaned, and held his hands out to me. The floor swayed, but I lurched over to him, my own hands outstretched, and breathed so deeply that my chest grew tight with exertion. A cold misty feeling flowed over me, and Val's cold tenuous grip fastened upon me.

Val's lips were so faint that I could barely feel them press against mine. I breathed deeply out until my lungs felt sucked and empty, then inhaled again until they felt like balloons. It wasn't until my second exhalation that he began to solidify. First he felt wiry and thin like

92

sinew, then tough and hard like bone, and then, finally, like solid flesh, warm beneath the grip of my hands.

I let go and pressed my hand on my chest, trying to hold my bouncy heart in, and gasped deeply. My insides felt as though my blood had been replaced with swirly giddy light, rushing golden through my veins. The dizziness was gone.

Valefor said happily, "Well, I feel much better! That was some good stuff, Flora. You are so full of lovely nice stuff: anger, guilt, sorrow. Yum!" He smacked his lavender lips and did a little dance.

"What was that with the Elevator, Valefor? It almost dropped us straight into the Abyss."

"That Elevator may go many places, Flora Segunda, but the Abyss is not one of them. I am sorry about the Elevator, but really you must take your complaints to darling Buck, for she is the one who has unstabilized me— Hey! Nice hat!"

This last was directed not at me, who was not wearing a hat, but at Udo, who was still sitting by the Elevator, looking slightly green. At the compliment, he grinned weakly and staggered to his feet, then made the courtesy that signifies Graciously Submitting before an Equal, which involved a bow so low that I was surprised his nose didn't touch the ground. Udo, like his hero the Dainty Pirate, is a fine one for manners.

"Thank you, sieur denizen."

"I love the bird wing, so beautifully cruel, and your kilt, what a divine shade of green. I do adore green, the colour of jade and jaguar blood." To me: "He could teach you a few things about dressing, Flora Segunda. He's got style and flash."

Now Udo was grinning and I could practically hear the sound of his head inflating. "You do me a great honour with your compliments, sieur."

"Your manners are very nice, too," Valefor answered. "Much better than Flora's, here, who has forgotten to introduce us."

"You have not given me a chance, Val, for heaven's sake. Udo Moxley Landaðon ov Sorrel, Valefor, denizen—"

"Valefor Fyrdraaca ov Fyrdraaca," Valefor interrupted, returning Udo's courtesy with Deference to an Equal, an even deeper bow. "I have the right to the name as much as you do, Flora Segunda, maybe more. I am very pleased to meet someone with such exquisite taste, Sieur Landaðon, and glad to see that Flora has some friends with style. Surprised, but well-pleased. Tell me, sieur – where are hems these days? Are they ankle or knee – I am so out of touch, and Flora is useless."

"Knee for day, and calf for night," said Udo, "unless you are super-ultra-formal, when they—"

I interrupted. "Do you want to discuss fashion, Valefor, or your restoration? We don't have time to do both. Udo has to get to babysitting, and Mamma is coming home tonight."

"Restoration, then fashion," Valefor pronounced. "I shall have an entire new wardrobe, then, of shimmering samite! How bliss to get out of this rag!"

So we sat down in front of the fireplace to discuss. Valefor ignited a warming coldfire glow on the hearth and produced a lovely little snack with tiny sandwies, double bergamot tea, and lime meltaways.

"So, according to *The Eschata*, to create a servitor –" I said. I had read the chapter on denizens in *The Eschatanomicon* three times, but sometimes it is good to think out loud.

"I'm a denizen!" Val protested.

"A denizen is a kind of servitor, Valefor. You know that. A servitor is a magickal entity created for a general purpose. A denizen is a servitor attached to a particular place. A domicilic denizen is attached to a House."

Val said snobbily, "Still, a denizen is better than a plain old servitor—"

"That's true. A denizen can act completely independently as long as its actions are in accordance with the parameters laid down by the adept—"

"Who was?" Udo asked.

I was annoyed at being interrupted. "Who was what?"

"Who created you, Valefor? Was it Buck?"

Valefor answered, quite loftily, "Of course it wasn't Buck. She is only fifty-two years old. I out-age her by far. I was created by Azucar Fyrdraaca—"

"*Which in Val's case*," I said loudly, to get them back on track, "the parameters laid down by the adept were to take care of the House of Fyrdraaca. And these parameters were laid into the fetish that is Valefor's centre. This fetish is the source of all Valefor's power, and now he's been disconnected from it, and that's why he is reduced and weakened."

"What's a fetish?" asked Udo. "Are you going to share those lime meltaways, Flora?"

I passed him the platter. "Every servitor has a physical item that binds it and links it to the physical world—"

"So it's kinda the physical representation of Val?" Udo interrupted.

"Ayah."

"Then shouldn't Valefor's fetish be Crackpot Hall?"

"No, the House is too big. No adept could charge something as large as an entire house. No one has that powerful a Will—"

"Azucar Fyrdraaca—" began Valefor, but Udo cut him off.

"So what's your fetish, Valefor?"

Valefor looked a bit embarrassed and mumbled something unintelligible.

I said, "What? I can't hear you."

"I have forgotten," Val admitted sheepishly.

Udo snorted. "You have forgotten? How can you forget something like that? That's pretty lame, Valefor. It's like forgetting your own name."

Valefor said plaintively, "I am insignificant and reduced, and I have been drained. There is so much about myself that I no longer know; why do you think it is taking me so long to write my memoirs? Buck has cut me off from much of myself, and, of course, my fetish, for with it, I should be whole and in command."

"So what do we do if we don't know what your fetish is?" Udo asked. "We can't reconnect you to it if we don't know what it is."

Val said eagerly, "You could kill Buck and let her heir take her place as the new Head of the House. Idden and I always got along quite well, I am sure *she* would restore me – oh ayah, it was just an idea. You don't have to get all stuffy about it, Flora. Remember, there will be Fyrdraacas in this House long after you are gone."

"I will not kill Mamma," I said, adding maliciously, as payback for such an awful suggestion, "I guess, then, you are out of luck."

Val turned the piteous all the way up to high and wrung his narrow hands together. "You don't know how it is, Flora. To be all alone in this empty room, to hear voices from so far away, lovely voices, and to know that they cannot hear you. To sit alone, with all these books telling the stories of other lives, not your own. And to feel yourself growing weaker and weaker every day, whilst your walls crumble and your family falls into ruin. And there is nothing you can do, alone, outcast, adrift, lost."

"There's got to be something that we can do, Flora," Udo said. "It sucks to be in lockdown; boy, don't I know it. I'm with Valefor on this, all the way. Wasn't

Nini Mo's motto 'Free the Oppressed'?"

"Thank you, Sieur Landaðon," Val sobbed. "You are so very kind."

"Quit crying, Val," I said. "We will find your fetish."

The sobbing stopped, and the tears on Valefor's pale cheeks were gone. "How?"

"We will use the Discernment Sigil."

11

DISCERNMENT SIGIL. SMOKE. SEARCHING. A TEA CADDY.

Rangers, of course, are always looking for things – information, people, clues – and so *The Eschatan-omicon* was full of sigils that find things. There was the Acquisition Sigil to find something you need but don't have; the Retrieval Sigil to find things you had but then lost. The Recovery Sigil, which seemed to be exactly like the Retrieval Sigil, only you had to have lost by your own fault the things you were looking for. The Discovery Sigil to find things that you didn't even know that you needed, and the Recollection Sigil to help you remember what you had forgotten. And the Revelation Sigil for things that were in front of your eyes but you were looking right through.

Some of these sigils were quite complicated. The Recollection Sigil was the obvious choice, but it called for several arcane ingredients (attar of crimson corn, starfish eyes, and a bowline knot), required that the adept prepare by drinking nothing but fizzy lemonade for three days before, and ended with the adept setting herself on fire. The Revelation Sigil would have also probably worked, but it called for six adepts and copious bloodletting. The Recovery Sigil required actions too disgusting to even contemplate.

But the Discernment Sigil, which helped you recognize what you were looking for when you saw it, seemed to fit the bill perfectly. It was short and sweet, required only two magickal Gestures, neither of which called for headstands or extra fingers, and it used only one very short and easy-to-pronounce Gramatica Word. No setting on fire and no bloodletting. It was not so much different from the Ignite Sigil, which I had done many times before. I was confident I could handle it.

"You will do it right, Flora Segunda, won't you?" Valefor said, worriedly. "If you do it wrong, your head could explode."

"If your head explodes, I am not cleaning it up," Udo said. He had grabbed *The Eschata* and was now flipping through it. "What about the Recovery Sigil; it looks like fun—"

"I've decided, Udo!"

"Who am I? Boy Hansgen?" Udo protested. "Who dropped and made you the boss?"

Boy Hansgen was Nini Mo's sidekick. When she died, he took over the Ranger Corps, and fought hard against the Birdies during the War. Afterward, when

Rangers were outlawed and the Corps disbanded, he disappeared and hasn't been heard from since. He was a good ranger, but no Nini Mo.

"You are not nearly tall enough to be Boy Hansgen," I said. "Give me the book back, Udo. My head will not explode, I promise you. I know what I am doing."

Udo tossed the book to me, grinning at my awkward catch. "You are lucky I am so easy, Flora. If Valefor is the one who is supposed to be recognizing the fetish when he sees it, shouldn't he be the one who does the sigil?"

"He can't. His only purpose is to act in regards to the House. He can't act in any other capacity. So I will charge the Word, activate it, and then pass it on to him, so that he'll feel its effects. Then he should know the fetish when he sees it. I would have rather done the Recollection Sigil, but this is the best we can manage."

"And once we have the fetish, then what?" Udo asked.

"We have to have the fetish first; then we'll be able to figure out how to restore Valefor. We won't know what Mamma did to disconnect them until we have the fetish."

"Well, let's fall to," Udo said. "I gotta be home by six, and I don't want to be late and risk another lockdown."

I didn't want to be late to meet Mamma, either; she frowns on tardiness as much as Sanctuary does, and after not seeing her in so long, I did not want to start out on the wrong foot.

So, Valefor cleared the table of its mess of papers, Udo took off his hat, and I reread the Sigil, to make sure of the steps. Read it another time, just in case. Udo arranged himself to one side of me, and Valefor across. Between us, I lay *The Eschata*, open to the Sigil, just in case.

My stomach was fluttering, in a very non-rangery way. I had never heard of anyone's head exploding from a wrongly done Working, but there is always a risk that problems will arise. *The secret to having confidence is acting confident*, Nini Mo said. I wiped my sweaty hands on my kilt and shifted so that my stays were not cutting so harshly into my back.

Strike hard, and with all your Will, Nini Mo said.

Closing my eyes, I rested my left hand on my knee and made the Invocative Gesture with my right. Pinching my left nostril closed with my thumb, I breathed in through my right nostril for four beats. Then I pinched my right nostril closed and exhaled through the left for four beats. Three times I did each side, and I started to feel the distant dizzy warmth that indicated the Current was building within me.

The fourth breath, I drew in through the right nostril, and then, pinching both nostrils closed, held the breath in. At first it was hard to focus; I kept hearing Valefor's cough, or the crunch of Udo's satin kilt as he fidgeted. Then my lungs began to grow tight and the urge to breathe started to build. I swallowed, feeling pressure in my ears, but ignored the sensation and focused my Will on the image of the Gramatica Word, focusing focusing focusing. The pressure grew, and the blobby darkness before my closed eyes bubbled and swam. Everything around me receded. The pressure burned; now there was nothing but it and the overwhelming urge to gasp.

Lungs scraping, I opened my eyes.

A thin light was spilling from the open pages of *The Eschata* lying before me. The light curled about itself, contracting into sparks, which in turn shifted and turned until they hung before me in the glowing sinuous letters of the Exhortation.

I opened my mouth and sucked in the glittering gnat-like letters. For a moment my mouth was filled with a sparkly crackling, and then, in shock and surprise, instead of expelling outwards as I should have, I swallowed. The letters burned as they went down my throat, burning hot and burning cold. I gasped and started to choke, redness dotting my eyesight. My stomach convulsed in a horrible searing pain, and I doubled over, then the letters were boiling back up my throat in a scream: "ℒℬℐℋℬℐℒ!"

The Word was as loud as thunder, as wide as the sky, as concentrated as a sword swing, as bright as a mortar flash. It flew as true as an arrow towards Valefor. He opened his mouth to receive it, and such was its force that he fell backwards, disappearing under the table.

"Wow!" I dimly heard Udo say. My mocha had had enough; it no longer wished to be friends with me, and its desire to depart was extremely urgent. I leaned over and let it go. Afterwards, my throat felt like it had swallowed a cat, a cat who had clawed all the way down.

"Valefor!" I croaked, wiping my mouth on my sleeve. My mouth tasted of fur; I spat, and spat again.

"I'm all right! I am fine!" Valefor popped up like a Springheel Jack-in-the-Box. "That was fantastic, Flora! Let's go, I feel great."

He danced his little happy dance, and I could see, clearly burning inside him, the glittery glow of the Sigil.

"That was something, Flora!" Udo said. "Did you hear that noise?"

"I didn't think it would be so big," I whispered. "Val, can I have some water?"

Valefor produced water and after about half a quart of guzzling down, and then a pint or so of spitting up, I started to feel better. My mouth still burned, and the rest of me felt as though I had been beaten with a stick, but it was a good sort of pain, and it was mitigated by the happy sensation of success.

"Hurry! Hurry!" Val sang. "Let's go a-hunting! It's near, I can tell, almost on the tip of my tongue, let's go! I have eleven thousand rooms, so there's no time to waste!"

So we went, wasting no more time, Valefor leading the way. My trek through Crackpot before had been a bare little jaunt, but now we were on a full-fledged expedition. Up narrow staircases and down broad staircases we went. Through antechambers, bedchambers, closets, parlours, dining rooms, sitting rooms, furnace rooms, bathrooms, water closets, attics, cellars, receiving rooms, and on and on. All the while, Valefor kept up a running commentary, like a tour guide:

". . . Slippery Stairs, where Anacreon Fyrdraaca broke his nose sliding down on a tea tray . . . Beekeeping Room, don't bother them, Udo, and they won't bother you . . . Formerly Secret Cubbyhole . . . Because it can't be secret if you know where it is, that's why, Madama Smartie . . . Luggage Mezzanine . . . I wonder if that salesman is still in the linen basket, I should come back and check . . . Eternal Atrium, look how large that tree has become, I must raise the roof in here or it's going to go right through the ceiling . . . The Gun Room, what on earth did Buck do with my .50 caliber Gatling . . . The Halfway Point—"

"Stop, Valefor, stop!" I said finally. I had a stitch in my side from trying to keep up.

"I gotta go, Flora," Udo said, halting as well. He's a championship fencer, but he also was looking a bit winded. Valefor, energized, was *fast*.

"I've got to go, too. *Valefor*, come back!"

Valefor slid back up the balustrade. "What? Why do you linger?"

"Haven't you seen your fetish anywhere, Val?" Udo asked. "We've been through half the House."

"Not even half. Remember, eleven thousand rooms?" Valefor said, "Come on—"

"Haven't you seen anything at all that could be your fetish?" I asked. "Nothing at all?"

Valefor hopped impatiently. "No. Come on!"

"I have to go, or Mam will ground me again," Udo complained.

I said, "And I have to go, too. We'll have to look more later."

"When?" Valefor cried. "Oh, when?"

"As soon as we can. It will be hard with Mamma around, but we'll think of something. Lead us back."

Valefor protested and whined and wrung his hands as he led us back through the maze of corridors, rooms and galleries, Udo and I both urging him to hurry up, and he insisting we were going as hurriedly as possible. But then suddenly Valefor's whine changed to hoots of surprise.

"Flora! I can feel it! I can feel it! We are close, very close!" He took off at a dead run, and we followed him, barely able to keep up. A doorway loomed at the end of the hall, and Valefor effortlessly passed through it. The door was locked. Udo pounded and banged, and I shouted for Valefor to open it, and after a minute, he did.

Inside, the curtains were drawn. Valefor's thin purple glow and the liquidy luminescence of the Sigil cast tremulous light over the small room, stretching monstrous shadows. Valefor was flitting about maniacally, tossing things hither and thither: a fishing net, polo mallets, old boots, pillows, dead flowers.

"Valefor! Cool down!" I ordered, dodging the footstool coming towards me.

"I can tell – it's near – I can tell, Flora Segunda," he said excitedly, descending upon the narrow gilt bed that was pressed up against one wall and tearing the sheets and blankets asunder. Great clouds of dust rolled up, and I put my hand to my mouth to keep from choking.

"The window!" Udo gurgled, retreating back into the hallway.

I stumbled my way across the room and pulled at the curtains; the fabric tore in my grip, and with a clatter, the rod came down and almost beaned me on the skull. The cloud of dust that came from this plummet made the dust Valefor was roiling up seem like nothing, but once Udo helped me wedge the window up, we had fresh air and light.

Valefor was dismembering the bed, tossing the mattress over and dislodging a sheaf of yellowbacks. The walls were pinned with prints torn from old *CPG*s and polo flags, and a model sailing boat perched upon the mantel. A yellowback whizzed by me and hit the wall, knocking a dartboard askew; I automatically bent down to pick the pamphlet up and grimaced. *Naughty Nan's Risque Review* was the title, and the illustrations were of scantily clad showgirls posing acrobatically.

"What room is this?" Udo asked, looking at a silver urn. Val had tossed it in his direction, and instead of dodging, Udo had caught it. "Hey, look, it's a trophy for best horseman at the Califa summer fair, and look who won it – Hotspur!"

"Bedchamber of Redoubtable Dreams." Valefor huffed, still chucking things. "Hotspur's bedroom, you know, when he was a kid. Can you believe all this junk? My fetish is buried in here somewhere under all this stuff. What a mess. I'll never find it."

"Poppy? This was Poppy's room?" I said, amazed. I looked around with new interest. Poppy had torn those prints out and stuck them on the wall? Those were Poppy's old cloaks hanging on the back of the door? Poppy's polo mallets in the corner and Poppy's hippo bank on the bookshelf ? "Why would your fetish be in Poppy's old room?"

"I don't know – but it's here somewhere, I can tell, I can tell!" Valefor said. "I can feel it so close, it tingles, it tingles!"

"Is it this?" Udo asked, seizing a stuffed monkey that sat in the rocker by the fireplace.

"No!"

"This?"

Valefor said indignantly, "No! Not a blackjack, Udo, don't be a snapperhead!"

"Maybe, Val, if you quit throwing things around and stood very quietly for a minute and focused, you'd be able to sense it better?" I suggested.

Valefor stopped his whirling and stood stock-still, clasping his hands under his chin as though he were praying, and closed his eyes. The Sigil burned inside him like a little sun, steady and bright, and its glow made his skin seem shimmery, like mother-of-pearl.

"Do you feel it?" Udo asked.

"Shut up, Udo – let me concentrate!" With his eyes still closed, Valefor extended one long arm in a point and began to spin. Once, twice, three times he twirled, his gown swirling around his legs and feet like water, his hair spinning out in a halo of purple. Then he stopped suddenly, his long finger pointing directly at the large trunk sitting in the fireplace alcove.

"There!"

"That dirty old trunk?" Udo said.

Valefor snorted. "No, my fetish is not the trunk, it's *inside* the trunk. Open it, Flora, open it!"

We dragged the trunk, which weighed enough to have a body in it, out of the alcove and towards the daylight spilling in through the windows. Its flat top was covered in about two inches of dust, but when I wiped the dirt away with the bedsheet Udo handed me, purple paint was revealed. Spidery silver letters spelled out *Reverdy Anacreon Fyrdraaca ov Fyrdraaca.*

"It's Poppy's Catorcena chest," I said. It's the custom that on your Catorcena, your family gives you a special chest with your name on it. You store your Catorcena clothing in it, and later, your heirlooms, the things that are important to you and that you wish to keep always.

"It's pretty beat-up," Udo said, and so it was, the paint rubbed off in places, and the wood rough and split. It looked like maybe Poppy had actually used the trunk as luggage. Valefor was already unlatching the clasps on either side of the open lock-face.

"Hold on, Valefor," I said, grabbing at his arm. I could tell he was just going to start flinging. "It's Poppy's important stuff, and we need to be careful."

"I'm surprised at your sudden interest about any of Hotspur's stuff, Flora Segunda," Valefor said. "But ayah so – we shall be very careful."

Ayah so. The minute the lid was up, Valefor elbowed me out of the way and started tossing. My protests ignored, all I could do was try to catch what he threw before it got messed up or broken: a tiny pink baby dress and two little knitted booties, a leather tobacco pouch full of coins, a green velvet smoking cap, a leather-bound book, a hairy piece of leather – ugh, a scalp – this I also threw, rubbing my hands on my kilt to take away the yuck.

"Come on, Valefor," Udo said impatiently. He caught the cadet jacket Valefor lobbed, and then the forage cap that followed.

Valefor's response was muffled. He was leaning so far into the trunk that he was in danger of falling in completely. I grabbed the back of his gown and pulled him out, and he came, sputtering ecstatically: "I have it! I have it!"

"A shoebox?" Udo said.

"Not a shoebox – a tea caddy?" I said, disappointed. Somehow it had seemed to me that Valefor's fetish should be more exciting than a tea caddy. Or if a tea caddy, at least engraved silver or solid gold, but this one was only plain wood.

"This isn't my fetish! My fetish is inside," Valefor cried. "I know, I know, I am sure – can't you feel it? Open it! Let's open it!"

We prised the caddy out of Valefor's grip to examine it more closely, but it appeared to be nothing other than an ordinary tea chest, slightly battered, made of dark red wood. It was locked. I shook it gently and it rattled slightly – whispering, like sand shifting.

"Smash it open," suggested Udo.

"You can't do that," Valefor said, aghast. "You might break me, inside—"

"Can we pick the lock? Isn't there a chapter in *The Eschata* about lock-picking?" Udo said. "Gesilher has a set of lock-picking tools he sent away for, from an advertisement in the back of the *CPG*. I could go home and steal them from him."

There is an entire section in *The Eschata* about lock-picking, but the problem, as I pointed out, was there was no lock to pick. Or, rather, there was a lock, but it had no keyhole into which tools could be inserted. Instead, the lock plate was just flat and round.

"How do you unlock it if there's no keyhole?" Udo asked.

"It's a seal lock." I'd never seen one before; they are old and quite rare, but a strongbox with a seal lock was described in *Nini Mo vs. the Kickapoo Dollymop*, so that's how I knew about them. "The lock is keyed to a seal. To open it, you press the seal against the lock plate, and that turns the lock open."

"What seal?" Udo asked. "The Fyrdraaca seal?" He and Valefor were leaning over my shoulder, breathing heavily and tickling my concentration.

I tried to squint the seal pattern into focus; the pattern incised on the lock plate was very thin, almost invisible.

"It's not the Fyrdraaca seal. I can barely see it, but it's not anything I recognize. I think it might be a bear holding a staff. Here, you look."

Udo pronounced the seal to be a bear holding a parrot, but Valefor, after getting so close to the lock that his eyes crossed, pronounced it a falcon in flight. I looked at it again, and this time it seemed to me that maybe it was a hand holding a short whip with a tendrilly lash.

Distantly, a clock tolled, and its chime brought both me and Udo out of our inspection.

"Pigface! I gotta go," Udo said. "We'll have to finish this another time. I'm gonna get popped for sure, but it was worth it. Good job, Flora!"

"I was the one who found my fetish," Valefor protested.

"Ayah, but Flora was the one who did the Sigil that helped you do it."

"I have to go, too, Valefor, but we'll figure out what to do next later." I wasn't going to have time to change if I wanted to make the horsecar, and Mamma was probably going to be annoyed I was late, but in my warm glow of success, I didn't care. My Sigil had worked, and we had found the fetish. We would find the seal, too, and Valefor would be restored!

12

THE PRESIDIO. A SNACK.
SNEAKING. ANOTHER DENIZEN.

When Flynn and I got off the horsecar in front of the Officers' Club, scores of canvas-clad privates were industriously polishing cannons, cutting grass, and bagging eucalyptus leaves. Maybe there was an inspection coming up, or maybe they were just trying to stay one step ahead of Mamma. All I can say is that I am grateful that she saves the white-glove treatment for work. Without Valefor, Crackpot would never pass her official muster.

Normally I am happy when Mamma comes home; it means that things will be as back to normal as they can ever be, and that while my chores don't lessen any, at least Poppy is no longer my problem. She'd been in Angeles for two weeks, a long trip even for her. But this time part of me wished that she had not come back for a few more days, just enough time to deal with Valefor.

114

Now that we had the fetish, all we needed was a way to get into the tea caddy. If we couldn't find the actual seal, there had to be another way to open the lock. *If you can't go in by the door*, says Nini Mo, *go in by the window*. The restoration was as good as done.

The Presidio is a pretty place, scattered with white buildings dappled by shade trees, surrounded to the south and east by sandy hills dusted with seagrass, and edged at the north and west by the glittering blue waters of the Bay of Califa. Despite being a place completely concerned with war, it always seems very peaceful.

Building Fifty-six, the headquarters of the Army of Califa, stands at the head of the parade ground, looking down its long slope towards the Bay. The parade ground is bigly huge, large enough to march ten regiments in unison, although the most I've ever seen is six, at the Fortieth Anniversary of the Warlord's Conquest, three years ago. In the middle of the parade ground four cannons guard the flagpole where the colours of Califa and the Warlord flap and snap in the perennial whippy wind.

Troops of soldiers were starting to assemble in front of the Adjutant General's office, preparing for the final afternoon Gun and Retreat. I hurried by, dragging the lollygagging Flynn behind me. If you are stuck outside within eyeshot of the Colours when Retreat starts, you have to stand at attention for the duration of the Colour Guard marching out, saluting the Colours, lowering them, folding them, securing them and removing them, while the Army band plays "Califa For Ever" and the cannons sound the end of day. I've seen Retreat a hundred times, and I didn't need to see it again.

Guards always stand in front of Building Fifty-six, but they never stop me. They never salute me, either, but that I can live with. If something is brewing, or a bigwig is on the post making trouble of some kind, then the front porch is crammed with aides, guards and strikers, and there will be a knot of horses out front, nipping at each other and kicking along the tie-up rail. Today the porch was empty, and so, too, was the waiting room, except for Lieutenant Botherton, who was standing behind the front desk, sorting mail.

He said, sharply, "Don't let that door bang— Oh, ave, Madama Fyrdraaca Segunda."

It was too late not to let the door bang, so I smiled sweetly and said, "Ave, Lieutenant Botherton."

Lieutenant Botherton gave Flynnie the evil eye. Dogs aren't allowed in official buildings, but I was willing to bet that the lieutenant was not going to point that out. Rank, or at least reflected rank, does have its perks.

"Has Mamma arrived yet?"

"The General's ferry docked safely earlier this afternoon, but the General has not returned from paying her compliments to the Warlord at Saeta House." Lieutenant Botherton swished his skirts away from Flynnie's friendly nose and sliced open another envelope. Yaller dogs, as everyone calls staff officers behind their backs, are notoriously stuck up. Their kilts are longer and their noses higher than anyone else's in the Army.

Daggit. Even after Valefor's tea, I was starving. And here I had rushed frantically, not bothering to change, sure I was late-late, and now no Mamma, no chow, zip. *Hurry up and wait*, says Mamma, *that's the way of the Army.* I think it's just plain rude.

"I'll be in her office, then." I scooted before he could say otherwise, dragging Flynnie away from the spittoon he was nosing. Building Fifty-six has been Army headquarters for ever, so it's stuffed with all sorts of martial mementos and portraits of old soldiers. The hallways are lined with cases full of conquest booty and the walls hung with faded battle flags, and thankfully it is someone else's job to do the dusting.

Mamma's office is large and has enormous windows that overlook the parade ground. There's her desk, a few chairs, a stiff horsehair settee, and walls and walls of file shelves containing walls and walls of files. *An army may fight on its feet*, Mamma says, *but it marches on paper*, and here were the pages to prove it.

To solace myself for having to wait, I sat down behind Mamma's desk and began rifling. Two sealed redboxes sat on the blotter, waiting for Mamma's attention, but I didn't bother with them. Redboxes are usually full of the most boring papers imaginable: requests for mule shoes, counts of blankets, reports on irascible horses and uppity sergeants, all endorsed, in triplicate, and tri-folded. They are not worth the hot knife it takes to slide their seals off. The red tape dispenser was full, so I cut a few yards off and tucked it away in my pocket. Red tape makes particularly good bootlaces.

The left bottom drawer of Mamma's desk is always locked, but that's nothing to me – a little pin and a little pop and Mamma's secret stash is revealed: a solid block of black chocolate. I made myself a little choco sandwie and tossed a biscuit Flynnie's gaping way. The first sandwie was so yummy that a second naturally followed, after which I put the much smaller block back and returned the locks to right.

Outside, the evening gun boomed dully, drowning out the echo of the retreat bugle. The clock in the hallway chimed seven, and my tummy, despite the two choco sandwies, rumbled loudly. Where was Mamma? I peered out the window. The Retreat Guard had marched off and a detail was slowly making its way down the sidewalk, lighting the lamps. The Bay had faded to a dark blue velvet and more lights were pricking the windows of the offices, just as the stars were beginning to prick the sky above.

The choco left my mouth dark and sticky, and Mamma's sideboard held only faceted bottles of bugjuice, which burns rather than washes. Mamma doesn't drink, but I suppose that hospitality requires her to have libations available for those who do.

A long narrow hallway runs the length of Building

Fifty-six, with a floor like polished silk. It's perfect for sliding down if you sit on a file folder, but if someone opens a door while you are flying, it's off to the Post Hospital and ten stitches in your grape. Believe me, I know whereof I speak.

The watercooler stands at the end of the hallway, next to the back door, which was open, in direct defiance of Mamma, who really hates draughts. Two figures sat on the back steps, haloed in cigarillo smoke, also in direct defiance of Mamma, who had made everyone else stop smoking when she did. I crept silently down the hallway, muting my footsteps by leaving my boots just inside her office. Stealth is made perfect only by practice, and besides, little ears can learn all sorts of interesting things when they maintain a low profile.

". . . I read in the *Califa Police Gazette* . . ." That was Crackers. He's chief clerk to the Chargé d'Affaires and can forge the signature of every officer over the grade of major. A very useful talent if it doesn't get you shot, and one which I had been cultivating myself, in my spare time.

"That rag! The *CPG* hasn't printed the truth in a hundred years." That was Sergeant Seth. She's a copyist, which has got to be the most boring job ever created by anyone anywhere. All documents that Mamma creates must go out in triplicate, and a copy has to be made and filed in the Commanding General's archives. That's what Seth does, sits at her desk and copies stuff all day long. I'd rather be eaten by bears.

"Maybe a rag, but they had witnesses. There's no doubt but that Paimon was up to something."

Today everyone had been discussing Bilskinir House and Paimon, its denizen – half the kids at school, the horsecar driver, and now the clerks. Supposedly, a group of Radical Chaoists, celebrating some obscure holiday on the beach nearby, had seen bright lights and heard distant roars coming from the House. Since the House had been closed for fourteen years, this was big news.

Sergeant Seth said, "Those Radical Chaoists were probably drunk, and that's where the lights came from – the bottom of a bottle."

"You can't deny that that group of kids disappeared last year, and there is naught explanation but that Paimon snacked them up. After being alone for so long, he must be very hungry. It stands to reason he'd grab a few edibles if he could get them."

Last year a school group from PS 94 had disappeared on a fishing trip, the wreckage of their boat later found on the rocks at Bilskinir's foundations. Mamma sent a squad to investigate, but they couldn't get near the House. A couple of weeks later, the school group started to wash up on the Pacifica Playa, in well-chewed bits. Sharks? Or a hungry denizen? No one was sure, but rumour seemed to favour the hungry-denizen explanation.

Seth said scornfully, "It's been fourteen years since Butcher Brakespeare died and Bilskinir House closed. A denizen couldn't survive that long alone. What would Paimon live on all that time?"

"Paimon was no ordinary denizen; he's an immaculate – self-contained. He must have still survived. Hadn't those bits been gnawed on?"

"That boat smashed against the Bilskinir rocks. Those kids drowned and were eaten by sharks."

"So you say, but show me the shark who'll cook his dinner before he eats it. Those bones were well charred—"

"Oh, there you are, Flora." Sergeant Carheña, carrying several redboxes, paused in the doorway of Mamma's office and totally blew my creepy cover. He said loudly, "Put those weeds out before the General sees you, or she'll smoke you herself."

Crackers and Seth scattered like buckshot. Evening had taken over Mamma's office, and my tummy was rumbling. Sergeant Carheña deposited the redboxes on Mamma's desk and lit the lamps, which cast a sunny glow in the dusk of the room. He's been chief clerk for as long as I remember and can make the most cunning hats out of linen paper and red tape.

"How are you, Flora?"

I sat back down in Mamma's chair and twirled once, just to see if it was still as fun as it had seemed when I was a kid. "Fine."

"How are your classes going?"

"Fine," I said. Twirling was not so fun. In fact, now I felt hungry *and* a bit sick.

"Are you looking forward to your Catorcena?"

"Oh yes, awfully."

"It will be a fine day, and you will be proud, I hope."

"Oh yes, awfully."

I looked out the window again. Two outriders on horseback reined up in front of Fifty-six; they were carrying Mamma's guidon and escorting a large black barouche.

Finally, Mamma.

13

MAMMA. WAX SEALS.
INCREDIBLE NEWS.

Mamma never just walks into a room. She strides into it and takes possession. Everyone stops what they are doing and looks to her, and now she's in charge. She says this attention is all about the rank, but I think it's more than that. The Warlord comes into a room and no one pays any mind at all, because despite the rank, he's just an old man with one leg. Mamma is so used to being the centre of everything, she just *is* the centre of everything.

So Mamma strode into the room, giving orders to Lieutenant Sabre, her aide-de-camp, who is almost always a foot behind her. When she saw me, she broke off and held her arms out: "Ave, Flora!"

"Ave, Mamma!"

She swept me into a giant squeezy hug and I squeezy hugged her back. She smelled of lemons, sea salt and the Warlord's tobacco. Her gorget banged against my forehead and her golden aiguillettes scratched my chin, but I didn't care. Suddenly I was superglad that she was home. Flynnie bounced up and began to jump, yipping like a squeaky door, but, thankfully, he didn't spray.

"And I missed you, too, Flynnie." Mamma kissed Flynn, also, although I had already gotten the full force of the lip rouge, and thus he avoided being smeared. "Ah, now my chapeau is askew. Here, can you reach the hatpin?"

When she bent over, I could, just barely. Mamma was in dress uniform: tricorn hat, tight black frock coat, white wig and red lip rouge. I hate the dress uniform because in it Mamma doesn't look like Mamma at all, but like a bandbox soldier, cold and aloof.

Mamma unbuttoned her frock coat and sat down on the settee, hanging her gorget over Flynn's neck. He jumped up next to her and laid his head upon her knee. All the dogs adore Mamma.

"Finally, I can breathe again. Flora, would you get me a drink? Just a tiny. And put the Command Fan on my desk, would you, darling?"

I took the fan, the symbol of Mamma's authority, and laid it on her blotter, then went to the drinks cabinet. "Water, Mamma, or tea?"

"No, just a tiny drop of whisky. Aglis, go tell Carheña to hurry up with those papers. I want them signed before I leave here today. And tell Botherton I want Captain Hankle's final report, ASAP."

"Whisky?" I asked, surprised at her request, and a wee bit alarmed.

"As Nini Mo said, 'There is always an exception to every rule.'" Mamma actually knew Nini Mo, way back when, when Mamma was just a girl. Unfortunately, about all she remembers of the great ranger is that she was very short and smelled always of patchouli perfume.

I poured Mamma a tiny teeny drop of whisky, and took it over to her. "What took you so long, Mamma? I've been waiting for hours." She took the glass and, in return, held her wig out for me to put on the wig stand on the sideboard.

"I'm sorry, darling. The meeting with the Warlord took longer than I thought it would. I have a splitting headache; that blasted wig weighs a tonne. Ah, that was just what I needed. Another wee drop?"

I refilled Mamma's glass with another wee, wee drop and sat down next to her, pushing the growling Flynnie off the settee to do so. He promptly tried to climb on to Mamma's lap; laughing, she pushed him down, scratching at his ears in consolation.

"How is Hotspur?"

"He's fine, Mamma."

"Orderly and well behaved?"

"Ayah." I had decided not to tell Mamma about Poppy's fit. That might lead to questions about damage, which would then lead to questions about clean-up. I was fairly certain that Poppy himself wouldn't mention it, either; he tends to forget such incidents almost as soon as they happen. I hoped he had forgotten all about Valefor, too.

"I'm glad to hear it." Mamma wiped off the rest of her lip rouge with her hankie and then looked like Mamma again. She is not beautiful, exactly, not like the Warlady or the Holy Headmistress, but she is better than beautiful, I think. Her nose is crooked because she's broken it twice, duelling and bronc-busting, but the slant gives her face character. Her eyes are vivid green, and her short curls are the colour of honey and they never frizz. Unfairly, I had gotten the Poppy end of the stick, the pointy chin and scowly mouth.

"How's your prep going?" Mamma continued. She kept looking beyond me, towards the door, as though she was in a hurry for something, or distracted.

A wee bolt of guilt stabbed me. "Fine, Mamma." Thankfully Valefor had mostly caught me up. He had even finished making my tamales, which was wonderful because I hate to cook.

"Did you get the invitations in the post?"

"Ayah, Mamma."

"I'm glad to hear that," she said. "Where is that Sabre? Listen, darling, do you want to run on to dinner and I shall meet you there? I have a few things to do here before I can leave, and they just can't wait."

The guilt was replaced with annoyance. I can't even say how many times this happens: I meet Mamma for dinner, she sends me on ahead, saying she'll be right there, and then I sit alone at the O Club, mouldering, until either she shows up just in time for dessert or some junior aide shows up instead to *present the General's compliments, and she is sorry she is delayed and instructs you to just go on home.* "Mamma, so you always say, and you never come! I've been already waiting for hours, and you've been gone for ever."

As I complained, Lieutenant Sabre returned, with yet more redboxes, and my heart sank deeper into irkedness. It would take hours to go through them; I might as well just go home. Only a little while earlier I would have been glad to go home, but now, suddenly, I felt forlorn and disappointed.

Mamma sighed and rubbed the frowny line between her eyes. "Aglis . . ."

"Sir?" Lieutenant Sabre kicked his heels together and practically saluted. Mamma runs through ADCs like water; she rides them so hard that they usually break after a few weeks. Lieutenant Sabre had been with her for over a month now, and his manners were so perfect and his posture so straight that he almost seemed prater-human.

"I'll deal with those boxes after dinner. Are the papers ready for me to sign? They should be ready by now."

"I will immediately ascertain, sir." This time Lieutenant Sabre did salute, then turned hard on one heel and fairly marched out the door. There's a saying in the Army: *he's so regular that he pisses at attention,* and if ever I had seen an officer who fit that description, it was Lieutenant Sabre. I'll bet he wore his hat even in the bath.

"Mamma," I pleaded, "can't it wait?"

Mamma sighed again. She looked terribly tired, as though she hadn't slept well, which was also unusual, as she can sleep even in the saddle. "Darling, here – as soon as I sign the papers, then we'll go to dinner. After, you go on home and I'll come back here to finish up. Ayah so?"

"Ayah so, Mamma," I said, slightly solaced. Maybe that was better, anyway. Once Mamma got back to her office, she'd work all night, which would give Valefor and me a chance to plan our next move.

"I just need to confirm a few court-martial sentences; it won't take me very long. You can seal my signature; I know you love to seal." Mamma rose from the settee and, after pouring herself another tot, sat at her desk and put her specs on.

I do love to seal, so I pulled a chair up next to her. There is something deeply satisfying about making a perfect wax impression; it takes more skill than you might think. Lieutenant Sabre, now returned, opened files and shuffled papers, and Mamma sharpened her pen. I lit the spirit lamp and set the wax crucible to the flame. Army sealing wax stinks of storax, bitter and pungent, but it smells good to me.

"All right, Aglis, let's go. We are burning daylight."

Sergeant Sabre read: "'Sergeant Micalah Tsui Sanford,

Second Dandies. Charges: insubordination. Specification One: on Flores 15, Sergeant Sanford, whilst drunk, did stand upon the squad room dining table, singing "Chicken on a Raft" to the dishonour and detriment of the service. Specification Two: when ordered by his superior officer, Lieutenant Felix Boyd, to remove himself from the table, Sergeant Sanford did call Lieutenant Boyd a square-headed—'"

"Just the verdict," Mamma said hastily.

"Mamma," I protested.

"Stay fresh and sweet as long as you can, my darling. Go on, Aglis, and skip the dirty details."

"I beg your pardon, General. 'Verdict: that Sergeant Sanford be sent down dishonourably from the service. Recommendation of the Judge Advocate General: sentence upheld.'"

"I agree. Dictate addendum: *Sergeant Sanford shall be held for thirty days' hard labour, on bread and water, and then dishonourably discharged.* If there is one thing that I can't abide it's insubordination."

Lieutenant Sabre blotted the addendum and handed the paper to Mamma. Her pen dipped and flew. Mamma's signature is ornate and swirly. Try as I might I can never quite get my *F* to look so curly. When I have to turn in signed sheets for school, I always use Poppy's signature, which is a wiggly blur and very easy to copy.

Mamma handed the paper to me, and I rolled the blotter over her signature, carefully so that the ink did not smear. The wax was just about the right bubbly. There's an art to making sure that you don't splatter when you pour, but I've got years of practice, so it's no trouble to me. I can put 'em on or take 'em off, no big.

"I need your seal, Mamma."

She fumbled in her vest pocket. Mamma wears her seal on her watch fob, and when she tossed it to me, it was nice and warm from being tucked so close to her heart. I poured a perfect round dollop of hot wax, then pressed carefully. The seal of the Army of Califa is the same as the Warlord's seal, of course, five arrows bundled with a swirling ribbon. It looks quite nice impressed in wax, very balanced and round.

"You are piling up, darling," Mamma said, pushing another paper towards me.

"You are squiggling," I said. "That could be anyone's signature."

"But only one seal." Mamma skidded her pen across the paper, splotching ink. "Chop-chop."

I blotted and sealed. Sometimes, court-martials are quite interesting – murder or mayhem – but these were all stupid stuff: drunk on duty, uppity in the ranks, kicking the captain's cat. Nothing yummy at all. Soldiers can't hardly do anything that is fun, and if they disobey an order, no matter how dumb that order is, they are in for it. Here was a sergeant spending thirty days in the guardhouse for having dirty buttons (Mamma dropped him down to time served), here was a corporal spending four months in the guardhouse for snarking off to his commanding officer (Mamma gave him another month and a flogging). There was nothing interesting at all, and my tummy was really burning with emptiness now.

"Hang in there, Flora. We are almost done," Mamma said, pushing her document over to me. "Where's Aglis with those papers?

Lieutenant Sabre had left the room, but now he returned with a folder. He handed it to Mamma, who flipped it open and dipped her pen.

"General, I beg your pardon but before you sign—"

"Ayah?"

Lieutenant Sabre was looking at me. Mamma paused.

"Flora," Mamma said, "my red-tape dispenser is low. Would you run out and get some more from Pecos? We are going to need it."

"Mamma—"

"Flora." She said my name in the Voice that makes colonels cry. I got up, a tiny part of me annoyed that she so obviously was dismissing me, but another part of me was suddenly apprehensively excited. Something was going on.

So I went, whistling cheerfully, as though going to fetch red tape was my favourite thing in the entire world.

"Close the door behind you, Flora," Mamma called.

I did, gently. Lieutenant Sabre has his own office, right next to Mamma's. They have an adjoining door, and this adjoining door, though closed, has a transom above it. The window was only slightly open, but slightly was enough.

". . . insists that you release the Dainty Pirate to his custody."

The Dainty Pirate? I stood on tiptoe, trying to get my ear closer to that open window. Not for the first time I wished I were taller.

"Not a chance in the Abyss. The Dainty Pirate is my boy. I got him, and I will spank him. You can tell Lord Axacaya's envoy to go home unsatisfied." Mamma's voice sounded hard, flat. "He's my prize and I shall keep him."

Mamma had captured the Dainty Pirate! Udo was going to absolutely die. The excited flutter in my tum became a full-fledged hurricane. But why was this incredible news a secret? For years, the Dainty Pirate had been the scourge of the coastline, robbing and plundering any vessel that crossed his path. Ayah sure, the Dainty Pirate had dainty manners and never actually killed anyone, but that didn't make him less of a thief. His capture would be a huge success for Mamma and increase her popularity even more.

Lieutenant Sabre coughed nervously. "I beg your pardon, sir, but Lord Axacaya's envoy made it clear that because of your previous association with Boy Hansgen, he doubts your ability to judge this case fairly. I beg your pardon."

Boy Hansgen? Nini Mo's right-hand man? No one had heard a jot from him since after the War, but he

132

remained the most wanted man in Califa. What did Boy Hansgen have to do with the Dainty Pirate?

"Lord Axacaya is wrong in this matter. Many years ago, Boy Hansgen and I were friends, but I have no such friendship with the Dainty Pirate. This situation must be resolved quickly. If the word gets out that the Dainty Pirate is Boy Hansgen and he's in our custody, it's going to get ugly."

Boy Hansgen was the Dainty Pirate? I almost spat with excitement; if I hadn't been trying to be cool as a cloak-twitcher I'd have shrieked. The Dainty Pirate's true identity is unknown, and although the press is always speculating, no one had ever speculated that he was Boy Hansgen. Boy Hansgen alive? A real ranger – alive!

Mamma continued: "I want this warrant carried out immediately, Aglis, the sooner the better. Until then, I want him held in complete secrecy. It will be a disaster if the press catches wind of this. And I want him disposed of before Axacaya has time to get the news back to Anahuatl City. And Goddess knows, I don't want the EI to hear about this. Who knows what stunt those idiots might pull."

The EI – the Eschatalogical Immenation – is a revolutionary society devoted to the eviction of all Huitzil influence on Califa. They are completely against the law, but are often in the newspapers, although they never seem to do much besides paint slogans and post anonymous broadsides.

"Ayah, sir," Lieutenant Sabre answered. "There's a batch of prisoners scheduled to be removed from Presidio Guardhouse to the Zoo Battery prison tonight. I've arranged for Boy Hansgen to be moved with the rest, and I've instructed the Zoo Battery commander to prepare the gallows for tomorrow night."

The gallows? The gallows! Mamma was going to *hang* Boy Hansgen, the last ranger? Nini Mo's sidekick? The heat of my excitement went dead cold.

"Is he secure? I do not want him getting away, Aglis."

"He is secure, General. There is no way that he can escape."

"Good. Would you see what happened to Flora, Aglis—"

I abandoned my eavesdropping and rushed back to Mamma's office, pausing in the hallway for just a second, to try to compose myself. Lieutenant Sabre opened the door and gave me a severe look, which I ignored.

"There you are, Flora! I hope you weren't goldbricking," Mamma said.

"I wasn't fooling around, Mamma. Sergeant Carheña was gone and I had to go to supply for the red tape," I said sweetly, waving the wad of red tape that I had oh-so-luckily stuffed in my pocket earlier. My tone was sweet, but my tum felt sick.

"Here's the last one. And don't peek. It's sensitive."

She slid the document over to me. The top half of the page had been obscured with a blank piece of paper, leaving only Mamma's signature visible. But I knew what it was, and after I poured, I hesitated. My hand had trembled, and the wax had splotched most unprofessionally.

"Chop-chop, Flora. What are you waiting for?" Mamma said impatiently. "The wax is hardening."

I sealed the Dainty Pirate's death warrant.

14

DINNER. SNEAKING.
EAGLE EYES.

Rangers have to learn to smile, and lie while they smile, and look content although they are grievous pained. But it's not easy to look carefree and blissful when your brain is churning like a flood. I could barely work my lips into a smile, and now I had an endless eternity of dinner time to get through before I could make my escape.

Lucky for me, Lieutenant Sabre went to the O Club with us. Normally I would have kicked up a fuss over sharing Mamma after she had been gone for so long, but tonight I was glad not to be the full focus of her attention. Even Flynn, begging under the table, was a welcome distraction.

Dinner with Mamma at the Officers' Club is always a prolonged affair. As soon as you sit down, ancient officers start hobbling over to the table to compliment

Mamma on this, or ask for her permission on that, or offer their opinion on another thing. Tonight was no different; in fact, it was probably worse because Mamma had been away for so long.

Between the endless interruptions, Mamma asked questions about the Catorcena, homework, Poppy and the dogs. I answered, trying hard to squeeze my voice into some semblance of normal, but it was hard. Continuing lucky for me, though, Mamma remained somewhat distracted, and now that I knew the reason, her "wee tot" and the lengthy meeting with the Warlord made perfect sense. But so many other things did not.

How could she? How could Mamma send the last ranger to the gallows? Boy Hansgen – he'd been her friend – he was no less a hero than Mamma herself was. He'd never surrendered, never given up. If his capture was a secret, why didn't Mamma just let him go?

If I had been a better ranger, like Nini Mo, I could have teased information out of her without her even knowing I was teasing; I could have scryed the situation in the smear of gravy she left on her plate, or I could have burned my Will through Lieutenant Sabre's smooth forehead as he sat there at attention, chewing his steak, burned it right into his brain and known all his thoughts. But being only just me, all I could do was sit there, churning with questions, and try to look blissfully ignorant.

"Did you get your dress done, Flora?"

"Ayah, Mamma." Brief stab of guilt, but I *would* have

it done next time she asked. In fact, Valefor might have finished it by now, for true.

"Are you all right, Flora? You seem a bit agitated."

Another sharp stab. "I think I am getting sick," I said, and then before Mamma could say anything more, the waiter whisked our plates away and asked if we wanted dessert. I did not, but alas, Mamma did, and of course Lieutenant Sabre followed her lead. I just wanted to get out of there before my facade completely cracked.

Mamma had finished quizzing me; now she turned her questions towards Lieutenant Sabre. Relieved to be off the hook, I sat there wishing dessert would hurry up – and then we had another interruption. A lieutenant in a red sash, which meant that he was Officer of the Day (the officer on duty when everyone else has gone home) and, thus, the interruption was official.

"I beg your pardon, sir," the lieutenant said, after saluting. "But I would not trouble you at dinner if it were not important."

"Ayah, so, Lieutenant Hulle?" Mamma asked impatiently.

The lieutenant leaned over and whispered into Mamma's ear. Her lips twisted and she put down the fork she had been fiddling with, then murmured something to Lieutenant Sabre, which I, darn it, could not quite catch.

Lieutenant Sabre whispered back. I tried not to appear attentive and twiddled my spoon, wishing I knew a sigil to enhance my hearing.

Murmur. Whisper. Murmur. Mamma. Hulle. Mamma. Sabre.

"Thank you, Lieutenant Hulle," Mamma said.

The lieutenant turned sharp on one heel and marched away, weaving his way through the tables that were now all staring at us.

Mamma sighed. "Will you excuse me, darling? I'll just be a moment, but I have something to attend to. Sit tight, Aglis, thank you." Lieutenant Sabre, half out of his seat, sat back down.

I could tell from Mamma's look that she was displeased. "What happened, Mamma?"

"Don't eat my cake, darling. I'll make it quick." She stood up, tossed her napkin on the table, and made her way towards the front of the Club.

"What is it?" I asked Lieutenant Sabre.

He was glaring at Mamma's back, the first real crack in his perfect yaller-dog facade I had ever seen. "Lord Axacaya. He wanted to speak with the General. He has the nerve to come here!"

Lord Axacaya is a powerful adept and Mamma's greatest enemy. He is not a true Califan; he came to the City many years earlier, fleeing from the Huitzil Empire. There he had been not just an adept, but divine. The Huitzils worship a hummingbird god, who feeds not on pollen and dew, but on blood and pain. The Flayed Priests of Huitzil take children from their real parents and raise them as the sacred offspring of this god. Then at a time ordained by the Flayed

139

Priests' oracles, these divine sons and daughters are sacrificed to keep the Waking World in balance. (Thankfully, the Huitzils didn't make us take up that practice when we made peace with them.) Lord Axacaya was one of those divine children. When he was fifteen, he should have died under a sacrificial knife; instead, he fled and came to Califa, and with him he brought war. The Huitzils wanted him back, but the Warlord, after granting him sanctuary, wouldn't turn him over, and thus the conflict between our countries began.

And then later, when the War was not going so well for us, Lord Axacaya plotted with the Huitzils to turn Califa over to them if his life would be spared. If Mamma hadn't found out in time about his plotting, we probably would have lost the War completely. Instead, Mamma was able to force the Huitzil Empire to make peace, and though the terms were more to their benefit than ours, still we remain a free country, thanks to her. I think Mamma would have executed Lord Axacaya if she could have, but he's under Huitzil protection and, therefore, untouchable.

"It must be pretty important," I said, fishing. *And*, I thought, *it has to have something to do with Boy Hansgen.*

Lieutenant Sabre said viciously, "Pernicious traitor. The General should have ripped his lungs out while she had the chance. Now he lords over us all."

"If Lord Axacaya wants something, why does he have

to ask Mamma for it? Why doesn't he just take what he wants? Mamma has no authority over him."

"It's not that simple. Under the Peace Accord, Califa maintains some independence and the right to conduct our internal affairs without interference –" Lieutenant Sabre stopped and looked at me suspiciously. "What makes you think that Lord Axacaya wants something from the General?"

Pigface Pogostick! I felt my face grow stiff and hard. I tried to arrange my mouth in an innocent smile. "Why else would he come here but to ask Mamma for something personally? I mean, he could have just sent a messenger if it wasn't important."

Lieutenant Sabre wasn't buying my feint. He looked at me so long that my face grew hot and my lips began to quiver. Rangers do not quiver, nor do they show they are caught. "I think I'll take Flynnie out . . ." I said hastily, before my facade collapsed completely.

"Ah, the transom," Lieutenant Sabre said suddenly, and he smiled a bit. "I have found it useful myself at times."

"Transom? What transom?"

He looked at me appraisingly. "You will remember, Madama Fyrdraaca, that this is a matter of state, and you will be discreet?"

"You won't tell Mamma, will you?" I asked hopefully.

"Not if you swear on the goddess Califa to keep silent."

I glanced around to make sure no one was in whisper

range, and then whispered: "Ayah, I swear, but I don't understand – the Navy's been chasing the Dainty Pirate for years. Why is Mamma keeping his capture a secret?"

"Shush—"

A plate of chocolate cake appeared before me, and then the waiter whisked around behind Lieutenant Sabre and plunked another plate in front of him, and then a plate in front of Mamma's empty place. A second waiter offered coffee, which I took, but Lieutenant Sabre declined for himself and for Mamma (which she wasn't going to be pleased about, I was sure).

As soon as the waiters were gone, Lieutenant Sabre said in a low voice, "When we sued for peace, what was the Birdies' first demand? The Ranger Corps be disbanded – the Birdies were afraid of the rangers' power and influence, and afraid of their magick. As Nini Mo's sidekick, Boy Hansgen was extremely popular. If word got out that the Dainty Pirate was captured, and that he was Boy Hansgen – think of the commotion. He'd be a hero and a rally for those who oppose the Huitzil overrule. At his execution, there would be a public outcry – maybe even riots. It's the General's job to keep the peace, as distasteful as sometimes that peace may be. And anyway, whatever Boy Hansgen may have once been, the Dainty Pirate is nothing but a common criminal."

"But why does Lord Axacaya want him?" I asked. "If Mamma's to execute him, isn't that what Lord Axacaya wants?"

"Ayah, but the General will execute him via Army regulations, and it will be short and sweet. Lord Axacaya would handle him according to Huitzil law, and that would be different."

"How?"

Lieutenant Sabre hesitated. "It would be messier. Also, Axacaya doesn't know that Boy Hansgen and the Dainty Pirate are one and the same, and the General thinks it best he remains ignorant."

"Have you ever seen him?" I asked. "Axacaya, I mean."

"Ayah."

"Does he really have an eye in the middle of his tongue?"

Lieutenant Sabre looked startled. "Gracious me, where did you read that, madama?"

"The *Califa Police Gazette*."

"You should elevate your reading habits. The *CPG* is hardly the proper reading material for a young lady of good breeding—"

"Does he?"

"No," Lieutenant Sabre said, "but his eyes are black as pitch."

"Lots of people have black eyes."

"Not like this. I mean, his eyes are *all* black, even to the whites. He has trafficked so long in darkness that it has suffused his body, and now it stains the windows to his soul, reflecting his inner impurity."

I'd never heard of an adept whose eyes had turned

to black, but then Lord Axacaya is a son of the Butterfly Goddess and he knows many dark and bloody arts.

It suddenly occurred to me that, though Lieutenant Sabre was being a surprisingly useful informant, I was missing out on an even more valuable opportunity to eavesdrop. Plus, maybe even get a glimpse of the boo-spooky Lord Axacaya myself.

"Excuse me, I have to go to the loo – I'll be right back." Before Lieutenant Sabre could comment, I bolted.

In the foyer, the Table Captain stood behind his stand, flipping through his reservation book nervously. The guards that normally stand outside the Club's front door were now standing inside, and they were holding their rifles at Port Arms, which is two positions away from Shoulder Arms, which is one position away from firing.

Earlier, the sliding doors to the Saloon had been open, though the Saloon itself had been empty and dark. Now those doors were closed, and two figures stood like sentries before them. They were heavily veiled, as formless as darkness, though their robes were a bright verdant green and fringed with brilliant feathers. The guards stared at these figures, and these figures – well, because of their veils, you could not see where they were looking.

"How are you, Madama Fyrdraaca Segunda?" the Table Captain said nervously. "Ready for your Catorcena? We certainly are." His eyes kept shifting from me to the veiled figures, then back again.

Normally, of course, people have their Catorcena parties at home, but in our case, that was out of the question, and so my party would be here at the Officers' Club. Ever since my sixth birthday, when Poppy ruined my party by standing on the roof of the garden shed and screaming at the goddess to strike him with lightning, I've had all my parties at the O Club.

"I am ready," I said, in a bright oh-I-am-just-a-harmless-silly-girl voice.

One of the figures swivelled in my direction, and somehow, just somehow, I knew it was looking at me. Suddenly I did not feel silly at all; I felt like someone was trying to rummage around in my head, picking through my thoughts, examining my teeth, poking my muscles, fiddling fingers in my brain. It was a horrible tickly feeling and made my insides feel all squirmy. I shook my head, but the feeling did not go away.

The veiling over the figure's head, I saw now, was sheer, but probably transparent enough to see through. The figure reached up a hand, long and graceful, bangled around the wrists with bracelets of jade and gold, and lifted the veil.

Two great eagle eyes stared at me, wide and unblinking, golden as an egg yolk. Above the eyes, iridescent feathers tufted upwards into a quiff, and below, curved a sharp black beak.

A Quetzal! A Huitzil sacred guard. Never had I seen one, except as crude drawings in *Nini Mo vs. the Eagle Guards*. They say that Quetzals are born to women

145

who lie with eagles, and they hatch out of huge green eggs, squirming babies with shrieking eagle heads. They say that the Quetzals tear out the hearts of sacrificial slaves, then eat them while they still beat. They say the Quetzals have no human feelings of mercy and love, only bloodlust and the killing instinct.

This Quetzal nerved my blood to shivering, with its unblinking golden eyes, the elegant narrow hand, the human form now evident beneath the robes. Valefor isn't human, but he seems human, he looks human, he acts human, and it's easy to forget that he's not. But this thing, despite its human attributes, had nothing in its eyes but a glittering hunger – the hunger of a predator. The Quetzal was unnatural, inhuman, and yet repellently beautiful, its sleek feathers shading from yellow amber into a deep yellow-red, the lethal beak as shiny black as wet ink. And those eyes, as round as two full moons, pitiless but also compelling.

I stood there, stock-still, caught in that gaze, unable to tear myself away. As mesmerized as a mouse who stands helplessly as death swoops down. Then the Quetzal let drop its veil and turned its great head away, dismissing me.

I turned and fled back to the safety of the dining room.

15

CASE TIGGER. UDO UPSET.
A PLAN.

Mamma came back a few minutes later, looking grim, and she did not eat her chocolate cake. Neither did I; for the first time in my life, chocolate cake held no charms for me. Dinner was officially over. Mamma and Lieutenant Sabre went back to Building Fifty-six, and Flynnie and I were sent home in Mamma's barouche. Finally, I was alone, which was good because I could pretend normal no longer.

Back in the City, I got the driver, Sergeant Ziniea, to drop me at Hayes and Ash, near Case Tigger. It wasn't terribly late, only around nine o'clock, but already the light in Udo's room was out. The Landaðons are fiends on curfew, which is the one great negative whenever I stay with them.

Udo's room is on the second floor, facing the alley, but there's a handy dandy tree right outside his

147

window. I have made the climb a zillion times, both up and down. I carefully opened the back-garden gate and stuffed Flynnie through, with stern instructions not to bark, and then swung myself upwards. Udo's window was open; the Landaðons are fiends for fresh air, too.

The street light across the road was angled just right to throw a few shadows on the floor of Udo's room, and it showed the dim outline of a dresser and three beds. Poor Udo shares his bedroom with two younger brothers, but Gernot wets the bed and Gesilher kicks, so they all have their own beds.

"Udo," I hissed. I banged my shin against the dresser and stifled a curse.

The biggest bed groaned. Kicking off my boots, I climbed over the trundle bed where Gesilher lay wadded under a mound of blankets. Udo's bed is shaped like a sleigh and draped with curtains that hang from the ceiling. He always closes the curtains, as he bemoans his privacy. I brushed them aside. "Udo!"

Udo grunted and moved, half awake. "Go away, Ges—"

I poked him. "It's me."

"Flora?" he mumbled. Waking up Udo is like waking the dead. Actually, waking the dead is probably easier.

"Ayah, it's me – wake up." I poked again, then resorted to pinching. Udo jerked and rolled and then sat up, muffling curses. "Move over." I crawled under the curtains and into the bed, and Udo drowsily made room for me.

"What are you doing here?"

"Mamma caught the Dainty Pirate!"

That news immediately snapped Udo alert. "What?!"

"Keep your voice down or you'll wake the kids!"

"Buck got the Dainty Pirate? When? Where—"

"Is the house on fire?" Gesilher said from the darkness beyond Udo's bed. He's a worrier, always expecting to be poisoned, or burned, or smothered.

"Go back to sleep, kid," Udo said, unkindly. "The house is not on fire."

"Ayah." Gesilher was quiet again.

I said, "I just came from the Presidio – Mamma is back from Angeles, and she's captured the Dainty Pirate. He's been held in secret, and he's going to be hanged tomorrow—" Here Udo groaned, but I continued, "He's Boy Hansgen! The Dainty Pirate is Boy Hansgen, Nini Mo's henchman – he's been incognito all this time!"

Udo gurgled at my news and bounced on the bed. "Boy Hansgen! You've got to be joking me! Why was Boy Hansgen disguising himself as the Dainty Pirate?"

"I don't know – but, Udo, they are going to hang him tomorrow night!"

"What about his trial? Doesn't he get a trial?"

"There isn't a trial, Udo. Mamma's already signed the warrant. She wants to make sure he's dead before anyone gets wind of it."

Udo protested, "She can't sentence him without a trial—"

"She's done so, Udo, to keep him out of the hands of

149

the Birdies. She's keeping the peace – do you know what the public might do if the news gets out that the Dainty Pirate is Boy Hansgen? They could rally around him; it could cause riots—"

"You act as though you are defending Buck, that you think she is right, and you say that you are going to be a ranger—"

"I am not defending Mamma, Udo, I'm explaining the politics to you."

"I don't care about politics. I care about the Dainty Pirate being hung. What are we going to do—"

The door from the hall cracked open, slanting light into the room. I burrowed down into the blankets, and Udo groaned and made the fakest snore I'd ever heard. I lay as quiet as a tiny crab and tried to hold my breath. For what seemed like the longest time, the light shone in silence. Udo snored again, and then the door closed.

I burrowed upwards. "You gotta keep it down, Udo! And I gotta get home; I don't want Mamma to make it there first."

Udo bent his head toward mine, so that our foreheads were almost touching, and whispered, "What are we going to do?"

"What *can* we do?"

"We have to rescue him. . ."

Rescue him! Was Udo *insane*? "We can't rescue him—"

"Are you kidding, Flora? You are always going on

about Nini Mo and what she would do. Do you think she'd let her own henchman go to the gallows? Put up or shut up, Flora!"

Udo was right about that, that's for sure. Rangers are loyal to each other and stick hard to the rule *Leave no one behind.* When Nini Mo's accountant was killed in a raid, she dragged his body fifty-five miles on muleback to return him to his family for proper burial. She would never stand aside and let her sidekick be executed.

". . . those guns in the gun room," Udo was saying, "and I have the pistol I got for my birthday last year; that's enough firepower to storm the guardhouse—"

I was only half listening to him. Why couldn't we rescue Boy Hansgen? All the way to Case Tigger, the knowledge that the last ranger would be executed tomorrow and I could do nothing about it had wormed and wiggled in my stomach like a bad egg sandwie. But Nini Mo says that what makes rangers stand apart from other people is that other people *don't* and rangers *do.* They act. Here was my chance to act like a ranger.

"No." I interrupted Udo's grandiose plan, which now involved two horse-drawn batteries and a squad of pike-men. "Nini Mo says you should only beard the bear in his den if you are coated in honey."

"Wouldn't that make the bear all the more likely to eat you?"

"She meant you should have the advantage before

151

you face the enemy on his own turf. We don't have the advantage. We will need to be subtle, and we certainly don't want to get caught." I had decided to act, and with that decision, my tum felt much better.

A desolate howl rose from outside the window.

"What the heck was that?" Udo asked.

"Snapperhead Flynn – he thinks he's been abandoned – I have to get going—"

"We could wear masks – or Glamours! *The Eschata* was full of Glamours – Glamours that Confuse, Glamours that Befuddle, Glamours that Disguise."

"Ummm . . ." I said, considering. Udo was on to something. *The Eschata* did have an entire section devoted to Glamours, which only made sense, as rangers often require disguises, and the proper Glamour can disguise not only your face, but your whole body, too. "Lieutenant Sabre told Mamma that the Dainty Pirate would be transported to the Zoo Battery guardhouse tomorrow night, and thence to the gallows—"

"That's perfect!" said Udo, bouncing the bed again. "The road to Zoo Battery goes out along the Pacifica Playa, and that's beyond the City's border and there's nothing out there – no spectators, no witnesses. We could hijack the guard and steal the Dainty Pirate away!"

"He'll be pretty well-guarded, Udo. I don't think just the two of us, even in Glamours, could take an entire squad, maybe two. But if we had a release order..."

The order itself would be easy. I have a copious supply of official letterhead, which I have been nicking from offices for years, because you never know when official letterhead will come in handy. Udo's handwriting is as good as any clerk's, and I know all the official lingo. An Army special order is always achingly polite, full of *presents compliments, commends to your obedience, your humble servant.* I could very easily construct a special order demanding that the Dainty Pirate be handed to our custody.

"Can you forge Buck's signature?" Udo asked. Another howl raised up in sorrow – a good reminder that I needed to get home before Mamma did.

I said, "It's hard. I might be able to do something that would pass a casual glance, though probably not close scrutiny. But it's not the signature – it's the seal. We could never fake that."

"Pigface Psychopomp. Can you kip her seal, then, while she's sleeping or something?"

"I could, but I don't know that it would be wise, anyway. I mean, the guard is sure to think something is fishy – why would Mamma condemn a man to death and then suddenly turn around and release him? They are sure to question. We need a release order from someone no one would dare question, someone whose word would be law unchallenged. Who ranks Mamma?"

"Lord Axacaya?" Udo asked.

I thought of the grim-visaged birds and Lord Axacaya's demand, and a tiny thrill of revulsion rolled up my spine. "No. Who else?"

"The Warlord?"

I grinned in the darkness, and thought Nini Mo would approve mightily of my plan. "Ayah. The Warlord."

16

HOME. BUCK.
DIFFERING OPINIONS.

I caught the horsecar at Octavia. It was late enough that Flynn and I were the only riders, and the driver looked half asleep. Luckily, his horse knew the way. I sat at the very back, Flynn curled up on the seat behind me, and thought about our rescue plan. At the time of discussion, it had seemed the proper thing to do, but now it seemed like an awful chance. And yet, what kind of a ranger would I be if I did nothing to prevent Boy Hansgen from going to his death?

The horsecar left me at the Way Out Gate, Crackpot's back door (or delivery entrance, as Valefor had informed me). When I stopped by the stables to feed the horses, I saw that they had already been grained and mucked, and my heart sank. Mamma had beat me home. And I just couldn't face her right now.

Though I had defended Mamma to Udo, I couldn't

defend Mamma to myself. I know she is sworn to uphold the Warlord, and that means she must uphold the Peace Accord, too, but how could she execute one of Califa's greatest heroes? A man who had once been her friend? She might have her reasons, but I did not understand them. Nor did I want to.

The dogs met me at the garden gate, carolling their pleasure at my arrival, and Flynnie flung himself forward to meet them. Any chance I had of sneaking in was lost in canine alarum. Still, maybe I could at least make it to my room. I very quietly opened the door, trying to slide in before the dogs could, but they leaped and pawed, and poured by me, almost knocking me down.

"Flora?" Mamma's voice drifted down the Below Stairs. "Is that you?"

"It sure ain't Nini Mo," I mumbled. The dogs scurried upstairs, which was well for them, because then I got a good look at the kitchen. When I had left to meet Mamma, the kitchen had been tidy and the dogs were locked up in the mudroom. Now the kitchen looked like the Flayed Riders of Huitzil had ridden through it once and then doubled back again, just for fun. The room was trashed. Someone, who could only be Poppy, had let the dogs out and unsupervised, and here was the result. Anger boiled up in me, so hot that it fair burned my throat. If I'd had a stick, I would have whacked something. Instead, I kicked the scuttle, which lay on the floor surrounded by spilled coal.

"Come to the parlour, Flora – I want to talk with you."

My heart, already low, disappeared into the depths of my boots. Mamma never actually talks *with* you; she talks *to* you. I trudged upstairs, a glassy sparkle of guilt glittering in my stomach. Had Lieutenant Sabre tattled after all? Or maybe Mamma had guessed? Or maybe she had found out about Valefor? I didn't know which was worse. No, I did. My knees felt rather weak. Nini Mo had faced the Flayed Priest Njal Sholto in a magickal duel, knowing that he was the greater adept, and thus she faced her own death. And yet she did not quiver. I would not quiver, either.

I would not quiver.

"Flora! Chop-chop!"

Mamma sat on the settee in the parlour, surrounded by a wash of papers. More were scattered over the low table before her, which also was stacked with the redboxes I had last seen on her desk at Fifty-six. The dogs had displayed themselves upon the hearthrug, like butter would not melt in their mouths. I could have kicked them all, a good boot right into the hinder. Violence is not the answer, I know, but it's a hard impulse to strike.

"Where have you been, Flora? I thought you were going home." Mamma peered at me through her pince-nez. She'd changed out of her uniform into her purple silk wrapper, and her hair was standing up in spikes, as though she'd been running her hands through it.

"I'm sorry, Mamma. I stopped at the chemist's; I still don't feel so well." It was easy to sound forlorn and sick, partially because I really *did* feel forlorn and sick. My cold was still lingering.

"Why didn't you have the barouche wait for you?"

"There's no place to wait without blocking traffic."

"I don't like your riding the horsecar this late alone."

"I had Flynnie, Mamma."

"Ayah so, I am sure he would be good in a fight, poor coward. Flora, I went up to your room looking for you."

My stomach, which had started to warm, turned to ice again. *Do not quiver!*

"I thought you said you had finished your Catorcena dress. What did I find, not finished? Your Catorcena dress. I understand that sewing does not come easy to you, but that is no excuse for not being truthful."

"I'm sorry, Mamma," I said, and I was sorry – that I hadn't put the dress away. But then, I hadn't planned that Mamma might snoop; it's not her usual habit. And even more than sorry, I was relieved that Valefor did not appear to be anywhere evident. Although, blast him, he was supposed to finish the dress before I came home.

"I can accept your apology, but apologies are not going to cut it at the Barracks, Flora. They expect cadets to abide by their word and be truthful in all things. It is a hallmark of leadership to never dissemble."

Ha! Mamma could say that, and yet was she not

dissembling in her dealings with Boy Hansgen? She did not practise what she preached. Rangers may lie, but at least they know that they lie. They are not hypocrites.

"I am sorry, Mamma."

"And the kitchen – you are supposed to make sure the dogs are in the mudroom before you leave, Flora."

Now, I would suck up the other stuff, but I was not going to take the blame for Poppy. "I did, Mamma, I did. Poppy must have let them out. They were in the mudroom when I left. It wasn't me."

"I stand corrected. In the future, then, perhaps you should put the dogs in the stable when you leave. Hotspur is not likely to go in there."

"Ayah, Mamma."

She sighed, and rubbed her forehead. She looked even more tired than she had at dinner. "I am sorry Hotspur is such trouble, Flora. You are good to look after him as you do. He has always needed looking after, poor boy."

In my mind, people stop being "poor boys" when they hit thirty, and Poppy was way past that mark, but I suppose Mamma has known him so long that it's hard for her think of him otherwise. Also, he does act very childish.

Mamma continued, "He has had a very rough time."

I didn't say anything because the only thing I had to say was rather mean. We must be nice to Poppy

159

because he spent three years as a prisoner of war. But other people have rough times and they suck it up and move on. Sergeant Carheña lost his leg at the Battle of Calo Res, and he gets along just fine. There's a girl in my gymkhana class at Sanctuary whose little brother fell out of the back of an ice wagon and was crushed. She gets along just fine, too. Why does Poppy have to be special?

"Can I go upstairs now, Mamma? I have a lot of homework."

"I wish you would sit with me for a few minutes, Flora. It's been so long since we have been home together, and now I have to leave again. A messenger arrived from Moro; the Ambassador from Anahuatl City requires me to wait upon him, and I have to leave first thing in the morning. I'm sorry, darling."

Leaving again? Was this a stroke of luck! Mamma out of the way, while Udo and I undertook our rescue plan. One worrisome detail easily taken care of.

"But I promise I will be back for your Catorcena. I promise. I'll be back in plenty of time. I promise."

"It doesn't matter, Mamma," I said. "Can I go? I need to get the kitchen clean before I go to bed."

"Leave the kitchen – I'll tell Aglis to send a squad over in the morning. And of course it matters. I promise I'll be back in time."

"It's fine. Good night." I turned around to go upstairs, and though Mamma called me back, I did not go. I didn't actually care about my Catorcena or whether

Mamma was there or not. All I cared about at this particular moment was saving Boy Hansgen. Even Valefor had taken backseat to that; he could wait a little longer. Boy Hansgen could not. Mamma's departure made things much easier. Once Boy was safe, then I would restore Valefor, and if Mamma found out and didn't like it, to the Abyss with her.

When I got out of the bathroom, Mamma was waiting by my door; she never gives up, which is what makes her the Rock of Califa, I suppose. Persistence may be good for a general, but it is not such a happy quality in a mother.

"What do you mean 'it doesn't matter', Flora? I thought you were looking forward to your Catorcena."

"I guess, Mamma."

"You have done an excellent job on your room, darling. I don't remember when I saw it this clean before, and the bathroom, too. I know you have a lot of responsibilities, and I am glad to see that you are, for the most part, handling them."

"Thank you, Mamma."

"I am sorry to have to leave again so soon, Flora, but I promise, before you go to the Barracks this summer, I shall take a nice long holiday and we shall do something fun, ayah?"

"Ayah, Mamma."

"I have to leave early, darling, so I won't wake you. Will you have cocoa with me before—"

A dog distantly barked, once, then twice, and then

the entire herd erupted into a yodelling volley. There is only one reason the dogs howl this late at night.

Poppy.

Downstairs, glass crashed and the barking turned to howls. Mamma whipped around, then ran downstairs.

17

ALONE. VALEFOR. NEXT.

Mamma left at oh-dark-thirty. She came into my room, but I pretended to be asleep and she didn't wake me – only brushed the top of my head with a kiss and slid the bed-door closed again. As soon as she was gone, leaving a faint whiff of sandalwood behind, I booted the dogs out of bed and ran to the window.

The outriders were already assembled; two of them were heaving Mamma's field desk into the back of a buckboard. Lieutenant Sabre stood by the back of the wagon, directing. The outriders finished levering up the field desk, then started on Mamma's trunk.

Usually I am sad when Mamma leaves, but not today. Today I was fearsome glad, and a part of me grimly wished she'd never return. This is very mean, I know, but sometimes my heart feels very very mean. Small *and* mean. Mamma could leave when she wanted to, but I'm stuck.

A striker held Jimmy's reins. The same wind snatching at the guidons was making Jimmy frisky, and he kept hopping a bit, so the striker had also to bounce, to keep him in place. The guidons dipped suddenly, and there was Mamma's bright head. She said something to Lieutenant Sabre, then took over Jimmy's reins, rubbing his nose soothingly. Mamma has a way with horses. No matter how wild they are, she can calm them.

I had not followed her all the way to the kitchen the night before. I had gone to the top of the stairs, and there I had stopped. Below, Poppy was shouting, the dogs were howling, and glass was smashing. Mamma's calm voice cutting through the clamour like thread cuts cake. Poppy's grating voice, rough with tears. "*The Human Dress is forged Iron!*"

"Shush, my darling, my sweet boy. Shush."

"*The Human Form a Fiery Forge!*"

"No, my darling, here, give the knife to me . . ."

That's when I ran back to my bedroom. I had slammed the door, crawled into my cold bed, and lay in bitter darkness the rest of the night, thinking bitter thoughts.

Now Mamma mounted, and Jimmy twirled a bit while she settled in the saddle, after rapping him on the withers with her crop. The last trunk was strapped down, and Lieutenant Sabre, who had been overseeing

164

the stowing, mounted. Here was revealed Lieutenant Sabre's one military flaw: he had a terrible seat. His stirrups were way too high and his knees stuck out like wings.

The guidons went first, and then the buckboard. Mamma fell in next, then Lieutenant Sabre, and the entourage jogged down the drive. Because Crackpot's main gate is too heavy to be opened without Val's effort, the drive now cuts away and veers to the back of the House, towards the freight entrance. At the split, Mamma paused and looked back. I ducked behind the curtain, although I know she was too far to see me. I couldn't see her face, just the bobbing feathers on her tricorn hat. For a few seconds, she looked at the House, and then she turned and rode away.

I went back to my warm bed, and there found Valefor, usurping my place and seeming pleased with himself. He looked not quite the worst I had seen him, but not the best, either. Somewhere in between, faintly sparkling but faded to lavender.

"How happy that Buck should have to leave again, and now here is our chance. I can still feel that Sigil rumbling around inside me. I know this time we shall find it, I know we shall, Flora Segunda – let's start."

"I can't, Valefor." I found my wrapper and put it on, then looked for my slippers. Now that I was up, I might as well stay up. Udo and I had agreed that we would be cutting school today; his plan was to leave Case Tigger as usual, walk the kiddies to school, and then hit the horsecar. I had plenty of time to take a long hot bath before he came, if I went now. We had a long day before us, and it would be nice to be clean for it. Plus, I was too hungry to sleep. I needed a big breakfast and then to start preparing.

Valefor said, "Why not? We are burning daylight, and Buck is gone. When will she be back?"

"Tomorrow afternoon," I said. "Just in time for my Catorcena the next day."

"That should be plenty of time to—"

"No, Valefor," I said, then told him about Boy Hansgen. When I was done, Valefor's brow was furrowed in a pout deep enough to plant potatoes in.

"But what about me, Flora Segunda? Have you forgotten poor Valefor?" The tears were welling. Val was a regular fountain; it was a talent that I should cultivate. Crying on cue should surely be a handy ranger skill.

"No, I haven't, but we have to rescue Boy Hansgen first. He's on a deadline, and you are not, Valefor. He's going to be executed at midnight tonight, so we can't lollygag."

"But you care more about a stupid pirate than your own family?" Valefor sobbed.

"No, I don't. Don't be silly. But I have to prioritize—"

"Your own family!"

"Valefor, look at it this way. Boy Hansgen is a ranger. I know he'll be able to help us open the tea caddy. And he's an adept, too. He will know exactly how to restore

166

you." I was making this up as I went along, but as I did, I realized that it actually made pretty good sense. If anyone would know how to open a seal lock without the seal, surely it was Boy Hansgen.

Val's sobbing turned into hiccups. "I might remember him, actually. Boy Hansgen, you said?"

"Ayah."

"Was he in a band? I think they played for Buck's twenty-first birthday – I do remember: The Infernal Engines of Desire, that was their name. It was a fancy dress party – come as your fear. I made the most wonderful cake in the shape of Horrors to Come and Delights to Pass, and real chocolate spouted—"

I cut him off. "So, see, Valefor, it's all part of the plan."

"Well, it could work," he said thoughtfully. "But you haven't forgotten about me, Flora? You will not forget. You promised you wouldn't."

I said soothingly, "I will not; I promise. But I can only do so much. Val, Poppy trashed the kitchen last night."

"I know. I heard him. Even in the Bibliotheca, I heard him. Oh, the noise. Well, I'll soon put a stop to that – it's first on my list."

"Could you fix the kitchen? And make me some coffee? Please. I'll give you more Anima."

So we bent our heads together, and this time I noticed that I could actually see my Anima. It was wispy and thin, a washed crimson that was almost pink, but I could see it. Again came the delicious feeling of sparkly well-being, and again I felt a whole lot better about the world – as though I had drunk two entire pots of coffee.

Valefor himself looked better than he ever had before; his form looked more solid and muscular, and his eyes were like chips of amethyst. For the first time, I noticed a family resemblance: Mamma's wide-set eyes and Idden's rounded chin. Poppy's bladed cheekbones and the Fyrdraaca nose, sharp as a tack. He really was quite good-looking in a matinee idol sort of way.

"You know, Flora Segunda," Val said, considering, "I think that perhaps I should make sure you don't forget me – and so I think that Valefor shall turn off the tap until you make good on your oath."

"'Turn off the tap'? What does that mean?"

"I mean, no more Valefor fixing everything nice and tidy. I mean, you are on your own until you come through, Flora."

"But you said you'd clean up the kitchen if I gave you more Anima!" I said indignantly.

"Well, now you know how it feels to be promised something and to receive it not. Turnabout is fair play."

"Valefor, I said I would do it, but all in good time."

"*Flora's* good time, and what time will that be? Well, Madama Fyrdraaca, you do as you please, and when you are ready, I shall be ready, too."

"I can clean the kitchen myself, Valefor," I said warningly. "I don't need you."

He was unperturbed. "Perhaps, but I think you've

lost the taste for cleaning. And I think perhaps that you do need me. I am secure in myself. Say hello to Boy Hansgen for me."

He wiggled a little wave in my direction and dissolved into a froth of purple. Well, he could pout all he wanted; my plan did not hinge on him, anyway, though I had hoped to get him to help Udo and me with our disguises, and maybe whip us up a nice snack before we went to tackle the Warlord.

When it came down to it, I'd warrant he needed me more than I needed him. Although, he certainly was right that I had now *completely* lost my taste for chores.

18

SEWERS. CLOWNS.
CHEERY CHERRY SLURPS.
SAD SONGS.

Trickery and disguise are the ranger's favourite tools. Easier to make a clean getaway if your target doesn't even realize it's been rooked. Easier to be given freely than to take by force. And the trick to getting what you want, Nini Mo said, is to make sure you phrase your request correctly.

The Warlord's favourite bar is a joint called Pete's Clown Diner, which is located in the most ruinous part of the City: South of the Slot. South of the Slot is famous for its hard-cases and blind tigers (or, to quote the *Califa Police Gazette,* "undistinguished personages and establishments of questionable clientele"), and not an area to be caught in at night unless you are suicidal or well-armed. Happy for Udo and me, who are neither, the Warlord's devotion to Pete's knows no schedule, and he's as likely to be found there at one in the afternoon as at one in the morning.

Early afternoon South of the Slot isn't pretty, but isn't life-threatening, either, as most of the dollies, mashers, twirlers, saltmen and other lowlifes are still passed out in their beds or on the sidewalks. Or, rather, in the gutter, as South of the Slot has only a scattering of plank sidewalks.

We took the N horsecar, which traverses along the Slot that gives South of the Slot its name (there's a North of the Slot, too, but it's all banks – thieves of a more respectable kind, says the *CPG*) and got off at Placer Street. Pete's Clown Diner is two blocks down, at Placer and Hazel, and within half a block, both Udo and I were wishing that we had worn shorter kilts and higher boots. Or better yet, ridden.

"Don't the garbage men come down here?" Udo asked. On the sidewalk the trash was ankle-deep; we would have walked in the street but that was knee-deep in mud, a rather unsavoury looking mud that reminded me, both in looks and smell, of something I did not want to be reminded of.

"I guess not. Perhaps they are afraid to." I veered around the half-eaten chicken that lay forlorn on the sidewalk.

"Cowards. This is a disgrace." Udo hid his nose behind a white lace hankie. Since he was dressed as a drover, in leather pantaloons and overkilt and an orange-and-blue-plaid smock, it made him look rather conspicuously suspicious.

"Put the hankie away," I ordered.

"But the smell—"

"We are supposed to be in disguise. How many drovers do you think use white lace hankies?"

"Ones that don't like the smell – ayah, Flora, you win, as always." Udo replaced the hankie with a stogie; the look was more in keeping with his disguise, but the smell was only marginally better. Smoking is a horrible habit.

South of the Slot really *was* a disgrace; I agreed with Udo there. Farther down the street, a dead mule lay on its side, as green as a grape and so gassy that I'm surprised the corpse didn't float off into the sky. The sidewalk planking soon disappeared completely, and then the trash turned out to be a good thing because the only way to get through the mud without losing your boots was to hop from broken barrel to discarded box to abandoned fruit crate. When a wagon went by, its driver cursing a blue streak and snapping a whip over the struggling team, its wheels tossed up rotting garbage and sludge.

The buildings that lined the street were little more than shacks, hovels in near danger of collapsing. Rat-faced children peered through broken doors and empty windows, and occasionally a rat itself scampered by. Sometimes followed by a cat. Mostly not. Grubby men lurked in doorways, staring at us as we walked by, but no one stopped us. Perhaps Udo's smock had blinded them.

Pete's Clown Diner was made obvious by the clown dangling over its front door and the coach parked in front, with the Warlord's crest displayed in gold on its side. The dangly clown was, I realized thankfully, not a real clown, but just a dummy dressed so, and strung up. Still, it looked awfully lifelike hanging there, and the painted red smile looked more like a grimace. Garish red light flickered through the grimy window.

"Oh, Goddess bless us for what we do," Udo mumbled beside me.

"Remember the plan?" I whispered, fiddling with my veil. It was hard to see through, making everything dark and blurry and slightly spotted, but it was necessary for my mournful disguise. What grief-stricken sister, about to lose her favourite brother to cruel fate, would show her face in public?

"I remember," Udo said.

We clicked closed fists. "Ready."

Palm to palm. "Steady."

Knuckles to knuckles. "Go."

In Nini Mo's yellowbacks, the doors to a saloon always swing, but Pete's had no doors, just a row of beads that clicked as we pushed through them. In the yellowbacks, saloons are always loud and smoky, full of gallant gamblers and luscious bar-girls with hearts of gold. Pete's was dark, the air stale with smoke, and dim. No cow-band warbled on the stage, so the room was quiet, and I didn't see any gallant gamblers or luscious bar-girls, only a waitress with a face as seamed as an old shoe. Men and women sat at scattered tables, their heads drooping into their glasses.

To one side of the room stood a bar, slick and long. Behind the bar, a giant mirror tilted, reflecting the half-empty room, and the drover and the mourning woman standing in the doorway.

"My skin . . ." Udo groaned, coughing. I shushed him. Now was hardly the time to worry about his complexion. "Confidence is as confidence does," said Nini Mo, so I sailed forward to the bar and leaned on it, very cool-like.

The barkeep looked over his glasses at me. "What'll it be, madama?"

For a second my mind was completely blank. What do you order at a bar? A drink. What kind of drink? I couldn't think of any kind of drink, and then—

Udo said, "Beer."

The barkeep rolled backwards and clutched at his chest as though Udo had punched him. "Beer? *Beer?* Young man, you insult me. Beer! This ain't no broom closet, no blind tiger, no gin joint. Pete's Clown Diner is a class establishment, with classy patrons, with classy palates. We make our own ice-cream and our own whip. Not to mention toffee syrup. And me, Thomas Yin Terry, known throughout Califa as a mixologist extraordinary, who can make any confection you can dream of, and yet you ask for *beer*? I am shamed." He bent his head down, and a tiny silver tear dribbled down his cheek.

As he spoke, I read the menu written on the mirror

behind him, and that's when I realized that Pete's was an ice-cream joint. The silver urn standing behind the bar, studded with levers, dispensed soda water, not beer. I was relieved that I was not going to have to choke down beer and pretend that I liked it. Ice-cream is much better, and besides, I was hungry.

I said quickly, "I apologize for my brother, sieur. He's a drover, and they have no class—" Here Udo's foot stamped on mine, but I ignored the spike of pain. "I'll have a Cheery Cherry Slurp."

The barkeep brightened up. "Ah then, a Cheery Cherry Slurp. I've not had a call for that in many a day. A fine choice. And you, sieur drover?"

"A Broad Arrow Sling," Udo said.

"Another fine choice. Be seated, and Lotte shall bring."

We sat, at a table that was grubbier than Crackpot's kitchen floor. Only a look from me had kept Udo from dropping his hankie on the chair before sitting down, but it was hard to blame him. Despite my tummy's rumble, I was thinking that perhaps it would be a good idea to just *pretend* to eat the ice-cream.

The Warlord sat in the back of the room, at a round table with three others, playing cards. I recognized him immediately, because, of course, his picture hangs next to Mamma's in every classroom and public building in the City. The Warlord wasn't exactly as his portrait showed: his hair was whiter, and his jowls heavier, but still, there was no mistaking him.

175

Once the Warlord was a fearsome pirate, who stole himself from the slave mills of Anahuatl City and then stole himself a small empire. Now he's pretty old and tired. I suppose final decay is unavoidable, unless you plan otherwise, which I do exactly – going out with a bang, like Nini Mo, long before my life descends into a whimper of old age.

Udo hissed: "There's the Warlord; what says your plan?"

"It says we should wait until we get our sodas!"

"We should move in—" Udo shut up while Lotte the Shoe-Faced Woman plunked the sodas in front of us, sloshing soda water and whip, and took my money. Now that the Warlord was sitting right there, just a few feet away, engrossed in his poker game, my nerve was sticking. The ice-cream looked pretty clean, and I was starving; maybe I should eat it first and then—

"Do you want to buy some flowers?" Something tugged at my sleeve: a small child with a smudgy face.

"Git, sprout," said Udo rudely.

The child stuck her tongue out at him, and repeated to me: "Do you want to buy some flowers?"

"You haven't got any flowers," I said. The kid's dress had giant holes in it, and her little bare feet were blue with cold.

The child looked at me as though I were an idiot. "They are outside. If you come, I'll show you."

"I'm sorry, but I don't need any flowers. But here –" I fished in my purse and found a coin. The kid snatched the coin out of my hand and said, "Pinhead!" before flitting off.

Udo mumbled, "That was smart. Now every beggar kid South of the Slot is going to be pushing on us! Don't you know never to give out alms?"

"She didn't have any shoes."

"She probably did at home. I mean, who is going to give money to a beggar with shoes?"

"Maybe she really is poor, Udo."

A choked sob came from across the table. Udo was sniffling into his soda, tears running down his face, his mascara blurring. I was momentarily confused. A second ago he didn't care about the beggar, and now he was crying over her? Then I realized – blast Udo – he had started the plan without waiting for my signal.

"Ahhhh," Udo said, loudly, dramatically. "It's too much to bear, hermana. It's just too much to bear. Our poor Tenorio, so young, so young."

Under the table, I kicked Udo a good hard swift one in the knee, but he didn't let up. "Give us a song, Felicia, give us a song to remember Tenorio by. Here, I shall play the tune and you shall sing –"

We rose and went over to where a rickety pianoforte stood against the wall. When Udo flipped open the cover, dust puffed up, and when he put fingers to the keys the pianoforte wheezed just like a cat. The original plan had called for me to play and him to sing, but apparently Udo was in charge now, and my plan was nothing.

"Sing, hermana, sing for Tenorio." He banged out the first chords of "Who'll Tell His Mother". I had no choice but to sing, and so I opened my mouth and hoped that I remembered all the words:

> "*Somebody's darling so young and so brave*
> *Wearing still on his sweet yet pale face*
> *Soon to be hid in the dust of the grave*
> *The lingering light of his boyhood's grace*
> *Somebody's darling, somebody's pride*
> *Who'll tell his mother how her boy died.*"

I'm not the best singer, but in this case, my wobbly notes were working for me, sounding like my voice was cracking with tears. The Warlord is notoriously susceptible to sob stories and sad songs – a susceptibility that our plan hinged upon.

The crowd, not fully appreciative, began to hoot and jeer, but Udo stubbornly played on, and I kept singing, even when someone threw a glass at my head. I ducked in time, and the glass slammed into the wall behind me, as explosive as a bomb.

19

A MÊLÉE. THE WARLORD.
AN AUTOGRAPH.

The glass-throwing got the barkeep to shouting, which made Udo play louder. I reached for a high note and didn't make it, my voice breaking into a jarring yowl. Another glass was thrown, which this time hit a mark: the Shoe-Faced Woman, who went down like a buffalo. The shouting increased, and things other than glasses started to soar: a boot, a pineapple, a spittoon. Udo ducked down and I ducked behind him, but we kept on with our recital. Ice-cream hit the wall above and showered down on top of us: goodbye, Cheery Cherry Slurp.

"Hey now, hey now!" This roar bellowed over the hooting, the piano, my wailing. The hooting stopped, Udo quit banging, and I let my wail trail away. We had finally got the Warlord's attention, though not in the way we had planned.

The Warlord rose up from the poker table. "That's enough of that – that's enough, there! I'll be taking apart the next man to throw something, with my own hands, for interrupting the lady's pretty song like that. Let the lady sing." The Warlord might be old, but his voice was booming, and there was an expectation in it that his orders would be obeyed.

They were. Some of the crowd grumbled, but they sat back down. The barkeep and another man picked the Shoe-Faced Woman up and carried her away. A potboy came in with a broom and began to sweep glass.

"Go back to singing, madama," the Warlord said. "I like your song fine."

"I cannot, Your Grace," I sobbed, snuffling into the bottom of my veil. "I can no longer sing, oh, Your Grace, pardon me." I started to make the courtesy that signifies Abasement before a Superior So Superior That No Abasement Is Abased Enough, but since it requires going down on both hands and knees and the floor was so very dirty, I pretended to stumble on my way down.

The Warlord caught me. "Now there, now there. Rezaca, get the lady a chair and a drink of water. Come to me, my darling, and tell me what is wrong."

I sobbed and moaned and sat where bidden. At first it was hard not to laugh, but then the more I pretended to cry, the more I found I was actually crying, and pretty hard, too, as though something had twisted a tap inside me that I didn't even know was closed. Now that I was going, I could hardly stop, harsh gasping sobs that made my internal organs ache.

"Now, now, poor lady, why do you cry so?" The Warlord patted my knee with a very large hand.

"Our brother, Your Grace, our poor brother, he has so little time left in this world," said Udo brokenly. "And we weep for him, Your Grace. He is the favourite of our mamma, and how shall we tell her?"

Someone shoved a glass into my hand, and I lifted the veil just enough to gulp down the stale water, turning my sobs into hiccups. I swallowed another big gulp of water, swallowing the hiccups, too. "Oh, Your Grace, can you not help us? You are so kind and generous."

"Now then, tell me exactly, my darling, what you mean, and perhaps I can. Come, come here, take my hankie—" Out of the Warlord's green brocade vest came an enormous lace-trimmed red hankie, already well used. I took it, glad that the veil covered my grimace, and dabbed.

The poker buddy who had gotten me the chair said, "Your Grace, the game—"

"Shut up there, Rezaca. Go on, then, darling."

I said brokenly, "Your Grace, it is this: our poor brother Tenorio enlisted in the Army, as our poor mother's sole support, her favourite child, too, and she with the goitres and the lumbago and the gout from a

181

whole lifetime of washing clothes to feed us poor little children."

"An admirable son," said the Warlord. He motioned for my glass to be refilled. "Go on, dear madama."

"And so poor Tenorio fell in with a bad crowd, who enticed him to drink and gamble, and soon he had gambled away all his earnings and more besides and was deeply in debt. And then, when desperate to send his poor mamma the money she needed for her lumbago medicine, he borrowed from the company funds –" I paused to sniffle and let the drama sink in. "And then he was caught and sentenced to be hung, oh, Your Grace!"

Here I let loose with a wail and another round of wracking sobs, waiting, hoping, praying that our plan was working.

"Your Grace, the game!" said the poker buddy urgently.

The Warlord raised his hand without looking away from me. He said, his voice catching slightly, "Tell me how I can help you, little lady. I cannot bear to see such a sweet face so sad."

All the blood that I had not realized had left my head rushed back into it. "Oh, Your Grace," I said, and this time the wobble in my voice was from relief, "I know it was wrong, and so does Tenorio, but does he deserve to die for it? Our poor mother."

"Your Grace, I really think—" said the same annoying poker buddy, but the Warlord waved another *shut up*, then patted my knee again, although this time his pat was a bit more like a rub. I smiled sadly at him.

"If we were all to die for our mistakes, Your Grace, who then would still live? And how should we then learn?" Udo said earnestly.

The Warlord said, "Have you spoken to General Fyrdraaca about this?"

"She would not see me, Your Grace. She is strict with the law. But is there no room in the law for mercy? The Warlord's rule has always been just and kind."

"Ayah, so it has been. And so it should be – Rezaca, if you say another word, I shall fry you." Again with the rubbing hands. Then, before I could protest, the Warlord hoisted me up and perched me upon his massive knee. He might be old, but he was still pretty strong, even for a man with only one leg. "I shall speak to General Fyrdraaca on your behalf, my little parrot. How shall that be?"

"But Your Grace." I let the tears well in my eyes. "The execution is tonight, and by then it shall be too late."

Udo interjected. "And General Fyrdraaca has gone to Moro. By the time she gets back, our brother shall be gone, and our mother shall die of shame."

The Warlord encircled one squeezy arm around me, and this I did not like at all, but there wasn't much to do but try to look sweet. I could smell his breakfast on his breath: pickled herring. I sobbed, bending my head and jabbing my elbow into the Warlord's chest. He eased up on his grip.

"Your Grace, can you not show mercy? Can you not save poor Tenorio?" Udo snivelled.

"I can and I will!" the Warlord declared. "Get me paper, Rezaca. I cannot let this little lady be sorrowed, and for such a trivial thing. Have we not all had our bad gambling debts, a horror to pay?"

The annoying poker buddy protested. "Your Grace, it's hardly within our purview to interfere with the law—"

"Whose law is it? Mine! And I shall do as I see fit!" the Warlord roared. "Get me that paper!"

Rezaca was not moved. "Your Grace, General Fyrdraaca—"

The Warlord rose up, dumping me off his lap. Compared to this, his earlier roar had been but a whisper. "Am I not Warlord of this Republic? Is not my rule law? If you do not want yourself to be drummed down to the Playa with the Rogue's March, then you should be doing as I say!" Even though his ire was not directed at me, my stomach quivered. In his prime, the Warlord must have been a force. In anger, he was a force still. Now I saw a glimmer of how his earlier reputation had been founded.

"I have a piece of paper, Your Grace," said Udo helpfully. "And a pen and ink, too."

The paper was an ordinary sheet of paper, and so, too, the pen, but not the ink in the inkwell. It was an erasable ink, the idea being that when we got home, we could remove everything but the Warlord's signature and write in our own pardon. It was a clever trick that Nini Mo used in *Nini Mo vs. the Ring-tailed Alphabet Boy*, and she had helpfully included the receipt in *The Eschata*. It rather surprisingly was made using very common household ingredients that Crackpot had actually had on hand.

The Warlord sat back down, and I made sure I was out of his grabby range. He lay the paper down before him, sweeping the cards and piles of money out of the way. Udo uncapped the inkwell and handed him the pen. "Now, my spectacles, where are they?"

"Around your neck, Your Grace? On a chain?" Udo pointed out.

"Ah yes, my boy, you are a good one. Here then, give me a moment now." The Warlord put his spectacles on and rubbed his nose. He pushed the spectacles on to his forehead and rubbed his nose again. Dropped his spectacles down again and dipped the pen. Wiped it on his sleeve, and dipped it again. Sighed and tapped his gold front tooth with one fingernail, and then, just as I was about to scream with impatience, began to write.

He wrote several lines and signed his name with a flourish, and then, after dipping again, drew his seal from his weskit pocket. Udo continued his helpful theme by producing a stick of sealing wax and a trigger. Within a second, a nice round blob of wax had fallen on the paper and was pressed into the Warlord's personal seal: a hammer.

"There you have it, my dear. Mercy has a human

heart, does it not? And let no one say that Florian Abenfarax de la Carcaza is not merciful. Blow."

I blew on the paper as directed, and then he rolled it up and handed it to me. "There shall be no more crying, eh?"

"Oh no, Your Grace, you are so kind, how can I ever repay you?"

The Warlord grinned and pinched my cheek. "Oh, we can discuss that later, my dear. Perhaps over an oyster supper?"

"Your Grace, we must hurry this to the Presidio," said Udo. "But after that, my sister would be most honoured to share an oyster supper with you."

I would have kicked him, but he was too far away. I could only smile and say through gritted teeth, "Of course, Your Grace. I would be honoured."

"I shall call for you. Where do you live, my dear?"

"Oh, I would be ashamed to have Your Grace call on me; it would hardly be proper. I shall come to Saeta House."

"No, no, my dear," the Warlord said quickly. "Meet me at the Empire Hotel on State Street, 10 p.m."

"Your Grace," I fluttered, and Udo fluttered, too, and then we fluttered our way out of there as quickly as possible.

We made it outside and were getting ready to make the return slog home, jubilant and crowned with victory, when a voice said, "You there!"

Our continued skedaddle was blocked by an

186

enormous barge of a man wearing the Warlord's livery; our about-face was blocked by Rezaca, whom I suddenly recalled as the Warlord's Chief of Staff.

Were we caught? My tum sank into the toes of my boots and there quivered.

"You will hold up and listen to me well," Conde Rezaca said sternly. "You have received the Warlord's graciousness this time, but don't let this be a precedent. If you are wise, little woman, you shall not keep that appointment with the Warlord. In fact, I don't ever want to see you or your brother ever again, do you understand?"

My nerves twanged with relief. I had been afraid the Conde would demand the paper back, but this order was easy to agree to: of course I had no intention of keeping the appointment. Udo nodded vigorously, and I said: "Yes, sieur, of course, thank you."

"Now get out of here before I decide to ensure your permanent absence from my sight. But wait –"

Our exit remained blocked by the Hulking Minion. Conde Rezaca stared at Udo, his lips pursed in consideration.

"Have I not seen you somewhere?" he said. "You do look familiar."

"I don't think so," Udo said falteringly.

"I am sure, sieur, that we are too low for your acquaintance," I said hastily. "Come, brother, and let us bother the august lord no more." I grabbed Udo's arm to hustle, but the Hulking Minion did not give way. As far as I knew, Conde Rezaca and Udo had never met before, but Udo does bear a striking resemblance to his two fathers, and Conde Rezaca probably knew them.

I pleaded, eager to get gone before Conde Rezaca's memory improved. "Please, sieur, let us pass and we shall trouble you no more."

Conde Rezaca nodded and the Hulking Minion stood aside. We put some speed into our skedaddle and were about half a block away, with the Slot well in sight, when another voice arrested us: "Hey!"

I turned and beheld the small beggar girl. Only this time she wasn't begging: she had a pistol and it was pointed straight at me.

20

JACKED. MUD. TUSSLING.

"What do you want, sprout?" Udo demanded. "Put that toy away."

The Stealie Girl said stoutly, "It's not a toy, pinhead, and I want your purses."

"You are too little to be a criminal," Udo retorted. I elbowed him in the ribs, hard. If there is one thing I don't need Nini Mo to teach me, it's that you shouldn't be uppity to people with guns. Even if those people look about ten.

"Come on, Flora, let's go." Udo made a move to continue on, but I grabbed his sleeve. The Stealie Girl meant business; I could see it in her narrow eyes.

Though we were standing in full view, with wagons jolting along in the street and people passing along the boardwalk, no one seemed the slightest bit concerned by our situation. Probably two greenhorns getting jacked was a common sight South of the Slot.

The Stealie Girl demanded, "Gimme your purses."

"I'm not giving you a thin—"

I cut Udo off. "I have five divas; you can have that."

"Slowly," she ordered.

I reached slowly into my purse and removed the last of my savings. The girl took the bills, her pistol unwavering. Well, she could have our money; cash was the absolute least of my worries. We had to get home and shift into the next part of the plan; already the sun was slanting low in the sky, signalling the end of afternoon, and I wanted to be on the Sandy Road to Zoo Battery before dark.

Also, I had just discovered that having a pistol pointed directly at you is very nerve-wracking. The mouth of the barrel seemed at least six feet wide, and at any minute it could spit a big huge nasty death right at me. My muscles were already clenching involuntarily, anticipating the pain.

I said, trying to sound soothing, "You can put the gun away, madama. We shall not argue with you."

"So you won't. Come on, Sieur Lug, give me your purse."

"I haven't got a purse," Udo said, which was true enough; he is so stingy that he keeps his money (when he's got it) tucked into one of his stockings. This makes it difficult for him to retrieve it, which makes it easier to get other people to pay.

"Well, then, I saw you all with the Warlord and I heard your drivel; it was sharp, to play on him that way, and I saw him give you that paper," the girl said. "Now you can give it to me."

"It's not worth a thing," I said, trying to keep the soothing smooth in my voice. "It's just a piece of paper. Here, you can have my veil. And Udo will give you his hat. They are worth something to a jobber. More than five divas, and more than a piece of paper."

"The Abyss I will," Udo retorted. "Listen, squirt, I'm one second away from blasting you. So turn around, march on, and leave us be. You got all our money, and that's all you need get."

"I want that paper," the girl said, stubbornly, "I saw the Warlord sign it, and his signature is worth a lot. I can get a fair amount for that. You can keep your ugly hat, but I want that paper."

"And I want a buffalo coat and a blue-tipped pointer — you've got all you are getting." Udo turned away, and the Stealie Girl cocked the pistol. The sound of the hammer snapping into place was awfully loud.

She said, "I will shoot you, and take the paper myself."

Udo froze, and then slowly reached inside his smock and pulled out the pardon. The Stealie Girl snatched the paper out of his grasp with one grubby hand.

My chest had gone tight with panic, but I tried to swallow the feeling away. *Be thoughtful, be quick, and overall be reasonable,* said Nini Mo. The Stealie Girl might have the gun, but I had my wits and could still be persuasive.

"Listen, madama," I said. "The paper is nothing; my friend here has ninety-three divas in cash at home. If you will accompany us there, it shall be—"

"You think me a ring-tailed baby, just been dipped in milk? I don't think so. What need do I have of ninety-three divas when I got this?"

Something elbowed me, almost pushing me off the sidewalk and into the Abyss of Trash that was the street: a masher on his way into the Azure Lagoon, the bar we were halted before.

"Heya, Ringie," the man said as he went inside.

"Heya, Cake," the Stealie Girl answered, and in her momentary distraction, Udo decided to act. He leaped. The Stealie Girl was small but she was sharp, and Udo was hampered by the tightness of his smock. They struggled, and the Stealie Girl dropped her pistol, which I managed to kick into the street.

Now all those people who had ignored us being jacked were interested in watching us fight, and a crowd quickly gathered, urging our melee on. Udo was shouting, and it looked like the Stealie Girl was biting. I tried to grab one of them, either of them, but only got an elbow in the chest for my troubles. All was confusion, with Udo and the Stealie Girl kicking and slapping at each other, screaming nasty, nasty things; the crowd hooting and hollering; and the paper – who had the paper? Where was the paper?

There – something white fluttered towards the ground. The Stealie Girl had dropped it. I grabbed and almost got kicked in the face; the Stealie Girl reached for it and was pushed aside by Udo. The paper flittered on the air and I lunged again, just as Udo did, our heads knocking together in a bright splurch of pain. Dizzily, I stretched and almost had it, but then a gust of wind snatched it out of my hand; the paper whizzed upwards, and a man in a blue-and-green ditto suit made his own grab but missed.

Udo pushed me aside, frantically grabbing, and he almost had it. But then the Stealie Girl rose out of nowhere and pushed him hard. He overbalanced and fell over me – the paper fluttered beyond our grasp, off the boardwalk, and out to the messy, mucky ick of the street, where it was promptly run over by a buckboard full of cabbages.

21

RECRIMINATIONS. REGROUPING.
HOT KNIVES. POPPY.

All the way home on the horsecar, I blamed Udo and Udo blamed me, and no amount of blame changed the situation or made us feel any better, but it didn't make us feel any worse, either. To be so close, and yet to have defeat snatched from the jaws of victory was bitter, bitter indeed.

As soon as the buckboard had rumbled on its way, Udo and I had rushed out into the mucky street. All our frantic mucky excavations turned up were muddy scraps, and then *we* were almost run over by an ice wagon and had to confess defeat. The Stealie Girl had not waited around to see the result of our search, but had legged it immediately, with my five divas, of course, and Udo's hat, which had come off in the melee.

Though I don't normally believe in whacking people,

I felt like making an exception for Udo and beating him with a stick. If only he hadn't bucked – I was sure that I could have talked our way out of the situation. Or let the girl have the paper and then jacked her back a few minutes later. Or something. But no, Udo had to jump in and act like an ass, and now we were completely and utterly screwed.

Udo said self-righteously, "I told you – if you hadn't given her that money, she wouldn't have thought we were easy marks."

"She thought we were easy marks, Udo, because we *were* easy marks. And you didn't have to be so fresh to her."

"She was just a kid—"

"Shush," I hissed. An old grammy was sitting directly in front of us, and there was an alert aura to her bonnet (garishly ornamented with a large orange velvet spider) that made me sure she was listening to every word.

"If you hadn't knocked into my arm, I could have grabbed it," Udo hissed back. "I had to do something – she was going to get away and you didn't seem poised to do any great deed."

This was so absurd that it wasn't even worth replying to, so I clamped my lips together, hard enough to hurt, and stared out the window. I was so angry, anyway, that if I spoke another word, that word would have burned my friendship with Udo to a crisp.

Not that I, for the moment, cared.

Rangers do not always meet with success, but they

195

don't let failure stymie them. They regroup. Of course, rangers didn't let themselves be jacked like stupid idiotic greenhorns. *Don't dwell,* said Nini Mo.

A ranger always thinks again and regroups.

I thought and thought, but my thinking was not regrouping. My thinking was running around and around the idea that Nini Mo would have done some extremely clever daring deed and saved the day. Turned the Stealie Girl into a pretzel, or kicked her in the nose. Bedazzled her with another paper or charmed her with flattery. It's only after it's all over that you start thinking of all the clever ranger things you could have done. Only when it's too blasted late.

"I say that you yield to my plan now," Udo said. The grammy had got off at Tradis Street, and we were alone in the back of the horsecar. "We just saw how effective a demand backed by iron can be. Let us learn by that."

"Yield to your plan, Udo?" I said incredulously. "You must be mad! After what just happened, I wouldn't yield to your plan if it were the only plan left in the entire history of plans. In fact, I am thinking that maybe I should cut you loose completely. You are a liability."

"What were you going to do?" Udo protested. "You were standing there like a slug waiting to be salted. I didn't see you—"

"Shut up," I said savagely. "Shut up."

Udo retreated into wounded silence and stared out his own window. Well, let him sulk. I would think of something. I *had* to think of something. The horsecar trundled by Saeta House, and by the Arrow Clock tower, and I saw that it was almost three. What were we going to do?

"What about Valefor? Can he cough up a forgery?" Udo asked, without removing his stare from the window.

"I don't think so. His talents lie in housework and whining, and anyway, he's on strike because I put him on the back burner while we took care of you-know-who," I answered, without removing my stare from my own window.

The horsecar was now passing the Califa Lyceum, and I noticed that the marquee was advertising Relais Evengardia (he who Idden once adored) in *He Should Have Stopped While He Was Ahead*, his latest play. A line had formed in front of the box office. Relais Evengardia is the most popular actor in all of Califa, renowned for his portrayal of General Hardhands—

And then – huzza! Oh cleverness! Oh blissful day! A fully fledged idea leaped into my head, as though it had always been there and was just waiting for me to pay attention to it.

I turned back to Udo, who was still sulkily fixed on his window. "Hey! Remember when you competed in the Warlord's Annual Histrionic Extravaganza—"

Udo abandoned his sulk. "Ayah! I won Best Actor for my portrayal of General Hardhands in *A Cold Day in the Abyss*. I was really good; sometimes I think I should go on the stage instead of to sea."

"Remember, you got that citation from the Warlord? Signed and sealed?"

"Ayah, so what?"

"*Forgery* is so what. Listen." I dropped my voice to a whisper, and Udo bent in closely. "I can copy the Warlord's signature, I'm sure. Particularly if I have a guide to go by. But it's the seal that's a problem – we can't forge that."

"Ayah so?" Udo whispered back.

"Remember how in *Nini Mo vs. the Mechanical Monkeys*, she forged the pass that got her into the Iron Mine of Arivaipa?"

"You know I don't read that trash, Flora."

"Ha! No trashier than *The Dainty Pirate Ahoy!*, I reckon, and a lot more useful right now, Udo. Look, she lifted the seal off the letter of invitation that Njal Sholto had sent to entrap her, and then put it on the forgery. It worked like a charm."

"Can you lift the seal off my citation?" Udo asked excitedly.

"I'll wager I can. Look, you go home and get the citation and meet me back at Crackpot. Go in the window, or something. Don't get caught, ayah so? And hurry about it. I think maybe we can salvage this yet."

Udo nodded vigorously. "I knew we'd think of something, Flora."

As far as I could tell, I had done all the thinking; no *we* involved at all. But now was not the time to get

Udo's dudgeon back up again, not with the afternoon running out and night fast approaching.

"Here's your stop – go –" I yanked on the bell, and the horsecar jangled to a stop, and Udo jumped off.

Two hours later, after a brief stop for a snack (I was light-headedly starving), I was at my desk, the citation before me, heating the knife Udo had just finished sharpening. The art to lifting a seal lies in the heat of the knife and the patience of the forger. You have to get the seal warm enough to slide off the paper, but not so warm it melts away completely. Sealing wax is more pliable and elastic than candle wax, of course, and has a higher melting point, but you can go too far. I've practised enough (Forgery 101) that if there is one thing I can do flawlessly, it's lift a seal.

But copying the Warlord's signature proved much less sweetie-pie. His letters are both quavery and legible, and these two qualities are very difficult to combine. All my efforts resulted in twiddles and squiggles, but nothing that would pass muster even in the dark. Udo tried, too, but he had no luck, either, no surprise.

"Let me have it back, and I'll try again," I demanded.

"I've almost got it, Flora. Quit leaning on me."

"We are running out of time—"

"That's because you are ragging on me," Udo said.

"Don't be a git—"

"What are you doing?" said someone else.

We lurched guiltily. There in the doorway stood

199

Poppy. He wore a tattered dressing gown, and the short spikes of his hair poked every which way. The mourning band painted across his eyes was blurred, as though he'd been rubbing at it. He had a terrific black bruise on his right temple, as dark as a thundercloud.

"Do you need something, Poppy?" I asked.

He came into the room and sat down on the settee to waste our valuable time. "Only my life. But I don't think I left that here. What are you doing?"

"Nothing. I mean, just working on a paper," I said. "Homework, you know. Are you hungry, Poppy? There's soup. I can make you soup."

"Soup makes my teeth hurt, Flora. Anyway, I eat the air." He sat there, as comfortable as bedtime, and he didn't look like he was going to move any time soon. Blast it! We didn't have time to waste dealing with Poppy, and he's so deceptive. He looked fine, albeit rumpled, but that didn't signify. Any moment he could break out in all sorts of horrificness; maybe last night was just a lead-up. The fireplace poker was out of reach. What would I do if he exploded?

But he didn't look as though he would explode. He scratched his chin, and said, "Forgery, eh? Didn't they used to boil people in oil for that once?"

"It's not forgery," Udo said. "It's an art project. I mean, it's a paper on—"

Poppy yawned and took a silver case out of his dressing-gown pocket. "I am no shavetail, Udo. I know forgery when I see it. What are you making? Letter of recommendation? Fixing a bobtail? Commandeering a battery? Trumping a jump?"

A bobtail is when the bottom of a soldier's release paper is clipped, removing the section where the recommendation should go. I didn't know what trumping a jump is, and right now I didn't care, either.

"A release, Hotspur, that's all; just a release," Udo said. "Here, let me light that."

Ignoring my dirty look, Udo lit a trigger from the fire and held the flame to Poppy's cigarillo. Udo is too casual around Poppy; having been spared the worst of Poppy's scenes and having normal parents of his own, Udo doesn't understand how bad Poppy can be.

"Someone in the calaboose?" Poppy asked.

I glared at Udo, trying to impart this glare with all the vigour of *Do not tell him a single more thing at all, shut up* that I could, but I could tell by the curve of his smile that he was not listening.

"Ayah so. Poor bugger," Udo said.

"He has my sympathy. Life is a prison if you cannot leave it as you like. It don't look like you are having much success. You got a mess of papers there."

"Well, it takes practice," Udo admitted.

The smoke wreathed Poppy's head like fog, and through it I could see only the thin line of his lips. "I used to be a dab hand. A handy talent for an ADC to have, you know, forgery. Sign the papers yourself and save your boss the trouble. And if you're skint, you can pay your bar tab off with your fakery. Here, let me see if I still got the knack."

An idea was forming in my mind that perhaps, for the first time ever, it might pay off to have a mad, irresponsible father. If Poppy were as good at forgery as he said, then one of our problems was solved, and if he mentioned it to Mamma later, well, who ever believes anything Poppy says?

Udo moved from the desk and gave Poppy fresh paper and a pen. He examined the pen, announced the nib had lost its sharpness, and demanded another. He sat straight as a ramrod and squinted down at the empty sheet of whiteness. He dipped his pen and drew a thin line on his forearm to test the flow, and thus I realized that he was left-handed, just like me. Mamma and Idden are right-handed both, and now I saw where I had got the trait.

Poppy dipped the pen again, and then sloped it across the paper, smooth and even.

"'Juliet Buchanan Fyrdraaca ov Fyrdraaca.'" Udo read. "That's pretty good, Hotspur. It looks exactly right."

"Oh, Buck is easy. Now here's a huckleberry. Watch this."

Poppy wiped the pen off on his sleeve and dipped again. This time his pen skittered and hopped, swirled and twirled, slithered and jumped, and finally skittered into a long black slide. The result was elaborate and complex, twisty letters that arched up and plunged down, entwining each other like snakes. Even though I couldn't read the name, I could tell that whoever

202

belonged to this signature was as big as boots, and firm in his or her authority.

"I wasn't sure I still had that one in me," Poppy said proudly. He blotted, then blew gently. "It's worth your life."

Udo said, "I can't even read it."

"'Banastre Micajah Haðraaða ov Brakespeare,'" Poppy said. "Old Hardhands himself. Ah, he'd have eaten my liver if he'd known I could copy him."

"Wow. What a signature." Udo was impressed, clearly thinking he needed to start working on a better signature of his own.

"He was a proper bastard, old Hardhands, but his warrant had class."

Now that Poppy's skill was established, there was only one signature I wanted, and I could wait no longer to get it. We had to be on the road within an hour if we wanted to make our interception.

"Can you do the Warlord?" I asked.

"I'm not sure. It's been a long time since I have seen it."

I pushed Udo's citation to Poppy, and he held it up, examining it carefully. "He has the handwriting of a five-year-old, our Warlord. It shall be easy as pie. Here, let me show you a trick."

He spun the citation around until it was upside-down. "It's easier to copy if you don't let the word get in the way. Think of it like a pattern you are drawing, like when your hair colours the sea."

I had no idea what he meant by that last comment.

203

"Can you do it, Poppy?"

Poppy closed his eyes and ran his finger over the spindly letters. He made a few wiggly lines with the dry pen, incising an imprint upon the paper. After dipping the pen, he turned the edge of the nib so that the lines were thick going up and thin going down. He made a few little twirls, then drew a little pig with floppy ears and dancing slippers. He pushed his scribble paper away, lay a new sheet down, and dipped his pen freshly.

Then, swiftly, he began to write. The ink slid across the paper, as smooth as skates on ice, without hesitation, without pause. He raised his pen, pressed blotting paper down, and grinned. "There! I am charmed!"

I flipped the citation around, and we stared at the two signatures, side by side. They were perfectly alike, right down to the monogram that came after the name: *Florian Abenfarax de la Carcarza, ADLC.*

"You are a genius, Hotspur," Udo said.

Poppy grinned, and this grin rounded his bladelike cheeks and crinkled his eyes. For a moment he looked almost handsome. Then the smile drifted from his face, and he was the same sad Poppy again.

He dropped the pen and said, "But you know, I think I have forgotten how to sign my own name."

22

STRANGE FACES.
A BLUE LIGHT. TEETH.

Nini Mo's yellowbacks always play up the excitement
and adventure – they never mention the anxiety and
alarm that comes before the excitement and adventure.
The hour you spend riding towards your target, while
your neck gets colder and your bottom goes numb. The
knot of nervousness in your tum, which only gets
knottier and more nervous as the place where you can
still turn back gets farther and farther behind.

We left Crackpot just at dusk, slightly behind
schedule but not by much. Broad-brimmed hats hid
our faces, and underneath our concealing cloaks, we
both wore stolen uniforms. Udo's was kipped from one
of his fathers, and it fit him perfectly. Mine was
borrowed from Idden's closet; it was the fatigue
uniform she'd worn the summer she'd spent as
Mamma's ADC, her third year at the Barracks. It was

tight across the shoulders and long in the kilt, but otherwise would do.

Zoo Battery guards the southern end of the Pacifica Playa, far out at the end of Sandy Road in what are called the Outside Lands because they lie beyond the City's limits. No horsecar went out that far at night, and even if it had, we certainly couldn't take it without compromising our disguises. So we rode, me on Bonzo, and Udo on Mouse.

It's a longish ride, through Portal Pass, which marks the City's official limits, and across the Great Sand Bank, which stands between the Pass and the ocean's edge, and so I had plenty of time to think anxious thoughts. Nini Mo says that the time for thinking is before you make the decision, and once you've decided, it's time to act. That's easier said than done. Particularly when not everything has gone according to plan.

I looked at Udo, or, rather, at his back, since he was riding ahead of me. Mouse is a tail-biter, and it's always better to keep her teeth out of temptation's way. From the back, he looked like pretty much the same Udo. But when he turned to say something to me, he had the face of a stranger.

After Udo's close call with recognition at Pete's Clown Diner, we had agreed that stronger disguises were required, and for that we needed Glamours. This turned out to be easier decided than actually done. A Glamour should be easy baby ranger stuff, not too hard, and not too complicated. And the first Glamour, though tongue-burning and headache-making, had turned out just dandy.

Udo's own parents would not recognize him. I *knew* he was Udo and yet could hardly believe it. Now he looked ruggedly efficient; his chest was broad, his shoulders even broader, and his chin as squarely carved as a bar of soap. His face, perched above a bull neck, was leathery and wise, and his black eyes had a humorous squint to them. The biggest shock was the hair. Udo's fondness for his own blond locks has kept them long and flowing, but now his hair was so short that the scalp beneath was as tanned as his face.

In fact, Udo looked a little too much like Sergeant Shanksworthy, the hero of the long-running yellowback series Sergeant Shanksworthy of the Steelheart Brigade. Though I wasn't a particular fan of Sergeant Shanksworthy, I guess the back of my brain had somehow decided that he was the perfect specimen of military manliness, and thus the Masking Glamour had so resolved.

"What are you goggling about?" asked Udo in a rumbling baritone that was as unlike his own boyish treble as the lion's roar is to the cat's meow.

"It's hard to get used to."

He pulled Mouse back so we were abreast, and the horses twisted their heads to snuffle at each other. "I know. It *feels* strange, too, as though my skin is too small. How do I look with a moustache?" He tugged one of the waxed spikes that stuck out at least two inches on either side of that stranger's mouth.

"I don't know what *you* look like with a moustache, but that face looks fine. Would that I looked so wonderfully different," I said, somewhat bitterly.

I was disguised not by a Masking Glamour, but by ten pounds of make-up that Udo had applied to my face with a trowel. This because the second Masking Glamour had failed utterly.

Magick is hard, I know that, and it takes long hours of practice to get things right. I thought I had been sticking to the easy stuff, the fail-safe stuff, but maybe I had just been lucky before. But what a time to fail! The Glamour had flickered briefly and then guttered, and all the Invoking, Evoking, and just plain Hysterical Entreaties to the Current had not got it to rekindle. I had tried other Glamours as well – a Concealment Glamour, a Dazzlement Glamour – but they only resulted in a pounding headache and the upchucking of my snack. Now, in addition to anxious, I felt rather dizzy and weak. I'd never realized magick involved so much urping.

"I swear I wouldn't recognize you in a hundred years, Flora. I swear that even Buck would not recognize you. You'll be fine," Udo said soothingly. "You'll be fine."

"I hope you're right, Udo. Get that horse over, she's squashing my leg. Do you remember the plan? You won't jump the gun like you did last time, will you?"

Udo edged Mouse sideways.

"I remember the plan perfectly, no fear, Flora. Don't worry. But remember, I will do all the talking. It will look odd if you keep piping up, when I outrank you."

The plan, of course, had been that I would lead and Udo would follow. But now he had the mature, authoritative face, and I, though disguised, did not look old enough to be an officer, even a shavetail lieutenant. There was no way around Udo's having to take the lead, and my insides quivered at the thought.

"I'll be quiet as long as you don't say anything foolish, Udo. Do not deviate from the plan even a tiny little bit, I'm warning you."

"Never fear – oh, and it's Captain Gaisford to you, Corporal. I think we should get into character now. That's the secret to great acting – you get inside the skin of your part and never leave."

"Udo—"

"Captain Gaisford, Corporal, and don't forget it, or I shall write you up for insubordination. Ride on, we are burning daylight." He spurred Mouse into a trot. Sometimes the only way to win with Udo is to ignore him, so I merely urged Bonzo on and fell in after Mouse.

After a while, the smell of wood smoke began to seep through the fog, and then the shadow of a squat building suddenly reared from the gloom: the Bella Union Saloon, as notorious a deadfall bar as you would never want to see. The Bella Union sits right across the

Califa city line, where the Sandy Road turns southwards towards Zoo Battery, near the Presidio's back gate, and this central location has made it a favourite hangout joint for drunken off-duty soldiers. Mamma has declared it out of bounds to the military and twice sent patrols to burn it down. Twice it has sprung up anew, a blot upon the landscape that not even fire will erase. The *Califa Police Gazette* is always reporting dire doings at the Bella Union: ear-chewing, bar fights, tar-and-feathering.

A high-riding covered wagon stood in front of the Bella, THE HORSES OF INSTRUCTION inscribed upon the canvas in luminescent paint. Grunts carried musical equipment inside as a tall man stood by, watching and smoking, a hurdy-gurdy slung over his back. The Hurdy-Gurdy Man was clearly going for a deathly, gothick look: greenish black hair straggling out from under a mouldering tricorn, sagging pink trunk hose. As I rode by, he looked up, his livid face wreathed in cigarette smoke, and flashed gold teeth at me, touching a salute to the front point of his hat.

The Bella Union behind us, darkness followed the fog's slow advance. My feet felt like blocks of ice, and my hands hardly gripped the reins. I wasn't sure if this feebleness was from the weather or all the Invoking I had done. Either way, I felt weak and tired.

Somewhere high above the fog, the moon must have risen, because the air was strangely light. I pulled up the collar of my sack coat; the wool rubbed the back of my neck, but moisture was dripping from my hat brim and I'd rather be raw than wet. Everything is always so much colder with a damp neck.

"Hey, Corporal –" Udo's blur made a vague gesture, and I turned around to follow his point. Just fog, thick and wet, but then, suddenly, there was a bright blue pulse of light, like a tiny fragment of sky cracking through the grey.

We reined in and watched as the light pulsed again. The horses shimmied, as though they could hear something we could not, and then distantly, we did hear something, a low rumbling that was as much vibration as noise. The horses shimmied again, squeezing together, and I kicked my foot out so Mouse wouldn't crush my leg.

"Cannon fire?" I guessed.

"Your ignorance astounds, Corporal Ashbury, but then what can you expect from a mere bouncer?" Udo answered. *Bouncer* is the Army nickname for cavalry, yet my hat brass proclaimed I was a webfoot, or infantryman. I started to correct him, but he cut me off. "Cannon fire does not spark blue. And besides which, that's north, and there ain't no guns to our north."

"Cannon fire can too spark blue if—"

Udo looked annoyed. "Your insubordination is grotesque. I do not know what the Army is coming to these days, with impertinence so common and respect so rarely valued. In my day, no mere corporal would ever dare contradict a ranking officer."

I almost answered Udo with something short and not

so sweet. But I bit my tongue, because there was some truth to what he had said about staying in the skin of your disguise. Didn't Nini Mo once say that the best way to impersonate a rustler was to *be* a rustler?

"I beg your humble pardon, Captain Gaisford, sir. I did not mean to contradict you. Please enlighten me. If then, there are no guns to the north, what does lie in that direction that could create such a singular sight?" I asked.

"You are overdoing it, Corporal. Not so heavy on the sop, please. And the answer is Bilskinir House."

Bilskinir House, indeed. Another blue note pulsed, and this time the ground really did tremble underfoot for a moment. A shiver ran across the back of my neck.

"I guess the papers were right," Udo continued. "Maybe Paimon is awake after all. What do you think he's doing in there?"

"Making dinner, I wager. As long as I am not on the menu, then I bid him good eating. Come on."

"I give the orders, Corporal Ashbury," Udo said curtly. "Ride on."

So we rode on, leaving the blue bursts of light behind us. The cold was biting, and my hinder was going numb – surely we were almost there? What seemed like an eternity later, but was probably only about fifteen minutes, Zoo Battery loomed so suddenly out of the fog that Udo almost ran Mouse right into it. The wooden gates towered over us, at least twenty feet high and wide enough for four riders to enter abreast.

Zoo Battery defends the southern end of the Playa and she houses sixty-five guns, so her red brick walls are high and thick. The gates were painted to look like teeth, giving the doors the appearance of a grinning, hungry mouth.

Udo dismounted, then advanced to bang heavily on the barred doors. His blows were tiny little puffs of sound, hardly louder than the distant crashing surf, but he had barely lifted his fist up from the third one when a cavity appeared in one of the lower teeth and an eye looked out.

"Who comes here?" the eye demanded.

"Friend, with the countersign." Udo sounded cool as lemonade.

"Answer, friend, with the countersign."

Here it was: no turning back. While Mamma had been attending to Poppy after his fit last night, I had spent a few minutes in the parlour, snooping through her correspondence book for passwords. I hoped that the Sign List I had copied hadn't been updated; I hoped that the passwords had not been changed. Here was the first test.

"Vilipend," said Udo, sounding rather bored.

The cavity closed.

Udo hitched his hat back on his head and scratched his nose. He tucked his reins under his arm, so as to adjust his sabre belt. He scratched behind Mouse's ear. The seconds clicked by. I thought I might scream. This was taking far too long; the guard should have recognized the countersign immediately, then opened the doors. They must have changed the password. My mind's eye saw through the Toothy Doors into the sally port beyond, where the guard was now assembled, rifles at the ready, to charge forward and blast the intruders: us.

"I will protest to Colonel Yangze," Udo said to me. "It's outrageous that we should be left lingering in the cold like this." Just as he raised his fist to hammer on the door again, before I could suggest we scarper, a crack appeared along the edge of one of the teeth. The crack widened and spread upwards and down, and then became a door, which opened.

23

INSIDE. ORDERS. SWAGGER STICK.

Nini Mo said that caution makes you careful, but panic is a poison that will kill you. I had plenty of the first and no intention of indulging in the second. My heart was thumping so loudly in my chest that I thought it might pop right out, which would probably be good, because it would save me the pain of being shot.

"It's about time," said Udo. "This is outrageous! How dare you keep us waiting! I'll have you on charges for this."

A face appeared around the edge of the door, bespeckled and abashed.

"I am so sorry, so sorry, so sorry. It's just that we had mislaid the key, and then Danbury was asleep, and he's the only one who can pull the chain up to open the door. He was a pugilist before the Army, and he's ever so strong – oh, I'm sorry. Advance and Be Recognized."

"This command is a disgrace." Udo swept forward as though he actually were a stuck-up staff officer. He left Mouse's reins dangling, and I dismounted and grabbed them.

Udo said, "Lieutenant, I am on urgent business and I have no time to waste. Come, come, Corporal Ashbury, you are dawdling again." This last, over his shoulder to me.

It is true that Nini Mo said that acting as though you have every right is one of the tricks to getting away with a disguise, but it seemed to me that Udo was not acting as much as overacting. Nonetheless, I hauled after him, towing Bonzo and Mouse behind me.

The portcullis door slammed shut behind Bonzo's tail with a rather alarming clang.

There's no way out but through.

Two guards with rifles stood behind the lieutenant, but their muzzles pointed down. In the fluttering lamplight, the lieutenant looked flustered and rumpled. His blouse was buttoned crooked and his hair was mussed. "I do beg your pardon for any perceived laxity, Captain, but also I must beg your pardon that you have not been recognized yet."

"Take my horse, and Corporal Ashbury's, too. I am Captain Seneca Gaisford, Judge Advocate General's Office. Escort me immediately to the Commanding Officer; I have a special order from the Warlord. Will you have me stand here all night?"

"No, of course not, sir. Lieutenant Wills Samson at

your service. Do come in, please do." The lieutenant scraped and bowed and ordered one of the guards to hold the horses. I released the reins reluctantly. It had occurred to me that the horses were in as much danger as Udo and I, and I wished we had left them picketed outside.

We followed Lieutenant Samson through the dank, dark sally port, then into the parade yard beyond. Udo was haranguing the lieutenant for taking so long to let us in, and the lieutenant was parroting apologies. I myself would have told Udo to jump off a log, but that's the thing about the Army; when someone outranks you and gives you some, you have to take it. The parade yard was lit only by a few dim lamps, but I didn't need much light to see the ominous shadow of the gallows in the middle of the yard. The open casemates rising above the parade yard looked like black empty eyes.

Lieutenant Samson led us along the covered walkway and into the guardroom. After the outside chill, the guardroom felt warm and cheerful. Happy red and orange firelight spilled from the huge barracks stove. Although the holding cell was empty, two guards sat on a bench against the opposite wall, drinking from tin cups. The door to the Commanding Officer's ready room was closed.

The lieutenant offered us chairs. "Do please sit down, Captain. Might I get you some coffee? A little nip of something warmer? It's a long journey from the City; you must be almost frozen. What a night to be out in, what a night. Hendricks, get the Captain and his aide some coffee."

Coffee sounded wonderful, and I did feel almost frozen, but we couldn't linger. Udo said dismissively, "Never mind the coffee. As I said, we are in a hurry. I have important matters to attend to." He pulled our forged document from his dispatch case. "Take me to the Commanding Officer. I have a special order signed by the Warlord for the transfer of one of your prisoners to my custody. You will get him ready for transport. The Warlord wishes to speak to him immediately."

The lieutenant rubbed his hands together pleadingly. "Oh dear, oh dear. This is quite strange, oh dear."

"Are you saying that the Warlord's orders are strange?" Udo asked in a quiet, dangerous voice.

The lieutenant looked alarmed. "Oh no, oh no, of course not, sir. It's just that—"

"Just what?" Udo leaned in. His Glamour's black eyes squinted into angry slits. He looked like someone about ready to cut.

The lieutenant rubbed his hands and yanked on his sleeve buttons. "Let me just present your compliments to Captain Honeychurch, she's in charge here, and you can give your special order to her. Do please have a seat."

"I shall stand," Udo said imperiously.

The lieutenant took the special order from Udo and hurried into the office, closing the door behind him. Udo stood, one hand tucked into his buckler, looking completely unconcerned, and I only hoped that my expression was equally nonchalant.

"I will be filing a report," Udo said to no one in particular. "A disgrace that a matter of such importance should be handled so carelessly."

Well, there he was certainly right. We had been left alone with two guards only, and the one sitting by the red-hot stove looked half asleep. In about three seconds, we could have disarmed them and taken control of the guardroom. Maybe two seconds. They weren't even armed. Their rifles rested in the rifle rack, which was locked. Of course, the guns Udo and I carried were not loaded; they didn't know that, and the threat might have been enough. But then we'd still have to find Boy Hansgen, and get the sally port unlocked. Better stick to the plan.

"You there!" Udo barked, pointing at the guard who was dozing by the fire. He strode across the room and grabbed the man by his collar, shaking him. "Are you asleep on duty? I'll have you shot!"

"I beg your pardon, sir, I beg your pardon!" The guard shook free of Udo's grasp and snapped to attention. Udo poked him in the chest with his swagger stick. I had tried hard to talk him out of the swagger stick – hardly any officers carry them any more, since Mamma banned the impromptu smacking of enlisted soldiers – but Udo insisted it helped him stay in character.

"And your tie is untied and your blouse unbuttoned.

I shall make a full report to the Warlord! Consider yourself under arrest as of this minute and report—" Udo raised the swagger stick like he was going to whack.

"Captain Gaisford, sir!" I said frantically, before Udo walloped the poor man and got himself arrested, and then me arrested, and then Boy Hansgen would hang, and that would be it for our plan. "Shall I see what is keeping Lieutenant Samson so long?"

The distraction worked. Udo turned back to me, and the guard sidled as far out of Udo's reach as he could, then stood at attention as though he were on review.

"I shall find out myself." Udo strode towards the office door, which luckily opened before he could kick it.

Lieutenant Samson beckoned to Udo. "Captain Honeychurch will see you, sir."

"I applaud her good judgement," Udo said, then, as I advanced to follow, "Corporal Ashbury, you may wait."

Not on your life, I thought, and made move to follow. Udo poked me backwards with the swagger stick, and I gave him a look that felt as though it should fuse glass but had no effect whatsoever on Udo's attitude.

"I told you to stay, Corporal Ashbury. I will have you on charges if you don't fall to."

I had no recourse but to stare desperately as the door closed behind Lieutenant Samson. Udo alone! We were doomed, doomed, doomed. What could I do? Nothing but hope for Udo's best, and somehow I could only imagine Udo's worst. My toes felt as cold as frozen grapes.

I sat on the bench, and the other guard, a small woman with grey-streaked hair, brought me coffee. "Those bosses. They are fresh. Here, this'll cheer you. I'm Hendricks, and that's Jam over there."

"Thank you," I said.

The coffee was hot, and as sweet as syrup, and it tasted like heaven. But the caffeine swelled up awful fantasies in my now-jittery brain. My eyes fixed upon the door, my imagination fired with dire possibilities: Udo threatening Captain Honeychurch with the swagger stick, poking or pointing, or perhaps even whacking. Udo can get carried away; that's exactly what led to Gun-Britt's broken nose, Udo not knowing when to stop. I should have held firm on that blasted swagger stick. Perhaps I should go interrupt them, with some excuse—

"A sloggy night to be out. And a sloggy night to die," Hendricks said. "Bad enough to end on the rope, but on a cold wet night as this, what's worse?"

"I can think of worse ways to go," Jam said. "There's always worse ways to go."

"You with the Dandies?" Hendricks asked me.

Mamma's regiment is the Enthusiastics, so why she had Dandy hat-brass in her insignia-box was a mystery, but it worked out well for our plan. The Dandy Regiment is currently stationed on the Trinity Line, so there was no fear of running into any other Dandies.

"Ayah so." The door remained closed. Udo, oh Udo, don't be a prat or a fool or a twit. Oh please, Udo, please.

"I thought they were up north," Hendricks said.

"Ayah, I'm on detach. Medical leave, but now I'm better and was supposed to report to my regiment, but I got stuck on this detail . . ." I could hear the sound of Udo's voice, but not his words. Any minute that door was going to open to eject a furious officer and we would be All Done.

Jam said, "I pity you, that officer of yours is a right twit. He could use a good fragging. I'd like to punt that swagger stick right up—"

The office door opened and here came Udo, the lieutenant, and behind them, another officer dressed in sangyn: a Skinner! In my tum, my coffee began to burn. Of all the people for Udo to get uppity with! Only one regiment in the Army is allowed to wear crimson uniforms instead of the ordinary black and gold: the Alacrán Regiment. They are nicknamed the Skinners because of their habit of marking their kills with scalps. They are the Army's oldest and most decorated regiment, but they have a ferocious reputation for being arrogant and bloody-minded – and ruthless cold-blooded killers.

Poppy is a Skinner, and that, no doubt, is part of his problem.

A Skinner is not someone to be messed with, but Udo had not toned his high attitude down. If anything, he had nudged it up a touch.

"Well, now, I am glad to see that you understand your duty so clearly, sir," Udo was saying to Captain Honeychurch. "And attend to it so promptly."

Where the Skinner's left eye should have been was a blackened pit. Each cheek was marred by a slashing mark: the zigzag scars that all Skinners get when they swear their Regimental Oath. It's a mark of courage, supposedly, to stand firm while someone slashes at your face with a sabre. I think it's more a mark of foolishness.

"I follow the Warlord's orders," the Skinner said.

"As do we all, though some of us do so with more alacrity. I want you to know, Captain Honeychurch, that I'll be making a note of the condition of your guard to the Warlord—"

Captain Honeychurch interrupted him: "Lieutenant Samson, take the guards and retrieve the prisoner."

The relief that flooded through me was so huge that for a moment I thought I might slide boneless to the floor. Udo had not got us killed; we were almost home, we were going to pull it off, bless the Goddess now and for evermore.

"Attend, Corporal Ashbury!" Udo ordered, and I jumped to obey.

Lieutenant Samson nodded to the two guards, then unlocked the rifle rack so they could take their weapons. Private Hendricks picked up a lantern and lit it with a trigger. I followed them out of the warm guardroom into the icy cold night. Back along the covered walkway, across the sally port, and into a small dank room beyond, empty but for a clutter of open barrels and cracker boxes. Beyond that, yet another dank room, completely empty.

My pulse fluttered so strongly in my throat that I could hardly swallow.

"You must be careful with him," Lieutenant Samson was saying to me. I snapped to attention. "He's been put under a geas not to speak Gramatica, so his magick is greatly muted, but he's still dangerous."

"I will attend." I wondered who had put the geas on Boy Hansgen. A geas is a kind of magickal interdiction, superdangerous and very difficult. It can easily backfire on the adept, who then might find *herself* the one constrained, caught in a trap of her own making that she cannot escape. Who in the Army had such ability – and more importantly, why was *that* adept allowed to freely practise?

"I am surprised the Warlord sent such a small detail, but I suppose it is not for me to question his orders," Lieutenant Samson continued.

"No, it's not," I said sternly. "We are all the Warlord's obedient servants."

Hendricks held the lantern high, while Jam bent to fiddle with a heavy iron ring embedded in the floor. A tug on the ring, and it pulled upwards, levering a square of the floor open to display the dark mouth of an oubliette.

"Stand back," Lieutenant Samson said. "Drop the

rope, Private."

Jam slacked the coil of rope and let it drop into the oubliette, and then leaned way in to shout, "Take the rope and I shall draw you aloft."

After a second, a distant answer came, unintelligible.

"He says he won't," said Jam.

Another unintelligible shout drifted upwards.

"He says he's fine where he is, the damp is extremely good for his complexion."

Lieutenant Samson wrung his hands and looked flustered. "Oh dear. What shall I say?"

Hendricks offered, "Beg your pardon, sir, but tell him if he don't take the rope and allow himself to be drawn upwards, we shall fill the oubliette with water, and close the lid. How will drowning be for his complexion?"

Jam leaned back over and shouted down the gist of Hendrick's suggestion, seasoning the recitation with some pretty spicy adverbs and adjectives, then relayed back to us. "He says that he wagers that he can hold his breath for a long time, and anyway, he'd rather be drowned than hung."

This time Hendricks leaned in and did the shouting. "You aren't to be hung yet, you fool – the Warlord wants to speak with you, and the execution has been suspended. Grab the rope and let us haul you upwards!"

Pause, and another shout from below, and Hendricks said to Lieutenant Samson, "He wants a wash and a clean shirt, first, before he goes to the Warlord."

"Tell him yes, anything, just let us pull him up," Lieutenant Samson answered hurriedly. "The Warlord will be angry we've wasted his time."

It took all four of us to haul the rope up; Boy Hansgen weighed a ton. It would have been easier with a winch, but I guess that is the thing about oubliettes – once you put someone in, you don't normally aim to bring them up again. (Which made me wonder why they had stuck him down there to begin with – perhaps it was the most secure cell at the Battery?) We heaved and ho-ed, and the rope burned my hands even through my gloves, but finally, eventually, a dark shape emerged from the oubliette, dirty and damp.

24

IN THE JAKES. CONFESSION.
AN AWFUL DISCOVERY.

"Thank you, sieurs," Boy Hansgen said, when he had achieved all the way out and stood up. He offered a sketchy courtesy – So Below Me I Hardly Bother – the manacles on his wrists and ankles clanking. "I hope that my poor starved weight didn't prove too heavy."

Boy Hansgen had a syrupy kind of voice, slightly accented, and musical. The lantern light was so dim that it was hard to make out many details; my over-whelming impression was of a white shirt and extreme grubbiness. And there was no way to get around his smell. The goddess Califa could probably nose him in heaven.

"I do hope you won't be complaining to the Warlord about your rations," Lieutenant Samson said plaintively from the position he had taken up behind Hendrick and her rifle. "You've had the same chow we've had."

"Ayah so, but perhaps your supper room is drier and your chow less sog. Or perhaps you are just used to hideous Army cooking. I will have that clean shirt now, and the wash." Boy Hansgen had the same easy tone of command in his voice as Mamma; even as a prisoner, he acted as though he expected to be obeyed.

"Do not try any tricky stuff." Lieutenant Samson was still safely behind Hendricks. "We'll be happy to shoot you and give the Warlord our regrets."

"I care for nothing at the moment but clean," Boy Hansgen said, "and wouldn't dream of blowing my date with soap. Lead on, and I shall follow as gently as a hairless Huitzil lapdog." He twisted the last words into a tone that suggested *he* was nothing of the kind, but the others were exactly that.

Back we went across the sally port, Boy Hansgen stepping jauntily, as though he were on his way to a lovely dinner rather than a supposed interview with the Warlord, and then his death. He must really like to be clean; I do, too, so there we had something in common.

In the warm guardroom, Udo and the Skinner stood at Lieutenant Samson's desk, Udo signing papers and saying: ". . . recommend you to the Warlord for your assistance, Captain Honeychurch—"

"Here I be, the man of the hour, the boy of your dreams!" Boy Hansgen said, and clanked his manacles together again so they rattled loudly. Now, in better light, he was shorter than I expected, and older, too. But of course that followed – he'd been Nini Mo's sidekick, after all, and she'd been dead for over twenty-five years, so he would have to be pretty old. In the Nini Mo yellowbacks, he's always illustrated as a young man, with short spiky hair and a bass guitar tossed over his back. No bass now, and the blond hair was matted, silver under the dirt, but he still looked pretty pugnacious and tough.

He continued, "Captain Honeychurch, dear brave Captain Honeychurch, my heart is pattering with pain to have to leave your tender care so soon."

Captain Honeychurch glared and said, "Would that my care had been as tender as you deserved."

"You is kind to me," Boy Hansgen said snarkily, and the Skinner gave him a look that seemed to say, *You aren't even worth the effort of my knife.*

Udo finished signing and threw the pen down. He gave the Dainty Pirate an arrogant once-over and said, "So this is the pirate who has caused the City so much ruin."

"I am that boy, and more besides. And perhaps just getting started!"

"I think you've come to the end, not the beginning."

"Hope springs, and who knows – maybe I will, too!"

Udo said, "The best you can hope for is a broken neck to save you the struggle of strangling."

Cut it with the snappy small talk, Udo, I thought, trying to telegraph that thought to him. *Let's get out of here.* But Udo was engrossed with his repartee and didn't glance in my direction.

Boy said, "You make such a dismal thought sound so cheerful, Captain What's Your Face. We have not been introduced."

"Captain Seneca Gaisford, JAG Office." As sign of his contempt, Udo made no courtesy bow at all.

"I am your obedient servant, Captain Gaisford." Boy Hansgen grinned and saluted with a closed fist to the chest. "But then, you knew that already. Lieutenant Samson here has promised me a clean-up before we go."

"I have no time for such things," Udo said. "We must leave at once. The Warlord is waiting."

"There's always time for soap. You don't want me to go stinky to the Warlord, do you?" Boy Hansgen smiled winningly at Udo. His teeth twinkled like ice cubes through the grime on his face. "We all know how delicate Florian is."

"Captain Gaisford," I said urgently, "we are late already." *Let us get going before we push our luck so hard that it breaks, Udo.*

"You do not need to remind me, Corporal," Udo told me. "I know my own schedule." He turned to the prisoner. "We have no time. I will see that you are given facilities when we reach Saeta. You have my word on it."

"At least let me piss. I promise I shall be quick. I'll be happy to do so in the fire if that's all the time—"

Captain Honeychurch ignored Udo's further protests and ordered us to take Boy Hansgen to the jakes. So

Hendricks led him out, with Jam and me bringing up the rear, Jam's rifle at the ready. We crossed the cold, windy parade yard and into the shelter of a casemate. At the door of the jakes, Boy went on, but the guards halted.

"You go," Hendricks ordered Jam. "Keep an eye on him."

"Not me," protested Jam. "Not me alone. We should all go."

Hendricks shook her head. "We'll guard the door. If he overpowers you, at least we'll still be standing firm outside."

"I don't want to be overpowered," Jam said obstinately. "Let him overpower *you*. What if he changes me into a polecat?"

"He can't change anyone into anything, Jam. He's under a geas – he's powerless."

"Then, why don't you want to go—"

"I'll go," I said, both to move things along and because it was a chance to tell Boy we were here to rescue him. I didn't really care to share Boy's potty experience, but I could close my eyes, or stare at my boots, or something.

Hendricks said, "All right, then, Ash. Better unholster, and keep your gun on him. If he does get you, holler, and we'll make sure to bar the door so he can't get through us."

Which wouldn't help me any, I thought, *trapped inside*, but I wasn't really worried about Boy getting me – not once he heard what I had to say. Still, I drew my pistol and cocked it. "If he pulls anything funny, I'll shoot him."

Hendricks nodded approvingly. "That'll save the Warlord the price of rope. Go on, then."

The jakes was the kind that has five holes in a row, with nothing to screen them, and across, a row of stone trough sinks. The Army is *not* a good place for the potty shy. A small stove smoked in a corner, but it did little to melt the chilly rime off the stone walls. Boy Hansgen was already leaning over one of the troughs, scrubbing soap into his face.

"Um, excuse me," I said. What would Nini Mo say? Something exciting and dramatic, like *If you want to live come with me* or *Let us fly and be free.* But I felt silly just thinking those things. "Um – sieur."

The running water was loud, but I didn't want to run the risk of the guards outside hearing me, so I reholstered and stood by until he was done. Boy Hansgen scrubbed and scrubbed, and then straightened up, holding out his manacled hands. I gave him one of the ragged towels hanging over the troughs, and he dried his face, revealing a fantastically purple shiner around one blue eye.

He regarded me as he wiped his hands, and said, "You are in bad shape, girlie. You won't be able to hide it much longer – and if they catch you, they'll hang you, too."

I stared at him blankly.

"Do you have a cigarillo? I am dying for a smoke. You don't have to be coy with me. I don't care what boo-spooky stuff you are up to, but your superior officers will take a dimmer view of your traffic in the Current. You should have stayed out—"

"I'm not in the Army," I said. "I'm here to rescue you—"

Before I realized he had even moved, Boy Hansgen was looming, pushing me against the wall, which was cold against my back.

"Who sent you?" His breath stank, and his grip on my collar was choking. Before, he had been so humorous that he had seemed harmless, his reputation perhaps overblown. But now, the jovialness had dropped from his countenance and pure steel had taken its place. Suddenly, I was afraid.

"No one," I gurgled.

"No one?"

"I came myself, on my own, with my friend, Udo."

"The one calling himself Seneca Gaisford? The one Glamourized?"

"Ayah."

He eased his grip, incredulously. "Just the two of you? To pull my feet from the fire, just the two of you, and both of you kids?"

There was a hammering at the door, and Hendricks's voice: "Hurry up in there! You've had time for twenty pisses!"

"My bladder is full!" Boy Hansgen yelled back.

233

"Ash? Did he get you?"

Boy relaxed his grip so I could holler, slightly hoarsely, "I am fine – we'll be out in a minute."

"Hurry! That Captain Gaisford is crapping bricks over your delay."

"We come!" I shouted.

Boy Hansgen was still regarding me with a hard blue gaze that seemed to bore right into my brain. "Just the two of you, and no one else?"

It was impossible to lie to that look. "Ayah – we have an order from the Warlord for you to be released to our custody."

"Where'd you get the order?"

"We forged it."

He laughed and released me completely. "Well, budding rangers! Nini could have done no better. What is your name, girlie?"

I loosened my collar and rubbed my neck. "Flora Nemain Fyrdraaca ov Fyrdraaca." His praise had kindled a happy little glow in me that made the burn on my neck feel like nothing. *Nini Mo could have done no better!*

"*Fyrdraaca?*" Now he really did laugh, low in his throat. "Now, this is precious – one Fyrdraaca sends me to the gallows and another Fyrdraaca cuts the rope! But listen to me, girlie – you've got one of the worst cases of Anima Enervation I've ever seen."

"Anima what?"

"Have you been trafficking with a galvanic

234

egregore – you know, a praterhuman entity, which gains its strength from human Will?"

A cold stream washed over me. I whispered, "Our denizen – Valefor – he's been banished and I was trying to help him."

"Banished? You mean abrogated? You've been letting an abrogated denizen siphon Will off you?" This time Boy's laugh was not amused. "Girlie, you are lucky I can see you at all – your denizen is sucking you of *all* your Will. Soon enough you'll be too far gone—"

The door thumped again, and then popped open. Hendricks, her rifle pointed, said suspiciously, "That is long enough. Come on."

That cold stream had become a flood that was threatening to wash away the last bits of my composure. I gaped at Boy Hansgen, who gave me a steady look that seemed to say, *Don't panic*, before obeying Hendricks's command. But he was too late; I was already panicking. His awful assertion had driven everything but panic right out of my mind. What had Valefor done? What did Boy mean that I would soon be "*too far gone*"?

Jam prodded Boy Hansgen on, and, now smiling again, he went, stepping lightly.

"Hurry on, Ash," Private Hendricks said over her shoulder. "The captains are about to get into a duello. Are you all right?"

"Ayah so." In a haze, I followed Hendricks across the parade yard, this time barely feeling the cutting saltwater wind. As we approached the sally port, the sound of Udo, loud and indignant, pulled me out of my daze.

". . . an absolute outrage. You can rest assured that the Warlord will be told in detail of this insult, and you can rest assured that the repercussions will be quite serious."

"Here I am again, all clean and sweet," Boy Hansgen said happily, "and ready to meet my ex-liege lord – well, now!"

My line of sight was blocked by Hendricks. I peered around her, and every atom of my body turned into freezing ice when I saw who Udo was hotly protesting to, his swagger stick poking ominously.

Lord Axacaya's Quetzal guards.

25

PANIC. A CONFLICT.
UDO'S LONG WIND. HAT BRASS.

Once Idden had tried to show me how Mamma killed that jaguar with a shovel, and in doing so, she punched me in the stomach. For a sickening second, I had wheezed and sucked, but my lungs would not inflate. That is exactly how I felt when I saw those Quetzals.

There were four of them, all unveiled, and their huge yellow eyes gleamed flat and iridescent in the flaring torchlight. Again I was struck by the awful combination of human and bird, the way the feathers shaded into skin. The unmistakable sharpness of those sword-edged beaks.

Udo and Captain Honeychurch had moved out to the sally port, and there we halted. Two Quetzals stood before the open gate, holding horses. Another stood with Udo and Captain Honeychurch, and it was with this one that Udo was arguing loudly. "My special order

237

is signed by the Warlord and must be obeyed. I hope you remember, Captain Honeychurch, you owe no obedience to Lord Axacaya."

Boy Hansgen said, his voice slightly quavering, "Now I know just how the snake felt when he saw those shadow wings circling above. Not eagles, but *buzzards*."

"We, all of us, are obedient servants to the Will of the Gracious Virreina, and Lord Axacaya is her dutiful son and his desires must be heard," said the Quetzal standing by Udo and Captain Honeychurch. Its voice was oddly sweet, and it sounded almost bored. "And he desires this man."

Cool, calm and collected, said Nini Mo. *Panic poisons; level-headed lives. She who holds out, holds all.* My chest felt light and airy, like I was breathing fog. I took a deeper breath, and then another. We hadn't lost yet.

"We are Califans first and foremost," said Udo. "And this is Califa still—"

A Quetzal interrupted. "Captain Honeychurch, you cannot deny a request by Lord Axacaya."

"Lord Axacaya has no jurisdiction here," Udo said hotly. "This is a military installation and under military rule. The Warlord is Commander in Chief." These last words were emphasized with sharp jabs of the swagger stick. I had a sudden vision of Udo torn into tiny shreds by those hooked beaks, but luckily for him, the Quetzal showed its respect for Udo's opinion by completely ignoring him and turning its attention to the Skinner.

"You shall not question Lord Axacaya's orders, Captain Honeychurch," the Quetzal said softly. "We will take the prisoner with us, and Lord Axacaya shall be pleased."

The other Quetzal had fixed its luminous gaze on Udo, and this gaze had apparently struck Udo dumb, for he did not now protest.

But Boy Hansgen did, a touch hysterically, "I beg you, Captain Honeychurch, as one soldier to another, do not send me to be torn apart by monsters. Let me hang, happy to die among my peers."

"You are no peer of mine," Captain Honeychurch said. "If it were up to me, I would have ordered you burned." The Skinner looked extremely unhappy, for which I could not blame her – either decision could end her career. Give over to Udo and let Lord Axacaya think his orders had been ignored, or give over to Lord Axacaya and risk the Warlord's wrath. Still, she was a Skinner and had taken the Warlord's oath – surely she knew where her duty lay?

"But does not mercy have a human face?" Boy Hansgen cried. "And look at them – there is no humanity there – no mercy. Please, Captain Honeychurch, can you not—"

"Captain Honeychurch, you have already ceded custody of this prisoner to me and, therefore, have not the power to grant Lord Axacaya's request." Udo had recovered, and his argument was actually a good one, though based somewhat on a technicality. "I am now in charge of this prisoner, and I say, you can go hang!"

"The Warlord owes obedience to the Virreina's representative," said the Quetzal.

"Ha! Lord Axacaya is hardly the Virreina's representative in Califa! What then is the Huitzil Ambassador?" Udo said doggedly. "And where's the order written? You cannot expect us to heed a verbal order—"

"I do not need a written order from Lord Axacaya," Captain Honeychurch said. "His servants are enough."

We were going to lose, I could smell it. Captain Honeychurch was going to give Boy Hansgen to the Quetzals, and part of me could not blame her. Which was worse, Quetzals now or the Warlord later? It's always best to procrastinate trouble.

If we were to come out triumphant, Something Had to be Done.

Who was going to Do It?

I looked towards Boy Hansgen, hoping he was poised to do something incredibly clever and flashy, to extract us all from the situation, but he did nothing. Standing between the terrified-looking Hendricks and Jam, he looked terrified, too. Maybe that was a ruse to throw us all off, so that any minute he could burst into some hideously clever escape attempt?

Any minute? Like right now? *Now?*

Boy Hansgen did not look like Someone Poised to Act. He looked like Someone Poised to Hyperventilate, or maybe Scream. His knees were practically knocking together, and only the firm grips of the guards kept him upright. He sure didn't have the nerve that the Coyote Queen had – I guess that is why he was just the sidekick.

Forget Boy Hansgen. What would Nini Mo do?

She would look for a Way Out. So, I looked.

The other two Quetzals – Minions, I suppose – stood before the gates, partially blocking that exit. Behind us, the sally port opened to the wide space of the parade yard, surrounded on all sides by three tiers of casemates, each alcove containing an extremely large gun whose barrel stuck out of an extremely small embrasure window. No exit there. If we somehow made it to the top of the parapet, there was nowhere to go but over the side, straight down into the pulverizing ocean surf. No exit there.

But Bonzo and Mouse had been brought up and now stood waiting behind me, a single groom at their reins. If we had a distraction and got by those Quetzals, perhaps we could just grab Boy Hansgen, leap on to the horses, and run?

The Quetzals' horses were Anahuatl Chargers, beautiful in a parade, useless in a fight, as nervous as chickens. Lord Axacaya sent Mamma an Anahuatl Charger one year for her birthday; I suppose he meant it as an honour, for they are very expensive. That horse was gorgeous, with a high narrow chest and the most beautiful bay colour. But he was so high-strung that he jumped at the slightest whisper. He kicked at his stall so much that he blew out a tendon and had to be shot. Mamma had never even ridden him.

Bonzo and Mouse, on the other hand, are Bulrush Shermans, a breed known for being solid and unflappable. Mamma rode Bonzo in the War, and she used to joke that Bonzo should be the one called the Rock of Califa, because it was she who always held firm when Mamma herself wanted to scarper. I'd wager my life that those Anahuatl Chargers would curvet and stampede at the slightest upset, but that Bonzo and Mouse would remain steady, no matter what.

I'd wager not just my life, but Udo's and Boy Hansgen's, as well.

Sometimes being of no account is useful. The officers and the Quetzals were still arguing, and the enlisteds were terrified, so no one paid me the slightest bit of attention as I inched my way towards the gates. I pretended, just in case anyone did look, that I was scratching my forehead, and in doing so, managed to unhook my hat brass. The insignia is held on to the hat with pointy brass prongs; there's a stupid Army tradition that when you take the Warlord's oath and are given your insignia, you are repaid by having your hat brass driven into your chest by your comrades' congratulatory punches. Idden reported to me that being brass-blooded, as they call it, *hurts*. I'd wager those fancy horses would think so, too.

The Quetzal minions holding the reins were paying

my sidling no attention, their gazes fixed on the argument. The groom holding Bonzo and Mouse was also staring agape at Udo, who was *still* in full-flood dudgeon. Captain Honeychurch was looking a wee bit more persuaded, but I wasn't going to risk it.

An Anahuatl horse flank was within poking distance. I was poised to punch, as soon as I was sure I would not be espied.

Then I heard: "Take him. And I bid Lord Axacaya joy with him."

Udo protested: "I will tell the Warlord!"

"You can tell the Warlord that I had to bow to the authority of our overlords," Captain Honeychurch said in a hard voice. "And if Califa is a client state and no longer has any Will of her own, it is no fault of mine, nor my regiment. You can tell the Warlord that!"

"I beg of you, Captain Honeychurch!" Boy Hansgen said desperately, but she turned away.

The guards shoved Boy Hansgen towards the Quetzals. He stumbled and almost fell, but they swooped in and grabbed him. They slung him over the back of one of those silly horses, and then they all rode away.

26

AMBUSHED.
GRAMATICA EXCLAMATIONS.
A COYOTE.

"Who the hell are you?" a voice whispered in my ear. I gurgled and wiggled, but someone was lying on top of me, squashing my kicks and muffling my squawks. My face was pushed hard against oily scratchy cloth that smelled of sour milk and grease.

My brain felt mushy, confused. Where was I? What had happened? Udo – Boy Hansgen – in a sudden rush, the confusion cleared and I remembered.

Udo and I had been riding hell for leather, trying to catch up with the Quetzals. Our plan? We no longer had a plan, just the intention that maybe we could ambush the Quetzals and steal Boy Hansgen back. In military strategy, they call any manoeuvre with not much chance of success a Forlorn Hope, and that about summed it up. But after we had beat a hasty retreat from Zoo Battery, we had put our heads together and agreed that as Forlorn as the Hope might be, we still had to try.

So we'd put the spurs to the horses and set off in chase. The Quetzals were in a hurry, and those Anahuatl Chargers can really run. Already they had disappeared. But Bulrush Shermans can run, too, and steadily. I was sure we could catch up. Then, suddenly, dark shadows had sprung up on the road, shouting and flapping. In Bonzo's sudden curvet, I had lost my seat – flown upwards. Then –*whompf* – darkness.

Now someone was pressing his arm against my face and hissing threats in my ear. Pain splotched my wrist, and I could barely breathe: my squasher weighed as much as a horse. Horse! Bonzo ... Mouse ... *Udo* – where were they? Were they all right?

The Squasher whispered in my ear, his breath meaty and warm, "I am dying to spit me some blackcoats, filthy bugger, but first I think we should have some fun. I need a set of ears to round out my collection." The cold edge of a knife wandered up the curve of my chin, and tweaked under my right ear, budding a spark of pain. My insides turned into slushy ice.

Then, thankfully, another voice hissed, "No ears – not yet."

"Aw, come on now, I been good," The Squasher whined. His weight eased up, and the arm across my face shifted, and I was able to turn my head slightly, uncovering my mouth.

"⊞𝓘𝒴▭ᴹ∕𝟺﹏," I whispered.

The Word exploded like a cork from a bottle, and for a second I thought I might explode, too. My brain went dark and tight, straining at my skull. My head throbbed, and I was engulfed in nothingness. Then my ears popped and I was myself again. The weight was gone.

I rolled over, forcing my stiff muscles to sit me up. My mouth tasted of iron sludge, and when I coughed, a giant wad of something nasty came up and out. A thin red glow suffused the air, and by this glow I could see the lee of a sand dune and trampled grass. Something lay upon the sand, moaning like a foghorn. A dark figure crouched over it, murmuring. There was no sign of Udo or the horses.

I started to crawl away, the sand cold against my hands. The dark figure looked up. In the thin red light, he was a blotch blacker than the night itself, which, now that the moon had risen and illuminated the fog silverly, wasn't so dark any more.

"Where did you learn that word, little blackcoat?" the Dark Man hissed.

I had no idea. The Word had appeared in my mind like it had dropped there from the sky, and once it was there, it had to get out somehow or my head would have imploded.

The Dark Man continued, accusingly, "You turned Hubert's blood into oatmeal."

"He shouldn't have tried to cut my ear off," I croaked.

"Lucky for Hubert that I was here and able to turn his

oatmeal back to blood. Else he would now be dead. It's strange to find a blackcoat with such a strong vocabulary. Who are you?"

Nini Mo says never to answer a question when you can ask one. "Who are *you*?" I asked, scrambling up and trying to keep one eye on the Dark Man while I looked around frantically for Udo and the horses.

"I'll trade you names, blackcoat."

"Keep your name, then, and get out of my way – I'm in a hurry."

The Dark Man stood. "Though I look more closely and see no blackcoat at all."

The slope behind me was steep, and sand is hard to climb. I could make a dash for it, but I'm not a very good runner, and in a chase, I wouldn't get far. Then I remembered the pistol at my hip. It wasn't loaded, but the Dark Man didn't know that. Nini Mo says sometimes the threat is enough.

I drew. The gun felt heavy in my hand, yet the weight was strangely comforting. That's the problem with guns: they pretend to be the solution to every problem.

"I have business elsewhere," I growled, "and so I bid you stand there while I go. If you seek to impede me, I'll shoot you."

The Dark Man answered, "I believe our business is the same. Are we not both hoping to get the candy and give the rush?"

"Give us the candy or we'll give you the rush" is the

traditional shout heard on the holiday of the Pirates' Parade, but I guessed he was using it as a reference to the Dainty Pirate. Still, I played ignorant.

"I don't know what you mean. It's not Pirates' Parade."

"Perhaps not a parade, true enough, but I do believe there is a pirate. Allow me to introduce myself." The darkness fell away from the figure, as though he had cast it away like a cloak, and revealed the Hurdy-Gurdy Man I had seen outside the Bella Union Saloon. "Firemonkey, at your service. And we should quit playing games if we are to have the slightest chance of saving Boy Hansgen."

"The Quetzals took him," I blurted.

"So I know. Others from my organization—"

"You mean your band?"

"The band is just a cover, of course. No, the Eschatological Immenation. Who else?"

The EI! Mamma had been right to be worried about them. They did more than just paint slogans after all.

Firemonkey continued, "When we heard of Boy Hansgen's capture, we knew we must act. Some of my group have already gone ahead to intercept the Quetzals. Hubert and I came back because we thought you were the Warlord's pursuit." He paused. "Listen!"

I listened. Hubert had stopped whimpering, and all I heard now was the distant throb of the ocean, the rush of the night air, and my own breathing. "I don't hear anything, and I don't have time—"

"Listen, not with your ears! *Listen!*"

What can you listen with, if not your ears? I stood, trying to listen but not to listen. And, gradually, I realized that I did hear something, a deep vibration that was more of a feeling than a sound. There was a rhythm to the sensation, ebbing and flowing with my breathing, but like a tide coming in, it grew stronger and stronger.

"What is it?"

"It's the whirlwind sound of the world turning round," Firemonkey replied.

"What?"

"Someone is rending the Current – come on!"

He ran, quickly, and I followed, less so. The sand slid under my feet and my empty sabre sling kept entangling in my legs. Ahead of me, Firemonkey swept up the sand dune and paused at its peak to wave an encouraging arm towards me. Halfway up, I skidded downwards, feeling my thigh muscles squeal, my arm throb. Firemonkey jumped the crest and was gone. A shout arrested my slide; teetering, I turned and saw below me a waving figure and the bulk of two horses. Finally, Udo.

I half jumped, half ran back down the dune, and only Udo's sudden grab stopped me from ending up flat on my face.

"Where the hell did you go?" he demanded. "Are you all right?"

"I'm fine, and the horses, are they all right? Where

did *you* go?" I pulled out of Udo's woolly embrace and squinted up. The jutting chin and heavy eyeliner were all too familiar: Udo's Glamour had worn off. It was good to see his face again.

"They're fine. Pigface, Flora, are you sure you are OK? Did you see those guys? Where'd they go?"

I answered. "I'm OK, but those guys, Udo, they're trying to rescue Boy, too. They are—"

"Pigface Psychopomp, Flora, *get down*." Udo gave me a hard shove, and I went sprawling. The horses jumped and scattered, and Udo himself hit the sand, half on top of me. A bitterly bright green light sped by us, barely missing our heads. It raced like a rocket, like hot shot, like a comet, and then got smaller and smaller until it winked out like a blink. The sand tilted up and tilted down, shifting like the deck of a ship. For a second, the whole world seemed to lift an inch and hover in the air. Then it jolted down again, with a tremendous thud. I felt as though every organ in my body had been pureed and poured back into my skin.

"What the hell was that?" Udo groaned.

"I'm not sure, but I know it was something Currenty. Come on."

"The horses – they've scarpered."

"Leave them; they know better than we do how to take care of themselves. Come on."

My feet turned in under themselves when I tried to stand, so I crawled my way up the sand dune instead, scraping my hands, tasting grit in my teeth, blinking away grit in my eyes. I started to slide back down, then felt Udo behind me, pushing. I paused at the top, bending to catch my breath, tasting iron on my tongue, my saliva too stringy to spit. The ocean ahead was a bright surge of silver, as fluid as mercury, and up the coast, Bilskinir House shone blue, like a malevolent morning star.

Distantly, a figure ran along the dark fringe of sand, pursued by Anahuatl horses. Udo, next to me, had pulled out his binoculars. "It's Boy; he's running hard, but they are gaining. Even if we got the horses, we'd never make it in time," he reported.

"Give me the binoculars," I demanded, yanking at the strap.

"Close your eyes," Firemonkey hissed in my ear. I started; I hadn't heard him crawl up next to me.

"Why?"

"Look beyond the Waking World."

I closed my eyes, and suddenly the steel-grey night was lit a glowing green, and the distant details of the chase snapped into clear focus. I saw then, not a man harried by a pack of horses, but a coyote, low and lean, running for his life along the shingle. And hot on his trail, four eagles.

Firemonkey said, anguish in his voice, "He hasn't got a chance."

"Can't we do anything?" Udo's free hand slid into mine, and I squeezed it tightly.

"No – they are too strong," Firemonkey answered.

"They've already got my comrades. Damn those bloody birds to the Abyss!"

The Coyote ran, his spine stretched long and his muzzle pointed like an arrowhead, but the Eagles flying behind him were like bullets. He was not going to get away. One Eagle rose up, then skidded downwards, snatching at the Coyote's back with outstretched claws. The Coyote stumbled, rolled in a tumble of legs, and writhed back to its feet, but another Eagle struck him down again. The others spun in a wide circle, darting and pecking, tearing with sharp beaks. The Coyote wove into the water, splashing, but the Eagles drove him back on to the sand, buffeting him with their huge wings. The Coyote lunged, his jaw snapping on to a wing, pulling the Eagle out of the air. The two dissolved into a blur of feathers and fur, the other Eagles swooping so low that their wings churned the sand up into a fine mist. Around and around the combatants they circled, and the mist became a whirlwind, so that I could see nothing but the spiral of sand.

My heart was beating so loudly in my chest that I couldn't even hear the thump of the surf. Udo was saying something, but I heard him dimly, all my attention focused on the now red-flecked sand devil, twisting and turning higher and higher. Udo's grip on my hand was crushing. The sandstorm flushed a deep crimson, then suddenly, as though an invisible hand whisked it away like a parlour trick, it was gone.

Now there was no Coyote, only a man on the bloody sand, so red he looked like he'd just been born. The Quetzals bent over him, their grotesque eagle-beaks tearing and pecking at his soft flesh. Then one stood, holding aloft something squishy and soft: Boy Hansgen's heart.

I opened my eyes.

27

HOME. STALE BREAD. VALEFOR.

Firemonkey and what was left of the EI did not linger. As soon as they saw that it was all over, they scarpered, warning us to do the same before the Quetzals noticed us, or the militia came, or whoever/whatever else the magickal battle might have attracted turned up. So, Udo and I rode back to the City in a daze, silently. It was so late that even the streetlights were extinguished, so early that the only other traffic we passed were milk trucks, and the occasional cab, ferrying someone home from a big night out.

So much for *our* big night out.

At Crackpot, we silently took care of the horses and went on to the House. When we had left so many hours earlier, the dogs had been locked up in the mudroom, but now, when I opened the back door, no dogs, eager to pee, shot past us carolling joy at their release.

Even before I stepped into the kitchen, I knew what we would see. Although I had not completely cleaned up the last kitchen mess, I had tidied up some before we left. Now, once again, the dim overhead light showed a scene of gigantic disaster. The table was covered in spilled sugar and broken crockery. Chairs were overturned. The kettle had been knocked off the hob, and the ensuing flood had turned the hearth into a soggy waterlogged mess. The floor was covered with jammy paw prints, and the butter dish showed clear signs of licking.

"Oh Pigface. Not again," Udo moaned. "Those dogs, I could shoot them, each and every one. And then Hotspur next."

"Do you want a snack before you go to bed?" I asked. I stepped over a broken jam jar and kicked some onions aside to get to the sideboard.

"Shouldn't we clean up?"

"It can wait."

"Then I think I'll hit the rack. We have to get up in a few hours for school."

The dogs hadn't gotten to the bread box; the bread inside was stale, but I didn't care. I was so hungry I would have eaten it mouldy. I took a knife off the knife rack and began to cut. Udo halted on the bottom stair, looking at me.

"We did everything we could," he said.

I chewed the bread; it made my jaw ache and tasted like nothing.

"Everything we could," he repeated.

I swallowed and tore another hunk off the slice.

"What more could we have done?" he asked.

"Nothing," I answered. "Nothing at all."

"You should go to bed, too, Flora. You look dead on your feet."

"I will, but I'm starving. I gotta eat something first."

Udo trudged up the stairs, and I righted a chair and sat down at the kitchen table, oblivious to the mess before me. Tea would have been nice, but I didn't feel like reviving the fire, and anyway, the teapot lay in pieces on the floor. I just sat there, staring into the shadowy darkness at nothing, chewing on stale bread.

Me and my happy splendid plan. My fabulous rangery skills, my magickal pride. I had thought I was so clever, and yet where had my cleverness gotten us? Nada, zip, *nunca mas*, nothing. I was an idiot, and a fool, and childish, and a failure. The long mirror over the sink reflected a sullen girl sitting in the middle of a huge horrible mess. Her eye make-up had smeared into pools of blackness, and her hair stood on end. Her lip rouge was blurred, making her mouth look almost bloody.

A nasty taste rose up in the back of my throat, bitter and burning, and I thought I might throw up. I leaned over, swallowing hard, and rubbed at my mouth with a gritty sleeve, scrubbing the rouge away. Now that girl in the mirror just looked washed out, a pale ghost. *She* would never be a ranger.

In a few hours it would be dawn.

In a few hours Mamma would be home.

Tomorrow was my Catorcena.

A little purple light shimmered, and became Valefor. He was looking pretty papery again, but I didn't care.

"Well," he said. "That was a fine time, Flora Segunda."

"Well-water," I answered. "Don't spoil with me, Valefor. I'm not in the mood."

"So much for heroic rescues. I am banished and even I could hear the screams. Such a magickal battle has not been seen since Hardhands—"

"Not now, Valefor!"

"Well, no matter. You did your best, which arguably wasn't really that good, Flora. But it's done."

"Go away, Valefor."

"Flora Segunda – you are far too serious. You give up so easily. Was it your fault that Boy Hansgen died? No, of course not. Your plan was perhaps not the best, and doomed to failure from the start, but it was kind of you to attempt it. He was going to die, anyway."

"Somehow you are not making me feel the slightest bit better, Valefor."

"Forget about Boy Hansgen. He's not the first magician to overreach, and he won't be the last. Let's move on to more important things."

"Yes, let's, Valefor. Let's, indeed," I said. "Are you familiar with the term Anima Enervation?"

Valefor shrank back a little, and his shape quavered. "Ayah so? What about it?"

"What is it, pray? Do tell me, Valefor. Enlighten me. You've always been quick to enlighten me before."

"I think, Flora Segunda, from your waspy tone, you know already."

"No, Valefor. I know that the Dainty Pirate thought I was fading, discorporeal, and he said that a galvanic egregore was sucking away all my Will, and I think he meant *you*, Valefor, and he said soon it would be *too late*. But perhaps you can explain it to me better, Valefor! Please do!"

Now Valefor wrung his hands, and his forehead wrinkled like a prune. "Is it my fault that your Will was so weak that it was so soon exhausted? And now we will both run back to the Current from whence we came."

"What do you mean, Valefor? Speak plainly and cut the mumbo."

"I was banished to the Bibliotheca and I had just enough stamina to keep myself strong from the wisps of Fyrdraaca Will that came my way. But then you came along and helped me out, Flora Segunda. It was so nice of you, and it enabled me to regain some of my former glory, though not a whole lot of it because, frankly, your Will was never really that punchy to begin with. But it was certainly better than nothing, though now your Will is running out, and so am I – I fear that I shall just dissipate back into the Abyss, and you shall go, too, for we are connected now—"

"Unconnect us, Valefor. Right now. Wherever you are going, you can go alone."

"Oh, but I can't, Flora Segunda. We are intertwined now; it's beyond my control, and there's nothing I can do."

"How could you let this happen?" I demanded.

"Me!? I am *weakened*, Flora—I could not help myself ! You are the magician; I am just the denizen. It is your responsibility to take precautions!" The hands were still wringing, but his eyes narrowed into gleaming slits, and I saw that his hands weren't really wringing as much as they were snapping with an audible crackle.

I stared at him. I should have been angry, but somehow, suddenly, I didn't care.

"You are pernicious, Valefor. Now I see why Mamma banished you," I said dully.

"Pernicious! After all I've done for you, Flora Segunda, you are so ungrateful. All you wanted were your own little comforts, no true thoughts of Valefor, poor Valefor, you only pretended to be my friend. You never cared for my needs at all, so it seems to me that you only deserve what you are getting, faithless Flora!"

"Leave me alone, Valefor, just leave me alone." I lay my head down on the table, not caring if I got butter or broken glass in my hair, and closed my eyes. If I vanished, then none of this would matter any more. No Catorcena, no Barracks, no Mamma, no failure.

"But, there is hope, Flora," Valefor said, eagerly. I felt him pat my hair hesitantly. "There is hope; we must not despair. You can save us still—"

"I don't care, Valefor," I said, without opening my eyes or lifting my head. "Just go away."

"But Flora, don't you want to redeem yourself? We haven't much time, but if I were restored, then I would be strong again and happy again, and so would you be, too, because we are connected. We are in this together, Flora!"

"I do not care," I repeated. "Go away, Valefor."

The little pats on my hair became little tugs, and I tossed my head against his grip. "Come on, Flora, just because you must be so morose doesn't mean that you should take me with you. Think of someone other than yourself for a change—"

I tugged away and stood up, knocking the chair down. Valefor hovered over me, his eyes white, his teeth white, his fingers long and pinchy.

"Leave me alone, Valefor, just go away and leave me alone!"

He tried to get in my way, but he was too insubstantial to make much of a roadblock. I pushed my way through him and ran outside.

28

BARBIZON. THE POND. A LEAP.

Valefor did not – perhaps could not – follow me. The sky looked like milky tea and the moon was a swirly smudge just above the tree line. The gate to the back garden was open, and I went through it into the tangled wilderness beyond. Valefor had bragged quite a bit about the marvels of his gardens – how perfect his hedge animals, how tall his cypress trees – but as with the rest of Crackpot, there was nothing left of the glory but the brag itself. Without his care, the foliage had become a tangle of branches, and the grass high and hiding. A small footpath beat its way through the wilderness, and I could just make out its trace through the gloam, leading towards the Sunken Puddle, Crackpot's ornamental pond.

Just beyond the gate, at the edge of the Puddle, stands the grave of Barbizon, my great-grandfather

261

Azucar Fyrdraaca's war horse. Her memorial is a statue so energetic that it seems as though Barbizon herself had turned to hard stone in the sudden act of curveting: she balances on muscular back legs, while an extended front hoof forever slices up at the sky, her teeth bared.

I sat down on a rock and stared up at Barbizon's shadowy bulk. The story goes that when my great-grandfather Azucar fell at the Battle of Creton's Harm, mortally wounded, Barbizon stood over him, keeping his enemies at bay with slashes of her sharp iron hooves, until at last my great-grandmother Idden fought her way through the rough din and helped Barbizon drag Azucar from the field. That, says Mamma, is true loyalty.

Something nosed against my leg, and I started, alarmed, before I realized it was Flynn. Dear darling Flynnie. I leaned over and squeezed him, and suddenly my emptiness was filled with a giant black sorrow, piercingly sharp. Now I was choking on tears that seemed to rip from my throat, leaving the taste of blood behind. Each breath I took cracked my heart a bit more, so that darkness spilled upward, outward, tearing my insides to shreds.

Flynnie's warm wet tongue lapped against my cheeks, slurped at my tears. He didn't care that I was a failure, an idiot, a baby. He loved me, anyway, no matter what. But who would feed him when I had entirely disappeared? Who would make sure Poppy didn't give him chocolate or leave the gate open so he could run into traffic and get squashed? Flynn squirmed, and I let him go, reluctantly. The sky had gone a thin pink – dawn at last – and Flynnie stood at point, quiveringly alert.

A gentle mist rose from the Sunken Puddle's surface, floating gently upward like cigarillo smoke. A small dark shape was moving fluidly across the water. Valefor, in his garden brag, had sworn three ancient turtles lived within the pond's deep, green waters, but if that was a turtle head, it was the biggest darn turtle head I had ever seen. And a big turtle could have a big head, but it would not stand up and clamber out of the water on hind legs, nor would it be tall and skinny. Or so white, either, like pale gleaming bone.

"Poppy! What are you doing?"

"Swimming," he answered, shaking himself like a dog. Flynn bounded up upon him, and he pushed the bounce down. "Could you hand me my towel? It's on that rock."

I tossed him his towel, then picked up the pack of cigarillos that fell out of its folds. He wrapped the towel over his shoulders, awkwardly, and sat down.

Mamma had warned Idden and me never to swim in the Sunken Puddle, but that was one warning she didn't need to make. I had never had the slightest desire to go swimming in it. The water smelled like yuck and Goddess knew what icky things swarm within its sour, green depths.

"You shouldn't swim in the pond, Poppy." I sat next to him and snuffled my nose against my sleeve, but he didn't notice that, or the catch in my throat. Would he

263

notice when I was gone? "You might get tangled in the weeds and drown."

"Not in this water. It's too buoyant. It's not really water, anyway. It's the Current, bubbling to the surface. If you dive down deeply enough, you can breathe the Current like air. It is marvellously refreshing, Flora – you should give it a try –you look like you need a little pick-me-up. It's delicious."

I ignored Poppy's crazy talk. I just wasn't in the mood for it. I should have gone back in the house, but I didn't have the energy to move.

Poppy put a cigarillo to his lips and muttered something under his breath. There was a small glitter of cold-fire, followed by a long exhalation of smoke.

"Was that Gramatica, Poppy?"

"Ayah," he answered, sounding pleased. "Ayah, it was. I don't know much, but I know enough to light a few fires and to maybe make it rain, if I'm on a roll."

"It's forbidden for soldiers, Poppy, you know."

"So is forgery, darling, and that comes in handy sometimes, doesn't it? Anyway, Flora, you needn't sound so self-righteous. You got Gramatica words in you, too. I can see them floating around inside you— and not just little ones, but big fat bright ones, the kind that burn. Once Gramatica gets into your blood, you know, you can't ever get it out. It grows and changes you, if you don't take care."

A tiny shiver ran through me. I remembered the Oatmeal Word – it had sprung into my head and out of my mouth, yet I could have sworn that I had never heard or read it before.

The little winkie cigarillo butt flew through the darkness and plopped into the water. "You know that if ever the Fyrdraaca family is in true trouble, Barbizon is supposed to come to life and to our rescue, just as she did for Azucar."

"Ayah, Poppy, I've heard the story."

"Well, I often consider that I've sat here many times, and often felt in true trouble, and yet Barbizon has never leaped to my aid. So you know what that makes me think?"

"That's it's just a story?"

"No, no. That my trouble is never true trouble. And things, though I think them bad, are not really so." Poppy turned his gaze back from Barbizon to me. "You should have a swim, Flora. You look as dead as winter grass. Come on. We shall jump from the Folly roof, and it shall do you great good."

The Folly is a summerhouse that sits right at the pond's edge, like a cupcake on stilts. For generations, Fyrdraaca kids have used it as a clubhouse, but I hadn't been there for ages. Now, I glanced toward its shadow. "It's much too high, Poppy."

"Nayah, not at all; it's perfect. You have to run, of course, to clear the gutters and the patio deck below. But it's like flying – just wonderful. The arc of the air and the smack of the water. And then the pull of the Current."

"It sounds painful."

"Ayah, but deliciously so. Come on!"

He grabbed my hand and yanked, and I was so surprised that I didn't yank back but came right off the rock. During the War, Poppy was wounded, and during his captivity he was tortured, and so one of his arms doesn't work too well and he limps badly. But there was no weakness in his crazy, hard grip now, and I couldn't get free.

"Poppy!" I protested, bushes whipping at me as we ran down the path, Flynnie bounding behind, barking his approval, the rat dog. We bumped up the Folly's front steps and into the musty interior. At the stairs, I took advantage of a solid banister and grabbed, with a sudden strength that I hadn't had earlier when I was deep in my despondency.

"Come on, Flora, don't be a stick," Poppy said, pulling harder. I clung, and he tore, and because he had me with his good hand, he won. We thumped up two flights of stairs, and my protests did not weaken Poppy's grip at all. When Poppy threw open the attic door, the dust our feet had raised gleamed like fog in the pink dawn light that spilled in through the open casement window.

"Last one in is the Man in Pink Bloomers!" Poppy crowed.

I gave one last yank, breathless from our hurtle up the stairs, and got free.

"Poppy, please don't—"

He turned towards me, and by some weird trick of the pale light and the streaky shadows, his face looked like a skull, bleached and grinning a white bony grin. "You have to burn in order to shine, Flora." He pounced with a grip as hard as iron, yanking me into his run, and I had to follow or fall. The window sill bruised my knees as Poppy pushed me over. I flailed about, grabbing empty air, and then I was jumping.

Immediately, my jump turned into a fall and then my fall turned into a plummet. The night blew by in a blur of shadowy trees, the sharp edge of the Folly roof, Poppy's loud shriek: *"Cierra Califa!"*

I hit with such a smack that all the air sucked right out of my stomach, and then I was twisting, turning, choking. Burning cold water weighed me down, pulling at me. In the darkness I could not tell which way was up towards air, which way was down towards death. My lungs swelled, my throat burned and pressure roared in my ears. The compulsion to breathe forced my mouth open, and suddenly I was sucking in water.

A cloud of pinkness lit up the darkness, surrounding me in a nimbus of light. A thick syrupy warmth flooded my mouth, soothed my throat, a yummy goodness that tasted like apples and nutmeg, vanilla and ginger. I wasn't drowning any more. I felt buoyant, almost frothy, as though my blood had been replaced with bubbly excelsior water. The water – the Current? – felt as warm as bathwater, curving over my body, caressing away all pain and tension. Other colours swirled in the pinkness – cerise, celadon, azure, umber, violet – and shapes, too, tremulous and serpentine. Below me, the light swelled into a brilliant glow of pinkness as bright as fire, and irresistible. I dove down toward this brightness, feeling the Current tingling and buzzing around me, but then my motion was arrested by a hard grip to the ankle.

I kicked the grip off, twisting and flailing, turning to see Poppy hanging in the Current beside me, as radiant as a star, his eyes glowing like green lamps. His movements were languid and graceful, with no sign of injury or crippling.

"Not yet." His lips shaped the words, and I could hear them as clearly as if we stood on dry land and he had whispered into my ear. "We must go back."

He grabbed my hand and began to pull me to the surface, which hung above us like a black ceiling, featureless and dark, and though I struggled and pulled, once again I couldn't shake free. The pink light was fading, and suddenly I was again choking on icy cold water, sputtering and panicking as my lungs began, again, to burn – and then my head broke the surface, and Poppy was pulling me to shore while I choked and coughed and splashed.

For a few seconds all I could do was lie on the sand, like a beached dolphin, spitting pond water and coughing, while a frantic Flynn licked my face and Poppy crouched next to me, laughing.

He crowed, "Did I not say? Oh, the Current is so sweet! I told you it was divine!"

"I almost drowned!" I pushed Flynn away and sat up, trying to spit the nasty taste from my mouth. "You could have killed me!"

"You can't drown in there, Flora. I told you, it's not real water; it's the Current. Do you not feel divine? Do you not feel better?"

Actually, now that my lungs were clear again, I did feel better. I felt drained and loose-boned, but better. Flynn pressed against me and I hugged his solid warmth. The air seemed less cold and the dark less dark, though perhaps that was just dawn coming on. The trees above me and the surface of the lake seemed edged in a pinkish glow, and my brain felt soothingly calm. For a few minutes I had forgotten about Valefor, forgotten about Boy Hansgen, forgotten about everything. Now I remembered, but somehow it didn't all seem quite as hopeless as it did before. My clothes felt heavy and wet, and yet that wasn't so bad, either.

"What was that light in the water, Poppy? Was it really the Current?"

"Oh, ayah. I told you, the wellspring of this lake is the Current. If you dive down to the very bottom, you can slip through the cracks into the core of the Abyss. All the Great Houses have their foundations in the Current, don't you know?"

But I didn't answer – he had stood up, and with that movement, the towel shrugged off his shoulders. In the thin dawn light I saw a large tattoo in the middle of his concave chest. A tattoo of a hand holding a whip. The same insignia as on the seal lock on Valefor's tea caddy.

"Poppy – that tattoo – what is it?"

He looked down his chin at his chest, grinning. "Like it, eh? It's my seal – the Flexing Whip."

"Your seal?" I choked. Suddenly I felt like an idiot. We had found Valefor's tea caddy in Poppy's trunk, so Poppy must have put it there. Why shouldn't the seal lock be his?

"Ayah, see." He tugged the cord around his neck up and over his head, and dangled it before me. "Take it. I don't need it any more."

I took it, and there was the seal I needed to unlock the tea caddy that contained Valefor's fetish. As easy as that.

Poppy ran his hand over his cropped skull and frowned. "I'm sorry, Flora."

"Sorry about what, Poppy?" I asked, still staring at the seal.

"I thought the Current would help you, but it didn't. I can still see right through you."

29

Udo Shouts. Restoration.
A Gramatica Word.

I flew from the garden into the kitchen, from the
kitchen upstairs, so quickly that my feet barely touched
the ground, set speedy on wings of panic and fear. Udo
lay snoring on the settee in my room, still fully dressed,
his big boots hanging over one end, his head almost
hanging over the other. He hadn't drawn the blinds,
and the room was already suffused with the slight glow
of dawn.

I still clutched Poppy's seal in my hand; now I
shoved it into my pocket and poked Udo, hard. "Udo,
wake up!" He moaned and threw up an arm to ward
me off.

"Uhhhh . . ."

"Can you see through me?" I hollered, yanking away
the shawl draped over him and poking him hard again.
"Can you see through me?"

271

Blearily he sat up. "What the hell is wrong with you—"

"Poppy said he could see through me! He said I was transparent! He said he could see right through me!"

Udo stood up, took me hard by the arms, and shook me. "Hotspur is crazy," he said calmly. "Calm down. And why are you all wet?"

I wrenched out of his grasp and flew to the mirror. I did look a bit blurry around the edges; my eyes were tiny blue marbles and my freckles looked rather grey. "I am blurry! I am fading! Valefor—"

Reflected in the mirror, standing behind me, Udo stared at me. He didn't look so good himself. His hair had disintegrated into a mass of matted elflocks, and his eyes were little slits of sleepiness. But he looked solid and firm, not insubstantial and flyaway.

I said hysterically, "Boy Hansgen said I had something – Anima Enervation – he said that Valefor was sucking all my Will. He said that Valefor would take it all and I would dwindle to nothing. He's done it, Udo! Valefor said we were connected, and as he goes now, so will I!"

Udo suddenly looked wide-awake. "Why didn't you tell me this before?" he roared. He grabbed me and shook me again, this time hard enough to clack my teeth together.

"I don't know. I just didn't. I forgot," I said weakly, knowing I sounded lame. "Anyway, never mind that. Valefor said there was no way to break the link between us, but that if we restored him, then he would be made strong again, and so would I."

"Do you believe him?" Udo asked. "You look all right to me, although maybe a bit wiggly about the edges. But perhaps I just need coffee."

"At this point he has nothing to gain by lying." I said. "And Poppy can see through me."

"Hotspur is crazy," Udo repeated. "What did you say the Dainty Pirate said you had?"

"Anima Enervation."

"Did you look it up in *The Eschata*?"

I shook my head. I had been too busy panicking to do anything that sensible.

Udo found an entire section on Anima Enervation – a section I could have sworn hadn't been there before or surely I would have noticed it and been warned. (Or maybe, Udo suggested, I had just not wanted to see it and had ignored everything that didn't suit my purpose? I doubted that, but didn't feel up to arguing with him.) The condition occurs when a galvanic egregore attaches itself to an energy source and then begins drawing so much Will that the source is completely drained and ends up with no Will at all.

Udo said, "Even if he sucked away your Will, that doesn't mean you would disappear, or be transparent – it only means you would lie around like a noodle, doing nothing."

"It is because I am abrogated," Valefor's voice said, from somewhere on high. We looked up from the book and didn't see Val himself, but his voice continued, "The abrogation is draining me, pulling me back into weakness, and now that Flora is connected to me, she'll be pulled, too, like me, from the Waking World to Elsewhere, and then to the Abyss of Nowhere."

"Break the link!" Udo commanded. "Leave Flora out of this!"

Valefor answered, still invisible, "I cannot; I haven't the strength to pull away, and neither does Flora. But if I were restored, we'd both be fine."

"Then we'll try the Restoration Sigil," Udo said. "If that's the only way."

"Finally, you all come to your senses!" Now Valefor's voice resolved into the rest of him. From the waist down, his figure had blurred into a purplish vapour, swirling and trailing like a train, and he looked airy and half transparent. "Finally, you do the right thing! Unlock my fetish, restore me, and I shall restore Flora!"

"You—" Udo made a lunge at him, but all for nothing, because Valefor whisked out of his reach, drifting up to float near the ceiling. "How could you do that to Flora?"

"Was it my fault she didn't know her own weakness? I'm just a poor redacted denizen, powerless and forlorn. I looked to you for succour, Flora – and look how I was taken in!"

"Taken in!" Udo shouted. He was balanced precariously on my desk chair and was trying to whack at Valefor, but Val was so wispy that Udo's snatches went right through him. "She was taken in by you, Valefor, by your promises—"

"I never promised nothing I didn't deliver! Didn't Valefor do your chores, Flora, and clean the house?"

"What price a clean house if Flora is gone?" Udo roared. "I don't want a clean house – I want Flora!"

"Stop it! Both of you. We don't have time for this!" I interjected. "Mamma will be home this afternoon, and my Catorcena is tomorrow!"

"Ayah so, but rest assured, Valefor, I'll be taking this topic up with you later," Udo said, climbing back down. "Where's that tea caddy? I'm going to get it open even if I have to smash it open. We've got to have Val's fetish."

"Smashing won't be necessary, Udo. I have the key." I fumbled in my pocket, withdrew the cord, and swung it before Udo's astonished gaze.

Udo grabbed at the cord and I let it fall into his grasp. "Pigface! Where did you get it, Flora? And why didn't you mention it earlier—"

"I got it from Poppy, just now. And, Valefor, how is it that you didn't recognize the insignia, when it was Poppy's seal all along?"

"Let me see that!" Valefor demanded, drifting down for a closer look. He snorted. "That's not Hotspur's seal! Hotspur's personal seal is Three Interlocked Rings Surmounted by a Star. I don't know whose seal that is, but—"

I cut him off. "Poppy said it was his seal, and

anyway, it doesn't matter, because it's the same seal as on the tea caddy, and so it could be the dæmon Choronzon's for all I care, as long as it works."

"Flora," Udo said. He looked up from *The Eschata*. "I'm reading through the Restoration Sigil – and I think we have a problem."

"What problem?" I asked, feeling dismay start to prickle. Just when I had started to feel hopeful again.

"Well, to activate the Sigil, we need a Semiote Verb."

"A what?"

Valefor said helpfully, "A Semiote Verb is a Gramatica Word that is so concentrated that it can only be in one place at one time. It's the most powerful type of Gramatica Word, very dangerous and not to be trifled with."

"In this case, we need the Semiote Verb *to Quicken*, in the Present Participle form," Udo said.

"And where is it?" I asked, dreading the answer.

"Bilskinir House."

30

UDO'S HOT WORDS.
A HOT BATH. MUFFINS.
UDO'S PLAN.

I sat down on the bed, my confidence dribbling away. Would this nightmare never end? Each time I thought we had a solution, another problem arose, and my energies were rapidly ebbing. Again I felt cold and empty, and as limp as a piece of string. "We can't do it, Udo. Paimon will eat us up! He'll gobble us down!"

"Oh, pooh!" said Valefor. "Paimon will do nothing of the kind."

"We can't give up, Flora. We can do it. We'll find a way," Udo entreated me. "We'll get the Word."

"I don't care if I disappear! Then I don't have to worry about going to the stupid Barracks, or stupid Poppy, or Mamma, or anything!"

Udo was horrified. "How can you say that?"

"It's the Fyrdraaca speaking," Valefor said. "It always comes out—"

I cut him off, shouting, "I don't care what happens to me! I just don't care! I'm a horrible failure and it's better this way. I thought I was so clever and rangery, and I wasn't anything at all but a *stupid heartless mindless snapper-head*!"

"Do you know who you exactly sound like, Flora?" Udo asked. He loomed over me with his arms crossed, looking lordly. "You exactly sound like Hotspur! Just exactly – 'I don't care,' 'I'm so tormented,' 'If I die it'll be all the same to me,' 'Oh, leave me alone to my darkness!'"

Anger bit at me, snapping with sharp teeth, for of course he was right, and yet it made me bitterly mad to know that he was. I turned away, biting my lip hard and wanting to smack him. So much for my belief in peace – when it came down to it, I was a Fyrdraaca all the way.

"She is her father's child. What do you expect?" Valefor interjected. "But you should think, for once, of someone other than yourself, Flora."

"Shut *up*, Valefor!" Udo shouted, and then to me: "You are always complaining that he won't suck it up, that he whines like a baby, and now you are doing the same thing, Flora."

"Leave me alone, Udo!"

"You are always talking about Nini Mo and how she didn't give up. You're right – you'll never be a ranger, but not because you fail, because you *do* give up! Nini Mo failed plenty of times, and yet she kept trying. That's what made her great!"

"Leave me alone! *Get out, Udo!*" I shouted, and even to my own ears, I sounded shrewish and stupid, and that just made me angrier. His words cut me to the very bone, because even in my blackest state, I knew they were true.

"What is Buck gonna say if she comes home and finds you disappeared?" Udo demanded.

I said wildly, "Maybe she'll be glad – one less stupid Fyrdraaca for her to worry about." I pushed by Udo, past Valefor, blindingly, wanting only to get away from them, wanting only to hide. I ran down the hallway, Udo following me, and slammed the bathroom door in his face.

My chest hurt like I might cry, but no tears came. I turned the taps on the tub and, while the bath filled, looked at myself in the mirror. I did look slightly transparent; if I stared hard enough at my reflection, I could see through to the stained-glass window behind me. I shivered, but from cold or fear, I wasn't sure, then turned off the taps.

It was a relief to get out of my soggy clothes and slide into the hot water. I was so tired that when I yawned, it felt as though my jaw would crack. I leaned back and closed my eyes.

"Can I come in?" Udo's voice asked through the door. I sank down until the bubbles tickled my nose, then called my assent. The door opened, and the steam parted, and there was Udo, with a coffee cup in one hand and a muffin in the other.

"I brought you breakfast. Valefor's in such a cheerful mood that he broke his ban on helping, and cleaned the kitchen up." Udo set the cup and muffin on the edge of the tub and flipped the loo lid down to sit. "I'm sorry I yelled at you, Flora."

"I'm sorry, too," I said in a small voice. I reached a soapy arm for the cup. It was perfect: hot, sweet, and milky. Udo always remembers how I like my coffee.

Udo continued, "But you drive me mad when you talk like Hotspur, and there is no reason for it."

"But we just get in deeper and it just gets harder, Udo," I said. "And I feel so tired and slow. I can't go on."

"That's because Valefor is sucking your Will away, Flora. You gotta remember what you feel isn't real. It's just a symptom of the problem, not the problem itself. You know, you aren't the only one who feels pretty bad about last night, Flora—"

"Maybe, but—"

"Let me finish – but I can't afford to feel bad right now. I have a plan and I'm gonna do it, Flora, and if you don't wanna go, then that's fine, I'll do it myself. I'm going to Bilskinir and I'm going to get that Word, and then we'll restore Val and you'll be all right."

I felt tears burn and hoped that Udo would think it was just the steam. He was really too good to me. "How are you going to do that? Remember what the *CPG* said about the kids on the field trip getting eaten?"

"The *CPG* is just trying to sell papers; you can't

believe anything you read there – remember last year when they ran that exposé claiming that the Warlord turns into a flamingo on the full moon? Valefor told me that Paimon was never that strong to begin with; he was really wrapped up with the Haðraaða family, and without them in the House to sustain him, he's probably withered away by now. I'm sure that he'll be no problem, and just in case, I'll be supersneaky. I reckon if I can get by Mam's curfew, I can get by some scrawny denizen."

"But what about that blue light we saw from the beach?"

"Valefor says there's a lighthouse. It's probably an automaton."

"But Bilskinir's a big House, even if there is no Paimon – how will you find the Word?"

Udo grinned and looked smug. "You should see how eager Valefor is now; he's practically rolling around like a hoop to be helpful. He found me this book." Udo displayed a small gilt-edged volume, *Califa in Sunshine and Shade: A Guide to the City and All Its Environs, Both Savoury and Sweet*. "It has an entire chapter on Bilskinir, with a map, even. See – " Udo opened the book and began to read – "'. . . and most assuredly not to be missed is the Saloon of Embarrassment of Riches. Here is kept the Haðraaða family's greatest treasures, including Banastre Haðraaða's gilded baby shoes, the Bilskinir Dollhouse, the Orb of Great Golden Weight, the Plushy Pink Pig, and several Semiote Verbs.' It will be as easy as pie, Flora. I won't be gone more than a couple of hours, and we'll have plenty of time to restore Valefor before Buck gets home, and you'll be as good as new. What do you say?"

I closed my eyes. Udo, alone, risking for me; Udo's plan, which actually sounded like a pretty good one. I guess not all my Will was gone, because when I dug down deep inside to the depths of my heart, I found that I did not really want to vanish, leave Flynnie, leave Udo, leave Mamma. Would Nini Mo give up? She was my role model. Poppy was not.

A ranger is made, not born, Nini Mo said. *A ranger doesn't give in, or give out.*

I was born a Fyrdraaca, but I could make myself a ranger. I was tired and I wanted to sleep, but what fun is sleep if you do not dream – and do not wake?

I opened my eyes.

Udo, looking damp and wilted in the steam, said, "Well?"

"Hand me my robe and get out," I answered, and he grinned in relief.

31

BILSKINIR.
THE CAUSEWAY. WAVES.

Rangers are masters at sneaking; it is their very rationale, their nature, their Will. Nini Mo snuck into the Virreina of Huitzil's seraglio and snuck the sixteen-year-old Infanta Eliade right out from under her mamma's nose before the Infanta could be sacrificed to the Huitzil goddess of rain. Then Nini Mo escorted the Infanta to Califa, where she married the Warlord and lived happily ever after.

If Nini Mo could sneak into the Virreina's seraglio and sneak the future Warlady out, then surely we could sneak into Bilskinir and steal a Semiote Verb. Of course we could, and then we would go home, restore Valefor, and live happily ever after, too.

Of course we could.

My heart remained optimistic, at least a little, but the rest of me was starting to feel pretty draggy. My head hurt, and my tummy growled with a hunger that even the maple-nut muffin couldn't satisfy.

We were going to miss another day of school, but that hardly seemed worth worrying about now. Even when Udo spends the night at Crackpot, he still has to walk the kiddies to school. So when he ran off to do that, I went down to the kitchen to try to plug the hole in my tum with a pound of bacon and two bowls of oatmeal.

An hour or so later, Udo returned, with egg-and-cheese on a roll and the extremely good news that a huge fog bank was moving through Ocean's Gate into the Bay and that Cow Hollow Harbour would be fogged in by noon. This meant that Mamma's ferry was sure to be delayed, buying us a little more time.

When we went to saddle the horses, we discovered that Mouse had thrown a shoe. There was no time to call the farrier; we'd have to double up on Bonzo, and this we did. Once again we rode out of the City, into the Outside Lands, via Portal Pass, only this time, when we reached the fork where Sandy Road goes south towards the Zoo Battery, we turned north on to Point Lobos Road.

The day, which started so sunshiny, had, as Udo predicted, turned cold and chilly. Even swaddled in Poppy's buffalo coat, I was cold, oh-so-cold, and glad that Udo rode behind me, for he radiated heat like a hot-water bottle. In front of me, Flynnie rode draped like a sock over my pommel. Twice we had tried to

284

return him to Crackpot, and twice he had somehow caught up with us; finally, we had to let him come, but he hadn't been able to keep up. Luckily, Bonzo is pretty strong, and Flynn doesn't weigh much, and he was warm, too, although boney.

The easy rhythm of Bonzo's walk lulled me into a haze. I felt drifty and half asleep, or maybe I *was* asleep and this was all a dream—

"Look!" Udo pointed.

We had crested the Point Lobos Hill, and there, ahead, Bilskinir stood, silhouetted against a hovering fog bank. The House sits on a tall promontory, at the northern edge of the Pacifica Playa, and the rocks upon which it perches looked black as the best dark chocolate. They rose straight up from the water, so sheer that I'd wager not even a lizard could find foothold upon the glassy stone, and where the cliffs ended and the foundations of Bilskinir began was hard to say. I had never been this close to it before, and it struck me now that the House looked dark and ominous, almost brooding.

"What style do you think that is?" Udo asked. Flynnie wiggled and kicked, so I pushed him down off Bonzo. He skidded down the sand dune and rushed to the waterline, flushing a flock of seagulls off the sand.

"I don't know. Early Awful Baroque? It looks a bit like a wedding cake," I answered, yawning.

"An evil wedding cake."

"How can a wedding cake be evil?"

285

"It can be black, and ominous, and evil."

A roadway, rotten and broken, started at the beach and undulated up the side of the cliff, becoming lost from view around the northern edge. The smooth sandy beach gave way to rocks, scooped with shallow tidal pools, clotted with seaweed. Seagulls swooped and curled, their yelping cries echoed by the distant barking of sea lions.

I urged Bonzo down on to the beach, towards the roadway. Flynn scrabbled ahead of us, nosing seaweed and splashing through the water, barking at any bird that had the gall to come too close.

Soon we stood at the very root of the House, and its height above us seemed enormous and pressing. When I tilted my head back, the perspective swayed and wavered, and for a sickening second, I thought the entire House – turrets, spires, domes, buttresses, gingerbread, and all – was about to slide down upon our heads.

The tide was coming in, a green scrim of water surging up over the beach. Each wave came a little higher, and fell back a little less. The bottom of the roadway had flooded out, but I hoped not very deeply.

"How long do you think it takes for the tide to come in?" I asked Udo, pulling Bonzo to a halt, just above the water's edge.

"Not long," he said. "It's rising awful fast."

I didn't ask Udo how high he thought the tide would get. By the damp discolouration of the sand and the seaweed on the rocks, I could tell this part of the beach would be entirely flooded at high tide, and a good part of the roadway, as well.

"And then how long until the tide goes down?"

"Six hours, give or take."

"I hope Mamma is very delayed," I said dolefully.

"Or maybe Bilskinir has a back door," Udo suggested. "The guidebook didn't say anything about one, but there has to be a way out other than across the beach. Look: Snapperdog!"

Flynnie had abandoned his sniffing and was now splashing through the surf. He climbed on to a piece of the broken causeway and turned to look back at us, barking.

"Snapperdog says we are falling behind," Udo said.

"Flynn! Get back here!" I shouted, but Snapperdog is notorious for ignoring commands, and he ignored this one, too. He bounced down off the broken bit of causeway, disappeared into a smack of surf, and when the wave pulled back, reappeared higher up on the road, shaking off water.

I could not let Flynn go where I would not follow, so I put heel to Bonzo and nudged her on. The water splashed around us, first just lapping the edge of the road, wetting Bonzo's hooves. If that had been all, it would have been easy as pie, just as Udo had promised. But it seemed that as the road rose, curving up around the side of the cliff, so, too, did the waves rise higher and higher, keeping pace with the roadway's ascent.

I gave Bonzo her head, trusting that she knew better than I how firm her footing was, and she moved toward the shelter of the cliff side, as far from the edge as she could get. Ahead, through the spray, Flynn could be occasionally seen bouncing from rock to rock. The ocean was surging ever upward, and falling back less and less, so that soon Bonzo's fetlocks were wet. We drew our feet up as high as we could, to try to keep our boots dry.

"Good girl, good girl," I cooed. Bonzo's ears flickered and she continued onward, her head down, her muscles rolling under my thighs. Once she staggered, sliding, and for an awful second, I thought we were done for. I dropped the reins and grabbed at her mane, clamping on to her as hard as I could. Udo nearly cut off my breathing with his squeeze. Icy cold water surged, soaking us, but then Bonzo recovered her footing.

I twisted, craning my neck, and saw that the roadway behind us had vanished into the swirling gush of the incoming tide. *There's no way out but through.*

"This totally sucks!" Udo shouted, and I could not argue with him. I'm not afraid of the water, but these waves were strangely insistent, like grabby hands trying to snatch us, to drag us under. I twisted the reins tightly around my hands and was, finally, glad for Udo's vicelike grip around my middle.

Bonzo, solidly, ignored the grabby water. Her head hanging low, she continued onward as surefooted as a mule. Now the sea was up above the stirrups, and I could not pull my feet any higher. Water slapped into my eyes; I blinked the sting away and wiped at my face with a wet sleeve. The coldness felt like acid eating at my flesh. My frozen fingers could hardly grasp the reins. Now the water was up to Bonzo's chest, swirling and sucking. The roar was thunderous.

Udo knocked me in the ribs, pointing, and I pushed my sodden hair out of my eyes. We had rounded a curve, and I could see ahead, at the top of a steep grade, the tall structure of a gate. A red figure posed in front: Flynn. If Snapperdog could make it, so could we.

Suddenly the waves fell back, and the water began to ebb. In a few seconds, the road was clear again, although still slick with seawater. The ocean had gone as flat as paper, the tide high, but not high enough to reach the road. And then a swell appeared on the water's smoothness, a swell that grew into a bulge and elongated upward into a wave.

With no urging from me, Bonzo broke into a jog, her hooves skittering on the wet rocks.

"Flora!" Udo moaned in my ear.

"I know – hold on. We'll be OK. Come on, Bonzo, come on, girl."

Higher and higher the wave grew, stretching like molten glass until it hung over us like a liquid ceiling, translucent blue and green, and still it did not surge downward. Even if Bonzo had been in the clear to canter, she would not be able to outrun the wave's break. But it did not break, only grew higher and higher. For a second, a minute, an hour, an eternity, the entire sea hung over our heads, heavy and smothering.

Then the wave collapsed. The noise was incredible, like the roar of a mob, or an avalanche, or a hundred cannons firing at once, or a thousand soldiers screaming together. My life did not flash before my eyes, like in books, but I thought of what Mamma would say when she found out that I had got Bonzo drowned, and that now she could not be mad about Valefor, and that I hoped I would see Udo on the other side, and I wished I'd been a bit nicer to Poppy, and—

Suddenly I realized the noise was receding and I was not drowned. I opened my eyes and saw that the water had been flung back by some invisible barrier. Bonzo had stopped and was looking about, bemused. Above us, around us, water thrashed and pounded, but not a drop touched us. Each time a wave rose, for a few seconds we were in a luminous tunnel of blue and green. Then the water would be repelled and the dreary daylight returned. The roadway was now smooth and dry.

"I think I just lost fifteen years off my life," Udo said. "And I almost pissed my drawers. Maybe I did piss my drawers. I'm so wet, I cannot tell."

A few more steps and we had reached the top of the road. Somehow I would have thought the gate to Bilskinir would be enormous and nasty, with spikes and bars and thorns and maybe gargoyles spitting boiling oil. But it wasn't. It was a plain white wooden gate, set in a plain white wooden fence, not so high as Bonzo's head. It was open.

Before this ordinary gate, Flynnie sat, licking his bottom while he waited for us. Beyond the threshold lay an immaculate sand driveway, as white and smooth as new snow. The sky ahead, framed through spreading trees, was as bright as blue paint, and the air was hushed and tranquil.

Looking over my shoulder, I saw that the waves had resumed their fury and were hitting the roadway hard. The crash of the surf shuttered us in, and I could no longer see the Playa below. In contrast to the bright day before us, behind us the sky was still grey.

Once again, Flynnie was point dog; while we hesitated, he bolted onward. No giant Butler swooped down to snatch him up as a tasty mouthful, and this emboldened us. But before I could touch her sides with my heels, Bonzo took matters into her own hooves and shot forward as though she had been spiked from behind.

She flew through the gate and down the path, hooves kicking up all the nice white sand. I yanked hard on the reins and not a whit did she slow down. We tore down the roadway, which curved through a copse of tall shady trees, and rushed through bright flower beds, blossoms kicking up around us.

"Whoa! Whoa!" I hollered.

Udo jounced behind me, his chin banging hard into

the top of my head, knees knocking into my sides. Bonzo shifted from the jarring trot into an effortless canter. That made it easier to stay on, but I could still not stop her.

"Hold on!" I could feel Udo starting to slip behind me, but I couldn't do anything other than saw back and forth uselessly on the reins. Ahead, the trees broke open to the blue sky and the bulk of a grey stone building.

"I am holding!" Udo shouted.

"Whoa, whoa, whoa!" Something loomed up in our path – a sundial, I think – and Bonzo bounded over it like a jackrabbit. Then suddenly she skimmed into a halt, but Udo and I kept going and tumbled over her neck, towards the hard ground.

32

KINDA CREEPING.
NOT SO CRAWLING. CAUGHT.

We were mussed, grass-stained, and breathless, but otherwise all right. My side burned from Udo's pointy elbow, and my back hurt from landing hard on the grass. The pain felt surprisingly good: it proved I was still solid. Flynnie stood over me, licking and drooling. I hadn't been dumped in years, and now twice in as many days; Nini Mo would not be proud.

"Get off !" I pushed at Flynnie, and heaved up to my feet. Bonzo had already recovered and was now tearing great gobs of grass out of the lawn, as though she had never done a snapperhorse thing in her entire life.

Udo clambered to his feet, grimacing at the grass stains on his jacket. "Now I'm wet *and* dirty." He wrung out the hem of his kilt and straightened his hat. "But at least I am alive."

"For the moment," I said sourly.

The way we had come was a wreckage of bent branches, torn turf and crushed flowers. So much for our sneaking in. I hoped hoped hoped that Paimon was truly puny and weak, or we would be in serious trouble.

"You'll dry," I told Udo. "Come on. We should keep moving."

I retrieved Bonzo's reins and pulled her from her chomping. The weather had completely changed. No longer chill and foggy, the air felt warm and springlike, and the sky sparkled with gentle sunshine. I took my soggy buffalo coat off and shoved it into one of Bonzo's saddlebags. Bonzo's stampede had led us deep into the gardens, and now there was no sign of the House itself.

"Come on – we have to find the House. We don't have any time to waste."

"Flora," Udo said, very quietly and carefully. "Look."

Flynnie, who had been twisting around my feet, went taut and anxious. His tail sprang up, and his back drew out, his nose pointing. I followed his point, then froze.

Three red dogs stood in the middle of the sandy white drive, staring at us. Each of them was nearly as high as my waist, and they had squat toadlike heads with huge wide-set eyes and ears clipped into batlike triangles. Their massive jaws looked like they could snap up Flynnie with one crunch. They looked like they could snap up *Udo* in one crunch.

"Don't move," I hissed to Udo without taking my gaze from the dogs. They stared back impassively. Out of the corner of my eye, I saw Flynn's brushlike tail cautiously move from side to side. Carefully, slowly, maintaining my stare, I reached for Flynn's collar with my free hand and got it tight in my grip.

"Good doggies, nice sweet doggies!" said Udo brightly, friendly. The dogs ignored him; their silent contemplation was all about Flynn. Bonzo had taken advantage of my distraction to go back to grazing, and I didn't dare make a strong enough gesture to pull her head back up again. But the dogs ignored her, as well. I wished I had a weapon, a stick, a rock, anything, but I was afraid to move.

"Sweet darling puppies," Udo said encouragingly. "Precious sweet *babies*."

Then, Flynn yanked and jerked in my grip, trying to pull away. Though he's wiry, he's strong, and he easily tore out of my hold.

"Flynn!" I shouted. But of course Snapperdog paid me no never mind, just continued his headlong hurtle toward the Dogs of Doom.

They broke formation and flung themselves forward with a sudden chorus of rumbly barking, which was answered by Flynn's hysterical yip. Flynn and the three strange dogs crashed together, and for one horrible sickening moment, I thought that was it. But instead of dissolving into a frenzy of snappy teeth and tearing jaws, they dissolved into a scrimmage of nose-licking and bottom-sniffing. Flynn began to spray with joy, turning around and around in ecstatic circles.

One dog bounced over to Udo and tried to lick his face, and another shoved his head under my hand to be petted: his thick silver-studded collar had an enamel badge on it that read BUMMER.

"You scared the stuffing out of me, Bummer," I said, rubbing his pointy ear. Bummer looked up at me, grinning a doggy grin, and licked my hand in a doggy apology. "Can you show us the way to the House?"

In answer, Bummer set off down the driveway at a trot, the other dogs falling in behind him. I tied Bonzo's reins to one of the lightposts that lined the drive, promised her we'd be back soon, and Udo and I followed.

Bummer diverged from the driveway on to a brick walkway. It curved around huge circular flower beds brilliant with ramrod-straight tulips, ambled through a copse of tall flame-tipped beech trees and droopy eucalyptus. The stillness was broken only by the purring of the fat doves preening on the close-cropped lawns and the papery rasp of the breeze-tossed leaves.

"The grounds look in awful good shape," Udo said, uneasily. "Don't you think if Paimon were really weak that they'd be a mess, like Crackpot?"

"Ayah." The same dismal idea had occurred to me. I

thought about the invisible wall that kept the waves from washing us away, and I looked at the dogs cavorting with Flynnie, so sleek and well-groomed. These were not hungry dogs, and this was not an abandoned garden. Outside Bilskinir's grounds, the day had been cold and grey; here were gorgeous sunshine and clear skies. These were not the signs of a paltry starved denizen. A little tiny fear shivered in my blood. To keep everything so nice must require a great deal of power, and Bilskinir House had been empty of its family for over fifteen years.

Something was nourishing Paimon and keeping him strong.

I just hoped it wouldn't be us. Nini Mo said, *If you can't be secret, then you should be speedy.* "Let's hurry," I said, "and then get out of here."

"Ayah, let's," Udo agreed, and we picked up our pace.

The dogs trotted by a shrubbery clipped into the shape of a rearing gryphon, and by another, shaped like a manticore. We went down a slow slope of wide marble steps and by a flat reflecting pool. In the pool's centre, the bronze figure of an archer stood tippy-toe, taut in the act of pulling back her bowstring. The water flickered with orange and white, and two bulbous eyes peered up at us: a fish the size of a large house cat.

"That's the biggest goldfish I've ever seen," Udo said. The fish flipped a fin against the surface of the water, splashing him, and he drew back in surprise. "I meant that nicely."

"Never mind the fish – come on."

But Udo lingered and the fish splashed at him again, this time smacking its tail and sending up a soaking sheet of water.

Then, behind us, a deep dark voice: "She wishes to be fed, but dinner is not yet ready. She must wait."

A chill started at the bottom of my feet and worked its way up, leaving my blood freezing cold in its wake. Udo stared at me, his eyes as round as marbles, his face a sudden sickly white. We were stock-still, and did not dare turn around. The back of my neck prickled coldly.

"Ave, Madama Fyrdraaca Segunda and Sieur Landaðon Uno." The voice was so rumbly I could feel the vibration in the back of my throat, and it reminded me, somehow, of chocolate, yet a silvery strand of lightness ran through it as well, like the gentle ring of a bell.

Udo and I turned around, and my hand groped for his. We squeezed, tight as death, and as damp.

Paimon loomed, taller than me, taller than Udo, taller than Mamma. He wore a blindingly white flannel suit, and white patent leather shoes, long and pointy, like loaves of bread. A white straw skimmer hid most of his face, but not the tips of the tusks, or the long moustachio protruding beyond the brim of the hat. The tusks looked very sharp, and the moustachio was a lovely shade of velvety blue. I wasn't sure I wanted to know exactly what the brim of that hat was hiding. One enormous blue hand held a basket of violets, and another violet was tucked in his lapel.

"Welcome to Bilskinir House," he said, and again I felt the vibration of his deep voice in the back of my throat.

"Ave, sieur denizen, thank you, ave," I squeaked. I made a deep courtesy and, despite my quaking knees, managed to make it down and up again without falling over.

"Ave, sieur denizen," said Udo. His voice had dropped about four octaves. He gave Paimon a courtesy bow that was deep and flourishing and involved much inclining of head and waving of hat. Blast, I'd given Paimon the courtesy Respect to an Elder. Udo had given him the courtesy owed to a ruler, or overlord. Better idea.

The dogs gave Paimon no courtesy at all. They frisked joyously around his feet, bouncing and licking, pawing at his knees. He pushed them down gently with an enormous hand, whose fingernails, I couldn't help noticing, were as silver and sharp as pins.

"Well then, Flynn, I am pleased to see you again, as well," Paimon said. "Sit."

Flynn, who had never obeyed such a command in his life, promptly sat, looking up expectantly. Paimon's hand looked like it could squash his skull like a grape, but instead Paimon used those pinlike fingernails to scratch Flynn's ears. Flynnie closed his eyes and looked blissful.

"Thank you for receiving us, sieur," Udo said. "Your House is magnificent, and we are privileged to be granted this honour."

"I am honoured by your visit," Paimon responded, and his courtesy was so low that his azure moustachio trailed on the ground.

Paimon looked as solid as bricks, as bright as noontime. He did not look the slightest bit forlorn or paltry – or hungry, for that matter, though this was no reassurance. To be that robust, he had to be well-fed, and what was he eating, then, if not trespassers and those who strayed too close to his boundaries?

"We made a bit of a – I mean, there was a mess. Bonzo got too excited. I am very sorry, sieur denizen," I said, not particularly suavely. "Very very sorry."

Paimon gazed down at me and rumbled, "Think nothing of it. Bonzo was just in a hurry to get home."

"Home?" Udo asked.

"Ayah so. Did you not know that she was born in my stables? General Haðraaða Segunda rode her, and then, upon the General's death, she went to General Fyrdraaca. Who, I hope, is well?"

"Very well, sieur." I was amazed at Bonzo's secret history, but now her stampede made sense. After her ordeal in the water, she was eager to get back to a place she recognized.

"Come. You are wet and bedraggled, and I would not like to see you become ill. Will you do me the honour of coming this way?"

300

We had no choice but to follow, and so we did, not daring to protest. Now did not seem a good time to mention that we were there on a mission of thievery. Now did not seem like a good time to say anything at all. *Silence is bliss*, said Nini Mo.

So we followed Paimon past the fountain and through an arch in an enormous boxwood hedge, thick as a stone wall. Beyond the hedge lay a huge lawn, as lush as a velvet carpet, its gorgeous deep green studded with yellow and gold daisies. And there, at the far end of the lawn, was Bilskinir House itself.

No longer as dark and ominous as it had appeared from the beach, now the House glowed brilliant blue, a shade darker than the sky above. The deep blue, I realized, matched Paimon's own hue. Silver-tipped spires and turrets pointed loftily, and above all, a huge dome floated, looking like nothing so much as a giant scoop of blueberry ice cream. The roofs of Bilskinir glittered like silver fire, and the House shone like a sapphire, almost too beautiful to be real.

The dogs scattered across the lawn at a dead run, to menace the fluffy white sheep peacefully cropping the grass, but with one stern *no!* Paimon brought them back to heel. Although the lawn seemed to be as wide as a polo field, somehow we crossed it in only a few steps, and then went up a long swathe of light blue marble steps, whose risers were lined with slender trees with silver trunks and silvery blue leaves.

The stairs opened up onto a long portico, upon

which sat a large round table surmounted by a cheerful blue and white umbrella. Next to the table was a tea trolley, and coming from it were the most scrumptious smells.

"Would you care for refreshments?" Paimon asked.

33

TEA. SANDWIES. EXPLANATIONS.

We were not on the menu. The tea was gunpowder, my favourite, and the sandwies were egg and cress, pea-butter, and red raspberry jam. There were little heart-shaped cakes sprinkled with red sugar, dark brown gingerbread decorated with gold foil stars, and lemon meltaways. There was a cheese rarebit, and fat sweet-potato chips, and vegetable stir-fried rice. All of my favourite things to eat, oh-so-delicious and warming.

We had been prepared, if caught, for the worst. Yet here was just about the *best*: yummy food to fill the cavern that had become my belly, and Paimon so exquisitely nice, even if also somewhat overwhelmingly imposing. Nini Mo would have advised, *Be guarded*, and I was trying to be so, but the atmosphere was so ordinary, and Paimon so gracious, and the food so delicious, it was extremely hard not to be lulled. It was also hard not to gobble. With each bite, I felt a bit stronger, a bit more optimistic. Perhaps Paimon would just *give* us the Word if we asked nicely and remembered to say *please*. But the time didn't seem right yet; Nini Mo says that to be sure you get the answer you desire, you need to phrase the question nicely and to offer it at the best possible moment.

Beyond the stretch of green lawn, the patio overlooked a splendid ocean vista. The sea was only a slight shade lighter than the sky, and the colour of both seemed faded compared to the House that twinkled behind us, as pretty as a spun-sugar treat. In the warm air, our clothes had already dried. The dogs had a table of their own, low to the ground, and each had a cushion to sit on and a silver plate off which to eat. Their manners were exquisite, too; they never barked or growled at each other, and even Flynnie seemed to be behaving.

While we ate, Paimon made polite conversation about the health of our families, various current events, and the latest polo scores. He was a big fan of the Monona Blowhots, who were already being called as the sure winners of this year's Pearly Mallet. Udo did most of the talking; my mouth was too busy chewing yummy delicious chow, and since Paimon was making sure that our plates never emptied, there was plenty of yummy delicious chow to chew. I felt much better.

Until I reached for my teacup, that is, and realized that I could see the vague pattern of the floral tablecloth right through my hand. I tried to pick up my knife, and it was soft in my fingers, gummy and hard to grasp.

"Ah," Paimon said, noticing my difficulty. He put the fish-shaped teapot down. "Please give me your hand, madama."

The hand he held out to me was as large as a dinner plate, blue as the twilight sky. His silver fingernails glittered. My own fingernails were purple, and Udo's were a garish cherry red, but Paimon's fingernails owed their shade to nature, not artifice, and, I noted again, they looked paper-cut sharp.

"Come now, it shall not hurt, madama," he chided.

His hand enveloped mine completely and the warmth of his grip, tight but not crushing, was reassuring. The wheeze in my chest loosened up, and some of the iciness melted from my bones. When he released my hand a few seconds later and I held it up to the light, my flesh had become blessedly solid again.

"How did you do that?" I asked.

"I gave you some of my Will, madama – but you needn't fear. You shall owe me no obligation for it. I have more self-control than young denizen Valefor does. And perhaps now is the time to discuss your problem and possible solutions to it. Please tell me all."

I let Udo tell the story, because I felt a bit foolish telling it myself. And also because my mouth was too busy chewing to talk. Somehow Udo managed to make me not sound like a complete and total idiot, and for that I was grateful to him.

"More tea, madama?" Paimon asked, when Udo had finished with a request that Paimon let us borrow the Semiote Verb, *for a while, a very short time, and we promise that we shall return it in perfect order very quickly, please, very pretty please?*

"No, thank you," I answered. I felt as full as a tick; I could not eat another bite.

"The tea was luscious," Udo said winningly. "We should hardly like to trouble you further, but the Semiote Verb is necessary to Flora's restoration. And we don't wish to sound hasty, but we are in a bit of a hurry. Flora has not much time."

"Please," I added, "please, sieur denizen, please?"

"I would be happy to give you the Verb," Paimon said. "But I cannot."

Suddenly I was hungry again. I reached for another egg sandwie, but this time it didn't taste nearly so good.

"Why not?" Udo asked.

"A Semiote Verb is extremely dangerous. Mispronounced, it could cause great harm, not only to the mouth that mangles it but also to the Waking World around it. I cannot allow it into untried hands. I beg your pardon for doubting your ability, but I must be careful."

I said piteously, "But it's my only hope. What else can I do? I shall disappear."

Paimon continued, "But besides the question of the Verb's potency, it would not affect Valefor's restoration, and therefore be of no help to Madama Fyrdraaca.

Valefor has been abrogated by the Head of Fyrdraaca House – General Fyrdraaca. Only she has the power to restore him."

"Mamma," I whispered. "Mamma will kill me if she finds out what I have done."

"I doubt that very much. General Fyrdraaca has a temper, it is true, but she does not have a reputation for bloodlust. No doubt she will be angry, but hardly homicidal," Paimon answered.

"You don't know Buck," Udo said darkly.

"I think it is you who underestimate General Fyrdraaca, sieur," Paimon said. "But then I understand how it is when one wishes to avoid censure for one's actions. Anyway, I suspect that that option is moot, anyhow. General Fyrdraaca's ferry has been fogged in off Point Lobos, and the fog is not reckoned to lift until midnight. Flora doesn't have that much time; by then it shall be too late."

"I don't see any fog," Udo protested. "The sky has completely cleared."

"Within my vista, that is so. I do hate the chill and prefer the blue sky, and thus I arrange my view within my environs as such. But I assure you that outside Bilskinir's boundaries, the day is drear, and the fog thick."

Paimon could control even his weather! And Valefor said Paimon was the lesser of the Houses in the City. Why had I ever believed a word Valefor had said? What a fool – me.

"Then Flora is pegged," Udo said in anguish. "There's got to be something we can do."

"There may be," Paimon agreed. "It may be possible to destroy Valefor completely."

"But wouldn't that destroy Flora as well?" Udo asked.

"It would depend on the sigil used, and the skill of the adept."

"But I don't think I want to destroy Valefor completely," I said. "I mean, he can't really help himself, he is not supposed to be banished and he is so hungry—"

"Why are you sticking up for that pinhead, when he tried to do you in, Flora?" Udo demanded.

"He couldn't help it, maybe. It's hard to be so hungry—"

"Pah! I don't care about Valefor," Udo said hotly. "I only care about you."

"In any case, we must not act hastily," Paimon said. He stood up and began to collect our plates, then to stack them on the tea trolley. I grabbed the last cake before he whisked the plate away. Flynnie, done with his chow, came over and lay his heavy head on my lap.

"But we are running out of time," Udo protested. "You yourself said we didn't even have time to wait for Buck. We *have* to act hastily."

"I have some small influence over the passing of time within Bilskinir's boundaries," Paimon answered. "And thus I can offer you some latitude. Enough to give us time to consider alternatives. I have an idea, but I must

308

seek advice before I offer it. Do not fear; my consultation shall not take long."

"Thank you, sieur denizen." I ignored Udo's protesting looks. "I could use a nap, and we do appreciate all your help. You have been so very, very kind."

"It is my pleasure. Come."

We followed Paimon through Bilskinir's humongous front doors, into a rotunda so lofty that the ceiling (if there was one) was lost in a sunny haze. I thought this must be the Hall of Expectant Expectations, where back in the day when the Pontifexa Georgiana Haðraaða ruled Califa, people would wait to be received by her. The hall was big enough to fit a crowd, but there was no place to sit. Here Paimon took our jackets and Udo's hat, and shooed the dogs back outside after giving them stern instructions to leave the sheep alone.

Califa in Sunshine and Shade had wasted few splendiferous adjectives in describing the House, but now I realized that no splendiferous adjective would ever do Bilskinir justice. The House was so splendiferous that I could not take all the splendour in; everywhere I looked, straining both neck and eyes, was such glory that it almost made me dizzy. We rode upstairs in an Elevator the size of a small boudoir, with walls lined in blue flocked velvet and mirrors that made it seem as though there were a dozen Udos and a dozen Floras. But there was only one denizen: Paimon had no reflection.

After escorting us down a hallway whose length was punctuated with portraits of dogs, Paimon halted in front of an enormous door. It opened, with no obvious action from Paimon, and he ushered us over the threshold. He clicked his heels together and bowed his enormous white-hatted head. "Rest. I shall return for you. Do not wander." The door closed behind him.

Udo reached out and tried the doorknob.

The door was locked.

34

SUNK. A WATER ELEMENTAL. FOOTSTEPS.

We are trapped!" Udo rushed to the window and rattled it, but that was locked, too. "We are trapped!" The bedroom was decorated in an oceanic motif – if the ocean were bloodred. Crimson walls were traced with silver lines to represent the flow of water, over which swam sinuous eels, languid fish. Crimson carpets were scattered with woven shells, coral, seaweed. A polychrome mermaid perched on the huge chimneypiece, her carved crimson hair spilling over her round white shoulders and down her white bosom, to wrap around a muscular blue-green tail. A blue enamel stove crouched below the mermaid, in the fireplace cavity. A huge wardrobe, inlaid with mother-of-pearl, took up one whole wall. The bed was silver gilt, with a huge wooden tester and sangyn red curtains. Burnished blue gargoyles perched along the footboard; the tall headboard was painted with a scene of a stormy sea.

I hardly heard Udo. I climbed up on the bed, and sank into a feathery comforter that did not smell like moths, cedar, or dust. Oh, the bliss of a nap. I felt yummy-full and very tired, and reassured by Paimon's reassurances. Surely he, a great denizen, could come up with a solution to save me, and keep Mamma in the dark, and all would turn out happily after all. All I had to do now was rest.

Udo said, "The chimney is sealed. There's no way out. We are trapped. Are you just going to lie there?"

"I'm not just lying here," I said. "I'm thinking."

"Of what?"

"Of nothing."

"If you are thinking of nothing, then you are not really thinking. You should be thinking about how to get out of this trap." From the thuds and rattling, I gathered that Udo was trying the door again, and then the window.

"It's not a trap, Udo," I said, without opening my eyes. "Calm down."

"Ayah so? Flora, come on. You believed Paimon, what he said?"

"Why should I have not? He was so nice, Udo, and kind, and he said he'd help us."

"Ayah, right to the stew pot. Didn't you notice how the table was full of food, and yet he didn't eat anything? And how he kept urging food on us, as though he was fattening us up? And he never took his hat off, either, so we could hardly see his face. Don't you wonder why – what's he hiding? Slavering jaws? Fangs? And then he says he can't help us, and it is too late to get Buck to help us, so we are at his mercy, and then he locks us in here, to waste our time, until it is too late for you. How can he be so strong if he hasn't been eating someone, something? Look at Valefor – he's been alone barely fourteen years and he was hardly there, and yet Paimon looks as good as new."

I had not noticed that Paimon hadn't eaten, actually, being myself so busy eating. And Udo had a point about Paimon's obvious stability. And yet, he had been so nice, and kind, and *sincere*. Surely Udo was just being paranoid.

"Didn't Nini Mo say to expect poison from standing water?" Udo continued. The bed creaked as he sat down on it. "Flora – it's classic – you lure the prey into the trap, baited with honey, lull them, and then when they are relaxed and at their most tender, *snap* the trap shut."

"If Paimon were going to eat us," I said reasonably, "why would he put us in the best bedroom in the House? I think from the design, this is the Bedchamber of Downward Dreaming. You should be excited, Udo. General Hardhands slept in this bed."

"And look where he is now," Udo said, which was stupid because even though Hardhands was dead, it had nothing to do with Paimon. The bed creaked as Udo stood, and then the window rattled again. "Look – Paimon said that he would slow time down, to give you more time, but the sun is going down. It'll be dark soon, Flora, and I don't want to be here after dark. Come on, Flora – focus. We have to get out of here – get that Word and get going—"

"Can I have a drink of water, Udo?"

"If I get you a drink of water, will you get up and help me figure out how to escape from here?"

"Ayah. I will, I promise," I said drowsily. Udo's footsteps stepped, then a glass clinked. "And with ice, if there is any—"

"Pigface Pogostick! Jumping Jethro-in-a-rattailed-kilt!" Udo yelped.

"You needn't swear just because I asked you for ice."

"*Hijo de mono y beso de naranja!*" I heard. "Who the hell are you, chupa?"

That wasn't Udo's voice. My eyes flew open. I crawled to the end of the bed and peered into the darkening room. Udo stood frozen, a jug in one hand and a glass of water in the other, and out of this glass something small and fishy was wiggling. It flipped up, and flapped a long tail as frilly and red as Udo's favourite crinoline, until it hovered in the air above the glass. It was only half fish; above where the waist would be if fish had waists was a humanish form dressed in a fancy black jacket covered with silver conchos, open to show a brilliant red weskit and a perfectly tied four-in-one cravat. Perched upon the cravat was an angry face surmounted by a top hat.

"Why did you disturb my siesta, idioto?"

"I beg your humble pardon, sieur," Udo said. "I didn't know you were in the jug."

The merman settled its top hat with a thump, then tugged on its weskit. "You never looked before you poured, did you, boy?"

"What *are* you?" Udo asked.

The merman scowled. "I am Alfonzo Guadaquevilla Ximenz Cimenes Perilla y Requesta, sieur." He made the tiniest of bows and tapped the brim of his hat. "I am not a *what*. I am a water elemental of the highest order, a direct descendant of Escarius of the Deep and of impeccable lineage. I need not ask what you are – that is obvious. You must be dinner. And about time, too. I am famished." The merman made a lip-smacking noise and slapped his tail on the air.

"Dinner!" said Udo. "Dinner!"

"Ayah, I can hear Paimon below, stoking the fire in the oven and mixing up marinade. And here you two are, so what else can this explain but dinner? You, sieur, look as though you might be a bit on the stringy side, but Madama –" and here Alfonzo flipped his tail and shot through the air toward me – "is quite nice and plump. A tasty little morsel, *muy dulce*. Though a bit waffly in the Will department, still tasty."

"I told you, Flora! I told you!" Udo shouted.

Alfonzo zipped around my head, flapping his tail as though he swam through water, not air, and poked at me with his cane. "You know, too, *dulcinea*, you look familiar to me. Have we met before? Elsewhere, perhaps? Madama Rose's Pirates' Parade party?"

I batted him away. "No, I don't think so. And Paimon isn't going to eat us. He said he'll help me! He was so nice."

The elemental answered, "He is a tender butcher, of course, and wishes to make your last moments happy."

"What did I say, Flora? I said so, didn't I?" Udo cried.

"I don't believe you," I told Alfonzo.

"Oh no? She who lives will see, eh? Or perhaps I should say, she who is eaten shall see. I think I shall go and I can lick the bowl. I hope there shall be sticky pudding for afters! *Mi favorito! Adiós, pequeños. Hasta la vista por cena!*"

The elemental flipped tail and hat and disappeared in a blue twinkle.

Udo looked triumphantly at me, and I looked woefully back. I didn't want to be eaten any more than I wanted to disappear to Nowhere. Would Paimon turn us on a spit like pigs? Boil us in a bag like pudding? The Huitzils sacrifice their enemies and make tamales with their ground-up bones, and mix their blood into hot chocolate and drink it. I thought of the Quetzals tearing at Boy Hansgen's bloody heart—

"I'll get the window if you get the sheets," Udo said. "We can tie them together and lower ourselves down, like the Dainty Pirate did when he was escaping from the Angeles calaboose."

My neck began to tingle.

"Udo—"

And then came the ominous sound of heavy footsteps in the hall.

35

THE WARDROBE.
A BALLROOM. ON THE RUN.

Paimon!" Udo gurgled. We clutched each other like a couple of shavetails, which didn't help a darn thing, but somehow Udo's grip was reassuring. If I would be eaten, at least I would not be eaten alone.

The door handle rattled. "Madama? Sieur Landaðon?"

"The wardrobe," Udo suggested in a strangled whisper.

Somehow we managed to stumble across the room to the wardrobe without making a huge amount of noise. Lucky for us it was so big. Despite its being stuffed full of clothing, we were both able to squeeze inside and pull the door shut behind us. We crawled as far back as we could, pulling the clothing over us, hoping for cover.

"I get points for being right," Udo hissed. "Next time maybe you'll listen to me—"

"Shush."

As the door creaked open, we froze, barely breathing in the lavender-scented mustiness. I surely hoped that Paimon could not see well in the dark, but I knew of course that he could. We huddled in agony, listening to the heavy tread enter the room.

"It is time for dinner," Paimon rumbled. Then, puzzled, "Madama? Sieur Landaðon?"

In my mind's eye, I could imagine it quite clearly: Paimon looking down in surprise at the messy bed, then lumbering about the room, lamp held high, examining each shadow for our cowering selves. He'd look under the bed, which of course would be innocent of us. He'd peer on top of the hard wooden canopy, for which he, naturally, would not need a ladder. He'd peek behind the billowing curtains; nope, we weren't there, either. We weren't crouched behind the fire screen; neither were we huddled inside the large clothespress at the foot of the bed, nor dangling by our sweaty hands from the window sill. That left only one place where we could be, and I could picture that, too, with disturbing vividness: the wardrobe door flung wide, ruffling clothes, awful hungry roar, claws that catch, jaws that bite.

I crabbed through the clothing, pushing at the heavy folds in a panic, my wheeling arms colliding with something solid yet crunchy – Udo's nose, I was later to discover. Fighting the heavy fabric felt disturbingly like drowning, and what little air I could squeeze into my lungs was stale and flat. Then I ran into something woodenly hard: the back of the wardrobe. There was no place else to go. We were trapped.

"Madama?" Clothing rustled and moved on a current of cold fresh air. "Sieur, what are you—"

"♀⊞⊁⚘⚹!"

Like before, the Gramatica Word popped into my brain and out of my mouth. It tasted like violets, and it whirled and gave off tiny purple sparks like fireflies. The bottom of the wardrobe fell away, and we were falling.

I landed with a hard thump, although something soft cushioned my fall. This softness was, of course, Udo, who swore at my weight and pushed me off him. I lay on my back, panting heavily. Above, a ceiling came into focus, painted with a riotous battle scene: screaming horses, spraying blood, clouds of smoke, and hacking swords.

"Pithfathe Psythopomp," Udo said, somewhat muffled. "I dink you broke by dose."

I sat up. There was just enough light to see that Udo's poor nose was a little spigot of blood, but it otherwise didn't seem too damaged. I shook out my slightly sticky hankie and tipped Udo's head back. After a few seconds of pressure (me) and grumbling (him), the bleeding subsided and we were able to take stock of our surroundings.

The grey light showed us to be in a wide room, bereft of furniture or other décor. One long wall of windows from floor to ceiling looked out over a pale silvery sea. Waves crashed out of the darkness, hammering on the windows as though they wanted to be let in.

The opposite wall was one long mirror, reflecting both the pearly water and the rumpled forms of Udo and me. A huge fireplace – big enough to roast an entire reg-iment – filled the southern wall; the northern wall sank down into an orchestra pit.

"I think this must be the Ballroom of the Battle for the City of Califa," Udo said, "which is good, because it's not too far from the Saloon of Embarrassment of Riches. Though how we got here, I don't know. Where did you learn that Word, Flora?"

"It just popped into my head. Come on – we gotta keep moving. We have to get that Verb, and then get Bonzo and Flynn and get out of here."

"So now she listens and believes. Will we leave my hat behind? I loved that hat."

"Your hat is a casualty of war, Udo. We all have to make sacrifices, and that hat is yours."

"You are a hard woman, Flora Fyrdraaca," Udo said, and he grinned a little bravado grin to show me that he didn't really care about the hat, he was just trying to sound cool. "Come on. That door should lead to the Hallway of Indefinable Munificence, and then it's just a short way to the Riches place."

A door was cleverly recessed into one of the panels of mirror at the far end of the room. It gave easily under my hand and swung open to reveal an ornate hallway, plastered with clustering vines and drooping tree branches, now dusty and dull. The coast was clear; there was no sign of any hungry denizen.

Pausing midway down the hallway, Udo asked nervously, "Do you hear footsteps?"

I did hear footsteps, and not just that, but my neck was prickling again, as it had before. Somehow I knew that little prickle was Paimon, hot on our trail.

"Come on!"

We ran. Ahead of us the hallway ended in an arch and plunged down a tunnel-like flight of stairs. The risers were made of white marble swirled through with pale green streaks, and so, too, were the walls, which curved up to meet a low ceiling. Down down down we galloped, ten stairs, twenty stairs, fifty, a hundred. Down down, deeper into the green twilight that was emanating from the marble itself, a cold watery light like coldfire. The smell of the sea and the distant surge of water.

Nini Mo says that most courage comes from being too tired and hungry to be afraid any more. If exhaustion and hunger were the hallmarks of courage, then I was the bravest person that ever lived. Yet, I didn't feel brave. I only felt sick and lost and like I had been hung out to dry in a rainstorm. Only Udo's painful grip was keeping me moving, that and the prickling on my neck that was growing more prickly by the minute. I put a hand out to touch the wall; it felt as warm as flesh, and it was vibrating slightly with the heaviness of Paimon's footsteps.

"I hope there's an elevator to take us back up," Udo said. "Going down ain't bad, but I don't relish climbing back."

"If Paimon catches us, I suppose he'll carry us back up," I said breathlessly. "I hope there's another way out."

"There's no way out but through," Udo said helpfully. "Hurry up, Flora, you are dragging."

"I'm coming, I'm coming," I puffed. Behind us the footsteps had grown louder and more rapid. Ahead of us, the stairs finally ended at an arched iron gate, its lintel twined with undulating luminescent letters that spelled out:

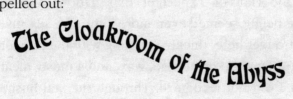

The Cloakroom of the Abyss

36

DEAD GENERALS.
DARK SPACES. CAUGHT.

Another rotunda, whose diameter was much smaller than the Hall of Expectant Expectations and yet whose height seemed even more lofty. The sea smell was stronger here, thickly mingling with the pungent smell of Opanopex incense, wax, and a musty meaty odour I did not recognize. Through the still hush, I fancied I could hear the low sweeping sounds of the surf.

The centre of the room was occupied by a small wooden boat beached upon a tall plinth draped in stiff red satin that obscured the boat's interior. A flickering lantern hung off the stern, and its bow took the form of a sinuous woman, her curved form and outstretched arms rising out of the wood, weed-green hair slick against her white sides. In the calm light, her eyes flickered with life and her red lips looked fresh and wet. She was, I realized, twin to the carved mermaid in the Bedchamber of Downward Dreaming.

The prickling on my neck was gone. "We lost him."

"How can you tell?" Udo asked.

"I just *know*. I don't know how but I do. I can feel him somehow when he is near, and I don't feel him now."

"Well, that's good, because I don't see any obvious way out other than the way we came, and if that way were blocked, we'd be pegged for sure."

"It's clear – he's gone – but I have to sit a minute, Udo, before I can go up those stairs again. I'm starving, too." I sat down on the bottom step and rested my head on my knees. My tummy was burning and gurgling, and my head felt as dizzy as a dust devil.

"I'm surprised that you can think of food when you are so close to being chow yourself."

"Leave it alone, Udo."

"Flora, come and look at this."

I looked up to see that Udo had paused in front of one of the alcoves. "I can't."

"Flora – I'm serious. Come on."

I slogged myself to my feet. The alcove contained a bier, and sleeping on the bier was a sallow young girl holding a wizened baby, so shrunken its face looked like a skull. An inscription on the arch of the alcove said: SERENTHA FRYDONIA HAÐRAAÐA & FRYDONIE HAÐRAAÐA.

"Why would you sleep down here?" I asked.

"She's not asleep, I think," Udo answered. "She's

dead. The Cloakroom of the Abyss is the Haðraaða family crypt."

Oh ugh and disgusting and yucky-yuck, but Udo was right. Each of the alcoves was occupied by someone who was sleeping a sleep from whence they would never awake. An old woman in a frothy blue dress, holding a perfect round orange in her hands: GEORGIANA HAÐRAAÐA I. A saucy little pug dog lying on a blue velvet pillow, its pink tongue poking from a slightly open black muzzle: HER GLORY'S FANCIFUL SHADOW. A man in full armour, his face hidden by a pig-snouted helmet, a sharp sword balanced on the length of his body: ALBANY BANASTRE BILSKINIR OV HAÐRAAÐA.

The bodies looked so alive, so perfectly asleep. It was hard to believe that our whispers would not wake them up. But they made me shiver. No matter how lifelike they appeared, it didn't change the fact that these pristine figures, so painted and curled and gussied up, were dead. They were cheats, facsimiles, and somehow it seemed indecent to allow them to lie there so exposed.

"I hope my hair looks that good when I have been dead three hundred years," Udo remarked, looking at an elegant old man in a flowery kimono and stiff elaborate upswept curls. EOS SABRE, according to the inscription.

The next alcove had no body, only an ivory-handled hunting whip, its slender snaky hunting lash twined around a copper-red braid, lying like a substitute effigy on the sangyn marble slab. The arch above had no inscription.

"I'll bet that one was for the Butcher Brakespeare – General Haðraaða Segunda. It's 'cause she didn't have any kids that Paimon got left all alone, I suppose," Udo said. "Wasn't her nickname Azote, and doesn't that mean 'whip'? I suppose there was nothing left of her to bury after the Huitzils ate her." He turned back toward the boat in the centre of the room. "And that leaves . . . who do you think, behind those curtains?"

"I don't know and I don't care, Udo," I said. "I'm ready. Let's get going. I am so tired now, I just want it over with. Fading, or restoration, I don't care, I just want to be done."

"Come on, Flora. This may be our only time ever to be here. Aren't you the least bit curious?"

"No, Udo. I'm not. I'm just hungry and tired. We still don't have that Verb yet. Come on."

"You are no fun," Udo said, and then craftily: "Or are you scared?"

"Udo." I moaned. "We don't have time for this."

"I think Flora is scared. Flora is scared!" Udo sang gleefully. "I dare you to climb up there and look."

"I don't have to take your stupid dare, Udo, or play your stupid games. Come on, if you are so hot on it, then I dare *you* to look."

"You can't block a dare with a dare, Flora. Come on, I triple-dog dare you!"

There's no block for a triple-dog dare, and no

backing out, either. And no point in further hesitation. When you must strike, strike hard, Nini Mo said, and strike them to the Abyss. I walked over to the boat – which, closer up, I realized was actually a fancy catafalque, not a boat at all – then climbed up the little flight of stairs and pulled aside the long billowing drape.

A prone figure lay under the slick shroud of a flag, not Califa's national flag, but a banner of sangyn silk that had no ensign. With one tentative hand, I gingerly picked up the edge of the fabric, drew it back, revealing a white face, a wide chest, and two folded hands.

I didn't need an inscription to know who this was. His portrait hangs in every civic office and schoolroom in the City, and though now that famous face was white and still, it was unmistakable. A tiny little shiver ran up my spine and into my tummy, which began to quiver.

Banastre Haðraaða, the Warlord's Fist.

"Hardhands," Udo breathed, now leaning behind me. "Look at him. He's a real stunner."

Hardhands was beautiful, it was true, but it was an icy-cold beauty, glassy, and I don't think that was just because he was dead. His hair, pulled back into a long braid tucked under his dark red officer's sash, was as white as snow. His taut lips were the palest pink, and his eyelashes lay like black feathers against his paper-pale skin. Long white hands with sangyn-coloured nails were folded on his chest, as though they had once clutched something – a sword, perhaps, or maybe a pistol – but now they lay empty, slightly cupped. He wore the sangyn-red Skinner uniform, its long sleeves trailing off the edge of the plinth, spilling to the floor like blood, but his cheeks were not marred by the Skinner scars.

"He looks pretty good for a guy whose wife shot him in the throat with an arrow," Udo said.

"No one ever proved that Butcher Brakespeare really shot him in the throat—" I stopped, caught suddenly by a glance at my hand, which still held back the curtain.

"Udo," I quavered.

The knobby lines of my bones shone through my flesh, like rocks at the bottom of a clear mountain stream.

"Pigface Pogocrud," Udo said. "Don't panic, Flora – we still have time, I swear. It will be okay. Come on."

He pulled the flag up over that cold beautiful face, and I was glad to see it disappear. It was exactly the kind of face that could haunt you in your dreams. And my dreams were crowded enough as it was.

As we clambered down the tiny stairs and struggled to put the drapes back as they were before, there came the faint sound of footsteps. A voice drifted down the stairwell, our only way out.

The iron gate at the top of the stairwell squeaked as unseen hands pushed it open. We wasted no time frozen in fear, but scrambled about, trying to find a safe spot. The funeral urns by the doorway were far too big; the little alcoves were not big enough, and I didn't fancy getting too friendly with any of the pallid dead.

"Hey," Udo hissed. For a second, I couldn't find him, then saw a frantically waving hand and part of Udo's head, poking out from underneath the drapes that hid the bottom of Hardhands's catafalque. "There's plenty of room – hurry!"

The footsteps were closer now, ringing like bells, and I thought that I could hear the ominous scrape of claws on the marble. I skidded across the floor, almost banging myself right into the edge of the catafalque. It was a tight squeeze, sliding underneath, but I made it, sucking in a lungful of dry dusty air. Udo dropped the drape, and again we were in pitch-blackness.

The space was cramped and the stale air tasted of sickly-sweet decay. The thought dropped into my brain that perhaps the figure above was merely an effigy, and down here, bony and sharp, was the real thing, twisted sinews and gritty bones, and perhaps it did not want to share its space. I buried my face in the back of Udo's jacket, trying to choke that thought down.

The footsteps tapped, tapped, tapped, stopped.

Tapped, tapped, stopped, tapped, stopped.

"Ave?" The voice, echoing off the marble, sounded as though it came from behind me, and I almost jumped out of my skin. I clutched at Udo, trying not to make a move, a sound, a rustle, a breath. We lay there in terrified silence, and only the mouthful of cloth I was biting kept me from screaming.

"Ave? Who's there?"

It was not Paimon's bell-like voice that spoke these words. But if not Paimon, who? The voice sounded distantly familiar. The footsteps came closer and I felt a swish of air as the drapes twitched.

"How about you, you old bastard?" the voice asked, and stairs squeaked. "Have you been gibbering around again? Snapperhead son of a bitch, it does my heart glad to see you lying there like a cold stiff log. I only rue that I was not the one who stretched you there, tinpot Pigface—"

The swearing stopped, and it was my fault. Udo's hair was tickling my nose, and though I tried to hold back the sneeze, I could not. It was a small sneeze, as muffled in Udo's back as I could make it. I held my breath and Udo pinched me, as though I needed any reminder to be quiet.

"Well now," the voice said. "I never heard of a ghost with a cold."

I stifled another sneeze, and then suddenly a hard hand was on my foot, yanking. I couldn't help it, my sneeze turned into a scream, and though I kicked and grabbed and Udo grabbed on to me, the grip was like iron and would not let me go. I slithered along the floor, underneath the drape, and then I was squirming and shrieking and kicking in the open air.

37

CAUGHT AGAIN. WHERE? PAIMON'S HAT.

What have we here, then? A little ghost? Or a little spy?"
The man with the grip inspected me at arm's length. It
was a hard grip and a long arm, and the man's face was
not friendly, though there was something familiar about
it. In his free hand, he carried a lantern, and this he
held up so its light shone on my face.

"Let her go," Udo said heroically, taking the wrong
cue to exit his refuge.

"Two little spies! A matched set." The man laughed,
and by this laugh, I knew him. It wasn't as hysterical as
the last time I'd heard it, but it was otherwise the same.

"Poppy!" I squeaked, for it *was* Poppy. A Poppy
strangely different, but Poppy all the same. No
mourning band was painted across his eyes, and
without its smudging, he looked younger, his face fuller,
less skeletal. The Skinner scars on his cheeks looked

vivid, fresh. His eyes were clear and steady, and the arm that held up the lantern showed no sign of injury or constraint.

And his hair! A copper-red braid the exact shade of a brand-new glory hung over his left shoulder and trailed down to tuck into the sash of his dressing gown. As long as I could remember, Poppy's silver hair had been cut razor short, almost to his skull. Mamma and Idden are both blonde, but my hair is red, and now I knew why.

"Poppy! It's me, Flora!" I cried.

"What are you doing here, Hotspur?" Udo asked.

Poppy squinted. "You know me?"

"Of course we do. You are Reverdy Anacreon Fyrdraaca, called Hotspur," Udo answered.

"Ayah so, but who are you?"

"But it's me, Flora – me. Your daughter, Flora, and Udo, too. See, it's Udo. Don't you know us?"

Poppy said grimly, "It is true that I have a daughter named Flora, but she is only six years old, and home, tucked safely into bed, I hope. And I don't know any Udo." Poppy let me go. "I think Paimon should explain what is going on here—"

"No!" Udo and I shouted, almost together. "Not Paimon."

"Look, Poppy," I said, desperately. "Look!" I yanked at my collar, and pulled out my identification badge. Mamma insists that Idden and I (and the dogs, too) wear our badges all the time. One side has my name;

the other, the Crackpot seal. It is to identify us in case we are ever lost. I guess I was pretty lost now.

Poppy took the badge and held it in the lantern light. "'Flora Nemain Fyrdraaca ov Fyrdraaca,'" he read, and then looked at me, wonderingly. "I recognize that badge; I had it made when you were born. Flora! Why are you so old? What happened?"

"I don't know, Poppy. We got lost in the House, running from Paimon, Udo and me, and somehow now we are here, and you are, too—"

Udo interrupted, "I think that time is out of whack here. Paimon said he'd slow it down, but maybe he's turned it too far back or moved it forward or something."

"How old are you, Flora?" Poppy asked.

"Thirteen – I mean, fourteen. Tomorrow," I answered.

"Look at you, Flora! Your hair was so fair, and now it's so red, and what on earth are you wearing? Is fashion so bad in the future? Come and kiss me, baby."

Normally I don't like to hug Poppy, but this time I went to his embrace willingly. Poppy's arms were strong and warm, and he smelled of pipe weed and bay rum. I kissed him, his cheek scratchy beneath my lips, and hugged him so tightly that he gurgled in mock alarm. He said, over my head, "And who, darling boy, are you?"

"He's my best friend, Poppy. Udo Moxley Landaðon ov Sorrel," I said into Poppy's soft woolen chest.

"Sorrel? Moxley has a son – wait until I tell him! He'll be so tickled!"

Udo said in a strangled voice, "My father! You know my father?" Udo's birth father was killed before Udo was born, and though he still has two fathers, I think it bothers him that he never got a chance to meet the one who engendered him.

"Of course. Damn, if only Moxley weren't at the War Department with the General, we could march straight up and say hello. I'm sure he'd be thrilled to meet you."

"My father was Buck's adjutant?" Udo said, bewildered.

"Buck – a general!" Poppy laughed. "I told her she'd never escape family fate! General Fyrdraaca – that's hilarious. No, not Buck, but General Haðraaða Segunda. Your father and I are her aides, which is why we live here at Bilskinir. And let me tell you, I've had some pretty strange things happen to me in this House. Once, I was on the way to the loo in the middle of the night, and a set of tiger fire irons chased me – and they would have got me, too, if I hadn't managed to beat them down with a hat stand. But never this strange as to meet my own grown daughter. Tell me, why on earth were you hiding under Hardhands's bier?"

"We were running from Paimon – he is going to eat us!" Udo answered. "He's still going to eat us if he catches us. You've got to help us, Hotspur!"

"Don't worry about Paimon, I can handle him," Poppy answered. "Now, darling, don't cry."

I couldn't help it. It was all too much. To be so hungry and then so full and then so hungry again. Being chased, hiding, and now this Poppy, tall and true and beautiful, and talking very fast but not the least bit crazy. Poppy as he once was, as I had never known him. Sane. Beautiful. Normal.

"Poppy," I gasped. "I'm in terrible trouble—"

"Ha! I doubt that any trouble you are in is any worse than any trouble I have been in. I am the troublemaker in this family, I'll have you know!"

Udo said, "Well, it is pretty bad, Hotspur."

Poppy squeezed me tightly. "I'll be the judge of that. Did you accidentally burn down the Redlegs' hay shack?"

"No—"

"Did you get caught stealing the Warlord's best hat for a dare?"

"No—"

"Did you lose twenty-five thousand divas at whist?"

"No—"

"Well, then, my title remains secure," Poppy said triumphantly.

I moaned. "It's worse than all that. Mamma shall kill me if she finds out—"

Udo interrupted, "Look – Flora's disappearing. We don't really have time to explain. We came to Bilskinir to get one of the Semiote Verbs – it's the only thing that will fix her, but Paimon won't help us."

"We'll see about that," Poppy said grimly. "If Flora is

336

in trouble, Paimon will be helpful, or he'll be sorry. *Paimon!*"

"No!" Udo and I yelled together. "He'll eat us—"

"Ha! I'd like to see him try to eat my child! *Paimon!*" Poppy hollered.

My neck began to prickle. With an audible pop, the air before us whirled into a Vortex, whose diameter grew wider and wider, until Paimon stepped out of the nimbus of blue coldfire.

Udo gave a little shriek, a squeaky little mouselike sound that didn't sound heroic at all. My own scream didn't sound particularly heroic, either. But I couldn't help it.

Paimon had taken off his hat.

38

PAIMON'S SUGGESTION.

Paimon's hat had only hinted at what lay beneath its shadowy brim: a peek of blue moustachio, a twinkle of tusks. But without the hat, the full monstrousness of Paimon was revealed in all its monstrousness. Two great curling horns, as thick as my neck, sprang from a broad blue forehead. Eyebrows as tufty as mice shadowed round blue eyes, whose pupils were narrow and slitty, like a goat's. Silver spectacles balanced on a leathery black ox-like nose. His jaw, big enough to chomp me up in one bite, supported the enormous tusks that sprang from either side of his enormous mouth, filled with equally enormous white teeth, as large as domino tiles. Long fringy ears, somewhat like a cocker spaniel's, framed this grotesque face, their prettiness making the rest of Paimon's face seem all the more horrible in comparison.

When he saw us and Poppy, Paimon's eyebrows lowered and his mouth opened, roaringly: "Major Fyrdraaca, what are *you* doing here? Flora, Udo, I have been looking everywhere for you."

"Poppy! Don't let him eat us!" I cried. Udo and I had scurried behind Poppy at the first sight of Paimon, and now I peered around his back, not able to take my eyes off the denizen. I had never seen anyone so big or so blue. The Quetzals were the marriage of bird and human, and each taken alone would be fine. It was this unnatural combination that caused their grotesqueness. But Paimon was like nothing else I had seen before, the monster from a nightmare, the horror under your bed, the thing that gets you on the way to the loo in the middle of the night.

"Eat you!" Paimon said in dismay. "Eat you! Where did you get the idea I would eat you?"

Udo answered, "That water elemental – Alfonzo – *said* you were going to eat us."

Paimon rolled his golf-ball-sized eyes and looked a little hurt. "Alfonzo is extremely untrustworthy. You should not listen to him. I have no intention of eating anyone."

"Never mind the eating, Paimon," Poppy said. "What the hell is going on here? Why is Flora here, strangely aged, and why is she disappearing? And why won't you help her?"

Paimon sighed, a sigh that was almost a roar. "There has been some terrible misunderstanding. I knew I was thrown off balance, but I didn't think it was that bad. Madama Fyrdraaca's current instability is disruptive, and this disruption has made your times overlap. I apologize for the confusion; this is really not good. You should not have met. It's bad precedent. You must go back, Major Fyrdraaca."

"No matter, that. It's only eight years," Poppy said impatiently. "We have met, and now I want you to help Flora. Give her what she needs."

Eight years? This could not be Poppy eight years ago. I remembered that Poppy well. That Poppy had ruined the slumber party I had for my sixth birthday by climbing on to the roof of the stables and howling like a coyote all night long. This was not that Poppy. With horror, I realized he thought I was the other Flora. He was trying to save the First Flora. He didn't know me at all.

"Poppy, I'm—" I started to say, but Paimon interrupted.

"What she asks for is useless. The solution she has suggested will not solve her problem." Paimon's words were directed at Poppy, but he aimed a glinty blue twinkle at me that clearly meant *Not another word*, and so glinty was that twinkle that I had to obey.

"And what exactly is this problem?" Poppy asked.

I will do the explaining, said that glinty blue twinkle, and explain Paimon did – an explanation that was basically the truth, with one big exception: He didn't mention that Valefor was banished, only that he and I had become intertwined and I was attempting now to extricate myself, before I disappeared. And he did not explain that I was the *Second* Flora.

If only that blue glint would glint elsewhere, I would protest, but then it occurred to me that Paimon did not want Poppy to know the details of the future, and I saw that was probably right. Would I want to know that my future was lost, that my sanity hung by a thread, that only failure and pain lay ahead? Probably not. But still, I wished that Poppy would know it was *me*.

When the story – still woeful for all that it was now shorter – was over, Poppy shook his head. "That Valefor is a tricky one. Watch him like a hawk. He's sweet, mostly, but boy, can he be trouble when he wants to be. Buck has to keep close tabs on him. Well, obviously, we need to call Buck. She'd get Val back in line pronto."

Udo said, "Buck's away, and she won't be back in time to save Flora. By the time she returns, it will be too late."

"Now, I could send Buck a letter. She'd get it and be forewarned about the future," Poppy said.

"Ayah, but you didn't, because if you had, then she'd know already," Udo pointed out. "And she wouldn't have gone anywhere."

"Ayah, that is true enough," Poppy admitted. "Paimon, can you slow Flora's evaporation down? Keep her from disappearing until Buck returns? Don't worry, honey. Hold on."

Poppy reached out to me, to pull me back into his embrace, but his arms went through me as though I were made of smoke, diaphanous and gauzy.

"Poppy!" I gurgled. I tried to clutch him, but my reach was just as tenuous.

"I can see through her now!" Udo yelped.

A geyser of hysteria was building inside me and about to blow, and then two large white flannel arms pulled and held me tightly to a hard silk chest. For a second, I could barely breathe, in that barrel-chested embrace, then I realized that I didn't have to breathe at all.

"I don't understand," Poppy said. "How can you touch her and I can't, Paimon?"

Paimon answered, "I can manifest in the Waking World, but I am actually of Elsewhere. I am manifested in both the here and the now – her now and your here. Thus she is clear to me."

"But I want to be in Udo's here, or Poppy's here," I gasped.

"Paimon, you are the oldest House in the City – you have to be able to do something," Poppy demanded.

"I have done all that I can do," Paimon said, "though I have a suggestion to make. But I do not think it will meet with your favour."

Poppy said, "I don't know that this is the time to be

squeamish. We shall do what we shall have to do. Let loose the advice, Paimon."

"There is only one person in Califa who can help Flora."

Poppy said impatiently, "Who is that? Don't be all spooky about it."

"Lord Axacaya," Paimon answered.

39

DESPERATION. DECISION. DEPARTURE.

Of all the suggestions Paimon could have made, this was the worst. My hope, which had sprung up when Poppy had proved to be so calm, so logical, so sure that we could figure something out, deflated like a punctured balloon. *Oblivion is only one step away*, Nini Mo said, and bitterly now did I understand what she meant. Perhaps there truly was no hope, and I should just give up. But I looked at Poppy, so straight and tall, and Udo, so faithful and true, and I did not want to give up, for them. I did not want to lose them.

"Axacaya!" Poppy echoed. "That tin-potted backdoor hornswoggling drummer? That jabber-jawed mincing malicho? He wouldn't help his own mother stay afloat in a stormy sea."

"He is the greatest adept in the City," Paimon said.

"He himself straddles the Line, with one foot on either side of the divide between the Waking World and Elsewhere. He is the only adept alive who has crossed the Abyss and returned again. If there is a way to save Flora, he shall know it."

I looked at Udo and Udo looked back at me, his jaw clenching. I knew he was remembering what I was remembering: Boy Hansgen's death. And wondering whether or not Lord Axacaya knew of our involvement in his failed rescue. How could we ask Lord Axacaya's help after that?

"But Lord Axacaya is Mamma's greatest enemy," I said weakly. "Why would he help me?"

"You do not know until you ask," Paimon said. "And do not think that your situation only affects yourself. You and Valefor are being pulled back into the Abyss – the denizen of one of the great Houses of the City is disintegrating. This affects all the Houses, and not happily, either."

"Sod Valefor – what about Flora?" Udo said rudely. "He can go if he wants. It is her we have to save."

"They are the same now," Paimon said. "As one goes, so, too, the other, unless they can be disconnected."

"And I hate like hell to ask Axacaya for anything," Poppy said doubtfully. "I doubt if either Buck or the General would like me to have that kind of a debt."

"For Pigface sake, Hotspur," Udo burst out. "Do you think that Buck is gonna like it if Flora evaporates?

What's she gonna say to that and if we could have done something to stop it and didn't? I'll go to Axacaya myself if I have to, and I'll *make* him help, Flora. You can count on it."

I blinked. When I looked straight at Udo, he was the same old Udo, but then when I blinked, it seemed that in his place stood a tall broad man, tanned from the sun, with fierce blue eyes, his waist girded with a heavy gun belt. Then I blinked again, and there was just scrawny Udo standing there. When I looked long at Poppy, I saw a skinny boy, pale face free of scars, ropes of blazing red braids looped about his neck and shoulders. Another blink, and there was Poppy, looking unhappy and lighting a cigarillo again. I couldn't believe how beautiful he was.

"We have no choice," the man who was Udo said, glowering.

The boy who was Poppy rubbed his face and blew a tendril of smoke. "Ayah, you are right, of course, Paimon."

Paimon, no matter how many times I blinked, looked the same as ever, towering and monumental, and now damp with my tears. I looked down at my hands; they were like glass, and all trembly. Never to touch Udo again, never to pet Flynnie. Poppy had smelled so deliciously of bay rum and pipe weed; Udo of cinnamon soap and muffins. Now I could smell nothing. I would never smell anything again, not wet-dog Flynnie, or Mamma's flowery hair pomade, or oranges. Never taste coffee, or maple-nut muffins, or chocolate. Paimon's coat was soft beneath my face, but he had no heartbeat. I could distantly hear Udo and Poppy arguing, but already their voices were becoming dim, and soon I would hear nothing at all. I would float through Elsewhere, like a ghost, and gradually even Elsewhere would fade and I would grow dimmer and dimmer and then be gone.

What could Lord Axacaya do to me compared with that? He could refuse to help me. Would I be worse than I was now? Nini Mo said that you must *dare, win, or disappear.*

"I will go see Lord Axacaya," I said in a small voice. And then, when no one paid any attention, I summoned up all the loudness I had left in me and said, in what turned out to be a shout, "I will go see Lord Axacaya!"

"An' you will," Poppy said firmly. "But not alone. I shall go with you – I wager I can influence Axacaya to assistance."

"And me, too," Udo said.

Paimon shook his massive head, his ruff flying. "I am sorry, but you cannot, either of you. Flora is almost gone into Elsewhere, and there you cannot follow her, neither of you being adepts. I will escort her, but you both must return to your proper places."

"I will go," I said. "Udo, you should go home, take Flynnie and Bonzo. Maybe you can stall Mamma, if you have to."

Udo protested, but what else could he do? Soon he would not be able to see me at all, and he could not follow me Elsewhere. So he agreed.

"But I do not want to have to explain to Buck what has happened," he warned. "Do not leave me holding the bag, ayah, Flora? It would be pretty mean to float off into the Abyss and leave poor me to get walloped. Ayah so?"

"Ayah so," I promised Udo, and hoped very much that I could hold to this promise. "And don't forget to feed the dogs and to let them out. They are probably explosive by now."

"As long as you are still bossy, Flora," Udo said, "there is hope. How do I get out of here, Paimon? Also, can I have my hat back?"

"Go back up the stairs and I shall meet you and escort you to my gates," Paimon answered.

At the bottom of the steps, Udo paused and looked back at Poppy. "Hotspur? My father – could you tell him . . ."

"Tell him what?" Poppy asked, when Udo didn't continue.

"Tell him I said hello," Udo said quickly and, turning about, disappeared up the stairs and into the darkness.

And so Udo was gone, and I hoped with all my heart that I would see him again, that this was not the last time for us. And I resolved, if I did return, to be a bit less snarky about his foibles, and also to give him the fuchsia umbrella I had got for my birthday the year previous and which he had been coveting. It is funny the trivial things you can think about, even when the situation is dire.

"Give us a minute, Paimon," Poppy ordered. "And then I will let Flora go."

"A minute only, Major," Paimon said. "We have a long way to go."

Poppy crouched down so that we were more of the same height. I had never realized how toweringly tall Poppy really was; my Poppy's permanent list made him seem shorter.

He said, "It is funny, young Flora, you seem too serious to be my child. Even transparent, I can tell that you are not a sunshiny girl. And you were so happy as a child, always laughing and singing. Flora . . . why did you not tell me what was wrong? I know you did not, or you should not be here now. For had I known, I would not have let it get this far. And yet – I know now, and still I did not help you when you needed me."

"Poppy . . ."

He looked at me gravely. "I wasn't born in a barn yesterday. I can tell that Paimon has withheld information from me. No doubt he doesn't want me to know the future, and if he doesn't want that, then I can only guess it isn't good. And yet, it cannot be all so bad, Flora, for you are grown so beautiful and strong. But I think there can only be one reason why I would not help you – but you needn't fear telling me. I do not fear dying, Flora. I expect it. Fyrdraacas don't die in their beds. I only hope that I make a good death. And I'm sorry that it means I will not be there for you. Will not see you grow up."

"Poppy . . . it's not that—" I choked.

"And even now I cannot be much help to you. And for that I am sorry, too. But you may trust Paimon, and, Flora, you must trust your mother, too. She loves you and Idden more than anything, and she will never let you down. I remember when you were born – you insisted on entering the world feet first, with the cord wrapped around your neck. You should have died, most babies would have, but you were too tough then, and you are too tough now – a true Fyrdraaca."

"Poppy, you don't understand –" I sobbed, "Poppy –"

Paimon chimed closer and cut me off before I could say more. "We must go, Major Fyrdraaca. I'm sorry."

"All right, Paimon. Now listen to me, Flora. Everything is going to be all right. Axacaya is spooky, but he is just a man. Remember that. He is just a man. But you are a Fyrdraaca. Remember Barbizon?"

"Ayah." I snivelled.

"Had she climbed off her pedestal when you left Crackpot?"

"No."

"Well, then, see, the trouble ain't so bad. Come on, girlie, don't cry – it only spoils your aim."

"We must go," Paimon said urgently. "Come."

Poppy kissed the air above my forehead, and I kissed it back. "Cierra Fyrdraaca, Flora."

"Cierra Fyrdraaca, Poppy." Paimon yanked me by the arm and sailed through the doorway. I turned back and caught a quick glimpse of Poppy, framed tall and straight, his hair glowing in the lamplight, and then he was gone.

40

A Balloon. Bath Time. Looking Good.

I stumbled after Paimon, with only his grip keeping me going. He dragged me onward, through endless hallways, up endless stairs, around endless corners, through endless galleries. I could barely keep up, huffing and puffing like a whirligig, then I stumbled over a riser, flew up in the air, and drifted like a kite, controlled by the firm grip of Paimon's hand. Now I really was bobbing along like a balloon, and it was actually kind of fun. Like swimming without worrying about getting water up your nose or some snapperdog cannonballing on to your back and almost drowning you. I bounced and flew, feet trailing behind, hair whipping, and the wind was such a blur in my face that I could not see a thing.

Finally, we stopped, and when Paimon let go of my hand, I floated to the ground with a gentle thump, and there I lay happily. The carpet was as soft as grass. I blinked and saw that it *was* grass, sweet and warm, dappled with white daisies and egg-yolk-colored buttercups. I flopped over on my back and looked up at the periwinkle sky, spangled with little green butterflies. A fresh breeze ruffled my hair.

"That was cool," I said. "Can we do that some more?"

"No," Paimon intoned. "You must get ready to visit Lord Axacaya. You cannot go to him dressed like that."

"I am afraid, Paimon," I said smally.

"Why is that?"

"Lord Axacaya hates Mamma, and his Quetzals tore out the heart of Boy Hansgen. What if his Quetzals want to do that to me?"

"They will not. Come, Flora."

I sat up reluctantly. "Why are things shifting back and forth?"

"You are Elsewhere now," Paimon said. He rustled around in a tree trunk – no, a wardrobe – no, a tree trunk. It was awfully confusing. "Where things can be more than they appear."

"So that was Udo as a man that I saw?"

Paimon turned, clutching a mass of red froth to his chest. "Ayah."

"If that was Udo as a man, then that was Poppy as a boy? Why did I see Udo forward and Poppy back, instead of both back or both forward? That doesn't make sense." Nothing in this House made any sense. It was enough to make you sick. "I am confused, Paimon."

"Udo has no past and Major Fyrdraaca has no future."

I followed Paimon by a leafy bower, invitingly plump with pink pillows and a trailing canopy of roses and grapevines. The bower looked so cool and delicious that I wanted nothing more than to fling myself into its depths, lie among the poppies and rose petals, and dream of long languid rivers, of floating aimlessly in a narrow lulling punt, trailing my hand in the cool water, and drinking gin fizzies. Then I blinked again and saw the bower to be a large overstuffed bed, heaped with pink pillows and covered by a carved wooden lattice.

Paimon heaped the dress on a rock and held out a hand to me. "In you go. The water is perfect." I blinked, and a pool became a steamy bathtub filled with glimmering bubbles.

"Can you make things be one or the other?" I asked. "I am getting rather dizzy."

"You must focus, madama. In you go."

I decided that I liked the glade better, and with that decision, there was no more bouncing back and forth. I threw my clothes at Paimon, and the splash I made jumping in was so big that he got drippy and wet. I floated and spun in the soothing water, staring at the serene blue sky, until Paimon started scrubbing. No matter how hard I wiggled and complained, or even bit, his right hand was like iron and his left hand was like sandpaper, and by the time he was done I felt like a shrimp that had just been boiled and peeled. But, Pigface, was I clean!

"I thought I was discorporeal now. Why do I have to have a bath and change clothes if I have no real body?" I asked. "What's the point?"

"You are seeing things as you are used to seeing them, in corporeal form, so that they make sense to you. But what you are seeing are symbols. It is not your body that you are cleaning, but your true self. You cannot go to see Lord Axacaya with a grubby soul, can you?"

"No," I admitted. "I guess not."

"You must go to Lord Axacaya as a supplicant, but yet you wish him to understand that your request is an important and serious request, made respectfully. Therefore you must look serious and respectful."

Nini Mo says that to get something you must look as though you don't actually need it. If you look hopeless, even if you *are* hopeless, why would anyone help you out?

Paimon plucked me from the pool like I was a sodden tea bag, then wrapped me in a fluffy towel the size of the City before bearing me back to the bower. There I was slithered into a chemise, stuffed like a sausage into stays, and laced tighter than a drum.

"I can't breathe!" I puffed, as Paimon cinched the laces tighter. He almost yanked me off my feet, and I grabbed at a tree trunk for support.

"Do not hold your breath," he ordered. "You do not need to breathe here."

Paimon the Merciless continued to tug until I thought I would break in two, and before I could protest, he tossed a froth of vivid red over my head. I emerged from the rosy foam coughing and gasping, and when I was done choking and Paimon was done lacing and tucking, my cheeks were almost as red as the dress.

"I look like a bloody nightmare," I protested when I saw my filmy reflection in the mirror. "I cannot wear this to meet Lord Axacaya. I don't look serious or important at all."

The skirt was huge and fluffy, like a giant blown rose or a waft of cotton candy. Sleeves puffed like balloons from my elbows, but my shoulders and neck were chilly and bare, and the neckline was cut awfully low.

"You look very fine," Paimon said, slightly hurt. "I designed this dress myself, madama, and it suits you perfectly."

"But I look all fluffy!"

"You look grown-up." Paimon descended upon me, with a brush in one long hand and a sheaf of combs in the other. He twiddled and twirled and brushed and bouffanted. When he was done, my hair, normally so frizzy, was a sleek mass of curls hanging in perfect spirals down my back, caught by each ear with a spangled diamond clip. The hairbrush was replaced by maquillage brushes, which fluttered over my face like little butterflies, dipping and swirling colour on my eyelids, cheeks, and lips. Last, Paimon handed me crimson gloves, soft as butter, and then a fan case.

Two thin chains unwound into my hand, dangling from a heavy silver clip. The fan withdrew from the sheath easily and when I flipped my wrist, it unfurled with a snap. Paimon clipped the fan frog on to my sash so that it hung on my hip like a sabre or a holster.

"There, madama," Paimon said, proudly. "It has been a while since I have acted as a dresser. General Haðraaða was quite particular about his attire, but General Haðraaða Segunda was very careless with hers. I am pleased to see that I still have the touch. You look fine."

He flipped a full-length mirror out of Nowhere, and there I was, reflected in its silvery shimmer, and I did look fine. I wouldn't say I was beautiful, but I wasn't bad. Udo is right – it's amazing what a little maquillage can do for you, particularly if you don't lay it on with a trowel.

And Paimon was right, too – I felt a whole lot more confident about facing Lord Axacaya.

"I hope I am irresistible," I said.

"You will do," Paimon said, with satisfaction. "Come."

41

MANY ROOMS. MANY TIMES. ADVICE.

Now I discovered that if I gave a little skip and swished my buoyant skirt in bell-like fashion, I could glide for several feet, at least, before I needed another little push to send me aloft and forward again. It was like flying, only instead of wings I had the huge poofiness of my skirts to keep me moving.

Paimon wafted down an enormous stairway, wide enough to march an entire squad abreast, his shoes making a delicate tapping sound on the porphyry steps, and I floated down after him effortlessly. A little snake's head at the end of the banister winked at me as I sailed by.

"Don't dawdle," Paimon said over his shoulder. "We have a long way to go."

"How are we going to get there?" I whisked my skirts faster to catch up with him.

"You shall see. Come!"

A narrow greyhound slid up to me, rubbing his head on my skirts, and when I bent down to pet his soft head, another cold nose shoved its way into my hand – a slender red dog who was not Flynnie. The greyhound growled, and I thumped him once between the eyes with my finger. "I have two hands. I can pet you both."

Paimon turned, wafting disapproval. "Get down, Kria, and you get down as well, Parzival. You are going to get dog hair all over madama's dress. Madama, please do not encourage them."

"How come I can pet these dogs and I couldn't pet Flynnie and the others?"

"Because these dogs are dead," Paimon answered.

"You mean they are ghosts?" They looked pretty solid to me, and they felt pretty solid as well, although Parzival seemed a little bony.

"That's a colloquial term. But yes, ghosts, if you will."

"Poor things. I'll bet they get lonely being ghosts all the time."

Paimon gently took my arm and drew me away from the disappointed doggies, who fell into a trot behind us. "We must hurry, madama, we are late as it is."

"I'm sorry, Paimon," I said. "It is hard to concentrate. I feel all drifty and dreamy – like none of this is real."

"In the strictest sense of the Waking World, madama, none of this *is* real. Although in the strictest sense of Elsewhere, none of the Waking World is real. Elsewhere is a place of shifting and constant movement, and it takes a great deal of concentration to hold yourself together in it. However, you must try, or else you will drift so far into Elsewhere that even Lord Axacaya will not be able to help you back, for there will no longer be any you to return. That which was Flora will have splintered into a thousand tiny bits and scattered into the Abyss, and you will be gone for ever."

For ever. The word shivered through me, spreading coldness. I focused on the hard heat of the dog's head beneath my hand, and Paimon nodded approvingly. "That's better. Come. We must go through some of the most distant reaches of the House. You must stick close to me, madama. Should we lose each other, it may take me some time to find you again."

I nodded. Now that I was used to his face, Paimon didn't seem monstrous at all. His ears were so silky and soft-looking, and his eyes were filled with kindness. And he was such a pretty shade of blue, damson twilight, blueberry dawn. I clutched his hand tightly, and on we went, the two doggies close behind us.

Through a solarium, weaving in and around elegantly dressed people clutching wineglasses and eating little snacky things, their chattering voices far and distant like a melody on the wind.

Through the Ballroom of the Battle of Califa, now

filled with rows of narrow beds, white catafalques for silently suffering soldiers, pristine bandages dabbled with blood, the silence broken only by the occasional stifled sob.

Through a dining room, the clink of glasses and dull murmur of conversation in pale candlelight. I caught sight of a bobbing gold feather – Mamma, with a huge pregnant tummy that kept her from pulling in close to the table.

"That's Mamma," I said, trying to pull away from Paimon. But he refused to drop his grip.

"No, it's just a memory of your mother and a meal here she had many years ago," Paimon said, drawing me onward past the head of the table where a Skinner sat, looking as though she could chew glass.

Down a darkened hallway, past a small child in a white nightgown, sleepily clutching a plushy pink pig, rubbing her eyes and crying distantly, "Bwannie . . . Bwannie."

Through the Ballroom again, this time thronged with dancers, the officers in unfamiliar green and gold uniforms, their golden gorgets gleaming in the lamplight. The civilians had towering hair, sculptured into swirls and crests, and inset with little trinkets – a ship, a castle, chirping red birds. Outside, the sea thrashed at the windows, and the sky was filled with falling red stars. Not stars, but hot shot – cannon-balls.

Then before us curled a familiar iron gate, familiar

green jade steps sinking downward into limpid darkness: the Cloakroom of the Abyss.

The flaring light and the dusty clothes were the same, only now the marks of death were all too clear on the still faces. Georgiana Haðraaða was flushed purple with poison, and the orange she held was shrivelled. Serentha Haðraaða's lips were locked in the rictus of travail, her skirts crusted with dried blood, and the malnourished baby was also malformed, with a crooked little back and flipper hands. The little pug dog Fancy's muzzle was flecked with foam, stubby paws and legs rigid and stiff.

I was awfully glad that the drapes to Hardhands's catafalque were closed. I did not want to see what was behind those sangyn curtains, which, as we passed them, seemed to move as though perhaps the thing they concealed had stirred.

We circled the room and then ascended the same steps we had just come down.

"Why are we going back the way we came?" I asked.

"You can never go the same way twice, madama," Paimon said. "The way may appear the same, but it is different and so are you."

He was right. Now at the top of the steps was a small door, narrow and not tall enough for Paimon to go through. It was closed.

"I can go no further," Paimon said. "You must go alone from here."

"Can't you go with me?" I asked hopefully.

"I cannot. This is the limit of my authority."

"Lord Axacaya is Mamma's great enemy."

"Does she say so, or does he?"

"She does. She hates him for what he has done to the City, and to the Republic. Do you think he'll really help me, knowing how Mamma feels?"

Paimon put an enormous hand on my head. His touch was as light as swan's down. "Sometimes we believe things to be true that are based not in truth but our own fears and desires. Sometimes things and people are not what they seem to be. Sometimes people have the same goals but different ideas about how to reach them, Flora."

"And Poppy—"

Paimon's touch became heavier. "The time for thought is past, Flora. You must not think. You have made your decision. You must act."

He held out a little red leather box, snapped shut with a gold clasp. "It is rude to visit someone and not take them a gift. Give this to Lord Axacaya as a token of your appreciation. And when he asks you to tell him your situation, do so clearly and truthfully. Be respectful and humble but not servile. Be polite, but do not grovel."

I took the box, and gratefully. "Thank you, Paimon, for everything. I am sorry that we ran from you. You have been so nice. Thank you very much."

"It is my pleasure to serve you. I hope perhaps you

will visit me again sometime. Remember, Flora: *Dare, win or disappear*. Now go forth."

Paimon's tusks brushed my forehead, smooth and cooling, and when I kissed his cheek, it felt petal soft under my lips.

I pushed the door open and stepped forward.

42

BLACK SAND. FLYING.
LORD AXACAYA.

Sand crunched under my feet, and ahead of me stretched a long beach: the Pacifica Playa. But not the Pacifica Playa as I had ever seen it before. The sky and surging sea were the same quicksilver grey, but the water pounded on sand that glittered black as soot. It was as though someone had reversed night, turned the light to dark and dark to light. The air was strangely still. The surf rolled silently up on to the sand, then silently surged back. If the sky above had stars, they were invisible against the silver.

I turned to look the way I had come and saw Bilskinir shining blue on the cliff above me. It was a cheerful gleam of colour in an otherwise colourless world, which despite the silvery glitter seemed drab for the lack of any contrasting shade.

There was movement in the sheen of the silver sky:

an eagle. The bird circled me, at first so high I could barely make out the sweep of its wings, but then swooping lazily lower to drift menacingly around me. Though a sizzle of fear shot up my spine, I did not give ground, even when the eagle wheeled up, then dropped into a screaming dive, claws outstretched, directly toward me.

At the very last minute, the eagle pulled up slightly. Then eagle legs stretched down into human legs, and the eagle body transformed into a lithe human form, and as elegantly as a dancer, it landed on the sand before me. The eagle feathers had translated into a knee-length feathery kilt and a feather cape, but the sleek eagle head, all enormous green eyes and hooked beak, had not changed.

"Ave, Flora Fyrdraaca," the Quetzal said in a soft fluid voice, then sank into the deep fluttering courtesy that signified Meeting as Equals, but Me Slightly Above. "I, Axila Aguila, give you greetings."

I responded with a courtesy of my own, a courtesy that said Before You and Better. "I, Flora Fyrdraaca, return those greetings with great pleasure. I am happy to make your acquaintance."

"We have met before," the Quetzal said, "at the Zoo Battery, when you tried to steal the traitor from us."

The Quetzal recognized me! Again I felt that wave of terror skitter up my spine, but I ignored it and said firmly, "You were stealing him yourself."

"Perhaps so," said the Quetzal, and it seemed like

there was a hint of humour in its voice. "*Cree el ladron que todos son de su condición.* A thief believes everyone else is a thief, too. Axacaya has sent me to act as your escort."

"How did he know I was coming?" I asked, wondering what exactly it had meant by the thief remark. That I was not the only thief, or that I was paranoid?

"He swims in the Current, and nothing there is hidden from him. He has been waiting for you. Will you come?"

There is no way out but through.

"I will."

"We shall go, then." The Quetzal spread wide its arms. The feathered cape fell away from its torso, and by the clingy drape of its thin white chemise, I saw, with a jolt, that the Quetzal was female.

"Come," she said impatiently.

I realized that she wanted me to step into her embrace, and I hesitated. The idea of touching the Quetzal made my insides quiver. I did not want to get close to that razory beak, those claws. Somewhere, once, I had read that eagles are so strong that they can crush bones with their talons. True, the Quetzal's talons curled at the end of human fingers, but surely they had the same strength.

The Quetzal turned her head in a smooth swivel left, then right, and her eyes flashed luminous green, like a cat's eye caught in a light. "Will you have Axacaya wait?"

. . . but through.

I no longer had any bones to crush, no flesh to tear, and what could she do to me that was worse than I had done to myself? Squeezing my shoulders together in a bit of a huddle, and twisting my hands together at my throat, I stepped forward into the Quetzal's embrace and closed my eyes. She folded wiry arms around me, clutching me to her chest, which, save for her soft breasts, was hard with muscle. She smelled faintly metallic, the odour of old dried blood, and also of acrid vanilla. The bare skin of her neck against my cheek felt downy.

With a sound like ripping silk, her wings tore at the sky. I felt the spring of her leap, and we were aloft. Air roared by, as loud as a train, and the darkness pressing against my eyes spun and whirled. The beat of her flight filled my ears with a rhythmic pulse that matched the throbbing heartbeat beneath my head.

Onward, onward, we soared, and time seemed to vanish into the tidal flow of our journey, the steady pull of movement flowing around me, over me, inside me. The sensation of speed filled me with a huge excitement that made me want to shout with joy.

Then, we spiralled into a descent, and lightly, I felt the bump of landing. I opened my eyes and saw that I stood in a large courtyard. Luminarias blazed in the dusk like stars fallen to Earth, and by their light, I saw glittering red and gold mosaic under my feet, a tall fountain, and flowering plants everywhere, climbing up the white mud walls, spilling over wrought-iron balconies: fuchsia and white bougainvilleas, yellow marigolds, blue chrysanthemums, lavender orchids, fragrant orange trees, and a dozen flowers I didn't recognize.

"Xochiquetzal. You say Mariposa. Lord Axacaya's House," the Quetzal said. She released me from her embrace and led me across the courtyard, through a carved wood archway, and into a narrow gallery. Butterfly lamps hung from the vigas overhead, and more luminarias lined the walls, illuminating a fantastic mural: a ceremony in which red played a prominent role, a jade-masked priest holding a knife aloft, four eagle-headed priests stretching a screaming figure over a plinth – a Birdie sacred sacrifice.

"I have brought her to you, Axacaya," the Quetzal said. I turned my attention from the lurid wall-painting toward the dais at the far end of the gallery, where a figure had stepped out of the darkness.

Lord Axacaya.

The Quetzal's wings fluttered and her head inclined: I Serve You at My Own Discretion. "I am done."

"Thank you, Axila," Lord Axacaya said, his words slightly slurred with a low musical accent. "I shall call you back when I am ready."

His hand flashed in a throw, and something soared through the air. The Quetzal caught the toss, glanced at her catch, and then continued the movement from her hand to her beak. When she turned back to me, I saw that both hand and beak were stained red with blood.

The Quetzal paused in her exit and stared at me with that fixed green gaze. "Go with the goddess, Flora Fyrdraaca." And then with a flutter of feathers, she was gone. Lord Axacaya and I were alone.

43

Courtesy. Gifts.
Chocolate. Please.

Aglis Sabre, Mamma's ADC, had told me that Lord Axacaya did not have an eye in the middle of his tongue, but the *Califa Police Gazette* often represents him as a hideous old man who has a skull face and snakes for hair and who drinks the blood of his enemies from a jade cup. And yet the man who stood before me was in all ways just a man, as Poppy had said, not old or hideous or skull-like.

Lord Axacaya was tall, with spiralling yellow curls cascading past his shoulders. Like the Quetzal, he wore a feathered kilt, but the feathers were iridescent green and blue, silver and gold, glittering and catching the light like jewels. A jaguar skin was tossed over his shoulders; the jaguar's head hung down over his chest, its glazed eyes gazing out at the world mournfully. A jade labret shaped like a butterfly pierced his lower lip.

He held in his left hand a jade mask, the kind that Huitzils wear on formal occasions, and, in his right hand, a feathery fan, whose golden quills were fully three feet long.

Aglis Sabre had been wrong about Lord Axacaya's eyes. They were not black voids but the galvanic blue of the hot summer sky, like the glowing heart of a coldfire spark. He looked young, in his twenties perhaps, but I knew him to be older than Mamma, and she is fifty-one.

"Welcome to my House, Flora Fyrdraaca," Lord Axacaya said. The words were clear and loud, but his lips had not moved. He bowed his head slightly and fluttered the fan sign that meant Honour without Reservations.

"Thank you for receiving me," I said, glad that I had got an all-perfect mark in the Fan Language section of Politeness and Charm class last term. I unholstered my own fan and ripped it open with one sharp twist of my wrist. I curtseyed Respect to an Elder and fluttered Gratitude from One Equal to Another.

Poppy had said to remember I was a Fyrdraaca, and I was going to remember it and hope that memory kept the trembles at bay, but it was hard not to tremble. Lord Axacaya looked human, but he also looked disdainful and arrogant, and there was no spark of kindness or compassion in his glittering blue eyes. They were as cold and calculating as the predator eyes of his Quetzal guard.

I held out the little box Paimon had given me and was glad to see that my hand did not shake. Neither, somehow, did my voice. "Please accept this token as a sign of my appreciation for your reception."

Lord Axacaya advanced toward me and took the box, his hand brushing against mine. Even through my glove, I could feel the heat of his skin. He radiated warmth like a stove, warmth and the thick rich smell of chocolate and cinnamon. It was a heady smell, dark and musky. His wrist was encircled by an intricate blue tattoo of a curling snake whose head came down over the back of his hand, its tongue extending the length of his index finger.

"How thoughtful of you," he said, and this time his lips did move, mouthing the words but turning slightly up in what might have been a tight smile.

When Lord Axacaya opened the box, a ladybird crawled out. It perched on one edge of the box, wiggling its antennae curiously, and then crawled down on to Lord Axacaya's hand. The insect was larger than a regular ladybird, about the size of a glory, and it had only two black splotches on its crimson back, shiny as enamel. Surely it wasn't really a ladybird, but what, then, was it? The bug fanned its outer shell, and a blur of brilliant coldfire light spilled out from under the red and black carapace.

"The Semiote Verb *To Will*, Indicative Past Plural," Lord Axacaya said. "Isn't it lovely?"

A Semiote Verb! Not the one we had been wanting

373

but equally as valuable. Hardly a gift. More like a bribe. I felt a wiggle of guilt that Paimon had given away something so costly on my account, and vowed then, if I got home – *when* I got home – I would be sure to write him a thank-you note.

"This is an extremely generous present, Madama Fyrdraaca." This time Lord Axacaya's smile was slightly more genuine, though it also, unfortunately, showed me that his teeth had been filed into points. I shivered involuntarily, but if he noticed, he didn't show it. Gently, he jiggled his hand, and the ladybird dropped back into the box, which he closed.

He said, "Come, I shall offer you refreshments, and then we shall discuss your situation."

I followed Lord Axacaya's gesture to a brazier stove shaped like a squatting monkey, which sat to one side of the room. Arranged before the brazier were two stone stools, one carved to represent a rabbit, the other a jaguar. The carvings were the Birdie style, angular and square, and vaguely I remembered that each animal was sacred to the Birdies. I sat where Lord Axacaya indicated, upon the jaguar, my skirt poofing like a marshmallow around me, and watched as he stirred the pot on the stove, frothing its contents with a whisk he held between his palms. He poured the liquid into a cup shaped like a skull and offered it to me.

Oh dear, the cup *was* a skull, its top removed and its brainpan lined with gold. *Don't let them see you flinch*, said Nini Mo, so I took the skull with no comment and no grimace. But this time, alas, my hand did shake.

"Love is all we Desire," Lord Axacaya said. It's a traditional blessing, which we never say at home because Mamma disbelieves in piety. But it precedes all meals at Sanctuary, so I knew the correct response.

"Will is all that we must Do."

The chocolate, I hoped, was not mixed with blood. It was thick as mud, hot, and spicy, and it tasted delicious. I drank, then licked my lips, hoping that I did not now have a chocolate moustachio.

Lord Axacaya drained his own skull cup and set it aside. He looked at me coolly and distantly, as though I were a specimen, interesting but maybe not *that* interesting. "Now, madama. Perhaps you will tell me why you have come to me."

Paimon had said to be clear and truthful. But where to start?

"At the beginning, perhaps?" he suggested. "That is where most stories begin."

"Can you read my mind?" I asked, startled. If he could hear the things I was thinking, he'd be even less likely to help me. "That's not very polite." Then I could have kicked myself. This was not the time for snark.

Now it was his turn to look startled, as though he were not used to people correcting him, which I suppose he wasn't, being almost a god and all. For a minute I thought I had blown it completely, but then he said, "I beg your pardon, madama, you are correct, of

375

course. In my defence I say that I was not so much reading your mind as your face. Elsewhere thoughts are as good as actions, in some respects, and your face is quite expressive."

Then I am sunk, I thought, trying to arrange my face into an attitude of blankness.

"Go on, I did not mean to interrupt you."

I plunged in. "Valefor, our denizen, is abrogated, you know, and I found him and tried to help him get a little energy, but then somehow we became intertwined and he infected me with his dissolution. Now he is fading back into the Abyss, and I am, too, that's why I am Elsewhere now. I thought maybe if I restored him, then that would stop my evaporation, but Paimon says that only Mamma can restore him, because she's the Head of our House. And he said that the only thing that would help me would be for the link between Valefor and me to be broken, and then I would not fade," I said. And because Nini Mo said that flattery was a useful grease, I added, "Paimon said you were the greatest adept in the City and that perhaps you could break this link."

Lord Axacaya listened to all this without comment, looking almost bored, and when I was done, he stood up and poured me more chocolate. Turning back to me, he said, "I am surprised at your magickal doings. It is no secret that General Fyrdraaca does not approve of the magickal arts."

"Mamma says magick is a trick that the goddess plays upon us."

376

Lord Axacaya answered by whispering a soft Gramatica Word. The Word danced in the air in front of me and twisted into a note of fire, then became a brilliant dragonfly that flitted away. "Magick is a trick we play upon ourselves. The only true power lies in our Will. All else is vanity and games."

I said impatiently, "It's a trick that Val has played upon me, and I don't like it one bit."

Lord Axacaya twitched his shoulders, and his movement made the jaguar's eyes flash with life. He said coldly, "A trick? Whose trick? And whose vanity? There is much of both in your story, madama, in the details that you left out in your telling."

He continued, "You say Valefor tricked you, yet your desire to help him was rooted in your own selfishness. You sought to spring Valefor from his prison only to relieve yourself of your chores – a mighty poor excuse to go against your mother's dominion. You dragged your best friend, your dog and your horse into a dangerous situation, and took little regard for their safety, and they easily could have been killed.

"But that is not all, is it? Let us see . . . Oh yes, you attempted a major magickal Working, with no preparation or guidance. There, not only could you have permanently damaged yourself and your friend, but you could have torn the Current, you could have thrown the Waking World off balance. What you set in motion could have destroyed us all.

"And that stunt with the Dainty Pirate? What right

had you to decide if he lived or died? What do you know of the facts of his case, the damage he has caused to Califa, to the Republic? The danger he posed to our future? Did you think you could hide your involvement? What will the Warlord say when he hears about that?"

Tears burned my eyes like acid, even as I bit my lip and tried not to blink, tried to hold them back.

"What else? Forgery, theft and falsehood. Deception, shirking and treason. You certainly have missed no vice, have you, madama? You have been nothing but thorough in your depravity. Why should I reward such behaviour? Why should I help you?"

"Paimon said that Valefor's disintegration affected all the Houses, that it could pull the Current off balance," I said, very small.

"Bilskinir, perhaps, and the other Great Houses, old and decadent, but your foolishness cannot affect me. My House was built by my Will and is strong enough to withstand your games. So why, then, should I help you?"

"I don't know," I whispered. *Don't reward failure*, said Nini Mo. Everything he said was true, and if true, surely I deserved everything I got. I bowed my head, feeling the tears dribble and feeling myself shiver and shrink. How could I have been so stupid? Why should I be saved?

He continued, "Your story fits well with what I have thought for years. The Fyrdraacas, as a family, have always lacked verve. Your entire bloodline is sour; there's no hope for it any more. Any spark that your family might have once boasted of has long since guttered out. No wonder it dwindles and dies out. Look to your mother, buried in her work, a slave to her enemies, ignoring her child, allowing her to run wild, no discipline, no guidance, no respect."

"Hey—" My protest was a squeak.

He said scornfully, "And then there is Hotspur, reckless and indifferent to the safety of others, now boiling in his own misery. When faced with adversity, he broke, his Will as thin as a thread but not half as strong. Incurably romantic with his falsely placed love towards the greatest criminal Califa has ever known—"

"Mamma is not a criminal!" I yelped, unable to keep silent any longer.

"Not General Fyrdraaca, you little fool. Butcher Brakespeare. Cyrenacia Sidonia Brakespeare ov Haðraaða. General Haðraaða Segunda. Didn't you know that he was her lover? All Califa knew and not you? Did he not snap after her death? Descend into madness because he could not live without her? Even the loss of his own child was nothing compared to the loss of his mistress."

"That's not true!" Even as I protested, doubt wormed at me. Like a flash came the memory of that empty slab in the Cloakroom of the Abyss – the whip twined with a braid of brilliant red hair. Poppy's hair, I realized. I thought he had clipped his hair short in mourning for the First Flora, but had he? Did he wear the black mourning band for her, or for someone else?

Lord Axacaya continued on: "Look at you now – you are no better than your father. The slightest bit of pressure and you snap like a twig. You cry and you wring your hands, and you disappear. And you thought to be a ranger. *Dare, win, or disappear!* You have made your choice, Flora Fyrdraaca, to disappear!"

These words stung me like poisoned darts. Was I no better than Poppy? I had scorned him because he gave up. He gave in. *A ranger*, Nini Mo said, *will never willingly dance with death.*

Dare, win, or disappear.

A red spark flared in my darkness. Anger at myself for giving in. Anger at myself for sitting helplessly while Lord Axacaya slandered my family. That spark was hot, and against the dampness of my despair, it felt good. It felt great. It felt *real*.

"No, you are wrong!" I cried. "I will not go. I will not disappear. And you are wrong about Mamma – wrong about Poppy!"

"Am I?"

Ah, that sharky grin, how I'd like to smack it off his face. With each second my anger grew, and so, too, my determination to prove Lord Axacaya wrong – wrong about me, wrong about the Fyrdraacas.

"Mamma and Poppy were loyal to Califa; they fought for her honour. What did you do? You betrayed the country that took you in, and you sold out Poppy, and

380

you would have sold out Mamma, too, if you could have! You work for Califa's enemies – it is you who are the traitor!"

Lord Axacaya's eyes blazed like cold fire. "You talk treason, to speak to me that way, girl. And yet, I know you are not responsible for yourself. You are a foolish child. And it is the parent who must take the blame for the foolish child. I can send my Quetzals to Crackpot and arrest Colonel Fyrdraaca. Is he not responsible for you in your mother's absence? I can have him killed, and no one shall resist my authority. He'll be dead by morning."

"You will not touch Poppy!" I cried. "I will not allow it!"

"How will you stop me, madama? Are you not diminishing and fading? Are you not weak-willed?" Lord Axacaya said scornfully. "Should I be afraid of you?"

"You pernicious pinheaded mincing malichō TRAITOR! I will see you in the Abyss before I allow you to bring the Fyrdraaca family down!" I screamed. Every drop of blood had turned to fire, and this fire was eating through my flesh, eating through my skin. My throat translated my anger into a shriek of rage that hung on the air like greasy smoke.

I was *furious*. And it felt good. It felt wonderful. It felt *fabulous*. Scalding heat flowed up my toes, into my legs, burned through my stomach, and into my mouth. Thick guttural Gramatica Words sparked and snapped in the swirling air, which now smelled thickly of my ire.

Anger consumed me like a fire consumes wood, and there was no room for us both inside me.

I opened my red mouth and let out an almighty screech of fury, a screech that tore my throat and burned my ears, and seemed to last for ever, a horrible sound that rent the air in front of me. My scream rose higher and higher, the noise translating from Wordlessness into the Oatmeal Word, magnified a hundred thousand times from whence I had last spoken it.

" ⊞🜍🜚⊞ 🜕〰!" The gash became a magickal Vortex, a roiling daisy wheel of fuliginous darkness that rolled forward to envelop Lord Axacaya.

44

WILL. MORE CHOCOLATE. A REVELATION.

The Vortex whistled as it blurred and gave off a spiky blue and green coldfire light, like gashes of lightning, acrid and hot. Then, with a sound so loud I could not hear it, but could only feel the tremendous buzz of its vibration, the Vortex flared into a blinding burst of coldfire and was gone.

My skull rang with a noise that made my spine vibrate, my ears buzz. My vision dissolved into sparkly whiteness. It felt as though *I* was turning into oatmeal, melting into a puddle of starchy goo – a horrible sensation, quivering and shivery, that seemed to be getting stronger and stronger. And then suddenly the world snapped back into focus again. The awful sensation of oatmealness vanished. Now I felt heavy, not with the weight of desolation and despair, but with actual weight, the feeling of flesh and bone. I held up one hand to the light; it was plump and white, and I could not see through it. I pressed my other hand against my chest, and felt the slight bump of my heartbeat. I felt alive.

I felt *real*.

Lord Axacaya stood where the Vortex had been. He stepped toward me, his now obsidian eyes blazing. He brought his hands together in a thunderous clap that seemed to shift the ground beneath me, and I scrambled backward, skittering away from him.

What had I done? I had thrown the Oatmeal Word at Lord Axacaya, and he had stood through it, and now he was going to smite me. A tiny voice said, *At least you don't go willingly*. But that tiny voice was an awful little consolation – all my troubles for nothing. I only hoped it would not hurt too much. At least he was not setting those Quetzals on me—

Then Lord Axacaya clapped again and again, and he spoke in a voice not furious but friendly: "Welcome back to the Waking World, Flora." He smiled, a genuine smile that wiped all disdain and arrogance from his face, which now looked much older. Thin lines radiated from his eyes and lips, and his butter-coloured hair was threaded with shimmering silver. And his eyes were so very black now, yet there seemed to be shimmering movements within their depths. Lieutenant Sabre had been right after all.

"What happened?" I croaked, bewildered. I was solid again, but how was I real?

"You are yourself again. You have regained your Will."

"How?" Each word felt like a razor blade, and my lips were sore, too.

"You asserted yourself. You stood up for your Will. Come sit down, and we shall have more chocolate. You look like you need it." He gestured toward the stools. Daylight now stippled the floor, filtering down from the *latillas* above, and hung in the still air like little clouds of sunlight. The luminarias were doused.

"By getting mad? By using the Oatmeal Word?" I sat down heavily on the jaguar.

"Oatmeal Word?" He sounded puzzled.

"What I said. That Gramatica Word." This time, I was relieved to see, the cup Lord Axacaya handed me was made of carved jade, shaped like a flower. But the chocolate tasted as rich and sweet as it had Elsewhere, and it smoothed away the pain in my mouth and throat. My tummy rumbled, but now my hunger was just plain old hunger, not ravenousness.

"Ah, you mean the Gramatica Adverbial form of *Convulsion*? No – that was just a symptom of your rage. You spoke it well, though; I was hard-pressed to withstand it. No, the solution to your problem, Flora, was Focus and Will. Nothing is stronger than your Will. Not even your little friend Valefor. He tried to pander your Will to his, but he could only do so because you let him. No one can take you from yourself, Flora, unless you allow them to. But you needed to be jolted

385

to that realization, and so I provided you with a spur. I am sorry to have sounded so harsh, but you were pretty far gone. I wasn't sure that you could come back."

"Am I still linked to Valefor?"

"You will always be linked to Valefor. He is a Fyrdraaca, too, and the bond between you cannot be broken. But I would advise not allowing him to siphon your Will in the future. He is hungry – he cannot control himself. But he should not be encouraged, and as you have learned, it takes a great deal of strength to keep a hungry denizen at bay. Best not to take chances."

"But will he keep fading away?"

"As long as Fyrdraaca House stands, he will remain."

I sat there, trying to wrap my jellied mind around what Lord Axacaya had said. It was my Will that brought me back, and that Will had been activated by my anger. That much I understood. But why had he helped me? He was Mamma's enemy, wasn't he? I had worked against him, as far as the Dainty Pirate went, and he knew it – didn't that make me his enemy, as well?

I said, "I don't understand, Your Grace. You said you would not help me. You said I was irresponsible and foolish."

"So you were," he answered. "But courageous all the same. It was foolish to go against your mother and try to assist denizen Valefor. But it was a brave thing, and it was the right thing, to try to free Valefor from his bondage. He may be a servitor, but he is a sentient being. Should he not have the right to his own Will?"

"You said my family was a failure, but the failure is all mine. Please don't blame Mamma and Poppy for my actions. I will take my punishment if I must, but don't hold them responsible. What I have done is not their fault."

"I hold you responsible for your actions; you and no other," Lord Axacaya said. "What I said before about the Fyrdraaca family – I stand by those statements. I am no friend of your mother's, nor is she a friend of mine. But there is a saying: The enemy of my enemy is my friend. We share a mutual antipathy toward our Huitzil overlords; I have no more cause to like them than she."

"But," I said, bewildered, "I thought you were allies with them. You act like you are their friend; you do their bidding."

"Can I not smile and lie while I smile?" Lord Axacaya said. "Sometimes, Flora, you must grit your teeth and bear it until such time comes when you can bite."

"If you are against the Birdies, then why did you want the Dainty Pirate? Why did you have him killed? Mamma had no choice – she had to uphold the Peace Accord or risk herself – but you? He was their bane. He made no secret of working against them!" I burst out. Even as I did so, I thought, *Oh Flora, you should probably keep your mouth shut and stay ahead while you can*, but my mouth would just not stay shut – I had to know. "Why did you have him killed, then?"

"Did I have him killed?" Lord Axacaya asked with a smile. "I saw it! I saw your eagles rip him apart! Udo was there – he saw it, too!"

"Did you? Things – and people – are not always as they seem. If you have learned nothing from your studies of Nini Mo, you should know that. Was she *ever* what she seemed? It is not enough to *see* something; you must know what it is that you have seen."

Now I was annoyed, and exasperated. Why couldn't he just say what he meant instead of having to be all mysterious and boo-spooky? Is there something about adepts that they just cannot speak plainly, that they have been too muddled by power and mystery?

Lord Axacaya laughed. "Well, then, I will say – unmysteriously and un-boo-spooky – Boy Hansgen is not dead."

45

UDO. PIE. SURPRISE.

I had thought I'd had all the surprises I could ever have, that nothing could ever surprise me again. But I was wrong. If Lord Axacaya had suddenly turned a cartwheel and set his own hair on fire, I could not have been more thunderstruck.

"He's not dead?" I repeated. "He's not dead? Why isn't he dead? I saw him die! I saw the Quetzals tear him to shreds and rip his heart out!"

"I'm afraid you and Udo stumbled into a little bit of sleight of hand designed to make it appear that Boy Hansgen had met his reward. You did complicate matters tremendously, and I have to admit that initially I was quite annoyed by your intervention. But then Boy persuaded me that you and Udo had done no harm and, indeed, had shown quite a bit of courage and initiative – qualities in rather short supply these days."

389

"But I don't understand. Why did you want us to think that Boy Hansgen was dead?"

"Not you, my dear, but others who were watching and taking an interest in his fate."

"You mean Mamma?" I was still confused.

"General Fyrdraaca – and the Birdie overlords – and others, perhaps, too. I'm sorry, Flora, but I can be no more specific than that. You understand that this is a deep, deep secret? I must swear you to silence. If it should get out that he yet lives, then it would be a great danger to him – and to our plans. Will you swear?"

"I swear," I said, thinking, *Well, I won't tell anyone but Udo, that is.* And also thinking, *I still am pretty super-darn confused, but what a relief to know that Boy Hansgen hasn't been ripped to shreds after all.*

Lord Axacaya stood and snapped his fingers. A spot of sunshine coalesced into a servitor with a sad camel-head and sad camel-eyes, who answered, "Your Grace?"

"Sitri, Madama Fyrdraaca is leaving now. She is in a hurry. Please have the closed coach brought around. She wishes to be both swift and discreet."

The next thing I knew, Lord Axacaya had kissed my hand and Sitri was practically frog-marching me down the gallery, through the courtyard now flooded with sunshine, and into a carriage. Thus an end to that ordeal, and I had, in fact, made it through.

The ride home, my brain boiling like a teakettle at high noon in the Arivaipa desert: Lord Axacaya— Mamma— The enemy of my enemy is my friend— Boy

Hansgen alive— The Quetzals— Poppy's dead general—

Poppy.

Though all these thoughts roiled within my brain, it was Poppy who kept boiling back to the top. Poppy as I knew him today and Poppy as I had seen him at Bilskinir. A crazy, shifty-eyed old man, bending and halting. A bright-eyed, bright-haired young man, tall and straight. Poppy with his shaking hands and his hollow eyes. Poppy laughing at the thought of burning down the Redlegs' hay shack. Poppy screaming and clawing at his face with his own hands. Poppy kneeling before me, trying to hold on to me. Poppy now. Poppy then.

And Poppy and Butcher Brakespeare, his dead general. Had he loved her? He'd been her aide and had been captured with her by the Huitzils and gone to prison with her. But that had nothing to do with loving her. What about Mamma? Had he never loved her?

When I came through Crackpot's back gate, Flynn was waiting. He yipped and curled with excitement, and tried to jump up on my poofy skirts. I pushed him down and kissed his nose, happy that I was solid enough for him to jump up on, never mind if he got paw prints on my dress.

The stables were empty of Mamma's horse, which meant, to my extreme relief, that somehow I had beat her home. Bonzo nickered, and pawed at the bars of her stall, in expectation of carrots and sweet feed. I fed her and Mouse, and made sure they had water. Never had horse chores seemed so satisfying, and never again would I complain about mucking out the stables.

I came in quietly through the mudroom and found Udo sitting at the kitchen table, eating pie. A pistol lay to one side of his plate, and a stack of papers and an empty inkwell were on the other. Although he was shovelling the fork in as fast as it would go, he didn't look like he was enjoying his food very much. A ring of dogs stood around him expectantly, and when they heard my step on the stairs, they broke into a belling bay and rushed me.

Udo looked up and choked, spitting crumbs. "Flora! Are you real?"

I waded through the dog pack, petting and kissing as I went. "Real enough to be pissed off with you! I am off facing my doom while you sit on your hinder eating pie?"

Udo abandoned the pie and vaulted the kitchen settle to squeeze me tightly, swinging me up in the air. "Oh Flora, you are a sight for sore eyes – I thought you were gone for good!"

"Put me down," I said, pummelling his shoulders. "I can't breathe!"

This demand only caused him to squeeze me tighter, and then I found that I was squeezing him back. He felt hard and real, and my eyes began to water in a most babyish manner. I no longer minded that he could toss me around, but I didn't want to encourage him further, so I said, "Put me down, Udo! You are mussing my hair. Paimon worked hard on it."

Hair mussing is a mortal sin in Udo's eyes; he sat me down gently on the edge of the kitchen table, then stood there, grinning like a fool.

"Flora! I'd given up hope! You look fabulous – where'd you get that dress? And your hair – you actually look like a human being! I thought you were gone for good, oh Flora! Flora – Flora! Guess what! The Dainty Pirate is alive!"

"I know, but how do you?" I got off the kitchen table and shook out my skirts.

"I saw him! He came here—"

"*What?!*"

"Ayah, see, I got back to Crackpot, and I sat here all night trying to think of what to do, but I kept thinking, *Wait, just wait another minute and she'll walk in the door.* Then, finally, this morning, I gave up, and I thought to myself, Udo, you can't stand this another minute. You have to go to Mariposa yourself and find out what has happened and, if you have to, gut Axacaya like a deer, if Flora needs revenge. So I thought I'd better fortify myself with pie before I went, and then once I finished that pie, I was going to march right over there, and Lord Axacaya and I were going to have strong words!" Udo said, in a tone I had never heard before. It was cold as ice and so, too, were his eyes. I was reminded of the vision I had of Udo as a man, the future Udo, and suddenly that Udo did not seem so far off.

"But what does this have do with the Dainty Pirate?"

"I'm saying, Flora – let me finish – so I was almost finished with my pie. There's a knock at the back door, and I go to answer it, and it's this guy, with a big pile of gifties, and he says, 'I have a delivery for Flora Fyrdraaca,' and I say, 'She's not here,' and he says, 'Well, you can sign for them,' and brings them in – and then suddenly I realize that he's familiar to me. And then I realize that it's the Dainty Pirate!"

"What did he say? Did he explain what happened? How did he get away?" I asked eagerly. The Dainty Pirate *here*! And I had missed him, blasted bloody blast.

"He didn't say, Flora – he just delivered the packages, then left."

My excitement deflated. "But how did you know that he was the Dainty Pirate, then? He could have just been some delivery guy."

"But I recognized him, Flora; I swear to you it was the Dainty Pirate. I mean, I couldn't just say, 'Hey, are you the Dainty Pirate?' because he's a wanted man, and supposed to be dead, and he'd deny it, anyway. But it was him, I swear, I know it. He winked at me on the way out – he knew that I knew, and I knew that he knew that I knew – we both knew."

"Did you open the packages that he brought?" I asked. "Where are they?"

"I put them in the parlour. I waited for you. Wasn't I nice?"

We stampeded upstairs and into the parlour, which was full of presents piled on the chairs, the sideboards, the tables. I had no idea I had so many friends, well, not really me, I guessed. People who wanted to keep on Mamma's good side. Still, it is cheering to get stuff, even from people you don't know. Udo threw packages around until he found the right ones: a big one and a small one, both wrapped in bright polka-dotted paper, green and gold – the Dainty Pirate's colours!

"See, this one is addressed to you, Udo," I said, pushing the large box to him.

Udo ripped paper and, delving deep into the box, withdrew a hat. Not just any hat, but the most marvellous bicorn hat, its brim pinned by a green and gold cockade, and its crown surmounted by a bright red feather – just the sort of hat a pirate would wear. In fact, it was the exact hat that the *Califa Police Gazette* always shows the Dainty Pirate wearing, right down to the garish plume.

"I told you! Open yours," Udo said triumphantly. "Pigface, what a gorgeous hat!" He put the hat on, points front to back, and I had to admit that he did look quite handsome, very piratical, even.

My box was smaller, and inside was the most beautiful compass I had ever seen, with a rosewood case and golden pointers and mother-of-pearl inlay. I held it in my hand, and the arrow jiggled and spun a bit, and then, head-steady, pointed north.

Udo said, tossing through the packing paper, "There's a note, but it's blank."

"Give it here." The paper did appear to be blank, but surely it could not really be. Why would Boy Hansgen have included a note and not written anything on it? "Wait a minute. Get a trigger."

I carried the paper to the parlour table lamp and removed the glass chimney. Udo lit the wick and I held the paper to the bare flame, close enough to heat but not enough to burn. Letters began to appear, pale yellow, darkening to brown.

"Well, now. Clever," Udo said admiringly.

"It's an old ranger trick. Lemon juice. Invisible until it reacts to heat. Here." I handed the paper to Udo, and he read aloud:

Dear Flora and Udo:
Please accept my most sincere gratitude for your
attempts to salvage me from an unsavoury fate.
As you see, although appearances may have
lent themselves to indicating otherwise, I was
able to make my escape. Someday I hope to
explain further. Until such times, please allow
these small remembrances to represent my deepest
thanks.

The Dainty Pirate

"Wow! Flora! See – we weren't in vain after all! See? It all worked out," Udo said, admiring himself in the mirror. "The Dainty Pirate is alive, and so are you – and ain't life grand? You have to tell me all about what happened at Mariposa. What was Lord Axacaya wearing—"

The hall clock chimed, and suddenly I forgot all about the Dainty Pirate— *Noon!* It was noon! My Catorcena ceremony was to start at two thirty. Noon! My stomach went cold, a chill that spread its way down my legs and into my feet, up my body, into my head. For a moment, the kitchen went black, and I actually thought I might faint like one of those silly greenhorns in a Nini Mo yellowback.

"Udo, it's already noon! What happened to Mamma?" I said, a touch hysterically. "Mamma didn't come home, did she, already?"

"Oh, ayah, we are lucky, so darn lucky, Flora. That fog bank that Paimon mentioned yesterday? It never lifted; it's sitting there still. No ships can get through the Gate. Maybe we might even have to postpone the ceremony, if she can't get through."

I resolved to send Paimon more than just a plain thank-you note. Maybe candy, or perhaps a smoking cap.

Udo turned away from his preening. "Pigface, am I glad to see you. Now you gotta tell me everything that happened with Axacaya – I hope you didn't sign anything. He didn't make you sign anything in blood, did he? What was he wearing? And what about

397

Valefor? Is he gone for good? But the House didn't fall down."

"Valefor should be all right, but he won't be making any more waffles. He's trapped in the Bibliotheca again," I answered. I knew that I was going to have to go find out how it was with Valefor, but I wasn't entirely looking forward to seeing him again so soon.

"Well, he deserves to stay there after all that, the little snapperhead. Why do you look so downcast, Flora? You are saved. The Dainty Pirate is saved. Everything is working out just dandy."

I said gloomily, "Ayah so, maybe, but there's still my Catorcena, and I haven't finished my dress, or my speech, and now there is no time."

Udo evicted a dog from the settee and sat down. "Don't be a snapperhead, Flora. Look at what you are wearing. It's the most magnificent Catorcena dress I've ever seen. It will do just as well as that other old rag, which wasn't half as nice. You even got cleavage. And the House, it's clean enough, I doubt Buck will notice if it's any cleaner – she won't be home long enough. The kitchen was the big thing, and I got that mostly done. And as for the speech – here—" Udo thrust a stack of papers at me. "Last night I was just sitting here, going crazy, and so I thought I had to do something, waiting for you to come back, so I wrote your speech for you."

"Really?" I read the top sheet: *First and Most Fabulous of all the Fyrdraacas, Azucar Fyrdraaca was known for his fashion sense and exquisite taste . . .*

"Well, I guess you'd have to say I didn't really write it, exactly, Flora. I mean, you'd already written a lot. I just fixed what was there. I lost the lines about being a slave, and how Crackpot only has one potty. Actually, I guess I had to redo most of it. You are lucky I'm a fast writer, and pretty good at the flattery, too."

"Thank you, Udo," I said. "It's kinda cheating, though, isn't it?"

"Well, it's really a collaboration. I never heard any rule about a collaboration, and besides, beggars can't be choosers, Flora. You speak it from the heart, like you mean it, and that's what counts, I think."

The rumble of cannon fire shuddered through the House, and the dogs jumped up, alarmed, and flung themselves out into the back garden, yelping.

The ferry-arrival gun.

Mamma would be home within the hour.

46

THE BIBLIOTHECA AGAIN.
AN UNDERSTANDING.

So Udo went home to change, for he couldn't go to my Catorcena, he explained, with me looking better than him. And I had two things to do before Mamma came home, both of which I dreaded but felt I should do. Had to do. *Must* do.

I was determined that the Elevator should give me no trouble, and after I told it so in no uncertain terms, it got the message, for it whirled me upward as though its cables were greased with butter.

The thin light streaming in through the windows of the Bibliotheca threw shadows, wavering and grey, but there was no sign of Valefor, or even sign that there ever had been a Valefor. The room looked anciently abandoned, dusty and derelict.

"⚷⧖⚸⬌⚶," I said, and a Gramatica flame kindled before me. A tall candelabra sat upon the library table, and I used the coldfire spark to light it. The candlelight projected cheerful warm light a few feet into the darkness, and that was all. The pages covered with Splendiferous script that I had seen on my first visit to the Bibliotheca were scattered on the table; I held one to the light and squinted until I could make out the title: *I, Valefor Fyrdraaca ov Fyrdraaca, This is My Story.* Val's autobiography.

"You should have learned by now to mind your own business," Valefor wheezed from high above me somewhere.

I let the paper waft down to the surface of the table and peered up into the dimness, trying to find a form to match the face, but he was hidden in the gloom.

"Come on down, Valefor, where I can see you."

He ignored the request. "What gloomy thoughts to match a gloomy face. I would have thought that you would have returned triumphant, the woman girt with the sword before her, and instead, here you are, as dumpy as an apple cake but not nearly so sweet."

"Lucky for you, Valefor, that I still don't believe in violence," I answered. "Otherwise, perhaps, I should rip you up into tiny little bits and throw you to the four corners of the earth. Come out where I can see you."

"And every corner girded with fire and ice," Val said, unimpressed. He drifted out of the murk, coughing. "I guess your pacifist nature works to my advantage, for once."

"I see, denizen Valefor, that you are not looking so perky now."

Indeed, grey and tattered, he looked more than ever like a ratty dust rag. His hair straggled grey, his gown straggled gray, and his eyes were the same colour as his skin: grey. Having been so recently flyaway myself, it was hard not to feel a spark of pity for him, but I didn't let this show.

"It's true," he said dolefully. "You are saved, and brilliant, but I am the same as I was before, forlorn."

He looked woeful, and within me, the pity warred with irritation. I remembered how desperate I felt when I thought I would blow away in the wind and never see Mamma and Poppy and Idden and Udo and Flynn again. Such desperation I would not wish even upon my enemy, and Valefor was not my enemy. He was, for better or worse, a member of my own family.

"However," I said, "that's no excuse for taking advantage of me."

"Maybe not," he agreed. "Does not your revenge feel good? You, free and clear, and me, still locked up, alone, quickly diminishing."

"Pooh," I said. "Revenge is not my motive. Despite your insidious little tricks, I would not see you diminish any further."

"You are not your mother's child, then, for sure," Val said. "But whether you wish revenge or not, revenge is surely what you will get, because without my restoration, I am lost. You may not be fading, but I still am." Here he sobbed and wrung his wasted hands together in a very melodramatic fashion.

"I couldn't restore you, anyway. Didn't you know that? Only Mamma can release you, just as only Mamma could lock you up. You, the Fyrdraaca House, and she, the Head of that House."

"I wasn't sure," Valefor admitted. "But it seemed worth a try. Well, Flora, you did your best; do not think of me when I am gone, though I suppose that you will perhaps miss my slaving, no?"

"Perhaps. Perhaps not. I cannot free you, Valefor, and I guess I ought not to have tried. But you are not diminishing further, Lord Axacaya said. You shall no longer grow strong, but you shall not further fade, either."

"Small consolation to be stuck like this."

"Maybe, Valefor. But it's better than disappearing completely, eh? And Lord Axacaya said that we are still linked, we shall always be linked, for we are both Fyrdraacas. If you focus strongly, you should be able to take some small solace in that, and perhaps it will strengthen you a bit." Lord Axacaya had not actually said focus would give Valefor strength, but it seemed to me that it couldn't hurt to give him a little hope, could it?

At this, Valefor perked up a little bit. "Are you still my friend, Flora Segunda?"

"If you behave, and no tricks."

"What about my fetish?"

"I will keep it safe, Valefor. And maybe one day I can get Mamma to restore you. But you must behave."

"I will try, Flora Segunda, I really will, but it is hard. My gift is rhetoric and confabulation, and it's so hard not to practice what I have no choice but to preach. You should understand something of exaggeration, being so prone yourself."

"We are not talking about me, Valefor, we are talking about you. Will you promise not to trick me again?"

"Trick you once, shame on you; trick you twice, shame on me," Valefor said, which I took to be as much of a promise as I could expect from him. "If we are still friends, will you bring me newspapers, and maybe a muffin or two? Even a little kitten or a mouse, if I am good? A tiny spark of Will to keep me perky?"

"We'll see, Valefor. We'll see."

And so Valefor.

And now Poppy.

47

POPPY.

Idden and I have never been expressly forbidden to go up to Poppy's Eyrie, we just never have any inclination to do so. Better to leave him alone. Today I was not going to leave Poppy alone. Today I *could* not leave him alone.

I can't imagine why the stairs were named the Stairs of Exuberance when there was nothing particularly exuberant about them. They were narrow and gloomy and lit only by slender slits in the heavy brick walls. Round and round they circled; wide on the outer edge, narrow on the inner. By the time I got to the top, I was dizzy from the spirals and, thanks to Paimon's tight lacing, breathless from the climb. I paused on the threshold of the half-open door (imagination would have it barred and bolted from without, like in a lurid mystery novel) and rested my burning leg muscles.

They didn't call the top of the tower the Eyrie for nothing.

"Poppy?" I peered around the doorjamb. When I got no answer, I sidled in, careful to keep the door to my back. A good ranger always knows what is behind her.

Four windows, one in each wall, stared at me like four wide eyes. There was a narrow iron cot, no wider than a grave but not nearly so deep. Since Poppy always looks like a corpse, I would have thought that the Eyrie would be an equal mess, all dank and crumpled, messy with blood and bottles, and Goddess knows what else.

But it wasn't. The cot was neatly made; the wooden floor was neatly bare. A small altar sat in the northwest corner, which is, of course, the direction from which Death comes.

Poppy knelt in front of the altar, his head bent, his shoulders hunched. The doors to the altar were closed, which is tremendously sacrilegious, even I knew that. The Goddess must be free to come and go as she Wills and it is an insult to her to shut her doors against her.

"Poppy," I said, quietly. My hands were shaking, and I scrunched them into the fluff of my skirt, clutching fistfuls of fabric. "Poppy."

"I'm sorry," he said, without looking up. "I'm sorry."

He turned his head then, though he did not raise his eyes, and I saw his face. It was masklike, his eyes sunken in the painted black band that bisected them. His eyes were dull and muddy. The contrast between that weary sad face and the handsome face, the bright green eyes, of the Poppy I had met at Bilskinir twisted painfully in my stomach.

"Sorry for what, Poppy?" I asked.

"Sorry that I failed you. Sorry that I could not save you. Sorry that I let you go – let you go on into the darkness, alone."

"I didn't go anywhere, Poppy. I am still here." I reached my hand out and tentatively, lightly, touched his shoulder, which felt fragile and bony beneath my fingers. "You didn't fail me."

Now, finally, Poppy lifted his eyes, and he looked at me, and with that look, his gaze sharpened like a knife, with sudden avid confusion and a strange sort of hunger.

"Flora? Is that you?" he asked wonderingly. "You are real? You are not a ghost?"

"I am not a ghost," I said firmly. "I am real."

Poppy stumbled to his feet and reached out to clutch me. I hugged him back, feeling the ridge of his ribs underneath his sweater, smelling the acrid odour of his sweat. Underneath that smell was another, one I remembered from the embrace of the other Poppy: pipe weed and bay rum.

He said, in a rush of words, "Flora, I tried, I told Valefor to leave you alone. I fed him to keep him off of you, and I took the fetish from Buck to give it to you, but then I forgot where I put it, and I couldn't find it in time. I thought you were the other Flora before, and when you were lost, I thought you were safe, but then I realized later you were not her, you were yourself, and I thought maybe if you swam in the Current it would fix you, but it didn't do any good. I'm sorry, Flora, I'm so sorry."

Suddenly it all made sense, although in a muddled Poppy way. He had remembered and tried to help, but so confused had he been that I hadn't even recognized his help *as* help. Poppy's warning to me about Valefor. Valefor's fetish in Poppy's Catorcena chest, locked with Poppy's seal. Poppy, dragging me off the Folly into the Current, hoping it would fix me – though it hadn't, it *had* given me enough jolt to go on a little longer. Poppy, even in his crazy confusion, had tried. He had done the best he could.

My throat closed in on itself, choking down the words, letting out only the most horrific gasping noises. Each wrack seemed to shake me to the core, dislocate my shoulders, wrench my ribs, but I could not stop. I closed my eyes, burning and blurring with running eyeliner, and Poppy's arms smothered me into the roughness of his sweater, holding me too tight to shudder any more, and then, at last, I could stop.

"I want . . ." I said into his chest, when I could talk again. "Poppy, will you come to my Catorcena?"

He didn't answer, only slackened his hug and let his arms fall. He sat down on the edge of the cot and bent his head again. Little lines of blackness ran down his cheeks. "I can't, Flora."

408

"Please, Poppy. Please."

"I can't, Flora, I can't bear the light. I can't see their faces. I can't."

I said, with more firmness in my voice than I felt in my knees, so tired and wobbly: "You can't mope for ever, Poppy. *Dare, win, or disappear!*"

"I'm sorry, Flora."

"I don't want your apologies, Poppy."

"But I don't have anything else. They took it all. I have nothing left," he said sadly.

"That's not true," I said, stung to hotness. "You have Mamma, and Idden, and me. And Flynn, and Flash, and Dash, and Lash, and Screamie. Even Valefor. Aren't we something? Don't we matter? We must matter; you must care, or you wouldn't have tried to save me. Poppy, don't you remember, when we were at Bilskinir and we said goodbye, and you said that you don't fear dying but you were sorry for not being there for me and for not seeing me grow up. Poppy! You are not dead! Remember you said that Fyrdraacas are tough? Fyrdraacas don't give up! You are Reverdy Anacreon Fyrdraaca. Poppy, *please*. Please don't give up. Please try."

He just sat there with his head bowed, and I wanted to whack him, which I knew was a totally useless want, not helpful at all, but it made me so angry to see him so forlorn. For a minute, in his arms, I had thought, foolishly, that somehow things might be different now. But no, that *was* a foolish thought. Poppy was just the same as always. Weak-willed and broken.

409

"You love your dead general, Poppy, more than you love Mamma, or Idden, or me," I said in a mean little voice. "Is that who you are mourning? Is that who you think about all the time? Not me, not Mamma, not Idden, not the other Flora. *Her!*"

He looked up at me, his face agonized, and I knew then it was true, what Lord Axacaya had said. He answered, "You don't understand, Flora—"

"Fine, Poppy. Have it your own way. I don't care. Sit in your tower and think of her. *I don't care!*"

Outside, a bugle sounded Boots and Saddles. I ran to the window. Below, looking like little toy soldiers, were Mamma and her escort, flags flying. The bugle sounded again, and abandoning Poppy, I tore down the stairs to answer its call.

48

MAMMA. ORDERS.
THE BARRACKS.

I met Mamma just as she swept into the parlour in a tide of yapping dogs, singing, *"With your rifle come and stand, with your rifle come and stand, gather round and assemble, gather round!"* to the tune of the Assembly bugle call. "Where's the birthday girl? Where is she!"

"Mamma!" I waded through the sea of dogs to meet her, and she enfolded me in salt-smelling buckskin arms and kissed my forehead with cold lips. I hugged her back, glad that I was real enough to do so, and also glad – oh, so glad – that she didn't know how close I had come to never being able to hug her again. "Mamma, I'm so glad you are home!"

"I'm sorry I am so late," Mamma said. "I thought I would miss the entire ceremony. That blasted fog, I was cursing the weather and the Goddess; the pilot said that he'd never seen such a fog bank before, so thick and squat; we thought maybe it would never lift. But it did lift and here we are, like the cavalry in the nick of time. Get down, wretched dogs, get *down*! Will you forgive me, darling?"

I hugged her tightly. "It's all right, Mamma. You are here now, that's all that matters. But Mamma . . ." Guilt twinged at me, and for one mad moment, I almost blurted out everything.

Mamma saucered her forage cap toward the bust of Azucar Fyrdraaca, but it missed its mark and was immediately seized by a chasing dog. "Dash – drop that hat – what is it, darling?"

"I skipped school!" If I had to confess something, that seemed the safest sin to admit to.

"Oh pooh! A little fault, I think, on this big day. Look at this room, it's so full of gifties there is almost no room for us! Are you ready, darling? I'm sorry to cut it so close – you look lovely, how well your dress turned out – but we need to redo your maquillage, darling. I sent Aglis on ahead, to make sure that everything was ready at the O Club."

With a flurry of commands, Mamma took charge. She ordered her outriders to load my gifties and the dogs into the barouche. She ordered me upstairs to get my cloak and hat, and not to forget my speech. She ordered herself upstairs to get her dress uniform, and then ordered me to help her find her silver aiguillettes, which we didn't find because, she suddenly remembered, they were in the luggage she had taken to Moro. Back downstairs, she ordered her outriders to get Flynn back into that barouche and keep him there. Twenty minutes and twenty more orders and we were ready to go.

"And now, do we have everything and are ready to go, darling?" Mamma asked, surveying the parlor one last time. "Your speech?"

"I have it. Mamma—" I had something to say and now seemed like as good a time as any to say it.

Mamma didn't hear me. She said, "I lost my Catorcena speech, what a disaster! My lady mother almost had apoplexy. I had left it on my desk and then that blasted denizen came and tidied it up, and couldn't remem—" Mamma stopped midword. She was looking beyond me, at the doorway, her face suddenly rigid and set.

There stood Poppy, his face white as paper but scrubbed completely clean. His eyes were muddy green, but they were clear. The Skinner scars on his cheeks were faint, barely visible. He had changed out of his ragged clothes into a green and gold brocade frock coat, black kilt, and polished black boots. His stock was untied. His hat, a gorgeous beaver bicorn, with black fur trim and a bright silver cockade, was on crooked. Poppy smiled at us, a small shy smile that lit like a lamp, and suddenly that beautiful young man I had seen at Bilskinir stood before me – bent, twisted, older, but still recognizable.

"Happy birthday, Flora," he said. "Ave, Buck."

"Ave, Hotspur," Mamma said. "What you are doing downstairs?"

"It's Flora's birthday."

"So I know," answered Mamma. They looked at each other and something passed between them, something I couldn't quite read. But one thing was clear: though Poppy may have loved his dead general, he loved Mamma, too. And Mamma loved him back.

"Can you tie my tie, Buck?" Poppy said. "My arm don't reach that high." He came forward and stood in front of Mamma expectantly. She quickly knotted his tie and tucked the ends into his weskit, then reached up to straighten his hat.

"Do I pass inspection, General?" Poppy asked, with the shadow of a smile.

"You will do, Colonel. There! We are all ready. You both look very nice," Mamma said brightly. "I hope I can get cleaned up well enough to match, or I shall be the disgrace of the family. Shall we go?"

Now or never. After I had faced Axacaya, after I had faced Poppy, what could Mamma say? It was my birthday. And Poppy had washed his mourning off and come out of the Eyrie to face life. Maybe things – people – could change after all. Or at least *try* to change.

"Mamma, Poppy – I want to say something."

"Ayah, darling? What is it?" Mamma said impatiently. "We don't have much time. Can it wait until later?"

"No, Mamma. It can't."

"They won't hardly start without Flora, Buck," Poppy said. "Let us sit down for a minute and listen."

"All right, but quickly." Mamma sat on the settee, and Poppy sat down next to her, taking her hand in his and holding on to it tightly.

I moved in front of the fireplace and took a deep breath. Somehow Flynnie had again escaped the barouche, and now he ingratiated himself between Poppy's legs. Poppy rubbed his silky ears absent-mindedly and stared at me. Mamma was looking at me quizzically.

Dare, win, or disappear.

"Mamma. Poppy. I don't want to go to the Barracks," I said in a big rush, the words almost blurring together. "It's not for me, I know it's not. I know that's probably disappointing to you, but I really don't want to go. I know all the other Fyrdraacas went, but please, not me. My Will lies elsewhere."

Mamma didn't answer. She looked at me, but at least it wasn't that cold *I'm in Charge and You'd Better Not Gainsay Me* look. It was more of a *Where Did This Come From; I Can't Believe I'm Hearing This* look.

Then she said slowly, "All Fyrdraacas go to the Barracks. It's our family tradition."

Poppy said softly, "Perhaps, Juliet, it's time to start a new family tradition."

Mamma turned her Look upon Poppy, but he only gazed steadily back.

415

"You never mentioned this before," Mamma said to me.

"You never gave me a chance, Mamma. You never acted like you cared what I thought."

"You have your duty, Flora."

"Ayah, I know, but there is more than one way to be loyal, Mamma."

"We don't have time to discuss this now. It's a serious thing you have said, Flora."

"I know, Mamma. I know that we don't have time now, and it's all right, but I just had to say."

"All right, Flora. Your objections have been so noted and will be discussed further at a later time."

"Thank you, Mamma," I said, relieved. "That's all I ask. I know it's a serious thing and must be discussed seriously, but that's all I want – to discuss it."

Nini Mo said talk was cheap and it is action that counts. She was right, but I now realized it takes a certain amount of words to get things done. I guess I wasn't a ranger yet, nor had I yet escaped the Barracks, but I had escaped something much worse – Nothingness. I was still me, and right this moment it felt pretty good, actually, to be me, Flora Nemain Fyrdraaca ov Fyrdraaca.

Behind Mamma and Poppy's heads, above the bust of Azucar Fyrdraaca, a purple spark glimmered briefly and then was gone.

AFTER

Later, after we had ridden in the barouche to the O Club – Mamma, Poppy, me, and the dogs, like we were a real family, with Mamma looking at Poppy as though she couldn't quite believe it, and the escort following behind, loaded with my gifties—

Later, after I had made my speech and sworn my oath, and curtseyed to the Warlord (who, thankfully, did not remember we had ever before met), and received the Warlord's beery kiss upon my cheek—

Later, after Mamma welcomed me to adulthood and presented me with my Catorcena chest, and the gifties were opened, most of them pretty good, except that someone had sent me a plushy pink pig, as though I had just turned four, instead of fourteen—

Later, after my Catorcena cake was cut, and slices handed around, and toasts made, and congratulations offered, and Dash and Flash stole a turkey off the buffet and were chased from the room by a posse of infuriated waiters—

Later, after I had danced with the Warlord, who trod heavily upon my toes, and then with Mamma, who was as light as a feather, and then with Poppy, who was surprisingly spry, and who had not gone near the punch bowl all evening—

Later, after all that, I was in the loo, trying to figure out how to wad my giant poof of skirts into such a small stall, when I remembered the small box Poppy had pressed into my hand at the end of our dance. Before I had been able to open it, Udo had descended on me and I had shoved it into my pocket as he whisked me away for a mazurka. And after Udo, Lieutenant Sabre and a waltz, and then Udo again, and so I had forgotten all about the little box.

Now I pulled it from my pocket. The box was small, made of worn red leather, and held closed with a small gold clasp. Inside, a tarnished silver badge lay on a crumple of velvet. Not a civilian identification badge, like the one Mamma makes me and Idden wear, but an actual Army-issue badge, enamelled in smoke grey and dusky purple, the kind you wear around your neck so they know who to ship you to when you are killed.

On one side was the logo of the Ranger Corps: the Unblinking Eye.

And on the other side, the name of the badge's owner:

REVERDY ANACREON FYRDRAACA OV FYRDRAACA.

Poppy.

Nini Mo's Tips for Rangers

TO DESTROY THE TASTE OF CASTOR OIL
A piece of the best dark xocolatl will kill that nasty oily flavour right dead.

TO SAVE ICE IN THE DESERT, EVEN THO' THE TEMPERATURE BE BOILING
Wrap the ice in best brown paper and tie with twine. Dig a hole six feet deep and two feet wide. Line with straw. Place bale of ice herewith. Cover with more straw and fill in with removed dirt.

THE TIME ELAPSED FOR DIGESTION
Homemade Sponge Cake: 2 hours
Salt Pork: 4 hours, 15 minutes
Pinole Flour: 5 hours, 12 min & 8 seconds
Mule: 4 hours, 15 minutes, poor Evil Murdoch
Best Shoe Leather: 3 hours, mighty tough
Grass: 2 minutes & keep a rag handy
Your Best Friend: 6 hours, 1 minute

ON TRAVELLING
If a coyote comes from the left & crosses your trail – GO HOME!